SCREW FRIE

Everybody needs friends

Thank you so much for ｐ

Your friend (but not in a creepy way)

RG Manse (rg@rgmanse.com)

metacircular.co.uk

# screw
# friendship

rg  manse

SCREW FRIENDSHIP by RG Manse

Cover design by The Chairman.

Edited by Caroline Smailes (BubbleCow).

First Published in Great Britain in 2014 by Metacircular Limited.

ISBN-13: 978-1-910641-02-6

metacircular.co.uk

*To Matt and Peggy*

*for making anything possible.*

# Chapter 1
# Fairy tale ending
## (Saturday, 28 May)
## Rosy

Rosy's rescuer had arrived, thank God. She watched the Fiesta right-turn into the car park: Findlay, her knight in dented armour, here to whisk her away from her handsome ex prince.

She shouldered the purple Karrimor she'd rammed with as many clothes as would fit—dirty along with clean, and likely some of Jen's in there too. Not that Jen would notice. Her flatmate had more lingerie than the Ladyboys of Bangkok. Rosy straightened her duvet, then joined her pal in the lounge.

"I can take little Justin if you like," Rosy said. "If you're worried about changing him."

Jen folded her arms. "He's a goldfish, Rosy. I'll manage."

"He likes the plant, not the diver." She picked a piece of fluff off Jen's sparkly cardigan. "The diver unsettles him."

In slippers, Jen had to reach up to help untwist the straps on Rosy's shoulders. "Wouldn't it be better just to tell Boog he's dumped?"

Rosy shook her head, eyes closing at the notion. "He's freaked me out now."

Last night, a shining-eyed Boog had shown her how to decode his cipher tattoo. She'd faked a smile, then retreated to Jen's flat, chained the door and bolted it, top and bottom.

"If he asks," Rosy said, "tell him… tell him my gran took a tumble, so I'll be staying with her for a while."

"Which gran?" Jen said, then shrugged. "He will ask."

Rosy was tempted to say Franny, Frank-the-Raper's mother.

Instead, she held her friend's arms. "I didn't say which."

Her flatmate exhaled a sigh, nodded, then eased open the front door. The crack and creak of the hinge made them both wince.

"Bye, babes," Jen whispered. "Take care."

Rosy mouthed a goodbye, then stepped out into the danger zone.

Two doors along, Boog's flat. A corridor and two flights of stairs between Rosy and sanity. Boog could be there right now, eye to the peephole, or ear to the letterbox. Boog with his tattoo. Waiting for her. Stalking her, as he must have stalked her from the start.

Rosy ghosted along the hallway, her trainers whispering on the carpet. Once through the fire door, she quickened her pace, and broke into a run to the stairwell where she checked herself, forced herself to slow down. Her story had to be credible: *Assumed you'd be studying. Didn't want to disturb you.*

All the way down the stairs, she expected to hear Boog call out to her.

When Rosy unlatched the main door, the sounds of cars passing on Edinburgh's Slateford Road rushed in, and her anxiety rushed out. Saturday. A fresh May morning and no university for months.

Forty feet away, Mum's Fiesta slouched across two parking spaces. Good old Findlay. She crossed from the red brick building, unslung her backpack ready to dump it onto the back seat.

The door handle resisted her fingers and thudded back.

Locked.

She knocked the window, then bent down and peered into the car.

Empty.

Rosy gnawed her lip, looked around. Where the hell did Findlay go?

# Findlay

Findlay walked around another corner and felt his stress levels fall, even before he'd cadged a ciggie. His fellow addict, dressed in jeans and a Nike T-shirt, must be Rosy's age. Handsome, athletic, a real pussy-magnet, no doubt—lucky bastard.

"Sorry," Findlay said. "I'm all out. How'd you like to save a guy's life?"

"No wuckas," the kid said, and tapped out a Marlboro. "You're Rosy's stepdad, aren't you?"

Findlay's eyebrows raised. "That's right."

"I'm at Heriot-Watt with Rosy," the kid said. "I stay in the flat two doors down." He smiled. "Stunning girl. Just beautiful."

"She certainly is," Findlay said.

The kid thumbed a light from his Zippo, then nodded across the car park and said, "Look at that fat bastard. As if cleaning that fucking car is going to help his chances."

Findlay looked across, straight into the hairy arse-crack of a fat guy hunkering down to clean the alloys of an Alfa Romeo. "Thanks for that," he laughed, and turned away. He inhaled and held the smoke, felt it revitalise him, then breathed out. "Classic car though."

"GTV, yeah. But look at the registration. That's 1997, for fuck's sake. Cost a fucking fortune." The kid's cigarette wagged as he spoke. "I drive a Clio. Three years old. Souped up a bit. It's the mutt's nuts."

"Rosy doesn't drive yet, hence Findlay to the rescue." Not that he minded.

"To the rescue?" the kid said. "You're not just through for a visit then?"

"No. Last minute change of plan. Not sure why. She wants to come home now."

"Does she? Interesting." The kid rubbed a balled fist—no doubt to show off he had biceps. The swirls of some indecipherable tattoo stuck out below the sleeve of his T-shirt.

Findlay always loved to see young guys ruin their looks. Honking big tattoos, rivets through the nose, earlobes stretched to busting over hoops you could pass a golf ball through, those were great. Welcome to Planet Ugly. Have a cigarette.

"Findlay. Findlay…?" The kid snapped his fingers.

"Dickson."

"Findlay Dickson." The kid pointed. "That's right. I knew it was Findlay. You live over the other side of Edinburgh, don't you? Over towards…?"

"Duddingston?" Findlay said. "Yeah, Northfield Terrace. Ex-council house."

"That's the one. Think that's just down the way from my aunt's," the kid said. "Northfield Terrace. Must key that into the sat nav. Small world, isn't it? Nowhere to hide."

"Not these days. People can zoom into your back garden."

The kid laughed. "I know. Isn't it great?" He flicked his cigarette. "Look, look." He nudged Findlay. "There's one for the ladies."

Findlay turned and the fat guy was reaching up, washing the roof, big hairy belly wobbling over his jeans.

Findlay tutted. "Must be twenty stone at least." He laughed. "He's so young too." Magic. Feed him more pies.

"Unhealthy lifestyle. Eating shit. No exercise. What would any woman see in that?" the kid said, then waved back in the direction Findlay had come. "Look, there she is," he said. "There's our beautiful Rosy… Oh, hold on. What's up?"

Rosy had come around the corner then stopped dead. She beckoned Findlay with her head.

Findlay's heart inflated. She'd been away all semester. Look at her. Just look at her. To think this was the gawky girl he'd raised from a baby. Having her back home would be like filling every room with flowers. Hot, sexy flowers he'd love to sniff.

Rosy beckoned him again.

"Duty calls." Findlay pinched out his cigarette, and looked down at his pasty legs poking from the bottom of his shorts and his sandalled feet with their nicotine yellow toenails. Oh, to be a young stud. Even a tattooed one. He popped the ciggie into his top pocket. "I'll enjoy the rest later. Thank you. Nice to meet you… er?"

Behind Findlay, somebody shouted Rosy's name, and he turned to see the fat kid wipe his dripping nose on his arm, then start to walk across, grinning.

"I'm Crawford," his young smoking pal said. "And that fat fuck is my flat mate, Boog. He's Rosy's boyfriend."

Findlay gaped.

Crawford grinned at him. "She's not interested in me. Believe me, I tried." He shrugged. "What's a man to do?"

# Boog

Boog waved at Rosy, then recognised the man standing beside Crawford: Rosy's stepdad. His picture was on Rosy's Facebook page—and in the photos Boog had sneakily downloaded from Rosy's phone—hence burned into Boog's brain like the days of the week, or the three-times table.

Vital to make a good first impression. Boog dusted down the front of his sweaty *Smile, Dipshit* T-shirt, drew in his gut, then skipped across the car park to meet the great man.

"Looking sharp, Boog," Crawford said, then clicked him a wink, deposited his cigarette butt, and said, "Great to meet you, Findlay," to Rosy's stepdad.

Rosy made awkward introductions and Boog's smile faded. Why the backpack? Was Rosy off for the weekend without telling him?

Findlay didn't shake Boog's extended hand. Turned his back, in fact.

"What happened to your other boyfriend," her stepdad said. "The good-looking one? What's-his-name…? Renoir?"

Boog's jaw set.

"Ruben?" Rosy said.

"Yes, Ruben. What happened to Ruben?" her stepdad said, then the little shit-stirrer moved between them.

Apparently, Boog had failed the audition.

"How can you have a different boyfriend already?" Findlay said.

Boog flinched. "What does he mean, *already*? And what's with the backpack?"

Findlay turned on him. "I mean," he said, through raggedy yellow teeth, "she already has a proper boyfriend. She's spoken for. And she's coming home—"

"Dad," Rosy said, loud enough to cut them both off. "Can you give me two minutes with Boog, please?" She raised her hands to the straps of her Karrimor. "I'll give you this."

Boog watched her shrug free of her backpack, all else forgotten for a moment, waiting for the tiniest glimpse of her bra... Damn it.

Rosy handed the pack to her stepdad. "I'll see you back at the car."

Findlay's mouth hardened to a slit and when he spoke, his voice trembled. "Two minutes."

Boog reached to pick up Rosy's hands, but she drew away, folded her arms. He rubbed the back of his neck. "You're not seeing Ruben again, are you?"

"No, of course not." She scowled.

Boog loved Rosy's scowls. He loved every expression her face could make. He tried to put his arm around her.

Rosy backed away. "Quit it, and listen, okay?"

Boog closed the gap she'd opened up, wanted her in his personal space, knew she couldn't resist the magnetic lure of the cuddlemeister, the safety of him. Earthquakes, bombs, zombie attacks. His body, her shield. Her impenetrable love shield. "Listening." He folded his own arms and smiled, leaned in.

"We need to turn the volume down. You and me. Both of us. For a bit."

Ice formed in his stomach. "Rosy? You're not... dumping me, are you?"

"No, 'course not," she said.

He followed her rapid glance to her bracelet. That was an old bracelet, not the Ortak one he'd bought her. Boog's eyes prickled. He waved his hand under her face to make her look at him. "So what does turning the volume down mean, exactly?"

"It means, get some perspective," she said. "Look what's happened to you. You're flunking out."

He shook his head. "I'll pass the re-sit."

"How, exactly? When you're not with me, you're at your car." Her brow wrinkled. "Why haven't you been studying anyway, Boog? Why do you need to re-sit?"

Boog leaned closer so they touched arms. "Rosy, you're more important to me than any university degree." She had to know that by now, surely?

"I think," Rosy said, and stepped back, "it would help if I

weren't here, distracting you—"

"But—"

"So I've decided to spend summer with my folks."

Boog's eyes widened. "Oh, no, Rosy, no—"

Rosy held her fingers to his lips then pulled them away before he'd even been able to kiss them. She folded her arms again, and the action pressed her breasts up. And even in his distress, the flash of white lace fulfilled him. White bra today.

"I don't want an argument, Boog," she said, and backed away again. "Listen, I have to go. I can't keep my stepdad waiting."

"Cuddle?" Boog said and assumed the position.

She frowned, then let him hug her. He kissed her hair. Midnight blossoms.

"Kiss?" he breathed into her ear, but she pushed him off.

"Forget about me and focus on passing the re-sit. One-hundred percent focus." She raised her hand in a tight wave.

Forget about her? "I could never forget about you, babe."

He waved. Boog's entire problem: He couldn't forget Rosy for even thirty seconds.

And if she was back with Ruben, the cuddlemeister would throw himself under a lorry.

# Findlay

Findlay checked the mirrors. No Rosy, yet. He unfastened her backpack and immediately struck the mother lode. Bras and panties. He pushed his nose in, breathed, and felt his crotch twitch.

The passenger door opened.

"Caught," Rosy said.

# Chapter 2
# Mum and Dads
## Rosy

Rosy watched Findlay's face redden.

He gestured at her open Karrimor. "I was only—"

She laughed. "What are you like?" She pulled the backpack off him. "No presents in there." He was worse than a child. She opened the rear door and flung her gear onto the seat. "It's just a little something this time," she said, as she rejoined him in the front, "and I didn't have time to wrap it."

Rosy worked her hand down into her jeans pocket to retrieve the key ring she'd bought on a whim. She presented it to him.

He squinted at the message. "I heart my dad," he said.

"Love. I love my stepdad." The only man left she could actually trust. She squeezed his knee.

He put his hand on hers. "You're a lovely girl, Rosy."

"I know," she said, and smirked. "Home?"

"Your mum needs screws," Findlay said. "We'll have to drop by B&Q."

Rosy sighed. "More DIY? The woman's an addict. Well actually, there's a builders merchant right next door. Shall we try there first?"

"Okay," he said, then squeezed and patted her hand. "Okay, Rosy."

Findlay showing affection. Clearly, he liked that key ring.

# Findlay

The builders merchant really was right next to the flats: Jewson, a whitewashed brick building with blue painted warehouse doors. Findlay headed under the raised shutters of the entrance into a shop section, hands still trembling. That had been too close. Almost caught sniffing his stepdaughter's undies.

Findlay's nostrils filled with the smell of wood. This was the right place for timber but not a lot of ironmongery on show. Shit. He couldn't be arsed with B&Q on a Saturday.

He joined a queue of depressed-looking tradesmen—still working for a living, the suckers—and fumbled in the pocket of his shorts for the note Irene had written.

*4 x 40 mm countersunk pozi (x 20)*

How the fuck did she expect him to work out what that meant?

Findlay was still scowling at the paper when he heard a voice he hadn't heard in over a dozen years. A voice that turned his intestines into a roiling liquid. A voice that cut off at the exact second Findlay's gaze snapped across toward the timber and locked eyes with—

Oh, Jesus, no.

Frank-fucking-Friendship.

And the monster's glare was already turning black with malevolence. "Findlay Dickson," he boomed, then pointed. "You. Piece. Of. Shit."

The big bastard strode toward him, snatched an eight-by-four-feet sheet of hardboard from a wide-eyed salesman, and kept on coming.

Findlay had a sudden and clear premonition of being buried in a hardboard coffin. Then he ran.

# Rosy

Rosy looked up, confused by a skittering sound coming her way. Findlay, almost at the car, dodged aside and a large sheet of hardboard twirled past at ground level, skimming away across the tarmac. Just before the boundary wall, the board tried to take off but didn't clear the top, hit the stone, bounced back and collapsed with a final judder and scrape.

While Rosy leaned forward to try to see the board thrower, the driver's door screeched open and Findlay flung himself in.

"Dad?"

He started the car, jerked away and bombed straight out into Slateford Road without looking.

Rosy covered her head at the roaring rasp of tyres and a horn blast behind, bracing for an impact that didn't happen.

Findlay floored it.

"Dad?" Rosy looked back but Jewson flicked out of view behind the flats. "What's going on?"

"Frank," he said, and his voice climbed an octave. "That psycho was in there."

Her biological dad? Rosy had just missed seeing Frank-the-Raper? God damn it. She twisted backwards and stared out the rear window.

"We lost him, Sweetpea. We're safe," Findlay said. "But screw Irene's DIY. We're going home."

Rosy faced forward and slumped back in her seat.

And screw Frank Friendship too.

---

Rosy moved her Tesco value orange juice—made from concentrate, yum—just to reassure herself that Findlay's eyes were focused on infinitely distant orange, not her cleavage. The eyes moved. Phew. Paranoia.

"Rosy?" her mum said. "Are you listening?"

"Sorry, no." Jeez. Home for less than two hours and miserable already.

Mum shook her head. "Do you have a start date with N-BioCom? If it's not for a month or so, maybe you'd still think about the biscuit factory?"

"Any day now," Rosy said. "I have to be ready at a moment's notice. No way I can commit to anything at Reward Biscuits, sorry."

Moving back home had not been part of Rosy's plans for this, the most important summer of her life. But after Boog's tattoo revelation last night, what choice had she?

"They should have given you a date by now, surely?" Mum said. "Call them. Don't delay. There's a good wage at Reward. God knows, I could do with some digs money from you."

Digs money for what? The grocery shop couldn't be a stretch: one tin of non-Heinz beans between three adults? One slice of white toast each? "If money's so tight, why not get your life partner here a job at Reward?"

That snapped her stepdad from his orange-induced—or maybe Frank-induced—trance. "Me?" Findlay said.

"Findlay? At Reward?" Mum said. "What do you want to do, kill him? Anyway, They're only interested in you, because they were so impressed with you last year. It's a golden opportunity, Rosy."

Said as if she really believed it. Jeez.

"They're not taking on any other students," Mum said.

"You'd better not have told them I'll start, Mum. I have big plans for the summer, none of which involves an endless conveyor of custard creams."

"That new boyfriend of yours," Findlay said, "must have polished off an endless conveyor of custard creams."

Rosy's mouth fell open and heat rushed to her face.

"You should have seen him, Irene," Findlay said. "Honest to God, I was so shocked. What do you see in somebody like that, Rosy? Are you poking fun at him? Surely you can't be attracted?"

Rosy held her hands up. "Boog is a nice person." Attractive too, damn it. Boog was lovely. For a stalker. She'd already had a text from him: *My head is full of aldehydes, ketones and you. Call me. B x*

"Leave her alone, Findlay," Mum said.

The last thing Rosy had expected from her mum was support. Mum was looking at her as though maybe even reassessing her.

But Findlay had his fangs in. "Look at her," he said. "Is this a girl who has to settle for fat?"

"Enough," Mum said. "It's none of your concern."

"It is my concern," Findlay said. "I don't want Rosy falling into his kind of habits, and getting type-two diabetes, losing fingers and toes. Or dying."

"His kind of habits?" Rosy said. "Like having a proper lunch, you mean, instead of a war ration?" She clattered her cutlery against the plate. "Least he doesn't smoke. And he's just chubby, okay? Plus he's only a boyfriend. It's not like I'm shackled to him, like some dopey teen drop-out carrying his sprog."

Mum pushed her chair back and stood. Rosy made a grab to squeeze her arm, to apologise, but Mum jerked away.

Her stepdad glared at Rosy, a *see-what-you've-done* glare.

"There's a bag of chocolate digestives to take to Franny," Mum said. "I expect you to do that, Rosy."

Rosy slumped. Franny. Frank-the-Raper's mum. What a great start to the summer.

"And Snuggy needs a walk."

"Now, hold it right there," Rosy said. "If I'm paying for digs, I'm not picking up all the odd jobs. I'll walk Snuggy. You take the biscuits to Franny. They're your biscuits."

"Fine. Why not?" Mum said. "I do everything else."

Findlay gave Rosy the evil eye.

So much for the I-love-my-dad key ring. "And you can give me one of those looks, *Findlay,*" Rosy said, "the day you actually do something, besides lounging in front of the TV, using cushions as fart mufflers. As if nobody notices."

Findlay's gaze dropped back to Rosy's orange juice and Rosy's own eyes drifted off to infinity.

Boog knew where she was now—he'd sent a card here once. Too many details. She'd shared far too much, far too soon. All for a cuddle.

But after Ruben, she'd so needed a cuddle.

---

*Rosy is officially still with Ruben, so when the chubby fellow-chemistry-student she's had her eye on looks across at her, she turns away to hide her flustered smile. She lifts two plastic cups of the orange juice Heriot-Watt Student Union has laid on for Freshers' Week and hands one cup to Jen.*

*But Jen isn't interested in the orange juice. "Uh-oh," her friend says. "Fat guy. Incoming. Two o'clock. Let's move it, babes."*

*Jen takes Rosy's hand and walks around to the comfy chairs.*

*"OMG," Jen says. "He's a heat-seeker."*

*Rosy frowns, turns and the chubby guy is right beside her.*

*Broad teeth shine in that wide smile of his. He's taller than Rosy—yay—but stretched to wide-screen format. Close up, his boxy nose is even cuter. "You're Rosy, right?" he says, and puts out a big hand. "I'm Boog."*

*His hand is a glove around Rosy's, soft and warm.*

*When Boog has gone, Jen laughs at him. "Oh, my God. As if. Imagine how you'd even have sex with that."*

*Rosy isn't imagining sex. She's imagining wrapping her arms around him and snuggling into him on the couch. Boog. He's lovely. Just lovely.*

---

Rosy wandered back downstairs, arms around her dirty laundry.

For Rosy, home had always been this place, an ex-council house her mum had somehow managed to buy on biscuit factory wages. Findlay hadn't worked in eight years and even before that his jobs were patchy. But eight years ago, he stopped describing himself as a bricklayer and became an entertainer. Findlay had been the one who waved goodbye to Rosy in the morning, and Findlay the one there for her at home time. Mum did everything else—including keeping the house in a permanent state of renovation.

Since her last visit home, the banister had been sanded and revarnished and the hall had acquired a swirly carpet and Jack Vettriano prints. Still, finding Mum was always easy: Just follow the smell of emulsion. And there she was, in the kitchen wearing old biscuit factory overalls, a paint roller in her hands.

"Is this colour too dark?" Mum said.

Rosy shoved her clothes in the laundry basket, then contemplated the orange stripe on the wall. "No. It's warm and rich."

Her mum widened the stripe with the roller.

"I almost saw Frank today." Last time Rosy almost saw him, she'd have been about four.

Mum stopped and looked at her properly for the first time. "Findlay said Frank tried to take his head off with a sheet of wood."

"More his feet. And hardboard, not wood. But yes."

Mum shook her head. She rolled the remaining paint on the wall, then dunked the roller in the paint tray and rocked it back and forth on the dimples until the fibres were evenly matted. Rosy suspected her mother was hooked on the smell of paint.

"Why did you ever marry Frank?" Rosy said.

Mum shot her a vinegar look. At Rosy's age, her mum had been married to Frank for two years but had already left him to live with Findlay.

"I mean, you married him," Rosy said, "but then just shacked up with Findlay. If it was okay to just shack up with somebody, why marry Frank?"

"Shack up?" Mum thumped the roller onto the wall and rumbled it back and forth, wet and sucking. "You have no idea what I'd been through."

"But Frank put you through it. So why marry him?"

Mum flapped her hand, and looked away. "It was the thing to do." She stood back and looked at the wall. "This is too dark."

"Why didn't you ever divorce him?"

"Rosy, what is this?" Her mum held the roller. They both heard paint drip onto the newspaper, and Mum dropped her hand closer to the tray. "I didn't divorce Frank because I didn't want to upset him."

Didn't want to upset a rapist? Jeez. This was frightening. Mum's head really was a logic-free zone. But maybe Rosy's was too. Because that hardboard spinning across Jewson's car park had rekindled her desire to know what the psycho looked like.

"This colour is far too dark," Mum said. "Twenty quid down the fucking drain."

Rosy's eyes widened. She hadn't heard Mum use the F-word before. It sounded clumsy in her mouth. "You can add a little white. You did that last time you redecorated my bedroom."

Rosy looked down at the paint tray. "Franny calls Frank a rapist," she said.

"Franny shouldn't be sharing details like that."

The dog whined.

"And weren't you going to walk Snuggy?" Mum said.

———————

Rosy dropped her gaze from a kite caught in the high boughs of a beech in time to see Snuggy squirt out a puddle of diarrhoea.

She scanned the parkland behind the houses, relieved there were no witnesses to film her humiliation. "You did that deliberately," she said.

Wasn't walking a Dachshund-terrier cross embarrassing enough? Rosy had wanted a dog she could cuddle, like an Old English sheepdog. Findlay had come home with this. Snuggy.

The Foo Fighters erupted from Rosy's cardigan and she pulled the phone out, snarled in a Tesco carrier bag. "Hey, Jen."

"Guess what arrived this morning, like an hour after you left?" Jen said. "Only a big fat N-BioCom envelope."

Rosy squealed back at Jen and stamped her feet on the grass in a rapid tattoo. "Yes, yes, yes! But how do I get my letter without negotiating Boog again?"

"You see?" Jen said. "This is what happens."

"Open it," Rosy said.

"Me? Open your special letter? Are you sure?"

"I'm sure, Jen. Open it."

Rosy's stomach turned a full cycle and her hands became slick. This was it. Her summer placement. The official start of her high-flying career. And she'd made it at eighteen. In your face, Mr Owen—saying she'd crash and burn if she went to uni straight from fifth year.

Now, she just had to pick the right moment to tell her folks that N-BioCom was based in Oslo. Boog didn't need to know.

Jen's muttering had stopped.

"Jen? You still there? What are they offering?"

"Oh, Rosy. Oh, babes."

"What? Is it only a pittance?"

Jen made a mewling noise. "There is no offer."

No offer?

Rosy's brow furrowed so much, she had to close one eye.

No offer?

She touched her eyelid and stared at Snuggy's lead. "Sorry, Jen, but are you sure? The CEO interviewed me himself. Jen?

The letter… it's a fat letter."

"Leaflets," her friend said. "It isn't you, babes, it isn't personal. They say it's across the board. No placements approved this year. It's the current economic climate."

No offer.

"They're re-evaluating their requirements. If the situation changes, they'll bear you in mind."

Snuggy—his eyes locked on Rosy's—hunkered down and dribbled out another shit pool.

Rosy hardly heard Jen. Biscuits. A summer of biscuits. Jam sandwiches, not gene sequencing. Overalls, not a lab coat.

Bastards.

Jen was talking. "Let's get smashed. Let's go out tonight and get hammered. Me and Crawford, you and Boog. How does that sound?"

Rosy's chin stiffened. "Perfect," she said. "Only let's not invite Boog."

Jen sighed. "The guy hid your name in his tattoo."

"Like that's in any way normal?"

"Take it as a compliment. Then either dump him or go back to being friends—ideally both."

Screw that. Rosy already had enough shit to deal with.

----

*Third morning of Freshers' Week and Rosy, sitting on the damp lawn outside the student union, watches Boog hover in the crowds, his hand on his stubbly chin. She raises her arm as though answering a question in class, then waves it. Boog thumbs his stubble, looking intellectual, then he makes an act of only just noticing she's sitting there. That's so endearing.*

*"Pull up a pew," Rosy says, and makes space—not too much, so that when he settles himself down on the grass and hauls his heavy-duty legs in, he's close by.*

*And once Boog gets over himself, he's easy to talk to. Rosy finds out his dad died a couple of years back. That's when she squeezes his hand and moves in to brush against him.*

*"My biological dad might as well be dead," Rosy says. "I have no memory of him."*

*He stares at her. "I can't imagine that. Don't you want to meet him?"*

*Rosy shakes her head. "My stepdad is my real dad. My biological dad is not a nice person," she says. "Bad blood on the Friendship side of the family, I'm afraid. I might go psycho and try to kill you."* She plunges a fist to his belly.

Boog gasps and flinches, then plays along, lolls his head back and sticks his tongue out one side of his mouth, making a strangulated noise in his throat. And now Rosy's hand is at his belly anyway, she flattens it out. She rubs—not long, just long enough to let him know she likes him—then takes her hand away.

His eyes are wide and she can see his mind whir behind them.

"Seriously, though," Rosy says. "My granddad was a murderer. Search for Gus Friendship, then decide if you want to speak to me again."

"I've already decided," Boog says, his grey gaze so sincere.

Boog is nothing but a lovely big teddy bear and Rosy's goal by the end of the week is to win a cuddle.

# Chapter 3
# Red lights
## Boog

A fist battered on the bathroom door. "Are you wanking again?" Crawford shouted.

Asshole. "I'm taking a dump. Want to check?" Boog shouted back, and resumed flogging his meat, but with greater urgency.

"I can hear you, slapping away in there," Crawford said. Another thump on the door. "C'mon, hurry it up, Moby Dick... I have to shave."

No good. The image of Rosy's white lace bra fled and all Boog could picture was Crawford's raggedy chin. He posted the toilet paper, flushed, crammed himself into his M&S trunks and zipped his jeans over his exhausted boner.

Evicted, Boog cuffed Crawford's ear. Crawford shoved him, but only managed to propel his own skinny ass backward into the doorframe.

"Some of us are going out tonight, and some of us are fat," Crawford said. "Which are you, Boog?"

"Asswipe."

"Tick-tock, drop-out," Crawford said.

Thank God Crawford would be gone from the flat in five weeks. Only Janek to distract Boog from his fightback.

Janek—wearing nothing but Y-fronts and size twelve K-Swiss trainers, yet never bare, poor bastard, with that pelt of ginger body hair—sank deeper into the sofa, headphones on, blowing up shit on the Xbox. Another doubled-over slice of toast and Nutella disappeared through the curtain of his hair. Those headphones were for Boog's benefit—a sweet gesture—but they did nothing for the clack and rattle of the controller and the crazy-ass flashing of the TV.

In all things, Janek had been Boog's benchmark. Boog didn't drink as much as Janek. He wasn't as fat as Janek. He worked harder than Janek. So maybe Janek was to blame. Janek had spent the bulk of two semesters in bars, in bed or in combat, blasting civilisations to vapour. Boog had relaxed. They'd shared no classes, so how was Boog to know Janek was basically just a giant brain embedded in a protective package of fat and fur?

Janek grinned at him. "Level eight, Boogieman."

No. Janek was blameless. There was only one person to pin this on: Rosy.

Boog made the sign for coffee.

"Yo." Janek strafed a truck. Boog flinched at the explosion and Janek guffawed. "Pussy."

The kitchen could be a scene from Janek's game. Dishes overflowed the sink, clambered up onto the worktop. A frying pan complete with sausage stuck in white fat lay on the hob. Cornflakes crunched underfoot. And the whole place stank of fish and chips. Per usual, Janek had left the knife standing in the Nutella jar. He'd also nicked three slices of Boog's past-its-sell-by ASDA wholemeal loaf, without bothering to seal the bag and shove it back in the freezer. Crawford, meanwhile, had draped his own jeans over a chair, but Boog's jeans were still a sodden tangle in the Zanussi, and somehow the jeans annoyed Boog more than Janek's after-dinner snack chaos.

No clean mugs, but Boog foolishly multitasked by boiling the kettle and washing a couple of mugs at the same time, thereby losing a precious few minutes of guilt-free procrastination.

And when Boog came back, his unpaid, full-time summer job sat waiting for him in the armchair: *Chemistry*, by Blackman et al. Twelve hundred pages of stuff he should have been studying all year, instead of Rosy Friendship.

He set his hairy flatmate's coffee down, then retreated from that Janek miasma of Right Guard losing the battle against body odour.

"Thanks, Boogie," Janek said. "You're a prize."

"No wuckas," Boog said. No wuckas at all.

Boog settled ass into armchair, and opened the tome at his

bookmark, a Foster's beermat rescued from his first date with Rosy. She'd written the drinks order on the back and thus turned the disc into a holy relic.

Chapter 21, Aldehydes and Ketones. But one look at a page full of erect little carbonyls and Boog's mind sprang back to Rosy.

Crawford began one of his Eminem raps, where he *d-dah-dah*ed through the hard bits.

Boog closed his eyes. He was so screwed.

"Forgot to tell ya," Crawford shouted, then opened the bathroom door and leaned over the chair to leer in Boog's face. "Rosy's coming out to play tonight."

Boog pushed him away. "Bullshit."

"Why else would Jen tell me to keep your fat ass in the dark?" Crawford said, and deodorised an armpit.

A knot gathered in Boog's forehead. Why would Rosy go out? Rosy wanted to turn down the volume.

"Don't worry, Fats," Crawford said. "I'll let you know if your woman strays." He grinned and shrugged into his G-Star shirt. "Of course, not if she strays my way, and she's certainly given me signals."

Boog raised his eyebrows. "Signals like *Stop* and *No Entry*?"

"Signals like she'd love to lose a whole lot of weight, fast," Crawford said. "Dead weight."

Boog bit his lip, shook his head then got up and followed Crawford to the front door. "Bullshit."

"You mean she hasn't sent you the same signals, fat boy? Maybe you need to pay more attention."

Crawford waved to Janek, then to Boog. "G'night ladies. Enjoy Xbox, or whatever it is you ineligible guys do to simulate having a life."

"Xbox is reality," Janek said. "You're the simulation, Crawfish."

The flat door banged.

Seventeen points out of fifty in the critical semester two exams. Seventeen points. Thirty-four percent. What was that? An E, for fuck's sake? A-passes his entire life, and now an E? Boog's dad would have taken him apart, atom by atom.

Boog deployed his inhaler.

An E.

But wasn't Rosy worth the sacrifice?

Why would Rosy go out without the cuddlemeister?

"We could grab a beer?" Janek said, scratching his balls.

Boog could do with a beer. "I should study."

"We could tail Crawfish," Janek said. "Find out where they're going. Then we could grab a beer."

Boog gritted his teeth. He had to knuckle down and study.

But he had to be sure Rosy wasn't back with Ruben. "Janek? Go excavate your clothes."

---

Boog and Janek waited on a yellow line, and watched the entrance to the Brass Monkey—a favourite of Jen's—through the windscreen. Tailing Crawford had been a scary gig but as soon as the destination became obvious, he'd been able to hang back. Crawford and Jen hadn't picked Rosy up. Maybe Rosy wasn't coming. Maybe Crawford had only been winding Boog up again.

"Looky-looky. Eleven o'clock," Janek said.

Rosy. Boog's heart gave that plaintive little tug. He wanted her so bad right now. So bad.

"You're a lucky guy," Janek said.

Boog frowned. "Why isn't she going inside?" He realised why as soon as he said it. "Shit, she's looking for the car. Get down, Janek." He tried to duck down himself.

"Down? Down where?" Janek whimpered, his legs already wedged under the dash.

"Too late. We've been rumbled."

Boog took out his phone, and became intensely interested in it.

Rosy rapped the driver's window.

Boog looked up, astonished to see her. The window hummed down. Her scent wafted in—Clinique Happy—and she bent over, giving him the sweetest of views if he but dare look.

Janek dared.

"Rosy?" Boog said. "What are you doing here?"

Rosy folded her arms. "Jen sent me a text to say you followed them."

Boog hoisted a thumb at his passenger. "Janek's stalking Jen, aren't you Janek?"

"Yeah, I have a problem," Janek said, and parted the drape of his hair, treating Boog to the tang of oniony armpit. "Stalking is tough with no wheels."

"Not funny, Boog," Rosy said, and she had that adorable little crinkle between her eyebrows.

"My fault," Janek said. "Boog's been studying his ass off all day. He just wanted a beer, honest. I spotted Crawford and thought it'd amuse to give chase."

Boog nodded, desperate, and patted Janek's back in lieu of a full-on chest bump and bear hug. "Truth. That's exactly what happened, babe."

"I don't know what's going on in your head, Boog," Rosy said, "but you'd better listen up because I'm not going to say this again." Her eyes were hard. "I have ambitions in life. I will not be carrying some worthless drop-out and making excuses for him."

"Rosy—?"

"If you pass your exams, maybe we'll talk. But until then, stay away from me. I don't want to see you." She backed away, arms folded. "Sort your shit out, Boog. You have all summer." She scowled and shooed him with her hand. "Now, would you just get lost?"

A total ban on the cuddlemeister. Licence to hug revoked.

Boog watched Rosy cross the road, desperate for every photon that reached his eyes, then she was gone, lost inside.

Janek leaned his head back in the seat and gave a big sigh. "I need to find me a woman to treat me that mean."

Boog had the woman. If he didn't pass his exams, she'd never treat him mean again. "Janek? You might just have witnessed the beginning of the end for me."

---

*All week long, Ben has been using his nickname from primary school— Boog—to introduce himself, establishing a new, cool persona to go with his new, cool haircut and his new, cool clothes. And his reinvention has worked, because all week long, an impossibly beautiful girl—the girl every guy keeps asking about—has been smiling at him, chatting to dull old Ben. But it's when he and Janek are in the queue, waiting to board the Get-to-Know Edinburgh bus tour, the last Saturday of Heriot-Watt's scheduled Freshers' events, when Boog gets-to-know he's fallen in love with Rosy Friendship.*

*It starts with a tap on his shoulder. He turns and she's two feet away. To Boog, she's the living definition of the word* radiance. *Rosy has an aura. From the tumble of her hair to her tight boots, a light separates her from everybody else. She's like a Marvel character whose disguise can't hide the superhuman within. A stray eyelash rests on her cheek, and that's the only way he can tell she's even mortal.*

*"Hey Boog. Need a partner?"*

*"Actually," he says, like the virgin he is, "this is my pal Janek."*

*Janek shakes Rosy's hand, then says, "Won't be room on one seat for the two of us, Boogie. You two should sit together."*

*Janek insists and Boog's new friend has saved his love life.*

*On the bus, Boog offers the window seat to Rosy.*

*Rosy shakes her head, a smile on lips perfect as petals, a smile that lights the gold dust halo in those infinite eyes. "You sit at the window," she says. "That way I'll always have a lovely view."*

*And Boog is hers. Boog is hers forever.*

# (Sunday, 29 May)

## Rosy

Rosy lifted her face from the pillow, aware that somebody was in her room. For a moment she thought the intruder was Boog until she spied the discoloured toenails and realised it was only Findlay, thank God.

Her woollen tongue managed an approximation of, "Dad?"

"It's almost nine in the morning, Sweetpea."

Almost nine? On Sunday morning? "Thanks." She waved him away. "Getting up. Go."

Somebody had driven nails through the back of her head at angles, then bent them over behind the headboard, pinned her onto the bed. God.

"Your mum's on early shift so she's gone to work. But she told me the bad news," Findlay's voice said, "about the placement."

The placement, gone. Reward Biscuits. Starting next Monday. Mum couldn't have been more delighted.

Rosy moved her head and the pain reminded her about the bottle-and-a-half of Pinot Noir last night. Eighteen was too young to drink. Somebody should change the law.

"Irene doesn't get the importance. But I do," Findlay said. "It's more than a job. It's your dream. We both have dreams, you and me, Sweetpea."

She managed to bring his face into view. "Dad? Not now. Please."

"Of course," he said. "But if you want me to phone N-BioCom, see if I can change their minds...?"

Yeah, like maybe he could drop into Norwegian and chew the fat about gene splicing.

"I'd do anything for you, Sweetpea," Findlay said. "Anything. Even if you just need a hug. Sometimes we need that, don't we? A great big hug, like when you were little. If you needed that."

He touched her hand.

Rosy gripped his finger, patted it. "I don't. But thanks."

He smoothed her shoulder through the bedclothes. "Think about it."

"I will," Rosy said.

Or she could go sniff an ashtray.

Not so long ago, she'd longed for a hug from her stepdad. Or from her mum. But now he'd only gone and given her a pang for a cuddle with the old Boog.

Thanks a lot, Dad.

# Findlay

Findlay stood with his back to Rosy's bedroom door, and his bald patch pressed against the wood. Beneath his bathrobe, his own wood pressed against his underpants.

He'd watched for twenty minutes before she'd noticed him. And the scene had been so hot. Just watching her lie on her front like that, the top of her breast lifting and falling, the curve of her buttocks—

Oh, Jesus, what was he doing?

Findlay shook his head and retreated to his and Irene's room to dress.

# Rosy

Rosy must have dozed because Boog had taken his shirt off to show her he had indeed sucked off his nipples with the Dyson. But Rosy's thinking brain woke her with a startlingly clear thought:

Screw N-BioCom.

Screw their CEO, the lying sack of Scandinavian seal shit.

And screw Reward Biscuits.

Rosy had other options. She could take a trip out to the campus tomorrow, visit her director of studies, and enlist his help to find a placement. Maybe with an English pharma company.

Yeah.

Fuck yeah.

She sat up—

— and became a child again.

On the wall, Rosy's old favourite, a poster from Disney's *Beauty and the Beast* tacked and re-tacked a half-dozen times, the colours garish now. Her Bratz doll, Cloe, in need of a good wash, dirty tramp. And the treasure of Christmas five years back—her dusty Technika portable TV and DVD player—just a cheap piece of crap. Kid's junk.

Rosy turned on her TV, opened up her *Beauty and the Beast* DVD, shoved the disk in the tray, then collapsed back in her tiny bed with her arms around Toff, her fat teddy. She clipped the DVD case closed and stroked the Beast on the cover. The beautiful Beast.

Rosy thought of Boog and how he'd followed Crawford and Jen last night. Crawford said Boog had driven like a madman.

It wasn't fair. First Ruben, now Boog. And she'd been so fond of Boog. She was all through with guys.

She watched her movie and when Belle sang about the baker, Rosy thought about those chocolate digestives just waiting for somebody to take them to Franny.

Not a pleasant prospect, admittedly, but Franny had to have a picture of Frank-the-Raper somewhere, surely?

Somewhere biscuit-related, perhaps?

---

*Rosy's mummy hands Franny a clear plastic bag full of reject biscuits, then Rosy holds her cheek out for Franny's wet kiss. Rosy wipes the slime from her face and Franny cackles, then shows them both into the lounge.*

*There on Franny's coffee table is a biscuit tin with a Christmas picture on the lid. Proper shop-bought biscuits, not factory rejects.*

*"Please, may I have a biscuit?" Rosy says.*

*"Oh, there are no biscuits in that my darling," Franny says, and pulls the tin from Rosy's prying fingers. Franny holds open the bag of crumb-speckled chocolate digestives. "Help yourself, my wee hen."*

*Rosy settles for a reject.*

*Franny puts the Christmas tin up high, way up high, way out of reach.*

# Chapter 4
## Biscuits
### Rosy

Rosy's mum once described Granny Friendship as so awful she was too scared to dislike the woman. Rosy had a certain fondness for the old girl. Even so, she felt her heart rate increase as she stepped onto the path between a garden of lawn and flowerbeds on the right, and its evil twin, ragged and ruined, on the left—Franny's garden.

Franny.

Even the woman's pet name originated from fear, when a four-year-old Rosy had stumbled over *Thank you, Granny Friendship*. Granny Friendship had laughed until tears came, then jabbed Rosy in the chest. "That's my name, now. Franny. I'm your Franny." Funny to look back on. Scary at the time.

The doorbell *ding-donged*. Rosy waited, the swag bag of biscuits behind her back.

Franny's letterbox rattled up so abruptly, Rosy teetered on the step.

"Bugger off," Franny said. "We're not interested."

"Franny? It's—"

"Rosy." The door clattered then swung wide. Franny stood there in a summer dress much too young for her, a pencil behind her ear, a cigarette stuck to her bottom lip. "Rosy. My Lord. You've blossomed. Come in, come in. You should have phoned." She scrunched her hair. "I'm a mess and I don't have anything to offer you."

The woman waved Rosy inside, through the hall and into the lounge, where a shiny road bike rested against the settee. The name on the bike read *Specialized*. An apt description.

Expensive. Franny pointed with her cigarette. "Chained to my back fence for a month. That makes it mine. You need a bike?"

Rosy smiled, shook her head then remembered the biscuits. She lifted the plastic bag. "Chocolate digestives."

Franny gave out a rattling laugh. "Good girl." She waved Rosy into a chair draped with washing. The woman shifted the bike forward and let herself fall back into the sofa, the biscuit bag clutched against her stomach.

The old woman opened the bag, grabbed a biscuit, broke it in her hand and pushed half in her mouth. She spoke over the biscuit. "Love these. Been ages." She chewed for a while, closed her eyes in pleasure.

Rosy wiped slick hands on her jeans, and smiled.

Franny gestured to the sideboard, a teak monstrosity packed with plates that wobbled whenever anybody walked past. "Thanks for the beautiful birthday card," she said.

The cat on the card had made Rosy laugh. Now it looked petrified and desperate to escape. The other card would be from Rosy's mum.

Rosy waved her hand dismissively at the card. "Bad taste," she said, "but glad you liked it."

"Nonsense," Franny said. "I always love your cards. You have an eye for a lovely picture. Your mother too."

Lovely picture? The cat had been photo-edited to goggle in a cross-eyed stare at its pink tongue snagged in a mousetrap. Still. As long as Franny liked it.

The second half of the biscuit followed the first, but into the side of Franny's mouth, like a wad of chewing tobacco. "His go straight in the trash."

"Frank's?" Rosy said, and sat forward. "He sends you cards?"

Franny raised her brow and nodded. "But broken hearts can't be patched with birthday cards." She chewed, knocked crumbs off her dress, picked up the newspaper, held it at arm's length. "Mr Geppetto or Island Song?"

Rosy shrugged, smiled. "Island Song."

"Good girl. That's a winner." Franny took the pencil from behind her ear then circled the paper before tossing it aside. "Time I had a win." Franny's amber eyes met Rosy's and, as usual, Rosy couldn't look into them.

"Findlay crossed paths with Frank at the builders merchant. Is Frank in the building trade now?"

Franny cackled. "Frank? Building something? He's useless. He can't even bang in a nail." She shook her head. "No, hen. He'd have been up to no good."

Like throwing hardboard.

"He still works for *her*. Phyllis Long." Franny spoke the name as though it scalded her mouth. "The devil has marked his own." That was a reference to Mrs Long's disfigurement. "She'll burn in hellfire." Franny sat forward. "You want to hear something awful, Rosy?"

Rosy nodded, leaned in close enough to smell the cigarettes on Franny's breath.

"I didn't offer you a tea and one of your own biscuits," Franny said, and rubbed Rosy's cheek.

The woman stood.

Rosy edged forward in the chair but didn't stand. Deliberately didn't stand. "I'll help," she said.

"Nonsense," Franny said. "You're the guest. Sit. Sit. Relax."

Relax. Right.

———————

Rosy waited as long as she dared then sat forward and let her eye rove Franny's lounge, up and down the shelves, looking for something, not even sure she could bring herself to act if she saw it again, already convinced this was her worst ever idea.

Franny, a wizard with the scissors, had dealt with all her son's pictures. The only one left intact was of a dark-haired, smiling three-year-old Frank in an oval mount on the sideboard. But maybe there were some other relics of Frank in...

That old biscuit tin.

And there it was. Red and gold. That old Christmas biscuit tin. Always in here somewhere. The tin sat on a coffee table now, half-concealed beneath a splayed library book. Rosy pursed her lips, rose to her feet, stepped over an ashtray and hunkered down.

The walls in this place were thin, as though maybe there were nothing behind the wood-chip wallpaper but cardboard. From the kitchen came the sounds of a basin filling. Never a clean cup. Same system as Boog: Just-in-time dish washing.

Rosy glanced at the kitchen door, then slid the tin from beneath the novel, couldn't help smirking at the dopey book jacket. *Rogue-hearted Son.* A redheaded heroine swooned against a bare-chested hero, helpless.

"Is a mug okay?"

Franny's voice made Rosy jump. "Perfect," she shouted back, picked up the library book, sat back up in the chair and waited. But the kitchen door remained closed.

Rosy swallowed, then moved in on the tin again. A cheesy Christmas scene decorated the lid: a golden-haired girl hoisted by an unseen adult to place the angel atop the tree. Yuck. Pass the yuletide sick-bag. Rosy shook the tin gently once, heard a muffled knock. Maybe pictures? Maybe the faces of Frank, cut from all the photos?

The kitchen taps shut off. Rosy waited. Heard a hand agitate soapy water. The bump and clack of submerging crockery.

Her own hands slick, Rosy popped the lid off the tin.

An odd smell wafted out. Musky. Not unpleasant. Inside, folds of white knitted wool. A doll's blanket or shawl. She lifted one side away, then the other. And her breath halted.

Oh. My. God.

The doorbell d-donged, and Rosy jolted.

"Who in the name of Christ—?" Franny said.

"I'll get it, Franny," Rosy shouted. Her hands shook so much she could barely shut the lid. "I'll get it." She plopped the romance novel back in place, dodged the table and ran for the door. If she could have, she'd have kept running.

---

In the half-second it took Rosy to wonder if the cyclist—balding and in grey Lycra—might be Frank, she remembered the bike in Franny's lounge. "Hi," Rosy managed, her mouth dry, pulse throbbing in her ears, heart still in full flight mode.

"Hi," the cyclist said. "Sorry to disturb you." He smiled. "I wonder—"

"Bugger off. Not interested, whatever it is," Franny said, and took charge of the door. "Sling your hook."

"Wait," he said. "Please. I'm looking for my bike. I chained it to the fence out there last night—"

"Oh you did, did you?" Franny said. "Let me guess,

somebody nicked it? Well, good. Teach you a lesson. That's a private fence, and that's a private road for residents, not a bloody park-and-cycle."

"Listen, I'm sorry," he said. "You didn't happen to notice anybody else with a black bike. It has the word *Specialized* on the down-tube—"

"No." Franny cut in before Rosy could open her mouth. "Now, bugger off before I get the police to you." She slammed the door so hard Rosy flinched.

Rosy gaped. "Franny, that's his bike. You'll have to give it back."

"Oh, no I won't," Franny said. "This is the only way they learn."

Rosy turned back, but Franny's hand clamped her wrist. "Do you want to get me in trouble?"

"Have you done this before?" Rosy said.

"No," Franny said, then shrugged, let Rosy go. "Once or twice."

Rosy covered her mouth, then—shaken and appalled— followed the bicycle thief into the kitchen.

———————————

Franny handed Rosy a mug to dry. Field mice, kissing. The same motif decorated the yellowed roller blind.

"Relax, my darling," Franny said. "Your pal will claim on his insurance. Some kid will get the bike of his dreams. I'll have another hundred quid to keep the wolf away. And the fat cat financiers get bloody noses." She reached up and pinched Rosy's cheek. "It's a virtuous circle."

Rosy stared. Was Rosy now an accessory? "Franny?"

Franny held her hands up. "Okay. Guilty. But I can't work, and benefit cheques don't cover my costs. Do you want your poor old Franny to curl up and die?"

Truthfully?

Rosy knew better than to ask why a woman fit enough to cut through a chain and lug a bike up four steps couldn't work. "Don't you get money from Frank?"

"Frank? Hah. Would you like to see what he gave me for my birthday? My sixtieth birthday?" She dried her hands on Rosy's dishtowel, then opened a cupboard and lifted down a clear plastic cake container.

A Victoria sponge filled the top layer.

Was that so bad? A card and a cake? "At least he remembered," Rosy said.

"Oh, he remembered, all right. He's like an elephant: never forgets and leaves nothing behind but shit."

Franny lifted the container lid. The icing sugar lay white and untouched.

"You didn't want to taste it?" Rosy said.

"I didn't want poisoned," Franny said. "I should have shown him what I thought of his birthday present."

Before Rosy could object, Franny flipped open the pedal bin. The sponge broke and flopped in. Franny tipped an ashtray on top, then the lid gonged down on Frank's cake.

"Anyway." Franny picked up the tea tray. "I assume you didn't come here to talk about a rapist."

---

Rosy had no desire to sneak another look in Franny's biscuit tin, so when Franny visited the ladies', Rosy behaved like a proper guest and just sat leafing through the same old doctored photos in the hope of finding something she'd missed.

Visitors to Franny's house had to pretend they couldn't hear every fart and splash from the bathroom, had to keep their own legs crossed until they got home. Judging by the noise, maybe Franny ought to lay off the chocolate digestives.

Rosy's search through the photos, meanwhile, was unproductive. The only intact image of Frank was a sheet of four duplicates of the big portrait on the sideboard. Four duplicates. A cuddly three-year-old kid and nobody had wanted a picture of him? Nobody?

The toilet flushed, and Franny rejoined her.

"My favourite picture of you is this one," Franny said. Her dirty fingernail tapped on Rosy looking like Queen Dork in a party frock. "Maybe 'cos I see myself in you, back when I was pretty."

Scary.

"Franny?" Rosy held up the four little Franks. "Could I keep one of these?"

Franny looked at her hard for a moment then nodded.

"'Course you can, hen," she said, "But that's not your daddy."

Rosy gaped. "It's not?"

"That's my wee darling. That's my wee Frankie before the devil twisted him into a monster." She poked her finger into another hole where Frank's face should have been. Her eyes glinted.

*The devil marks his own. Twisted into a monster.* Frank must be disfigured. That's why Mum and Findlay never let Rosy see him. Disfigured, like Phyllis Long. And if Rosy wanted to see Frank, maybe Mrs Long could arrange that.

Rosy picked up the photo: Frank in the shed with his dad, Gus Friendship. Still little more than a toddler, head snipped out. "What I don't understand," Rosy said, "is why you kept granddad's face, but cut out Frank's?"

Franny leaned back to fix Rosy with a stare. "Because, Rosy, all the evil in this family is rooted in Frank."

Rosy looked down at the missing face.

"Frank drove the wedge between Gus and me," Franny said. "Frank is the curse. Frank is why Gus isn't here today, the reason Gus did what he did. Gus was no killer."

Oh, but Gus was a killer. Rosy's grandfather's deeds were all over the internet. Frank could only have been six at the time and no six-year-old kid, no matter how malevolent, made Gus Friendship do what he did.

"I'll go cut off one of these for you." Franny waved the photos and stood.

Rosy lifted her mum's wedding photo. Their only wedding photo. Mum stood smiling, leaning against a ragged hole. Franny had been especially thorough in her excision of Frank in this one, had even snipped into Irene's image where there'd been overlaps. They'd had to wait until Frank turned sixteen before they could marry, so Rosy had already been born, and wasn't in the picture. Her mum wore nothing shiny. Rosy had checked for any reflection of Frank. Nothing. Nothing at all. And nothing of Frank in this house, Rosy felt sure now.

Phyllis Long was the route to Frank.

Rosy shuffled to the picture of Mum, pregnant. Clearly still a schoolgirl, her mum was huge with Rosy. Huge.

Franny returned and handed Rosy the picture of Frankie.

"Stay away from Frank, hen. He's not right in the head. Sees things that aren't there. You have a dad who loves you. His name is Findlay. Stay away from that monster."

---

*Findlay lifts Rosy off his back, and sets her on her feet on the wooden boards that thread their way through one of the marquees at the Royal Highland Show. The whole tent stinks of poo. Rosy reaches through the pen and lays her hand on the sheep's flank. The wool is soft but pushes back against her fingers. The sheep walks away.*

*Rosy's stepdad takes her hand.*

*She smells her fingers and rubs them together. "I want a baby sheep for the garden, Daddy," Rosy says.*

*"A sheep would eat all Mummy's flowers," Findlay says. "Now, a dog…"*

*"Don't put ideas into her head, Findlay," Mummy says.*

*Rosy is about to ask for a dog when her stepdad stops, turns back the way they've come. "Take her outside, Irene," Findlay says.*

*"What? Why—?"*

*"Frank. Dead ahead."*

*Mummy grabs Rosy's hand and together they run along the planks, back towards the daylight. Rosy tries to look behind, tries to see the bad man Frank, but Mummy brings down a hand to block her view.*

---

Once Franny had phoned in her bet and the horse racing started, no earthly force, not even chocolate coated, would separate her from the telly. Rosy left without asking, even obliquely, about the biscuit tin, too afraid her tone would betray her. She waved at the net-covered lounge window—empty, she knew—and started down the path.

The neighbours had emerged—a couple in their eighties or maybe nineties wearing matching green aprons—out to weed their side of the garden, the weeds seeded, no doubt, from Franny's rampant tangles. Rosy said hello and was opening the gate latch when something cracked hard across her skull.

"Bitch."

Another blow fell. Rosy ducked, lifted her hands to protect her head. Tried to turn to see her attacker. Pain bloomed as the wooden pole of a hoe thumped Rosy's lip. The swing would have cracked teeth if an old hand hadn't grabbed hold.

"Stop, Isabelle. Stop it." The old man stepped between his wife and Rosy, twisted and shook the hoe free of her grip. "That's Rosy," he said. "That's Frankie's daughter. Little Rosy."

The woman—Isabelle—stared at Rosy, then at nothing. "Frankie's daughter?" She shook her head. "Poor wee Frankie."

"It is Rosy, isn't it?" the man said. "Are you okay?"

"I'm fine," Rosy touched her aching bottom lip, where a lump was already forming, and inspected the blood on her fingertip.

The man winced. "I'm really sorry," he said. "She's getting worse. She's never hit anybody but me before." He sighed. "She gets… confused. She's stronger than me, but her mind…" He shook his head.

"Wee Frankie?" Isabelle said.

Rosy's photo of Frankie had fallen face up onto the path, and lay at the woman's feet, ready to be trampled.

"Go," the old woman said and made a shooing gesture. "Run. And don't come back." She broke wind trying to bend over. "Don't come back. Don't come back."

To Rosy's relief, the old man retrieved the picture.

"Pay no notice," he said. "She doesn't even know what she's saying anymore." He looked as though he might cry.

"Sorry." Rosy squeezed his hand, opened the gate and slipped past.

———————

On the bus home, chilling her fat lip with a Wall's Mini Milk, Rosy played back the image of the thing in the biscuit tin, the thing wrapped in the tiny shawl.

A child. A girl. A mummified human foetus.

From the child's back bulged a tumour like a second head.

Rosy was born in Franny's house. And in that photo, Mum's stomach had been huge.

# Chapter 5
# Beast awakened
## (Monday, 30 May)
### Rosy

Rosy's director of studies at Heriot-Watt campus was good enough to see her with no appointment, only to acquaint her with the Latin for eggs—*ova*—and basket—*calathus*. He said he'd email her a few contacts, but doubted that at so late a stage she'd be successful in her search for an alternative placement. He advised her to revel in her youth and cherish her vacation.

Rosy had wanted to tell him he'd wasted half a day of her vacation and she'd aged just listening to him, but had instead told him he was wonderful.

She called Jen to check she was remembering to feed Justin, the goldfish, and with the morning squandered, why not make a day of it?

---

Every birthday, every Christmas since Rosy could remember, there'd been a card with gift tokens or book tokens and a little packet of sweets from Phyllis Long. Rosy had always meant to write, but never got around to it.

The tree on Rosy's last Christmas card from Mrs Long had been taken from an illustration in a 1930's limited edition *Stories of Hans Christian Andersen*, apparently. And above that inscription was the sticker Rosy had been looking for. She dialled the number.

"Good afternoon, Shawford Group," a female voice said.

"Sorry, I had this as the number for Phyllis Long?"

"That's right," the voice said. "I'm Heidi, Phyllis's PA. Can I help?"

Rosy blinked. Phyllis had a PA? "This is Rosy Friendship—"

"Oh, you're Frank's daughter?" the woman said in a rush. "Hold on. I'll put you straight through to Phyllis's mobile."

Rosy waited, and the PA must have introduced Rosy because Phyllis answered, "Hello, dear."

---

Phyllis Long clearly had a different idea of discrete than Rosy. After the short ring from her phone that announced Mrs Long's arrival, Rosy stepped out of the house to see a sparkling, deep blue Aston Martin DB9, its engine murmuring.

Rosy ran to the car before every kid in Northfield Terrace descended. She pulled the door open and got in, careful with her feet so as not to leave any marks. "Hello, Mrs Long."

Mrs Long turned. "Hello, Rosy." The words and the eyeless half of Phyllis Long's face told her the woman was trying to smile. The side with the eye hung slack. "Look at you. You're so grown up. So beautiful."

Rosy managed to stop herself from saying the woman looked well. The woman looked as scary as Rosy remembered. That half-paralysed face and permanently closed eye seemed somehow more ghastly with such feminine clothes—the lacy-collared blouse, the poppy print midi skirt. A Halloween mask in diamond and sapphire earrings.

The car pulled away with a throaty rumble, and because Phyllis's missing eye was this side, Rosy had the disconcerting impression the woman was driving asleep. But from here, she also appeared more human, more normal, the sagging cheek and mouth hidden. Younger too, though she must be in her mid sixties.

Rosy fumbled for something else to say, then realised a little gratitude was long overdue. "Thanks for all the tokens and sweets, Mrs Long."

"Call me Phyllis. Please. I feel foolish now for sending those," she said. "You're too grown up for chocolate Santas."

"Are you kidding?" Rosy said. "Nobody's ever too old for chocolate Santas."

"Your dad doesn't like them," she said. "Calls them dog chocolate."

And by dad, she meant Frank. Frank-the-Raper.

"As I said to you on the phone, Mrs Long—Phyllis—I'd sooner just see his picture than meet the man."

"Nonsense. Your dad would love to see you." Phyllis said. "He talks about you all the time."

"My dad sees me often enough," Rosy said. "My real dad." She felt her neck bristle as she said that but it was too late.

"Of course," Phyllis said. "I meant your natural father. Frank talks about you endlessly."

Rosy ran her hands through her hair. "We live in the same city, and Frank has never come to see me. I can't imagine any thought of me ever crosses his mind."

"Oh," Phyllis said, "you'd be surprised."

Anger rose up from nowhere. "Frank raped my mum."

"Frank was fifteen and drunk—fourteen, actually," Phyllis said. "Your mum was drunk too."

Mum had been drunk? At fifteen?

"You can't ever have the full facts," Phyllis said, and briefly turned her demolished face on Rosy, "so don't go holding grudges. Especially not someone else's."

That brought more anger, but Rosy controlled herself. "I only want to see him. That's all. I have no intention of ever forgiving him."

"That's fine, dear," Phyllis said. "It's your pain. You may hold onto it, or let it go."

Rosy glared out at the traffic. Of all the people to stick up for Gus Friendship's son.

———

Rosy sat silent while Phyllis parked on a hatched rectangle marked *Private* in a cobbled area for permit holders only. Rosy had lived all her life in Edinburgh, but visited Stockbridge maybe three times, aware this was Frank's haunt, and not, therefore, anywhere for her.

Certainly, Rosy had never heard of St Bernard's Place, the street Phyllis had driven down, but she hadn't missed much: St Bernard's Place was just another Edinburgh street of elegant Georgian buildings, businesses giving up one at a time to the creeping mould of charity shops.

On the drive past, Rosy had spotted the cafe where Frank

must work. At first glance, she'd thought the place was called *Nasty Bite* and, by the looks of it, the name fit perfectly. But the first letter T of the sign had come loose, and hung at an angle.

*Tasty Bite.* Tasty. Yeah, right.

"Ready?" Phyllis said.

The woman's voice in that muffled leather interior startled Rosy.

"Just to be clear," Rosy said. "I only want to say hello, have a private word with him, then leave."

"Fine by me," Phyllis said.

"And he's definitely not expecting us?"

"As you requested, Rosy, I've said nothing to Frank. Not a word. You'll see him at his worst."

"Okay," she said, and her innards slackened. "I'm ready."

---

A bell above the door of the Tasty Bite betrayed them with a ding that made Rosy cringe. She followed Phyllis inside, trying to hide behind the little woman. Bleach, toast, stale coffee. The smell of the place hit her, dizzied her, threatened to topple her.

Brown.

Everything. Even the light that fell across the floor, dirtied by the blistered film on the windows. Frank's world. Shit brown. Shit hole.

Rosy wanted to escape, but Phyllis's arm snagged her, held her, drew her into the cafe's dingy bowels.

A retired couple stood by the cash register, engaged in directing the shadow that squatted behind the counter to something in the glass cabinet. Rosy could see the tongs. Frank must be holding those tongs. Rosy hated that her heart had started to hammer, as though this place, this person were in any way significant. The tongs closed on a scone.

"Sit," a ponderous voice said. "I'll bring it."

The customers moved aside and there, straightening up and turning his back on her, loomed Frank. She watched hands big as a farmer's attached to forearms thicker than Findlay's legs deposit the scone on a plate, then poke a teabag into a china teapot.

Rosy's breath stalled and if the hard hook of Phyllis's arm hadn't held her steady, she would have turned and run.

"Gimme a minute." Frank's words struggled around a thick tongue. Had something happened to his face? Damaged his mouth so he couldn't talk? He glanced over the bulk of his shoulder, recognised Phyllis, turned, then his eyes met Rosy's.

Rosy's heart clutched tight and forgot the beat.

"Rosy?" Frank said. The teapot tumbled from fat fingers, exploded on the floor. "*Uh*. My baby."

Oh shit.

Why did nobody ever tell her Frank was retarded? Why did nobody ever tell her Frank was beautiful?

---

*On a school trip to the National Gallery of Scotland, Rosy has traipsed past countless canvases, growing ever more convinced that, like opera and blue cheese, art is something people only pretend to like. Then she stops dead in front of a painting of a young man.*

*He wears a high-necked coat of kingfisher blue and a frilled shirt with upturned collars. He is crowned in dark curls, and his perfect lips almost smile. But it's his eyes that arrest her. Eyes that bridge two hundred years.*

*She searches the gift shop postcards until she finds the painting, then she kisses it and holds it to her chest:* Portrait of a Man *by François-Xavier Fabre.*

*Later, emptying the remains of Rosy's packed lunch, Mum claims to be humiliated by her twelve-year-old daughter's inability to eat crusts. Rosy's mind, though, is on feeding her soul, not her body.*

*"Forget the Mona Lisa," Rosy says. "I'd have this over a million Mona Lisas. Look at his eyes."*

*Her mum takes the National Gallery postcard, studies it and smiles a smile that makes Rosy frown. "I think," her mum says, and hands back the portrait, "somebody has discovered boys."*

---

"We'll have a seat over here, Frank," Phyllis said. "Join us when you're free, and bring your daughter a… tea?"

Rosy nodded. "Tea." Rosy's eyes were still trapped in his.

"Okay," Frank said.

Rosy had fallen backwards from a swing once, thumped her head but told everybody she was okay. She'd taken half-a-dozen steps, then the world had gone grey, shrunk to a tunnel and she'd fainted. That's how she felt now, like she'd smacked her head on asphalt, and at any moment, reality would shrink to nothing.

The little woman drew out a chair for her. "Are you all right, dear?"

Rosy was fine. Fine. Wasn't she? "Mum didn't tell me he was…" Rosy searched for the least-offensive word: "Simple."

"You want something, Phyllis?" Frank yelled, oblivious of the customers and their glances.

Phyllis cringed. She signed a C for coffee.

"Frank's far from simple," Phyllis said. Her eye sparkled. "But he's not entirely normal either."

What did that mean? Rosy wanted to look at him again. To see for herself. This was Frank? This was her dad? He was the antithesis of Findlay. How could Findlay and Frank even be the same age?

Phyllis was studying her, and Rosy fumbled for something to say. "How long has… Frank worked here?" she said.

"Since sixteen. That makes it… eighteen years? Goodness." Phyllis lowered her voice. "Shhh. He's coming."

"A coffee for you, and a tea for Rosy. I don't know if you like crisps, Rosy, baby, but I brought you some to munch."

And again, that awkward speech. Frank's eyes weren't quite straight, or were they? His eyes… his eyes pulled at her… like that postcard.

He set a tray on the table, handed the coffee to Phyllis. He then reversed a chair, sat down, propped his chin on his hands and sighed. "Oh, Rosy. I want to look and look and look at you."

Phyllis shoved Frank's arm. "Stop that."

But Rosy wanted to look back. "It's… it's okay."

Frank was big, like Boog, but not like Boog. Frank was like a rugby player, or a weightlifter.

"See?" Frank said, and propped his chin up again. "She's my daughter. We're the same."

He glanced sidelong at Phyllis's unwavering glare, defying her at first, then seeming to think better of it. He hauled himself upright and sat inspecting his fat fingers.

"Thank you," Phyllis said, and tutted at him. "Honestly."

The sound of a throat clearing made Rosy look up.

"Tea and a plain scone?" the pensioner said. This was the

man Frank had been serving when Rosy arrived.

Frank rolled his eyes. "Tea and a plain scone. Tea and a plain scone," he said, met the old man's glower then pushed his chair back and stood. Six-feet-three versus five-feet-nothing, a standoff between an American Football player and a referee. "Sit." Frank pointed. The referee caved under the pressure. And Frank stalked back to the counter.

Phyllis shook her head.

"He has a way with customers," Rosy said. She watched Frank's back as he poked a fresh teabag into another teapot and filled it. What was he doing in this job anyway? Why wasn't he out on a construction site, the big brainless guy they called in to swing a sledgehammer or lift a girder off somebody's leg?

Frank put the teapot on a tray, noticed she was watching, and wiggled his fingers at her. The wave was the kind an adult directs at a baby in a buggy.

And that thought snapped Rosy from her daze.

The bastard hadn't been there to wave into Rosy's buggy, had he?

She looked away, annoyed that her initial shock had let him sneak beneath her defences, steal the initiative.

"I'll leave you to have your catch-up," Phyllis said, "if you feel comfortable enough on your own with him?"

"We've caught up," Rosy pushed her chair back. "I wanted to meet him. Now, I've met him."

Phyllis's wreck of a face became harder. "You can't go before you give him a chance."

"Can't I?" Rosy said. "He did that to me, remember?"

Phyllis shook her head. "No, that's not what I remember at all."

"Tea," Frank said, loud even from here, "and a plain scone. Happy now? Can I go talk to my long-lost daughter now?"

Long-lost. Long-lost in Edinburgh. Bastard.

"What do you remember, Mrs Long?" Rosy said.

"Why don't you ask your father? He's coming back."

Rosy stood, stuck out her hand. "It was nice to put a face to the name, Frank."

His smile faltered. "You're leaving already?" he said. "When are you coming back?"

Rosy crossed her hands. "Never."

"Okay," Frank said, and looked at Phyllis, his smile gone. "Well, can I give her a hug now, then?"

Phyllis covered her mouth, distraught, nodded.

Frank opened his arms.

Rosy stiffened, embarrassed, didn't want a hug and yet took a half-step toward him, and then he was all around her, surrounding her. He smelled of soap and the outdoors.

---

*Autumn air fills Rosy's lungs as she emerges onto the open top deck of the tour bus, her hand around Boog's. The bus turns past the statue of Greyfriars Bobby, then leaves the National Museum of Scotland behind. They take a seat one row back from a pair of Chinese students.*

*"Brrr," Rosy says, not cold in the least, and moves in closer to Boog.*

*Boog stopped watching the tour some time back. He looks all around as if somebody might be ready to arrest him, then lifts an arm, and lays it across Rosy's shoulder. Rosy leans into him. He gets the idea. The guy's a natural. Rosy has just met her cuddle goal.*

*Time to dump Ruben. Way past time.*

*They turn onto South Bridge.*

*"Blackwell's bookshop there," their guide says, "and for those who have memories of Freshers' Week they never want to forget, Outkast Tattoos is just along there."*

*Everybody laughs.*

*Boog's arm draws Rosy closer. It's the I-care-about-you hug she's tried to coax from her mum or from Findlay for as long as she can remember.*

---

"Be happy, baby," Frank said into Rosy's hair. "Your daddy loves you."

# Chapter 6
## Another approach
### Rosy

Marching wordlessly back to the car beside Phyllis, Rosy should feel exhilaration. She'd stuck it to Frank, good and proper. Why, then, did she feel like such a complete shit?

"Happy?" Phyllis said.

"Not particularly."

The woman stopped. "So go back."

Rosy thrust her hands backward through her hair, grabbed and tugged till it hurt. "Why am I the one to make the concessions?" she shouted.

Phyllis folded her arms, anger clear on her lopsided face. "Oh, and you've made a ton of those, haven't you?"

Rosy lifted her arm, tried to say something, then pointed at the cafe, held her head, covered her mouth and—humiliation of humiliations—she began to cry. Right there in the street. "I'm so confused," she said but it came out as a great honking wail.

"Come here, you silly girl," Phyllis said.

The woman put her arms around Rosy, patted her back, and for the first time in forever, Rosy allowed herself to just cry.

A young mother with twins in a pram passed them. The children's eyes tracked Rosy for a second before their faces crumpled and they started to cry too.

"I'm sorry," Rosy said, and flapped her arms. "I'm sorry."

"Now, here's what we're going to do," Phyllis said. "We're going across to my offices, and you're going to visit the ladies' and when you're back in control and you've knocked those chips off your shoulders, we're going to go back in there.

Okay?"

Rosy nodded. "Yes." A gob of snot ran from her nose.

"But listen to me, Rosy Friendship, and listen well. What happened was between your mother and Frank. Not you and Frank, okay? Not you two. You two have a relationship to build."

---

Rosy sat in a cubicle more plush than in any hotel she'd visited, and dabbed at her nose, feeling so stupid.

How could she go back in there now? Why had she even come? Silly little girl.

She blew her nose again.

Heels sounded on the floor then a voice, not Phyllis's, called to her. "You okay in there?"

"Fine," Rosy said.

The sandals beneath the door had an adorable rose print. "It's Heidi again," the lady said.

Phyllis's PA. "Hi," Rosy said. "Pleased to meet you." That had to be the dumbest way in the world to introduce yourself.

"I have this eye spray. I'll leave it here. Works like magic when you've been crying."

"Okay," Rosy said, and began to tear up again.

"If it's any consolation, honey," Heidi said, "he's had me crying too."

A laugh escaped Rosy's throat. "Yeah, it helps, thanks."

The sandalled feet hesitated, then turned, and Heidi was gone.

Rosy shook her head, dabbed her nose, told herself to buck up. This was how girlie girls like Jen behaved, this was so not Rosy. Rosy didn't even cry when she broke her arm and the bone stuck through. Rosy was tough, like her mother.

Time to try some of Heidi's magic eye spray.

---

As soon as Rosy stepped back in the cafe, the counter flapped back and Frank was out.

"I'm sorry, baby," he said. "Please don't go away."

"Don't crowd the girl, Frank," Phyllis said. "Not everybody's built like a Sherman tank."

Frank's eyes swept right then left, as though waiting for a line from a prompter. "Okay," he said, slowly, then waved at Rosy. "Hi."

"Hi," Rosy said, waved back.

"We should have dinner," Frank said.

"Now, what did I just tell you?" Phyllis said.

"Sometime." Frank held his hands up. "We should have dinner *sometime*. When you're ready. When you're hungry. You can come too, Phyllis. Oh, and Irene."

"That would be nice," Rosy said. "Except, I don't think Mum will come."

"Why not?" Frank said.

Phyllis pushed him like a keeper shoving an elephant. "Maybe you want to talk with your daughter? While I mind the till?"

Frank pointed Rosy to the same table as before, and hoisted a thumb at Phyllis. "She's crusty, but she's okay."

"Crusty." Rosy laughed. "Yeah."

Frank dressed well, she realised. None of Findlay's Tesco value range. Timberland boots, Dockers and a Crew Clothing Co. T-shirt.

"You look beaut'ful," Frank said. "Like Irene…"

Not like her mother. Rosy could see that now. She was Frank's daughter. His hair, his complexion, his eyes.

"… more beaut'ful than your pictures."

"Pictures? You've seen pictures of me?"

"At my mum's," Frank said. "That's where I soak up news about you and Irene. I know a lot about you. You're at university to be a scientist. Real smart. You play the violin and the cello."

Rosy shook her head, cringed. "I gave up music lessons four years ago. Sorry."

"You won't eat crusts or green vegetables," Frank said.

"That was a while ago, too, Frank."

"You went to Prague last year on holiday, but you thought the money would have been better spent on Festival tickets," he said.

That brought memories of Ruben, losing his temper on Charles Bridge.

"Frank?" Rosy said, and dared to touch his hand to stop him. "I know about me. I don't know anything about you."

"Okay," Frank said. He looked at Rosy with those not-quite-straight, not-quite-squint eyes, and took her hands in his. "My name," he said, "is Frank Friendship. I'm your real dad. And I'm Irene's legally wedded husband. *I* am. Not Findlay Dickson, not anybody else. Me."

His face had taken on the same belligerent expression as when he'd squared off against the customer.

"This," Frank said, and pointed to his wedding ring, so tight it seemed to have crushed the bones, "has been on my finger since the day Irene put it there. And it's *never* coming off. Never. Because I'm going to get her back."

He released Rosy's hands. "Now, you know everything about me."

Rosy gazed up at him, confused by how looking into his eyes could be so like looking into her mother's. Then she realised that the feeling of deep familiarity wasn't with her mum's eyes at all, but with her own, and that she and Frank Friendship had just peered into the depths of one another's soul.

———

"Thoughts?" Phyllis said, once Rosy was back in the Aston Martin.

Rosy just closed her eyes and exhaled. "Intense," she said. "I'm... my head is all over the place."

"Hard part is over, so now you two just need to keep in touch," Phyllis said, and patted her leg. "Let's get you home."

The woman edged the big car forward, and growled out onto St Bernard's Place.

Rosy looked back at the Tasty Bite. "I have to be honest," she said. "I'm not impressed by your cafe. It's a dump. If I owned that, I'd bring in the bulldozers and turn it into offices."

"Funny you should say that," Phyllis said. "Sadly, I'm now of the same opinion."

Rosy turned in her seat. "Seriously?"

"The cafe's no longer breaking even. Not when it's adequately staffed," Phyllis said, that closed and sunken eyelid lending her face an exhausted look. "But I can't keep it staffed anyway." She glanced at Rosy. "Frank has become more intolerant. He isn't always rude to customers, but coworkers..." She gave a grim little laugh. "My biggest frustration is that I'd cracked it.

"I'd hired a Polish man six months ago. Marek Borkowski. Horribly arrogant, but Frank didn't faze him."

"So what went wrong?"

"Marek quit a week ago," Phyllis said. "Not attracting enough young female customers, apparently."

Rosy drew her head back. "Can't fault him for his honesty," she said. "So you're shutting the place down?"

"Frank doesn't know yet, and I'd appreciate if you didn't tell him."

Eighteen years' service. Rosy couldn't quite believe she was already concerned for Frank. "What'll happen to him?"

Phyllis shrugged. "There's work to keep him occupied out at my estate."

Rosy sat back and watched Stockbridge go past, trendy little places swarming with people. If businesses here could make a go of it...

"What about modernising and taking the cafe upmarket?"

Phyllis shook her head. "Good money after bad. More customers means more staff, somebody else I have to find who can work with Frank."

"Wouldn't a different clientele convince that Polish guy—Marek—to come back?"

The old woman took her eye off the road for a brief glance at Rosy. "Would you be interested in a summer job, Rosy?"

Rosy laughed. "Me? Working in a cafe? No offence, but I'm really after something better than 'Part-time cafe worker' on my CV."

Like *Biscuit factory dogsbody*.

"How about, 'Business start-up consultant for a new cafe chain'?"

Rosy's eyebrows lifted. Was this for real? "Cafe chain?"

"A chain has to start from a pilot," Phyllis said.

Rosy stared straight ahead at the road. It couldn't touch Junior Research Assistant for N-BioCom. But it beat the pants off the biscuit factory.

And she'd see Frank every day.

"Wait a minute," Rosy said. "Start-up consultant? Why would you want me?"

"You'd be cheap," Phyllis said, "you'd be motivated, and

Frank wouldn't tie the toilet door with you inside and leave you there all weekend."

"Oh, no. He didn't?"

"Don't tell Frank I told you that either, please," Phyllis said. "I assured him it was forgotten."

Business start-up consultant. Ruben would have killed for a role like that on his CV.

The sun seemed brighter, the car more luxurious.

Of course, Rosy could never tell her folks. Findlay hated Frank with a passion, and the flying hardboard had demonstrated the feeling was mutual.

"Can I think about it?" Rosy said.

"Please do," Phyllis said. "Very seriously. But to be clear, I don't waste money. I expect a return on any investment. And please do not underestimate the magnitude of the challenge."

---

*Second day in Prague, Ruben wants Rosy to sit with him on the Charles Bridge for an artist to charcoal their portrait. The artist takes Rosy's hand and pulls her toward the folding chair but Rosy shakes free and holds her hands up.*

*"No, thanks," she says. "You have a solo portrait done, Ruben. I'll wait."*

*Ruben's face goes from sunny to sullen. "What is wrong with you, Rosy?"*

*Rosy doesn't want to be in a picture with Ruben. That's what couples do. If they have their picture drawn, Ruben will expect more of her, more than she's ready to commit to. "Let's find a coffee house or an ice-cream shop or something," Rosy says.*

*Ruben stalks off and she has to run after him.*

*"Ruben?" she says.*

*He turns around and there are tears on his face. "Why must you keep denying me, Rosy?"*

*Ruben, Rosy has just realised, is unstable. "Let's get an ice-cream," she says.*

# Chapter 7
## Lies
### Rosy

Rosy beat Snuggy back to the house, and ran inside. The dog cannoned in behind her, claws skittering on the lino.

"Whoa, careful," Mum said. Suds filled the sink, and sparkled on her yellow rubber gloves.

"Hello, Mum." Rosy puffed. She grabbed her mother around the waist, then surprised herself by hugging her. "How was work today?"

Mum laughed and writhed free. "Same old, same old."

"Well, somebody's happy," Findlay said. "Doesn't Dad get a hug?"

"'Course you do," Rosy said, catching her breath. She hugged the little man, patted his bony back and frowned that his face had wound up in her cleavage.

Now she smelled of cigarettes.

"Guess who found a decent placement for the summer?" Rosy said.

"Wait a minute." Her mum leaned back from the sink. "What do you mean, a decent placement? You're starting at Reward next Monday, remember? I found you a seat on a factory bus and everything."

"Sorry, Mum. I really can't. Not now," Rosy said. "But this will be much better for my CV."

"I made commitments, Rosy." Her mum pulled off her rubber gloves, threw them in the sink. "On the strength of your commitments to me. How is this going to make me look?"

Rosy blinked. "Excuse me? Hello? We *are* only talking about a biscuit factory. Biscuits?"

"We're talking about the place I work," Mum said. "The people I work with. The company that put a roof over your head and sent you to university."

"Nobody sent me to university," Rosy said. "I earned my place. And I've worked at Reward before, Mum, remember? I think my *career* is a bit more important than putting Doug McKinnon's lecherous old nose out of joint." Doug was the only reason Rosy was a special case at Reward.

Her mum folded her arms. "What is this new placement?"

Rosy breathed in. "My director of studies found it. It's not as good as N-BioCom, but it is a lab, a small Edinburgh lab, associated with cancer research at the Royal Infirmary. They're in Stockbridge." The lie just unfurled. "I start tomorrow."

"Tomorrow?" Mum sighed, resigned. "You can't put them off for a month? Even just a couple of weeks, so I don't look like a complete idiot?"

Findlay slapped his hands on the table, so they both looked at him. "Irene. Stop. This is Rosy's dream, and I will not have you stand in her way."

Rosy frowned at him. Mum wasn't standing in her way. Mum was a pushover, had already capitulated.

Her mum stared at him. "Pardon me? Rosy's dream? To be a hospital lab assistant? Since when?"

"Irene," Findlay said. "I don't demand much in this household, but I do demand…" He swiped a tear away, and Rosy felt her toes grip the lining of her shoes. "I do demand that this wonderful girl is free to follow her dreams wherever they may take her." He'd begun to cry.

And because Rosy's flood defences had already been breached today, she felt tears well up. "It's okay, Dad." She held Findlay's hand. "Don't upset yourself."

Her mum gaped at the pair of them.

"But I am upset," Findlay said. "You, Irene Friendship, should be ashamed. Look at the state you've got us both into with your brutal intransigence. Us. The people you claim to love."

Brutal? Mum? What was Findlay on about? Rosy wanted to disappear now.

"Okay," her mum said, eyes wide. "Rosy: Do what you want.

Findlay: Your demand has been heard and met."

Findlay nodded. "Well… I should think so, too." He sniffed and squeezed Rosy's hand. "See? Together, we're unstoppable."

Rosy cupped her hands over her nose and mouth.

That went well.

# Findlay

Findlay was still shaking with passion at the stance he'd taken for Rosy, and he needed fresh air. He picked up his ciggies and lighter.

"I'll walk Snuggy," he said, and he could see the surprise on Irene's face. Yes, Findlay was full of surprises today.

"But Rosy just took…" Irene said, then caved. Caved to the might of a man in charge.

Snuggy tugged ahead and Findlay allowed himself to be pulled in the general direction of Arthur's Seat. Findlay would walk Snuggy more, if he could ignore the shit-bag fascists. Findlay would be sick in his mouth at even the thought, the very notion of picking up lumps of smelly dog—

Findlay choked and swallowed the bitter taste.

His little dog pulled him further on.

Rosy had cried at Findlay's eloquence. Wasn't that something? If God were recording Findlay's finest moments, that would be somewhere near the top. She'd held his hand.

And sticking his face between her breasts would be somewhere near the bottom. Along with Sunday morning's incursion into her room. But both hot as hell. If God were playing those scenes back, Findlay would point out that Rosy wasn't his natural daughter, so of course he wanted sex with her. She was just so fuckable. He could do her doggy-style right this second, right here on the pavement.

Snuggy had stopped to sniff. Findlay tugged him away before he got any ideas about shitting on this walk.

Findlay had picked Snuggy out himself, picked him because he was the littlest and ugliest in the home, and Findlay'd had a horrible feeling they might do the little guy in. As Findlay well knew, little, ugly ones needed just as much love. More.

If Irene's baby had been Findlay's own, she'd have been plain. He held no illusions about that. But, oh, Findlay would have loved her. In the truest sense, without the baggage.

Without resentment.

And then this whole situation wouldn't have arisen, would it? These fantasies. This lying awake beside a woman as good-looking as Irene, but with thoughts of Rosy pulling at him. Rosy in the next room, so young, fresh and abundant, lying there. So fuckable.

Rosy had hugged Findlay. Had held his hand. Findlay wasn't that much older. Fifteen years. Slimmer than that boyfriend of hers. That fat fuck of a boyfriend. And if that kid could be Rosy's boyfriend, looks clearly didn't matter to her. Clearly. There was already a bond between Findlay and Rosy. Such a strong bond. And they weren't related.

Would Rosy consider Findlay? Even as just a fuck daddy?

Snuggy had stopped and a greenish brown gunge was spurting and frothing from his backside.

"I hope you've got a bag for that," a voice said.

Findlay turned to see a lardy cow in a red blazer like a hand-me-down from Butlins, her arms folded. Then he caught the scent of Snuggy's business and was promptly sick in his mouth.

---

*Findlay undoes his school tie and shoves it in the pocket inside his blazer. He walks in the wrong direction, heading away from home, and then he sees her: Irene, pushing the pram. Findlay hears the baby's cries already—Frank's spawn, Frank's parasite, yelling and squawking.*

*Findlay runs his fingers through his thick brown hair, hair Irene has complimented more than once, and crosses the road diagonally to intercept her.*

*"Irene?" he says.*

*Irene turns and studies Findlay's face.*

*"Noisy, isn't it?" He points at the baby.*

*"It's a she. Her name's Rosy."*

*"Rosy. Beautiful name." He looks in at the repulsive, red-faced little screamer, already with Frank's dark hair. He can smell its shit too. He smiles at it although he's struggling not to barf. "Beautiful baby."*

*"How's school?" Irene says.*

*Findlay puts his hand on hers—a married woman's. "Lonely. So lonely."*

*Irene looks at him. Her eyes are liquid. "Lonely?"*

*"Without my beautiful, beautiful Irene."*

*Findlay can hardly believe he's said it.*

*And Irene's legs buckle and he has to steady her.*

*"Oh, Findlay. I made such a bad mistake."*

*Findlay finds he is crying too. Crying with joy. "Mistakes can be fixed, Irene. I'm here for you. I'll always be here for you."*

# Rosy

Rosy couldn't remember the last time she'd had mince and potatoes, but did remember that horrible texture, like somebody had already chewed everything before her.

"Not hungry?" Mum said.

"Not so much." Of course, excitement over tomorrow didn't help. Excitement about Frank.

A drop of gravy fell on her mum's blouse. She tutted, stood then wiped the smear at her little pot belly.

Rosy thought of that photo, that pregnant belly so huge. She frowned, then said, "I had a really weird dream last night."

"Oh yes?" Mum said, and sat back down, still dabbing the gravy stain with kitchen paper. "And you're blaming my cooking, are you?"

Rosy tutted. "No, but this dream was so weird. So, so weird."

Findlay stroked Rosy's arm. "What was your dream, Sweetpea?"

"I dreamed," Rosy said, and watched for her mum's reaction in particular, "I had a sister."

Her mum laughed. "A sister to eat your mince and potatoes?"

Rosy shook her head. "No, a sister who had a deformity. A big hump on her back."

Mum grinned. "Was your sister called Esmeralda?"

Findlay laughed at that but Rosy didn't get it.

"Esmeralda. The Hunchback of Notre Dame's sweetheart." Mum shook her head. "Never mind."

If the foetus in Franny's tin had been her mother's stillborn child, there was no sign of grief. Of course, maybe they wouldn't have shown Mum.

"Was she pretty? I mean, ignoring the hump," Findlay said and squeezed her leg.

Findlay had become more tactile after getting so emotional, and that wasn't a change for the better. "I don't really remember," Rosy said. She tried adding another detail to see if that produced a reaction. "We were twins, born at the same time."

Again, nothing.

Findlay rubbed Mum's hand. "Irene dated an identical twin at school, didn't you?"

Rosy's eyebrows lifted. Must have been pre-Frank. "Was it hard to tell them apart?"

Her mum shook her head. "Not really," she said, then laughed. "Mine had a broken nose." She laughed again then dabbed her eyes. "Oh, dear. And I haven't even been drinking."

Oh, so funny. Rosy scowled, got up and tipped her mince out for Snuggy.

"That'll go straight through him," Findlay said.

Mum shook her head. "It's not the mince. Snuggy gets overexcited whenever Rosy comes home."

"Pardon?" Rosy stared at Snuggy.

Snuggy stared right back.

The dog had a thing about her? The dog?

"He'll be fine in a day or two," Mum said. "First time I realised was when you came back from Scout camp. Snuggy had a major dose of the skitters."

Findlay made a little choking noise in his mouth, shuddered and swallowed.

Clearly, her stepdad didn't like mince and potatoes either.

———

Rosy had long been the only person in the house who could right-click. And also being the only person in the house who could follow step-by-step instructions with giant balloons and pictures, Rosy had ended up with the job of setting up a new wireless router to replace one that had plinked out like a bulb a month after Mum changed internet service providers.

She sat on the telephone table and tested that the installation worked by ordering *The Beancounter's Cafe Handbook*, a top-rated book about running a successful coffee business.

The phone began to ring. Anybody phoning Rosy would use her mobile, but she was right there, so picked up.

"Hi, baby," Frank said.

Rosy held her mouth, then ran upstairs with the handset, and closed her bedroom door.

"Frank? Why are you calling this number?"

"Phyllis told me you were starting work at the cafe tomorrow."

"Do you have a pen?"

"Sure," he said.

"Well, write down a new number."

"I'll remember. I have a good memory," Frank said. "Shoot."

"Write it down, please. It's my mobile number."

She read the number out and he recited it back to her.

"Don't call me at the house again, please," Rosy said.

"Okay," Frank said. There was a long pause. "Why not?"

"You'll upset people. You'll upset Findlay."

"Good," Frank said. "Because know what? Findlay upsets me. He upsets me by living with my daughter and my lawfully wedded wife."

"You'll upset me, Frank, okay? Don't call this number or you'll upset me. I want you to call my personal number only."

"What? Now?" he said.

"If you like, yes."

The line died. Rosy patted her pockets. Where had she left her phone?

She dashed downstairs to the lounge.

"Your phone's singing," Findlay said. "I hope it's not that big fat boy."

Rosy picked her phone up and ran back upstairs to her room.

"Rosy?" Frank said. "Are you there?"

"I'm here, Frank. And, yes, I'm starting at the cafe tomorrow. What did you want to say?"

"Nothing," he said. "I just wanted to talk to my baby."

Rosy laughed. "That's nice. What shall we talk about?"

"Let me think," Frank said. "Did you know a cat can't taste sweet things?"

Rosy rolled her eyes. "I had heard that somewhere."

"Did you know, the human gut has almost as many working neurons as a cat's brain?"

Rosy rubbed her forehead. "Did you buy a book about cats?"

"No," Frank said. "I thought you'd like to talk science. The cats tumbled in there by accident. I feed a guy who keeps cats."

Rosy's brain hurt. There was an odd noise in the background. "What are you doing, Frank? I can hear splashing."

"I got all messed up out on a job for Ernesto. I'm in the bath."

"And you had a pen in the bath to write down my number, like I asked you to?" Rosy said. A job? Out on a job for Ernesto? A robbery? A mafia hit?

Frank was talking. "You asked if I had a pen, I said sure, which I do. Just not in the bath," he said. "You asked me to write down a new number. I told you, I'd remember. I have a good memory. You asked me to write it down anyway, and I'll do that later. But I remembered Irene's number from seventeen years ago, didn't I? And I only ever dialled that once to prove I knew where Findlay was hiding so I could come snap his neck anytime I fancied. I think I'll remember my own baby's number."

Rosy turned her back to her bedroom door, and dropped her voice. "Rewind, Frank. Snapping Findlay's neck. That was just an idle threat, right?"

"Lost the soap," he said. "Whoa, found it."

She frowned. "Why are you calling me from the bath?"

"Efficiency. I prefer to do two things at once."

She smiled again. "I'm looking forward to starting at the cafe, Frank. I'm sure we'll make major improvements."

"Improvements?" Frank said. "What do you mean?"

Uh-oh. Hadn't Phyllis told him? "I mean, little touches."

"You said major improvements."

"Little touches that make major improvements," Rosy said, and sat down on her Mr Men stool. "Over time."

"Don't go messing with things. You're only here for summer. I made everything quick and slick, so I can do it all myself."

"Tell you what," Rosy said. "You have your bath, and we'll talk about everything once I start. You can explain your system to me then."

"You'll be fast as me in no time, Rosy. You'll whiz," he said. "That's why we don't do real coffee. Real coffee is slow. And I can't stand the stink."

Oh, jeez.

"Can you put Irene on now?" Frank said.

Rosy gasped. "What? No, I can't put Irene on. And you mustn't call her."

"Ohhh, you didn't tell her we met, did you? That's why you don't want me to call you at the house."

"Correct," Rosy said.

"I'd better tell her," Frank said.

"You'd better not, or you'll put the kibosh on me working at the cafe."

There was a long pause. "Okay," he said. "Just don't tangle me up in your lies."

Rosy scowled. "What's my mobile number, Frank?"

He repeated it and she could just picture digits written in steam, dripping down his bathroom mirror.

"Good. I have to go. Enjoy your bath."

"I will," he said. "I'm onto my belly now, saving the best bit for last."

She hoped that meant the best bit was his belly. She hoped.

---

*November and there's snow everywhere. It would be too cold to sit in Princes Street Gardens if Boog weren't here. They cuddle on a stone seat at the war memorial, and Rosy calls Boog her hot-water Boogle, but he frowns.*

*"That just makes me self-conscious about my weight," Boog says. "And when you touch my belly all the time, that makes me feel fat, too."*

*Rosy puts her hand up his jumper, leans in and takes her first real kiss. Each tongue explores a new mouth.*

*When she pulls away, Boog's breath steams out, his cheeks are redder. Snow from his woollen hat has fallen and now dusts his long eyelashes. "Awesome. I didn't know I could do that," he says and swallows. "Your teeth are so big."*

*Rosy laughs. "My teeth are tall, yours are wide."*

*He looks down at his belly. "I want to get rid of that for you."*

*Rosy shakes her head. "Don't. I love your belly. I love your cuddles. You could give cuddle lessons at university."*

*"I'm the cuddlemeister," Boog says.*

*"You are." Rosy laughs and watches her own breath puff out. "I need another lesson," she says.*

# Chapter 8
# Germs
## (Tuesday, 31 May)
### Rosy

Rosy rapped on the glass panel of the door to the cafe.

Frank loped across and bear-hugged her over the threshold, breathing in her hair. "You taste like peaches."

"Smell, you mean."

Rosy could get used to one of those hugs every morning.

Now with her renovation eyes on, she realised there was something in the middle of all this dinge she could turn into a feature. That big mahogany counter. It bowed out slightly and appeared to float. Rosy crouched low, and tipped her head to look beneath. She could see right through to the wall behind and through the door into the kitchen. Legs at either end— pesky gravity—but otherwise, yes, the counter just floated. With a light underneath, that would look awesome.

Frank was frowning at her. Best to leave off taking pictures of everything until the afternoon. She followed him into the kitchen and hooked her jacket next to his.

"That's Phyllis's peg." He moved Rosy's jacket to the next hook, looped an apron over her head, spun her around and tied the tapes tight. Next, he walked her to the sink, turned on the cold water, squirted soap on his palms, then, standing behind her, he took her hands and washed them with his own.

Rosy should have objected but emotion choked her up. Odd, yet wonderful at the same time, his breath steady in her ear, his arms around her, looking after her, washing her hands as though she were three years old. When he'd done, he picked up the towel—rough and stiff as cardboard—and dried their hands together, to leave her skin tingling.

"That's the first thing you do," he said, "soon as you come in."

"Yes, boss," Rosy said.

Frank turned her to face the cafe and gave her a little push. "Deli tubs. Take all the lids off. Check the date on the lids. Yesterday's means deadly poison. Pull 'em but don't chuck 'em. They're our lunch. Today's date means specials."

She stepped into the cafe. A giddiness, a sense of not belonging here, made a short-circuit in her head, a *zub* in her ears. Alone here with Frank, drawn into his world.

The big floating counter was split-level, high shelf facing the customers, and a wide workspace behind. That counter was awesome. She found the switch to turn on the light for the deli. The fluorescent tube flickered on in the refrigerated display, illuminated three banks of discoloured plastic tubs on top, grey with white stress marks. Those tubs had to go.

She should note down everything that needed fixed, before she became indoctrinated. "Frank? Do you have a pen and some paper?"

"Till," he shouted through. "Under Happy Henry."

Above Rosy's head, another fluorescent light buzzed and struggled to come on—must add lighting to her list—but Happy Henry was hard to miss. On a pile of three order pads sat a gonk with faded and matted pink fluff. His red nose might have been cheery but for his brooding scowl. She picked the toy up, then snatched the order pad and gaped at the sketch there.

Rosy walked back into the kitchen, grinning like a fool while she studied the drawing on the pad—the face of a gruff space explorer, helmet visor raised, scowled back. At school, Rosy had been good at drawing. A chasm separated that kind of good from this. This piece wouldn't look out of place in a Marvel comic or a graphic novel. "Frank? Did you draw this?" She stepped up to him and held the pad out.

"Yeah." He ripped the leaf off, scrunched it tight and lobbed it in the bin. "Sorted."

She stared at the rubbish and the gap where the precious little ball had disappeared. "But—"

Frank pointed outside, toward the road. "Bread's here."

---

The bread truck said *Maclay's, Family Bakers Since 1947*, but the dumpy Indian man who used his butt to close the sliding door didn't look like he was a Maclay.

Frank relieved the older man of the plastic tray.

"Oh. Is this your lovely daughter, Frank?"

Frank nodded once as if to say, *What of it?*

"Hello, doll. I'm Jay." The man dusted his hands on white trousers.

"Rosy," she said, and held out her hand.

Frank blocked their handshake. "Germs," he said and shoved an empty blue tray at Jay, then hoisted his thumb at Rosy. "Back inside."

---

The bell on the door clunked as the door shut.

"There was no need to be nasty," Rosy said, and scowled at him.

Frank pointed at the deli. "Lids." He clapped his hands. "Thirty-five minutes and we're open."

Rosy's jaw clenched but she kept quiet. She heard him wash his hands again. Germs.

Egg mayonnaise, tuna and cheddar all had yesterday's date. All deadly poison. Egg. She shuddered. That might as well be deadly poison.

Rosy put the lids and the expired tubs on the kitchen worktop and again felt a little giddy.

Frank's eyes bulged at her. "Oh, baby, what have you done?"

She spun around. "What?"

He pointed at the pile of lids she'd brought through. "The lids have the dates," Frank said. "The lids have to stay with their tubs."

She covered her mouth with her hands. Stupid, stupid, stupid.

Now Frank was pointing at her face. "And you just touched your mouth. Germs."

Rosy bit her lip. "I'm so sorry, Frank. I wasn't thinking."

"Go wash your hands."

"What about the food?" Rosy could see her first day's pay disappear.

"*Pfff*," he said, and waved a hand. "Doesn't matter. Labels are for people with bad memories. I remember all the dates."

Anger rose up in Rosy. "You remember? So why scare me like that?"

"Don't make mistakes," Frank said. "People can die. Keep your hands clean. Check and double-check everything. Use your nose for sniffing." He pointed at his wide wedge nose. "Use your eyes for peeping." He looked side to side, the words and action comical but his delivery serious. "If in doubt, chuck it out."

"How about this for an idea then?" Rosy said. "Start putting the date on the tubs, instead of the lids."

"Nope." His answer was immediate and final. "Thirty minutes to make soup, egg mayo, tuna mayo and grate cheddar. Let's go, baby."

———————

Tuna mayonnaise didn't strike Rosy as a topic requiring special instruction, but Frank had a problem with everybody else's tuna mayonnaise.

"Some places don't drain right," Frank said, "so it sounds all wet…"

*Sounds* all wet?

"And most places mush." He wagged his finger. "We don't mush here at the Tasty Bite."

Rosy averted her face so Frank wouldn't see she was laughing.

"We open the tin both sides." Frank demonstrated with the biggest tin of tuna Rosy had seen. "Get rid of these…"

Don't serve up the ends of the can. Useful to know.

"Then we push the block out, like so, into the straining bowl…"

Like so.

"Then we flake—don't mush, don't press—flake, see? And when we've separated it all out to flakes, like so, we set it aside to fully drain." Frank smiled, satisfied. "We'll leave that for ten minutes then fold in the mayo. Fold. Not mush."

Rosy nodded. And after laughing at first, she realised his deadly poison tuna mayo did look one hell of a lot better than the usual fare.

We don't mush here at the Tasty Bite. She picked up the tub.

Very appetising. Apart from the tub itself.

"You can have some of that for lunch. Saladised if you like," Frank said.

"Saladised?"

Frank shrugged. "English has missing words. Learn Franklish."

---

Frank treated customers with the contempt Rosy had only seen before at airport passport control. Even then, she'd never heard an immigration official refer to anybody as *baldy*.

"Hey, baldy," Frank had said and whistled to call a customer back as though he were down in the paddock with an unruly herd. "You forgot your juice."

Frank held up the bottle of Tropicana orange juice. And when... *baldy* came back, Frank slapped the bottle into his hand as though passing him the baton in a relay race, then waved the man aside—"Go!"—and pointed at the next customer.

"What do you want?" Frank said. "Cheese? Again? That's three cheese you'll have had in a row. Are you eating right?"

The customer stammered.

"Eh-but-eh-but-eh-but," Frank mimicked. "Never mind. But think up a different filling next time. And not cheese and tomato." He shook his head and made up the roll.

Once he'd finished, he bagged the order then held it out of the customer's reach. "Cheese, again. Three in a row. Don't make it four," he said, and only then did he hand the bag over.

"You," Frank pointed at the next customer. "Are you two together? Is she your girlfriend? Man, the Turin Shroud isn't the only miracle. Okay, Worzel, what do you want?"

"Frank?" Rosy said at the first break. "Do you have any regular customers?"

He frowned at her. "Most customers are regulars."

Rosy gaped. "Well, if I came into a cafe and they treated me the way you're treating these people, I'd never be back."

He looked off to one side, frowned, then looked back at her. "Why not?"

"Baldy?" Rosy said. "You don't call people baldy. You just don't."

"He didn't have hair. He forgot his orange juice. I did him a favour, baby," Frank said, then put a warm hand on the small of Rosy's back and rubbed. "Don't worry. It's your first day," he said. "You'll learn."

Rosy rolled her eyes.

The next customer to come in, was a young woman with frizzy ginger hair who looked so frail, Rosy thought her shoes would chafe the skin off her ankles. Watching her approach was like watching a toddler wander onto a railway track. Rosy closed her eyes.

"Hello, Twiglet," Frank said.

"Hello, Frank." The woman's voice was a croak. "The usual, please."

"I'll give you a good mix."

Frank took out a piece of food wrap and began to layer meats and cheeses on top.

"That's enough," the woman said.

Frank held up a finger. "One more slice. I need a nice pink background." He added a slice of ham, then took a mayonnaise squeezer and piped out… an elephant. A bloody amazing one, too. He picked up a segment of black olive, put it down as the eye. "How's that?"

The girl nodded, smiled. "Beautiful. Thank you."

Frank swept his creation into a polystyrene tray and told Rosy the price to ring up.

"Twiglet needs to eat more," Frank said, when the young woman had gone. "She won't eat bread, so I started adding backgrounds and drawing flowers and stuff on there so she'd eat the mayonnaise." He settled his arm snug around Rosy's waist. "If customers look short of cash or in need of a good old feed, be heavy-handed with the fillings," he said.

Maybe Rosy could see why Frank had regular customers after all.

And Rosy began to wonder if there might be biology at play in his touches. If some other man were to pull her against him like a rag doll, or put an arm around her shoulders and lean over until his cheek touched her hair, or stand there, drawing doodles, his free hand resting between her shoulder blades, he'd earn himself an angry red handprint on the face—a foreign body, triggering an immune response and rejection. Frank was

Rosy's flesh and blood. The result? Acceptance. No, more than acceptance. Anticipation and comfort.

Besides, Frank didn't touch her breasts or fondle her butt. Frank didn't ogle her. Unlike Findlay these past few days, Frank didn't look away either. Frank looked her in the eye.

———————

*Rosy sits in the cinema beside Boog, watching cars tumble on the screen and thinks how nice it is there's so much of Boog. She leans into him, and he's cosy and soft. He lifts his arm and wraps it around her, then looks into her eyes and smiles. His face is wide and happy and so much sweeter than Ruben's.*

*This is all Rosy wants, to snuggle into him. This is her ideal lazy Saturday afternoon.*

*Then Boog's hand brushes Rosy's breast.*

*An accident? Rosy's not sure but gives him the benefit of the doubt.*

*In the dim light she watches his big fingers spread then close slowly, slowly on her boob and squeeze.*

*"Don't." Rosy hits his hand away, annoyed that he would bring sex in to ruin the simple joy of being together.*

*But Boog doesn't stop. Back comes the hand to close on her breast.*

*Rosy pushes his arm off then exits, dodging her way past others seated in the same row. "Sorry… excuse me… sorry".*

*Boog follows her and she hears people swear.*

*She exits into the foyer.*

*"Rosy?" Boog's face has lost its colour. "What's wrong? What did I do?"*

*Rosy looks at Boog but she's thinking about Ruben. "When a girl says no, Boog, it means no. Understand?"*

*He holds up both hands and nods frantically. "Yes. I'm sorry, Rosy. I'm so sorry."*

———————

The prospect of cleaning toilets made Rosy squeamish. She'd had to learn at Jen's but she'd hoped Frank would take care of that part of the business. Frank didn't need to.

"Rosy, that's Ellie," Frank said, pointing at a woman in her late fifties who'd just walked in. "She's based at Shawford but comes over to do the toilet."

"He means to *clean* the toilet." Ellie said, shook her head, and set to work.

"She's on speed-dial two if there's a real mess," Frank said. "Just think emergency number two. Get it?"

"Easy to remember," Rosy said. "Who's on number one?"

"Shawford maintenance. And, yes," Frank said, "they're pish."

On Frank's order pad, a sallow goth teen struggled to drag a puff from his cigarette, ear buds dangling beside thick soles. This was the kid whose breath Frank said stank of cigarettes and who then asked Frank for a packet of Polo mints.

"Do you think I could keep that drawing?" Rosy said.

"Nope." Frank tore the sheet off. "Because that's pish too." He crunched it up like all the others and cast the perfect little study into the bin. "They're always pish."

# Chapter 9
# Nasty bite
## Rosy

Frank's dislike of the stink of coffee clearly wasn't shared by the large number of potential customers Rosy had already noticed, who would leave the Shawford office just across the road then come back carrying Starbucks and Costa cups. Easy revenue, lost.

And if the Tasty Bite had proper coffee, maybe things wouldn't have turned nasty just after the trickle of lunchtime visitors died down, when Frank was having his own lunch and a team of council workers parked their van outside the cafe to come in search of caffeine.

"A latte and a cheese roll, darling," the wiry driver said to Rosy.

Rosy winced. "We don't have an espresso machine, sorry. Would filter be okay?"

The driver's jaw dropped. "You're kidding, right? No *expresso* machine?" He circled his finger in the air and jabbed his thumb backward over his head. "No coffee guys." They trooped back toward the door.

Frank came through from the kitchen, tipped his head back and whistled so loud, Rosy had to clamp her hands over her ears. Their only seated customer—a businessman on his phone —ducked as if a surface-to-air missile had taken out a Chinook, then glared across.

"We do filter coffee and tea," Frank said. "And I'll throw in free crisps with every two filled rolls."

The driver screwed his face up. "Feck off, pal. No sale." He looked the counter up and down. "No wonder it's a ghost town." He pointed to Rosy. "If you threw in a piece of her, I might consider it."

Rosy frowned, as the door closed on the last guy. "Annoying."

Frank's face was stone. "He's gonna apologise."

Rosy grabbed his arm. "Whoa, what? Apologise for what? For wanting proper coffee?"

"No." He pulled free. "For his smut."

Frank threw the shop door open and the bell sang. Rosy held her face and watched him open the door of the council van and gesture with a thumb. Then Frank was reaching into the van.

Rosy covered her mouth, remembering that sheet of hardboard flying across Jewson's car park.

The driver got out of his own volition. He wasn't a small man himself, and he had a van load of men to back him up but Frank stood out there, one hand in a fist by his side, the other pointing, and Rosy could hear his voice, though not what he said. The driver, meanwhile, cowered back, his hands raised to his chest in a tight surrender gesture.

Next thing, the council worker was heading back into the cafe, Frank beside him like an arresting officer.

The driver looked down at his knees. "I apologise for my smutty remark about you, Miss."

Rosy's gaze flicked to Frank, then to the driver. "Well, there's no harm done, is there?" she said.

Frank held the door open for the man, who left without so much as a glare.

She waited for Frank to close the hatch in the counter. "What did you say to him?"

"Nothing much," Frank said. "I just told him to apologise." He gave her a sidelong look, then hugged her against him, then went back to finish his lunch.

---

When—too soon—Frank locked the door and flipped the sign to *Closed*, Rosy experienced the I-shouldn't-be-here sensation again and the *zub* that threatened she might faint. She turned her back to him deliberately and waited by the kitchen door... for what? For Frank to hug her again? For Frank to put his arm around her waist? For Frank to make a move on her, now he'd flattened her defences?

Rosy really, really shouldn't be here.

She closed her eyes and felt the draught of him pass.

"You re-lid the deli tubs, I'll do the till," Frank said. "The faster we clean up—" He stopped.

Rosy opened her eyes and, when they met Frank's, her heart trembled.

Frank turned his gaze toward the ceiling, lifted a hand to grip the back of his neck and the great ball of his bicep swelled his T-shirt. "Baby, I—" He trailed the hand up his neck then rubbed his head so his hair stuck out in a new chaos. "You're not going to stay, are you?"

Rosy looked at her hands. "I want to stay."

Frank took a step toward her, frowned and showed her his clean, empty hands. "I want you to stay. I want that." He studied her. "What's wrong, baby? Something's wrong."

*Baby.* Rosy closed her eyes. "This has all just happened so fast. This job... You." She struggled for the tangible. "I'd rather you called me by my name."

"Okay." He nodded. "Okay, Rosy."

"And I'm not comfortable... hugging."

"Oh, don't worry about that," Frank said. "You're my baby. It's okay to hug me. I'm very comfortable with it. I like hugging you. I like that a lot."

"It's too soon for you to be hugging me."

He frowned. "Okay."

She smiled. "You say *okay* a lot, Frank."

"Okay—" He grimaced. "*Pfff.* That's gonna be a tough one."

"It's... okay." She inspected her fingernails because it was easier to look there than at his face. "I want our..." She couldn't say the word *relationship.* "When we're in the shop, I want to be absolutely professional. And I don't want you to... defend my honour. If guys pass remarks, let me deal with them myself. I'm used to it."

Frank began to say *okay* but stopped himself. "Professional. When we're in the shop," he said. "And when we're not in the shop?"

"Doesn't matter. We'll be in the shop pretty much all the time anyway."

"Pretty much," Frank said. "Except when we're not."

Rosy swallowed. "I'll do the deli tubs."

Frank wasn't retarded but, no, Frank wasn't normal. Words like *innocent* and *childlike* kept presenting themselves but didn't sum Frank up any more than *simple*. The incident with the van driver wasn't innocent—whatever Frank had said, that guy had been terrified.

She lifted Happy Henry and looked at another scribble on the order pad. This one was a brain. A brain, stewing in liquid, electrodes inserted.

Proceed with caution. Extreme caution. Franny, Mum and Findlay all knew things—bad things—about Frank Friendship. But did she dare to ask them more questions?

She put Happy Henry back down and watched Frank count the money from the till. He told her what the total should be without even totalling up the till. His hands moved fast. He didn't write anything down, didn't say out the denominations under his breath.

Phyllis had told Rosy to direct her questions to Frank, but Phyllis had confided that Frank had tied somebody in the toilet all weekend. Who else knew stuff about Frank? Heidi? Phyllis's PA, whom Rosy had yet to meet but who'd loaned her eye spray. He'd made Heidi cry. Then there was Marek, of course, Frank's arrogant, womanising ex work colleague. Marek had stood up to Frank, which made him a pretty special guy. Phyllis had given her Marek's number. Rosy must call him as soon as she was done here.

Frank declared the till was in balance and Rosy felt relieved, since mostly that had been her job.

"What do we do with the money?"

"Float stays in the till," Frank said. "I take the rest to the office."

"How much float?"

"I'll show you tomorrow." Frank beckoned her with his head. "C'mon, Rosy. Let's go."

Rosy hung her apron back up, retrieved her coat and joined him at the door in time for the rain to come on. Just 4:35 p.m. They sheltered in the lea of the building, like a couple of smokers who'd given up the habit, but wanted to inhale.

"Hungry?" Frank said.

"Mum's on early shift. She'll have made dinner."

"Okay," Frank said, then smacked a fist to his forehead. "I said *okay* again. Damn it."

Rosy shook her head. "Forget I said anything about that."

"Little things get annoying."

Was that a hint? "Am I doing anything that annoys you?" Rosy said.

Frank shook his head. "Not one single thing. You're perfect. You're my baby."

Before she even realised what she was going to do, she hugged him. "Thanks for making my first day easy," she said into his shoulder. "Thanks for looking after me." His arm closed around her waist but she pushed free and ran to the bus stop and didn't look back.

# Chapter 10
## Marks
### Rosy

On the bus home, Rosy flicked through the *before* photos she'd taken of the cafe. Not nearly as many with Frank as she'd have liked. He'd kept moving out of the frame, then he'd taken her phone from her and shot her instead. "You don't want me in your pictures," he'd said.

A text came in as she was zooming in on Frank's face. A message from Jen that jerked Rosy from her seat, and sent her dashing downstairs to change buses.

*In Outkast Tattoos. Where r u?*

———

The bus heading up the Bridges was full, the traffic bumper-to-bumper, and Rosy had to stand next to a gym dude in tracksuit bottoms who thought it was okay to adjust his genitals in public. The gym dude stared down her cleavage all the way to South Bridge, got off at the same stop then followed her until she ducked into a shop with black corsetry and support stockings in the window.

Rosy watched him dither about outside, then walk back toward the bus stop. She smiled at the shop owner, a woman in an orange sari, and flipped through some well-dodgy lacy underwear with printed hearts.

Once satisfied the genital rearranger had gone, Rosy stepped back out into sleazy sunshine.

"Gotcha." A hand grabbed her arm and her own hands leapt to her throat.

"Jumpy." Jen looped her arm through Rosy's. "I thought you'd abandoned me."

"I picked up a stalker on the bus," Rosy said.

"Uh. Why can't I ever pick up a stalker? Was he cute?" Jen waved her hand. "Scratch that. You're into bellies."

Rosy rolled her eyes.

"You need pepper spray." Jen led Rosy across a side street. "I carry one in every handbag. I'll give you one of my spares."

Pepper spray from eBay? "No thanks," Rosy said. "It won't be pepper spray, it'll be for athlete's foot."

"It's like nuclear weapons—the threat is enough," Jen said, then signalled a right turn with her fake Louis Vuitton. That clutch bag looked so tacky, it could be the genuine article. "I've had my chat with the tattooist, by the way. And I've decided what I want. I know you hate tattoos, but you're going to love this idea."

"Let me guess…" Rosy moved a hand over each of her boobs in turn. "Left… Right?"

Jen laughed. "It's lace. Delicate lace. Very classy. I'll show you. C'mon."

Outkast Tattoos. Oh yes, it'd be very klassy.

---

Rosy realised retrospectively that she'd had an ambition in life never to set foot in a tattoo parlour.

Tattoo *studio*, Jen corrected her.

Freaking tattoos. Rosy didn't get it. She just didn't get it. In a curtained booth, but with the curtain looped over the pole, a youngish guy—twenty-two, twenty-three at a push—clamped his grinning jaw while the tattooist happily scarred his back for life. A machine that reminded Rosy of a soldering iron buzzed at the outline of grotesque gothic letters—*NEVER SAY NEVER* —and left a trail of inky destruction. The tattooist—his own skin as vandalised as a motorway underpass—wiped with a bloodied, grubby-looking cloth.

Nazi.

The mutilation made Rosy want to whimper, the way she'd whimper at pictures of emaciated greyhounds on charity letters, but Jen's eyes shone bright. Excited. Hungry. Jen was a goner. Like Boog.

"Tattoos are forever," Rosy said. "Why do something like that?"

"Nothing's forever, babes. Enjoy your body before it's all stretch-marked."

Rosy thought about her mum's stretch-marks and shuddered. "One more reason I am never having a baby," she said. "But I was talking about Boog."

"So was I," Jen said and sighed through a pout. "When you dumped the gorgeous Ruben—if only I could have had *his* babies—I couldn't see what you liked about Boog." She tweaked a mascara-fused eyelash free. "But I like him now, and I feel so sorry for him. Such a sweet gesture, and you are totally overreacting."

"It isn't sweet. It's horrifying." Rosy shuddered at the memory of Boog using a photo editor to slide the bands of his tattoo down. Superimposed, they created four letters: ROSY.

"He shows you how desperately he loves you," Jen said, "and you think it's horrifying?"

"Jen, I repeat: It's horrifying because he had that tattoo done at the end of Freshers' Week. Before we'd even been on a date. We were almost strangers."

The tattoo meant it hadn't just been happy coincidence that Boog wound up in a flat two doors down from Rosy. He'd been stalking her from the first.

"Love at first sight," Jen said. "That's the truest love of all, and you are shitting all over it, shitting all over somebody who thinks the world of you."

Rosy remembered Snuggy's diarrhoea. "Enough about Boog's big mistake. We came to talk about yours."

Jen grinned. "You'll love it."

"Love it enough to risk losing my best friend to AIDS?" Rosy said. "Uh-huh. One dirty tattoo needle…"

"They can treat AIDS," Jen said.

# Boog

Crawford's ass was distracted in the kitchen, making his infamous Fiery Ring Chilli—infamous only to him—and Boog took the chance to shimmy his own ass into the bathroom, his little tube of miracle cream tucked in his pocket.

Once Boog had checked the lock, he checked it again, shrugged out of his T-shirt, loosened his belt, then—hands clammy—took out the tube: *Materna Smoothing Stretch Mark Cream.* That name wasn't nearly emasculating enough, though. No, they'd had to stick a picture of a pregnant lady on the side.

Fuck, but this was embarrassing. One of these days, Crawford would catch him and that truly would be game over.

Boog squirted out a centimetre of the white goop, and the smell of cloves rose up. Already disgusted, he worked the cream into his belly with upward strokes, into those repulsive pink stretch marks that wandered up his skin like snail trails.

He stopped and fingered another blemish. Was that a new mark starting?

His shoulders collapsed. Rosy deserved better than this. Rosy, deserved an immaculate pillow—skin like fresh fallen snow, not this scarred mound of lard.

Was the cream even doing anything? Possibly, but probably not.

He'd thought of a surer, manlier way to hide those bastards: a tattoo. A great big fuck-off tattoo. Rosy wasn't a tattoo fan but maybe he could strike the balance with a swirly design. What else was he going to do, if he couldn't lose the weight?

But a tattoo was bound to distract him from his studies. And if he failed the re-sit, Rosy was gone anyway, stretch marks or no.

The sight of his ever larger reflection always made him feel ashamed, but he manned up, held his belly and examined his profile in the mirror.

He'd kept telling himself as long as Rosy was happy with how he looked, he could be happy too. But, fuck, was he ever packing it on. He'd started to wake up at night, panicking.

Boog washed his hands and sprayed himself with deodorant to disguise that clove smell.

Dressed again, and with the evidence hidden, he opened the door and—.

"Busy, were we?" Crawford said.

"Busy?" Boog said. "No." Every red blood cell in his body had set a course for his face.

"Busy wanking?" Crawford prodded the tube in the front pocket of Boog's jeans. "Just call me Sherlock Holmes."

"More like Inspector Clouscau," Boog said, his relief a tremble in his voice. "A gay version who fingers guys' junk."

"My package was bigger than that in primary school."

"As all the boys in dance class will attest," Boog said. "No wonder you're infamous for your Fiery Ring."

"Asshole."

"Exactly."

Boog staggered back to his bedroom and flopped onto the bed. He hoped to God Rosy was missing the cuddlemeister. A reply to one of his texts sure would be nice.

# Rosy

Rosy switched off when Jen showed her the tattoo design—an embroidered-effect Celtic circle. She then had to hear all the reasons why her friend's shoulder would look hot crowned by an Iron Age cake doily.

When Jen finally shut up, Rosy tried one last time. "It'll ruin the line of your clothes. It'll clash with everything. And in five or six months, will you still love it?" Rosy took hold of Jen's shoulders and turned her to face down the full length of the shop. "Open your eyes and look at this dump. Really look. Look at the businesses around it. Tattoos are seedy, tasteless, tacky things."

"They're hip."

Screw it. "Fine. Listen, I tried to save you. I'm kinda grossed out, so I'm going to leave now."

"Oh, no, you're not." Jen said, and folded her arms, drew herself to full height on her outrageous heels to almost eye-level with Rosy. "Not until you explain why you, Miss Organised, forgot all about my consultation, and why you've been orbiting another planet all through this conversation."

Rosy shrugged, busted and helpless. "Because I've met Frank. I've met my dad. And Planet Frank is blowing my freaking mind."

# Chapter 11
# Heidi and mountains
## (Wednesday, 1 June)

### Rosy

After a heart-to-heart with Jen and with the benefit of a night's sleep, Rosy had a new perspective on the whole hugging thing with Frank. Frank was comfortable with the hugging. And why shouldn't he be? Rosy was, as Frank had pointed out, his baby.

Frank was only hugging his baby. There was nothing sexual on his side, or she'd know.

When Frank opened the door for Rosy, she spread her arms —

— and Frank hugged her again.

"*Mmm*," Frank said. "Morning, baby."

And—just like that—they were back on track.

———————————

Just after midday, Rosy watched a twenty-something natural blonde dash to the door, pause to fix her skirt, then come into the cafe.

"Heidi," Frank said over the head of the woman he was serving, "this better not be another rush order, or you can about-turn and march your disorganised tits back to where they came from."

Rosy blinked.

"Go sit down," he said to his customer. "Go on, shoo. My daughter will bring your tea and pancake. Shoo."

He then turned his glare on Heidi, his arms folded, chin raised.

Rosy took her time to find a teapot.

"Not my fault this time, Frank," Heidi said, "so lay off. It's a reschedule."

Rosy waved her fingertips, "Nice to see you, Heidi."

"Hey, honey. Oh, look at you." Heidi tipped her head to one side and pursed her lips. "You're so like Frank."

Frank clapped his hands under Heidi's nose, and Rosy flinched. "Hey," he said. "Do I look like I have time to waste?"

Heidi's lip stiffened. "We need lunch for six people."

Frank folded his arms. "Six people? When?"

"Soon as?" Heidi said, her voice small. "Twelve-thirty?"

Rosy took the tea and pancake to Frank's customer, apologised for her dad, and practically sprinted back.

"No," Frank said. "I told you, didn't I?" He made a little dismissing gesture with his fingers. "Sorry, lady. We're busy."

Rosy put her hand on Frank's arm. "Would twelve rolls be enough, Heidi?"

Frank opened his mouth.

Heidi nodded and her shoulders slumped in relief. "Perfect. You are a life-saver."

Frank grabbed his head.

"Germs," Rosy said, and pointed at the fingers tangled in his hair.

For a moment Frank stood there, looking off to the side as though there were somebody there he needed to consult. Then he took hold of Rosy's wrist, pulled off and dropped her disposable glove, and with his big pink tongue licked from the palm up to her fingertips.

"Germs," he said, tasted his tongue like he'd just licked an envelope, then folded his arms.

Rosy closed her eyes, shook her head, then smiled at Heidi. "Excuse us, please," she said "Back in one minute." She grabbed Frank by the apron string and led him into the kitchen.

———

"Hello?" Rosy said, still not believing what just happened. "What was all that about?"

"She keeps doing this," Frank hissed. "She forgets to order, then comes over at the last minute."

"So what?" Rosy said. "We're a cafe. We can cope with food for six people, for goodness sake."

Frank shook his head. "That's not the point. She's supposed to order the day before."

"It's a reschedule."

Frank wrinkled up his nose and forehead in a scowl. "No it's not. I can tell by the whole—" He rolled his hands in a weird shrugging gesture. "I can tell. She makes me so— *Ugh.*" He shuddered.

"As a favour for me, would you help her out?"

———

In the time it took Rosy to prepare four rolls, Frank had the rest ready and Heidi was only waiting for Rosy to finish. Throughout, Rosy watched the young woman. But it took no effort to work out what was going on. The woman's eyes were glued to Frank. Glued. And she kept adjusting her skirt, her hair, her watch, her bracelet.

Frank tore off a carrier bag, put the rolls in, shoved in six packets of crisps and held it out on one finger to Heidi like a pooper-scoop bag. "Don't ever do that again."

Heidi snatched the bag. "I can't help it, can I, you big bully?"

"No," Rosy said. "No, you can't. We're happy to help, aren't we, Frank?"

Frank said nothing. Heidi pursed her lips, looked at Frank, gave Rosy a tiny wave and a thanks then hurried out.

"*Pfff.*" Frank shuddered again. "She bugs me."

Rosy smiled. "Don't you get it, Frank? She fancies you."

"Of course she does—"

"And so modest about it—"

"But guess what?" Frank tapped the wedding ring strangling his finger. "I'm a married man."

"But—"

"But, nothing. Why can't she leave me alone with her hungry eyes? I told her."

Rosy smiled at the hungry eyes and shrugged. "Maybe she sees you on your own all the time."

Frank massaged the knuckle of his ring finger. "That's why I have to get Irene back."

———

Shop closed, Rosy stared out of the cafe kitchen window onto the cobbled bin area, at the dumpster with *Tasty Bite* painted on the side and thought of Frank, standing here night after night for all these years, washing up, stuck in his narrow little world with his narrow little dream of Mum one day coming back.

She heard him walk in.

"What would be different if you had Mum back?" Rosy said.

He thought about that for a while. "I'd have somebody. We could do stuff."

"What stuff?"

"Go someplace at the weekend," he said. "Look at a mountain."

That made Rosy think of Ruben and hill walking. "Couldn't you do that with Heidi?"

He shuddered.

"What about with me?" Rosy said. "We could look at a mountain. We could go hill walking."

Frank breathed out. "Yup, I'd like that. Me and my baby. We could do that. I'd like to do that." He stepped up behind Rosy and put his hands on her shoulders, then rested his chin on a hand and looked out. "Or you could help me get Irene back."

---

*Rosy waves two things at Ruben to show how clever she is: a* Moulin Rouge *DVD to watch while they're here, house-sitting for his sister, and an unconditional acceptance for Heriot-Watt.*

*"No surprise to me," Ruben says and he closes in on Rosy. "But I don't mind celebrating." His fingers clamp on Rosy's buttocks and he pushes her toward the sofa.*

*"Stop it, Ruben." Rosy squirms free. "Don't you think about anything besides sex?"*

*"Aw, fuck off, Rosy. Don't pull that shit on me again. Are you a lesbian or something?"*

*Rosy scowls. "That's right, turn your problem back at me."*

*Ruben sticks out his jaw and slaps his hand over his eyes. "My problem? Here's a news update for you. I'm a guy. Guys need sex. All the fucking time. That's normal, okay, Rosy? That's what normal is." He tips his head back then slumps down in the sofa.*

*Maybe he's right. Maybe that is normal. Jen would be all over Ruben by now. What's stopping Rosy?*

*"I was thinking about buying boots," Rosy says.*

*Ruben's head falls back against the cushions. "Go. Go buy boots."*

*"Hiking boots."* Rosy joins him on the sofa, picks up his hand and rubs it.

He looks at her.

*"You wanted to go hill walking,"* Rosy says. *"I'll buy boots and we'll go hill walking. This weekend."*

*"Hallelujah."* Ruben pulls her close so he can kiss her. *"You're gonna love it."*

# Chapter 12
## Fiddle
### Rosy

With wood everywhere she looked, the Widower's Fiddle, the cramped pub just off St Bernard's Place where Marek Borkowski had suggested they meet, might very well be inside a fiddle. The vague smell of socks suggested it was high time the widower considered remarriage.

"I'll be the most handsome man in the bar," Marek had said when she'd called him, reminding her of Crawford, so full of himself. She remembered the reason the Pole had given for leaving the Tasty Bite: not enough skirt. She'd enjoy letting some air out of his ego.

The moment Rosy stepped in, the roving eyes of a sandy-blond guy at the bar settled on her. She pretended not to notice him, took a stool at the opposite end of the bar and ordered a bottle of Miller.

The sandy-haired guy cleared his throat a couple of times and both times Rosy looked up at him, then at her watch and then at the door. The barman delivered both her beer and a shy smile. Rosy smiled back at him and picked at the label on the bottle until at last, the guy at the bar got off his butt and walked across to her.

He stuck out his hand. "Rosy."

"Oh." She looked him up and down "You're Marek? I was expecting somebody... good-looking."

He took that badly and she shoved the bottle to her mouth to hide her smile. He was kinda cute. Athletic build, broad chest but otherwise not enough meat. Jen's type, not Rosy's. But cute. Definitely cute.

"I can see you are Frank's daughter, anyway. I'm relieved he did not make up this wife and child of his." Marek spoke very clearly, his accent pleasant, not thick.

"Frank mentioned me?"

"Mentioned you?" Marek laughed. "Yes, Frank mentioned you. He mentioned you... *a lot*."

Rosy smiled. Good.

Marek beckoned Rosy to follow him across to a table by a hexagonal wooden pillar, as if he were a talk-show host inviting an audience member to join the guests. He pulled out a chair for her, then pushed it in as she sat, timing perfect. She marvelled at his manners—assisting a lady who slugged beer from a bottle.

"Per my phone call," Rosy said, affecting boredom, "I'll be making improvements to the cafe over the summer to increase footfall and target a more well-heeled clientele. Phyllis was pleased with your work, and suggested I speak to you to see if you'd consider coming back to us." Us. Nice. She arched her fingers.

"I admire your confidence, Ms Friendship," Marek said. "You are Ms Friendship?"

"Miss is fine. Not being from Eastern Europe, I prefer words with vowels." She drew her lips into a smile. "You admire my confidence? Why confidence?"

He waved a long-fingered hand in front of him. "You've discussed these improvements with Frank, have you?"

"Not yet." Rosy said.

"Ah." Marek watched her watching him, then put his glass down. "Frank is somewhat... resistant to other people's suggestions."

"That'll be my problem to worry about," Rosy said. "He does listen to me."

"Well, that is one small positive grain to pick away from the negative mountain. But, you see, the cafe job was always only a filler for me. I'm more of a night person."

"You mean you're more security guard material?"

"You are funny." He shook his head. "Funny girl. But, no. I perform. I have a show. And I have my platform. All of which consume a considerable amount of my time."

"Your platform being…?"

Marek shrugged. "My online presence."

"Like a blog?" Rosy said and tried not to laugh.

"A channel. Many media." He flicked his fingers and produced a business card the way a magician would conjure up the queen of hearts.

"Neat trick."

"Look me up," Marek said. "If you like what you see, become a subscriber, tell your friends."

"Maybe later." She pushed the card, unread, into the back pocket of her jeans, knowing already she'd forget to take it out, and picturing the tatters it would make in the washing machine. "Is this… *channel* a new commitment?"

"No. But it is picking up in popularity."

"Meaning, you'd be far too busy for a mere cafe now?" Rosy rolled her eyes ceilingward then pinned him. "Are you trying to negotiate an extra fifty pence per hour, Mr Borkowski, while you ogle young ladies?"

"Are you trying to patronise me, Miss Friendship?" He steepled his hands and pressed his index fingers against his chin. "What is your master plan, since you find mine so amusing?"

"The proven one." Rosy acted bored again. "Hard work. First class honours degree from a prestigious university, join a leading company."

"Hard work?" He smiled. "Hard work for somebody else's business?"

"Hardly an alien concept to a Pole, I'd have thought," Rosy said. "Isn't that what you people are so good at? Working hard, doing the jobs the British turn their noses up at? Or is that just a ruse to get over here, learn the language, then start some internet scam?"

"Learn the language," Marek laughed. "Sorry, but I find that amusing. Do the locals even speak English? *Goat a wee boatle a cola tae go wi' that, mister?*"

Rosy laughed. "See? Phrases like that have got to come in handy."

Marek tapped his fingers on his chin again. "How to say this without offending?" He raised a finger. "Ah, yes." He leaned forward in his chair. "You are an ignorant, racist bigot."

That hit Rosy like bucket of ice cubes over the head. Then the ice became steam as embarrassment brought heat to her cheeks.

"My '*ruse*' to come here," Marek said, "was a scholarship. My degree—first class honours in Psychology—is from University College London. I am told that institution carries some prestige, even in Scotland." He spoke matter-of-factly, his voice pleasant, calm, and that gave his message more bite. "No matter. It allowed me to walk into, then walk straight back out of, my imagined dream job—a London advertising agency even you may have heard of—because in my first week, I realised something important," he said. "When you work for somebody else, you are a cog. I need to be my own machine." He smiled. "I have big plans that do not include cafe or security guard jobs. Or first year undergraduate students playing business executive."

Rosy's face must be bright red by now. "I'm sorry."

"Don't be," Marek said. "Students are always arrogant. It's part of growing up. I was arrogant, too."

"But not any more?"

"I can afford a little arrogance. My show sells out every performance. In eighteen months, my email list has grown to forty thousand subscribers. I have a conversion rate of seventy-nine percent—that's how many people open my weekly emails and follow the links—over thirty thousand people who are interested in what I have to offer."

Rosy set down her empty beer bottle. "Let me buy you another beer, Marek."

---

Rosy was glad for the settling time of Marek's Guinness. It gave her a chance to regroup, try a different strategy. Her toes curled in retrospect at her behaviour. She glanced over at him. He'd been watching her. He wasn't difficult to look at. Definitely not her type—wrong build and she'd never been a fan of blue-eyes and blond hair—but he was smart and had a bucketload of confidence, for sure. Would be great to have him back at the cafe.

"There we are, love," the barman said.

Rosy ferried the drinks back to the table, slid the Guinness his way. "You said you have a show. Is it a comedy?"

"No, but you will laugh, I hope, after hearing my qualifications." His eyes glittered. "I do magic, with a twist. The twist is, my clothes are the first thing to disappear."

Rosy gaped.

"Yes. I do magic… naked. I not only have a big ego." Marek wiggled his middle finger. "I have a big wand."

Rosy's gape widened and became a grin. "Oh. My. God. Get out of here. That's got to be perfect for the Edinburgh Fringe."

"Sell out last year," Marek said. "Bigger venue this year, performances planned every day of the week."

She pulled out his card: *Marek: The Naked Magician*. "You should talk to my stepdad. That's his dream."

Marek laughed and widened the gap between his knees. "To wave his wand in front of two-hundred strangers?"

Findlay's scrawny legs came to mind and Rosy shuddered, held her hands up. "Ewww, no." The shudder hadn't finished. "But his dream is to put on a show at the Fringe."

"The Fringe?" Marek tutted. "Anybody can do that. Your stepdad needs a bigger dream."

"Yeah," Rosy sighed. "He needs something, all right."

The man took a sip from his Guinness, then set it down. "Why don't you give me Findlay's number? Maybe I can inspire him."

Rosy froze. "You said Findlay. How did you know his name?"

"I used my magical powers," Marek said, then raised his hands. "Okay, I will be a bad magician and reveal my secret: I heard it every time Heidi came over to the cafe, every time a customer asked Frank out, or flirted with him." Marek balled his fists. "I'm her lawfully wedded husband, not Findlay. She's my daughter, not Findlay's."

Rosy laughed, but, jeez, Frank really had a problem with Findlay.

"Give me Findlay's number," Marek said, flicked his eyes down to her breasts and hips then back to her face, "and give me yours."

Rosy had withheld her number deliberately, didn't want random people to have it. "I'll give you Findlay's number," Rosy said, "but I'm afraid I have a boyfriend and I'm not into naked magicians."

"Assumptions, again?" Marek said. "I do have a girlfriend, you know—the lovely Katrina—who doubles as my naked assistant."

"And so you want my number, why?"

"In case Katrina is taken ill and I need another assistant." He leaned forward. "I shall need your number, Rosy. How else do I call you? With a decision about coming back to the cafe." He shrugged. "But I suppose Findlay could relay a message."

Ouch. Moron. What had she been thinking? "Better if you don't talk to my stepdad, just in case. He doesn't know I work at the cafe, yet." She raised the beer bottle to her lips. "I'll tell him, of course, but not yet." She wondered if, as a psychologist, Marek knew a lie when he heard one.

"Do I still get your number, Rosy?"

"Yes, of course."

He swept his hand across the table, spreading a dozen business cards. "Pick a card, any card..."—he grabbed at the air beside her ear and handed her the pen that appeared—"... and write your phone number on it, please."

When she was done, he took the card and held it up. "You are one-hundred percent satisfied with your boyfriend?"

She shrugged. "No problems we can't work out."

He raised and lowered his eyebrows at her. "Problems are still problems."

---

*Rosy finishes her tutorial assignment in the university library, then looks out at bare trees. She hasn't been out with Boog since he tried to fondle her breast in the cinema. Her phone vibrates and she reads the message:* The cuddlemeister is missing his protégé.

*Rosy sends him a message back:* Where is the cuddlemeister?

*Back comes a reply:* Behind you.

*Rosy looks over her shoulder and smiles at him, then moves back to take the chair beside him.*

*"Does this mean I get to sit next to you in class again?" Boog says.*

*She misses the little things he thinks up to try to make her laugh during lectures. Rosy nods. "Maybe."*

*He folds his arms. "A boy needs a yes. When a girl says no it means no. When a girl says maybe, a boy just don't know."*

*Rosy smiles. "Yes."*

*He puts his arm over her shoulder. "I won't paw you again, I promise. I'll wait for a yes."*

*"Good." She has to stay in control so the Ruben situation never happens again. And Boog isn't Ruben. Boog is adorable.*

*"Shall we do our tutorial assignment together?" Boog says.*

*"I've done mine already. We could go for a walk. Lovely day out there."*

*Boog looks at his notepad, then closes up his laptop and grins. "Tutorials can wait," he says. "You, Miss Friendship, have an outstanding assignment for the cuddlemeister."*

———————

Rosy refocused on her companion then stood. "It would be good to see you at the cafe."

"I do miss the fireworks," Marek said. "The constant threat of violence."

Rosy remembered Frank's confrontation with the driver of the council van and Findlay running from Frank at the builders merchant. "You don't think Frank is capable of violence, do you?"

Marek smiled. "Rosy? I think Frank is capable of anything."

# Chapter 13
# Lair of the beast
## (Thursday, 2 June)
## Rosy

Last summer, every day in the biscuit factory had dragged, and Rosy had told herself she was far too intelligent to enjoy a repetitive manual job. And yet here she was, another day at the cafe gone, feeling as satisfied as if she'd completed a lab report and the graph of her titration matched the textbook.

"How am I doing?" Rosy said. "Am I doing okay compared to Marek?"

"Marek was good, until he started trying to make me look bad to Phyllis."

"He's naturally ambitious," Rosy said, then when he raised his eyebrows, added quickly, "so I've heard."

Frank worked through the drawers in the till, counting as fast as if he'd broken in and the cops were on their way. "Marek thought he could push me aside and walk into the top job."

Top job. Rosy suppressed a smile.

"Twenty-seven pence out, baby," Frank said, and pulled the spewed-out till roll toward him.

Rosy winced and bit her lip. Looked like her results didn't match the textbook after all.

"Here," Frank said and pointed at a line on the roll, circled it. "Finger-trouble," he said. "That was £4.58 not £4.85. Table order, table six. She's given you the exact money but you rang it up wrong. A number fourteen, hold the mayo, a cheese scone with raspberry jam and a black tea." He took the cash from the tip dish. "Sorted," he said.

The only thing on the till roll was the total. How did he remember the order? How did he spot it so fast? "Frank...?"

"Sorry, yeah," Frank said. "Marek told Heidi bad stuff about me so she'd tell Phyllis."

Rosy forgot about the till. "Bad stuff? Like?"

"Like he told her I hurt a kid," Frank said.

"That's terrible," Rosy said.

"Hey," Frank said, "the kid deserved it."

Rosy's mouth fell open.

Frank closed the till and walked into the kitchen. Rosy followed.

"Anyway, it's not like I hit him," Frank continued. "I just picked him up by the hood and dumped him outside."

Rosy winced. Physical contact with a child? "You need to be extra careful with kids," she said. "Keep your hands off."

"Not if they're tramping dog shit over the floor," Frank said. "It wasn't just the shit shoe kid. Every little argument with a customer, Marek would snitch to Heidi, so I'd get it in the neck."

Frank picked up a cloth and wiped around the sink.

"Maybe Marek had your best interests at heart," Rosy said. "There's a way to treat customers."

"*Pfff.*" Frank snorted. "I treat customers right if they treat me right," he said. "If they don't, they'll get what's coming."

"Frank," Rosy said. "About the till..."

"Forget it," Frank said, and threw the cloth into the sink. "Would you come home with me, Rosy?"

Rosy felt her face redden. "What?"

"I want you to come home with me. Come home to my flat and keep me company tonight. I'm fed up always being on my own," he said. "Come home with me for dinner."

Dinner. Rosy let go of the breath she'd snatched.

"You said you'd come sometime," Frank said. "Well, now is sometime."

"Now is a bit sudden. Mum will have made dinner."

Frank shrugged. "So what? Can't she put it in the fridge? Oh, come on."

"It's still early days, Frank. I don't know..."

"Sure you do," he said. "You know. If you didn't know, you

wouldn't stick around. I feel it. I see it. Look at me and tell me you don't. We already bonded, Rosy." He snapped his fingers. "Like that. All those years apart and we bonded in less than a second."

Frank didn't take a single step closer yet he filled Rosy's vision until there was only him.

"There's no way back now. Call Irene, baby. Tell her you won't be home for dinner tonight."

———————

Rosy followed Frank as he hurried across the road away from the darkened cafe, slipped between buildings on the opposite side, then powered uphill. Followed a rapist home.

They cut along a dog-leg alley formed by garden walls and high slatted fences until they reached an arched tunnel through a building that ejected them into a cobbled street full of lock-up garages. A few metres further along, Frank came to an abrupt halt.

"Welcome back home," he said.

They stood before a black door between two steel-shuttered garages. The door entry system had three buttons, the faceplate for the middle button empty. The bottom said *Service*, and the top *Frank & Irene Friendship*, both in Frank's crazy-neat block letters. Frank unlocked a mortice, then a Yale. He swung the door open and a chill escaped, as from a cave. Concrete steps and a painted iron banister led straight up to a lightless landing.

"Just me here now," Frank said, and for a spooky moment she thought he was telling Rosy her mother no longer lived there. Then he pointed at the vacant button on the door system. "Mr Kerr across the hall passed away. He smelled of cabbage and pee. You'd have liked him."

Rosy laughed, heard the tremor, and only then understood she was terrified.

"It's okay, baby." He picked up her hand, and pulled her over the threshold. "You can tell Irene I made you," he said, his voice reverberating.

Rosy followed him toward the darkness above.

———————

Even the top landing was concrete, with only a doormat as decoration. Frank unlocked the door of his flat then told Rosy to wait. "Just need to check something."

He opened the door only wide enough to squeeze through, which—for a man of Frank's size—was pretty far. But his body blocked Rosy's line of sight and all she saw was the carpet. She guessed he was checking for porno magazines.

The door swung wide. "Come on in," Frank said.

There, right in front of her, stood an iron-framed double bed with a puffy white duvet. And nothing much else. A wardrobe against the near wall. A chest of drawers with healthy-looking pot-plants beneath the window on the far wall, and bedside cabinets at the bed head, tidy to the point of sterility. Not at all what she'd anticipated. But her eyes had already left that behind, because the bedroom was little more than an afterthought.

Bulging from the bottom half of the room was a kitchen that looked like a hurricane had torn it from another building and landed it here. Forty years ago, judging by the appliances.

"Great, isn't it?" Frank said, shoving his boots into the base of a wardrobe bulging with clothes. "Everything in one room. Except the bathroom. That'd be dirty. It's there if you need to go." He pointed at a door on the opposite side of the bed.

"That's a lot of kitchen," Rosy said.

"The kitchen used to be small. But I cook in big batches to save time, so I needed a freezer. And who needs a settee when there's a bed, right?"

No settee? OMG. "Yeah," Rosy said.

The freezer—in fact all the appliances—though ancient, looked spotless. The whole flat was spotless.

"I got these from a kitchen renovation up at the manse. They cleaned up like new," he said, answering the question before she'd even asked.

Rosy inhaled and could almost taste the gravy of whatever Frank was cooking. "Something smells—" Rosy turned and realised Frank had pulled his T off. She jerked her gaze away. "Incredible." She swallowed.

"Just chicken stew," Frank said. He hauled a rugby jersey on and Rosy's heart clambered back down her throat. "Do you like jigsaws?" He went down on all fours, pulled out a black case the size of an artist's portfolio case and laid it on the bed, unzipped it to reveal a three-quarters done peacock jigsaw. "This one is tougher than it looks."

"Looks pretty tough."

"I love jigsaws, but they're sneaky. They try to hook you. I do a bit whenever I come home. I have to set the timer for ten minutes so it doesn't pull me right in."

Jigsaws.

Frank clapped his hands, grinned at her. "It's too early for dinner, baby, and we're not doing anything else anyway." He wiggled his eyebrows. "So why don't you and me have some fun?" He patted the bed.

# Findlay

Findlay sucked on the end of his Bic while Irene set out dinner.

"What do you think of this one?" he said. "A man goes into the doctors and says 'Doctor, I'm having terrible trouble with my eyes.' And the doctor says, 'You're telling me. This is a cheese shop.'"

He watched Irene's half-hearted smile. "It's okay. Did you make that one up?"

He shrugged. "I think so." He penned a face with a flat smile next to that one. "How about this then? Why is a waist called a waist?"

"Don't know," Irene said.

"Because you could have squeezed in another pair of tits."

Irene had a good laugh, then said, "You didn't make that one up, did you?"

Findlay shook his head. "But I can disguise it." He cleared his throat and put on his cheeky chappie performer's voice. "Here's one for the ladies in the audience. When you reach a certain age, your husband will stop seeing your waist as a waist. Because that's where your tits are."

Irene laughed, but not much. "I don't think I'd have got that if I didn't know the funny version."

"The funny version?" he rolled his eyes. Why the fuck did he even bother?

One of the frozen lasagnes beeped. Irene swapped the trays over. She must be saving for something again. Two lasagnes between three.

"Surely you have enough jokes by now to put on a show, Findlay?" she said.

Findlay's stomach lurched at the thought of it. "I need the full act, Irene, not just the jokes."

"Well, I think you have enough." She patted his back. "You have the pagoda joke."

"You're the only person who's laughed at that."

"Why wouldn't the Chinese girl get married?" Irene said. "Because she wouldn't let her pagoda." She hooted. "Don't you get it? Wouldn't let her pa—"

"Of course I fucking get it," Findlay said, "it's just not fucking funny." He looked at his watch and scowled. "It's after six. Rosy's normally back before now, isn't she?"

"They're having to rerun a sequence or something."

"Hope that's not your daughter's fault," Findlay said. "Hope she's insured."

Rerun a sequence. Sounded like a euphemism. Likely the lab manager wanted to peer into her cleavage. The lab manager wasn't the only one. Where was Rosy with his little dinnertime treat?

"How can you tell when your little sister—?" He clammed up. "No, that one's not funny."

"Try me," Irene said. "I liked the pagoda."

"It's an old one and it's not mine."

How can you tell when your little sister has had her first period?

Your dad's knob tastes different.

# Rosy

The bed creaked with each slow rock of Frank's body and Rosy looked up at him again.

He sat cross-legged at the top of the bed, an intense look on his brow, Rosy at the foot. Between them lay the jigsaw that commanded all Frank's attention.

"*Pfff.* This really is a tough one, but I think the secret is the focus." He picked up the box lid. "Look." He leaned over, pointing a thick finger. "The feathers over that side are more blurry and over there, they're really sharp. Which means," he said, and picked up a joined-together section of three pieces, "that... probably goes..." He tapped it in and grinned at her. "See?"

Rosy grinned back.

He shoved the sleeves of his White Stuff rugby jersey back up his forearms.

Look at him sitting there. Could Rosy's mind have conjured a face more masculine yet more flawless? Strong, wide, smoky-stubbled jaw, yet skin smooth and shining like a schoolboy's out throwing snowballs. A short, broad nose, cheeks poised to smile and eyes to coax and keep any secret. Even Frank's ears fascinated—flush, compact artworks in mathematical proportion. Perfect. This was her father. Rosy remembered sitting in the school orchestra, hugging her cello, hoping to God that Findlay wouldn't hang around at the end to embarrass her in front of the other parents, in his pilled tank-top and turquoise cords. All the time, Frank had been here. Beautiful, beautiful Frank.

He reached forward for a jigsaw piece and Rosy heard a fart.

"Oops," Frank said, and closed one eye. "Sorry about that. That one saw its chance and made a dash for it."

Then again, there were some universals.

Rosy found some blue pieces that fitted together and without even knowing how she knew, she placed them straight away into the main puzzle. Everything just fitted.

Frank smiled at her, and began to rock again, and Rosy turned her eyes back to the jigsaw.

---

"See?" Frank said. "What did I tell you? Sneaky jigsaw just stole two hours. That's why I always have to set the timer."

He bounced off the bed, and stood up. "I'll make dinner. You can do more jigsaw, or I have an old TV in the garage. Think it still works. I could bring that up for you to watch while I cook."

Not a soap fan then. "I'd rather watch you, Frank."

He smiled like a little kid. "Okay. That's allowed. But I'm bulky, so it's gonna be tight for space."

A neat steel strip separated carpet from linoleum, and Rosy stepped across. "I think you need a bigger place."

"Nah," Frank said. "When Mr Kerr over the landing croaked, Phyllis wanted to renovate—gut the building, top to bottom, and make one big flat. But I don't want my things disturbed. Everything's exactly how I like it."

Didn't bode well for Rosy's summer task. "Phyllis is your landlord?"

"Landlady," Frank said. "This was my dad's place for a while."

Frank's dad. Gus Friendship. Rosy didn't want to think about that awful man prowling around in here and Frank may have picked up on that because he shook his head and the conversation lapsed. Rosy watched his big back, his shoulder muscles, thick neck, those arms.

"It's nothing fancy to eat. Sorry. I didn't think that far ahead." He looked awkward. "I watch for yellow labels and special offers. I don't buy crap like sausages, burgers, pies—anything that might have cardboard or cat brains. I only buy things if I can picture it on an animal. These are organic chicken bits. They were at the use-by date, so I put them in the slow-cooker straight away."

How appetising. Mind you… "Smells delicious."

"I was going to fry up some leftovers. Potatoes and cabbage. Bubble and squeak."

Gag. Rosy hated cabbage. "I'll have what you're having. Just pretend I'm not here."

Frank reached around her back, drew her against him briefly, then rubbed her arm. "I don't want to pretend that. You're my baby. I want you here. I always wanted you here."

For some reason, that hit Rosy right in the gut. She stepped back and clapped her hands to rid herself of the threat of tears. "What can I do to help?"

"*Pfff.* Set the table?"

"Great." Rosy looked around. "Where is the table?"

He lifted a flap on the wall. It locked in place to make a tiny table. "I usually eat standing up, but folding chairs are in the garage. Wait. I'll get them."

The door banged behind him. Rosy was alone.

What could the flat tell her about her mysterious father?

# Chapter 14
# Snipped away
## Rosy

Rosy studied Frank's flat while he was gone. What did he do with himself all the time? Not jigsaws. He said he set the timer to limit those to ten minutes. No sign of a computer. No TV. No books. No CDs. No movies. Did he really live here? With nowhere to sit down?

He had a radio in the kitchen and clearly he liked to cook.

No.

Frank cooked in batches to save time, that's what he'd said. But to save time for what? Maybe he went out. Womanising? And once again, no. She'd seen him give Heidi—quite a babe —the cold shoulder, and Marek had confirmed as much.

Unbelievable though it seemed, Frank was staying faithful to Rosy's mum. Not womanising. Not drinking—when she mentioned the Widower's Fiddle, he said he wasn't into beer and alcohol. What then? Training? Nobody could have a physique like Frank's without heavy-duty exercise. At the gym?

No sign of Frank, and Rosy had to pee. She pushed the bathroom door open and here was the first sign of normality— a drying rack, full of clothes. Clothes seemed the only thing Frank spent money on. Everything branded. Superdry, Sergio Tacchini, Diesel. She locked the door and pulled down a big Canterbury T-shirt—white, with three black kiwis—pressed it to her face and breathed him in.

But as Rosy draped the T back on the rack, she noticed a nametag, sewn into the collar: *Alan McAdam.*

Rosy looked inside the Sergio Tacchini.

*Alan McAdam.*

Tags with the same name, sewn into everything she checked. Why would Frank's clothes—?

Were these Frank's clothes? Or was Frank… living here with another man?

---

The urge to pee forgotten, Rosy ran back into Frank's bedroom. She could search the place. It would only take a minute. But if she were to find something like condoms, a porno magazine… or a machete…

The front door juddered open. "Two chairs," Frank said. "And look what I found." He tossed Rosy a child's bowl. Little elephants looped trunks, like on a beaker at home. "Irene left that in the draining rack when she stole you away."

Stole her away. The image of Rosy, beaker in hand, sitting beside her mum on Franny's doorstep, flashed into her thoughts and with it the realisation something else was missing from this room. "No photos, Frank?"

"I keep them safe," Frank said. "From people with scissors."

---

After they'd eaten, Rosy took a seat on the end of Frank's bed and watched him slide the top drawer in his chest of drawers open, then lift out a brown A4 envelope.

Photos. The perfect way to relax after food. For the first time since she'd come home for the summer, Rosy felt pleasantly full after dinner. Frank's stew held no surprises, had been as tasty as it smelled, and he'd given her a portion her mum would have divvied up between three. Who knew the word tasty could ever apply to cabbage? The second revelation was his stewed raspberries with mushy homemade ice-cream. Yum. He could really cook.

Frank sat beside Rosy on the bed and gingerly opened the flap on the envelope. "I only have three pictures."

Rosy had to hold back the sigh of disappointment when he set down a picture she'd seen before. Just her mum brushing Rosy's hair.

"I managed to sneak that one out. It's a beaut'ful picture. She doesn't know I have it."

"*She* being your mum, Frank?"

"Yeah."

"What's the deal with Franny?"

"Franny?" Frank frowned. "Who's Franny?"

Rosy shrugged. "My baby name for Granny Friendship, your mum. Why does Franny cut your face out of all the pictures?"

Frank fidgeted with the envelope. "She doesn't want to look at me."

"Yeah. I'd worked that out. But why? Why doesn't she want to look at you?"

"Because," Frank said, meeting her eyes, "her good son drowned, and all she got back in his place was me."

# Findlay

Findlay gnawed his lip, unable to even enjoy an advert for Always Ultra pads. Where the fuck was that stepdaughter of his? "Re-running a sequence, Irene?"

"I have no idea what it means, Findlay, but I guess it's time-consuming."

Findlay scowled. "We could have a coffee and a biccie…"

"You know how to work the kettle, Findlay."

"A milky coffee? Whenever I do those they froth up. I don't have your magic microwave touch."

Irene stood. "Sure."

Third day at work and Rosy was working late? Findlay should have let Irene drag her off to the biscuit factory.

# Rosy

Rosy blinked. "You *drowned*, Frank?"

She studied him. He looked away.

"Frankie drowned," Frank said. "He fell in the bath. He was dead for too long. I came back in his place."

Rosy shook her head, felt sick. "I don't understand. You're talking like you and Frankie are two different people."

"Frankie died. He was gone too long and he slipped away. I came back. I'm not Frankie, I'm somebody else. I'm not smart. Frankie wasn't in school yet, but he could read and write. I couldn't even say my name." He looked at the ceiling. "Can we please change the subject?"

Rosy wanted to hug him, needed a hug herself, but she could feel through the bed how tense he'd become. "You're a better cook than Mum."

He smiled. "Is Findlay a good cook?"

"No," Rosy said. "Findlay doesn't cook." Findlay didn't do anything anymore.

"You should tell Irene I'm happy to cook," Frank said. "When she comes back."

When. Oh, God.

"I was hoping to see a picture of you, Frank."

He opened the envelope again. "I have one Phyllis took. She gave my mum—Franny—a copy but my mum took the scissors to it."

He laid the picture on her lap. The wedding photo. Rosy pinched the bridge of her nose, overcome. Reeling, in fact. "My God, Frank. I don't understand your mother." She shook her head. "Phyllis took this?"

"Irene was happy. You can see that. I don't think she was only smiling."

"It's a beautiful picture. You're right: Mum isn't just smiling. She's happy. It's in her eyes."

"She told me she loved me. Then she was with Findlay, and

she wouldn't give me another chance."

Rosy thought about Boog. She'd come so close, once, to saying she loved him.

Frank picked the photo up by its edges and slid it back into the envelope.

"No more photos, Frank?"

"I have a real nice one of my dad here, but I'm guessing—"

"No," Rosy said. "I don't want to see that."

He sighed. "Phyllis takes pictures of me sometimes and puts them in with a card or something. But I don't want pictures of me on my own. They make me feel bad so I throw them out."

Frank clapped his hands and looked at his watch. "Time's up. I'll walk you to the bus stop. Ernesto has another job for me. Can't be late. One bad word from him, and I'll roast in hell."

---

Rosy waited silently with Frank until her bus arrived. When he hugged her, she pecked him on the cheek, but instead of returning the kiss, he screwed his nose up and wiped his face with the back of his hand, cat style.

"See you tomorrow, Frank."

"Yeah," Frank said. "And tell Irene you'll be having dinner with me every night from now on. Tell her she has to come too."

Rosy shook her head. "Nice try, but I can't. See you tomorrow." She squeezed his hand. "Bye."

"Bye, baby," he said.

Rosy clambered aboard the bus.

Frank wasn't normal because Frank had suffered brain damage. There'd been no monster standing next to Irene in the engagement photo, just a kid—a big, beautiful, lost-looking kid. But the real shock was what Frank had been holding, what Frank had been gazing at.

In that photo, a little pink-faced bundle nestled in his arms, eyes closed.

Franny hadn't just cut Frank out of that wedding picture. She'd snipped out baby Rosy with him.

And what had Frank gone and got himself mixed up in?

*Ernesto has a job for me.*

As Rosy sat, she remembered her exchange with Marek:

*Is Frank capable of violence?*
*I think Frank is capable of anything.*
She watched him wave at the bus.

"Bye, Frank," she whispered, then, quieter still, "Take care, Daddy."

---

*On Boxing Day,* Beauty and the Beast *plays on the video in the lounge, and Findlay—eight-year-old Rosy's darling Beast—holds her hands as they whirl around the ballroom for the third dance since Christmas morning.*

*When the movie is over, Rosy unrolls her* Beauty and the Beast *poster. She studies the Beast. "I don't think he was ugly, even to begin with."*

*"He was ugly, but inside, he was good," Findlay says. "That's the lesson of the story. No matter how ugly you are outside, somebody can see the good in you." His eyes go wistful.*

*Rosy rolls her eyes. She gets that. She's not a numptaloid. "What I mean is, the Beast is handsome. A bit like a lion."*

*Findlay frowns at her. "He has tusks and horns, Sweatpea. And a nose like a bull. He's hideous."*

*Rosy hates to break it to Findlay, but she'd rather look like the Beast than look like Findlay.*

*"You sure can't tell from the outside," Rosy says. "Granddad Friendship was handsome and look what he did."*

*"Exactly," Findlay says and points at her. "In fact, you can bet if they're attractive outside, they're ugly as sin inside. But don't worry that your teeth are too big and you're all elbows and knees," he says. "Most girls are ugly ducklings at your age. You'll be a looker when you fill out."*

*Findlay has just told her, following his logic, she's only ugly on the outside, but not to worry because when she's older, she'll be ugly on the inside.*

---

Snuggy barked at Rosy as though she were an intruder. So much for a quiet entrance. She shoved the kettle on, then walked into the hall and stuck her head around the door of the lounge. "I'm making tea, if anybody wants—"

Findlay grabbed her arm, hauled her off balance and shoved her into the settee. She landed hard on her wrist and pain shot up her arm.

Findlay's face, blotched purple, loomed too close to even focus on. "What the fuck were you thinking?" A gobbet of saliva landed on her lip. "Frank Friendship? *Frank-fucking-Friendship?*"

"What about him?" Rosy looked past Findlay to her mother's white face. Rosy had to wipe off that droplet of saliva. Germs.

"Your little game is up, madam" Findlay said.

"Game? What game?"

"He called us, Rosy," Mum said.

This conversation didn't make any sense. "Who called? Marek?"

"Marek?" Findlay said. "Who the fuck is Marek? Another fat boyfriend?"

"Frank called," Mum said.

Rosy gaped. Frank phoned? When she'd told him specifically not to? "Why?"

"Why?" Findlay stuck out his chin, shook his head. "Duh. Because he's Frank-fucking-Friendship, that's why. What the fuck were you thinking?"

"Findlay, calm down, please." Her mum said. "You're not helping."

Rosy swallowed "Why did Frank call?"

"To let us know you'd be late but you were safely on the bus," Mum said. "And to tell me not to be angry with you because it was his fault."

Rosy let her head fall back. How much did they know? How much had Frank told them?

"Have you nothing to say for yourself?" Findlay said.

"I wanted to meet him, and I didn't want to upset you—"

"Upset us?" Findlay said. "Oh, well thanks for that. Now I feel much less upset about you having secret liaisons… *with a rapist, a criminal—*"

"Findlay," Mum said, "she's old enough to make her own decisions."

"What? Like a responsible adult?" Findlay turned his fury onto Mum. "You don't get it, Irene. If she'd come to me and told me, that's one thing. But lying to me? Manipulating me with all that… *shit* about a lab job?"

Rosy closed her eyes.

"Treating me like a prize fool," he said, "letting me stick my neck out for her? And all the while she's siding with a man whose threatened to kill me in my bed?"

Rosy slitted her eyes. "He's my father. I have a right to see my father."

Findlay's face turned purple. "We've been protecting you from your father—"

"Shut up!" Mum yelled.

Rosy and Findlay both looked at her. Mum held her head, fingers spread in her hair, rubbing her own scalp, thumbs on her jaw.

"Mum, I—"

"Shut up, the pair of you."

Rosy looked from her mum to Findlay, then back to her mum.

"It's your life, Rosy," Mum said. "If you want Frank in it—"

"Irene, no—"

"If you want Frank in your life, that's up to you. But do not—*do not*—bring him back into ours. You tell him to stay away from me, and away from Findlay—no more phone calls—nothing, understand? Or I'll have the police onto him. You hear that?"

# Chapter 15
# Bruised
## (Friday, 3 June)
## Rosy

Mum was still on early shift so only Findlay was in the house next morning. Rosy poured herself some cornflakes, but her stepdad's eyes were on her as though to make sure she didn't steal any of the cutlery. Rosy sat down, then rapped her spoon on the table. "What?"

"You know what. You're going back to that cafe, aren't you?"

"It's my job." Rosy started to pour milk over her cereal.

He grabbed her arm. "Your job, Rosy, is to leave. That's your job, if you're part of this family."

"That's not happening." Rosy pulled her elbow free. She already had a bruise from where he'd grabbed her arm last night. She'd worn a long-sleeved blouse to cover it, but if she were to show Frank… She took out her anger on a mouthful of cornflakes.

"Why are you doing this? To me? To your mother?"

Rosy chewed her cereal and ignored him.

"I'm scared, Rosy. I'm really scared."

"What?" she said over a half-chewed mouthful. "Because he skimmed a bit of hardboard at you? You seriously think Frank is out to get you? After seventeen years?"

"No, I'm scared Frank is out to get you." Findlay looked behind him as though Frank might be there, waiting.

Rosy pushed her cereal bowl away. "I have two minutes. Tell me about Frank."

"Two minutes? Two days wouldn't be enough."

"Edited highlights."

Findlay pulled his dressing gown tight on his scraggly chest. "Where do I even start?"

# Findlay

What hurt Findlay most about Frank was the betrayal, and as he explained everything to Rosy, he gained fresh clarity himself, could see more clearly the cause and effect, could even see that his depression was linked back to Frank. Frank Friendship had ruined his and Irene's lives.

"Even though we'd gone to the same primary school," Findlay said, "it was secondary school before I got to know him. I wasn't the most popular kid and Frank was a misfit too. I was just shy, but Frank…? He was never right in the head."

Rosy looked like she was about to object, but she let him carry on.

"My parents said he was brain-damaged. I know he didn't speak until he was five or six. And you know all about his dad and the murder. But what you won't know is that Frank stopped talking again after they nailed his old man."

"Frank is the same age as you, isn't he?" Rosy said. "So how could he be in the same classes? If he stopped talking, I mean. They'd have to hold him back a year or two, surely?"

Findlay frowned. He'd never really thought about that. Frank had just… "He kept up. Somehow," Findlay said. "But Frank would do stuff. Crazy stuff. I mean really crazy." Findlay broke into a sweat just thinking about his stunts. "He climbed the school building—three storeys—to do a shit on the ledge of the art room window. When he wanted a new coat and his mother wouldn't buy him one, he soaked the sleeves of his anorak in meths and set them on fire." He saw Rosy hide a smile. "Frank drank the crystals we were growing in science class. The chemistry teacher had to go with him to hospital to list everything he'd swallowed. And kids being kids, we did what you're doing now, Rosy. We laughed. Ha-ha. Isn't Frank a character? A real character."

Findlay poured himself another cup of tea. "The irony is, I think I actually loved the guy. I mean, he was nuts, and he scared the crap out of me but he was a laugh and I loved him. So I confided in him, the way boys do. I told him about this one special girl."

Rosy rolled her eyes. "Mum?"

He nodded, annoyed. "Irene. She was way out of my league, I mean way out. And she was spoken for. Dating Mr Wonderful, brainiest guy in our year, twice my size, captain of the rugby team—he was the twin with the broken nose."

Findlay shrugged. "Like I say, Irene was way out of my league. But I found I could talk to her, and against all the odds, we sparked up this amazing friendship. And then one day—get this  she dumps Mr Wonderful. She dumps him. And she asks me—Findlay Dickson—to a Halloween party." He held up his hands. "Girls. I'll never fathom them. But didn't I have to go and ask if my pal, my best mate Frank-fucking-Friendship could come?"

Findlay clawed what remained of his hair. "Frank only raped your mother because he knew I loved her."

"Dad," Rosy said, and put her hand on his arm. "I want to hear the whole story, honest I do. But I'm going to have to dash, or I'll be late."

Findlay blinked. Hadn't he just slit a vein so she'd understand? "Late?"

"Sorry. I'll see you tonight."

# Rosy

Frank had sketched a picture of a dog in free-fall, looking up as it tumbled down a well, and Rosy knew how the beast must feel. Frank had said not a word about making the call. Not one word. He acted as though nothing had happened.

When a man who'd been nursing a mug of filter coffee for forty-five minutes left, Rosy grabbed what might be her only chance to shout at Frank.

"Why," Rosy asked, "did you phone the house, Frank?"

He shrugged. "I wanted to."

She pulled the pen from his fingers, and folded her arms. "Because you knew it would drive Findlay apoplectic?"

He grinned. "Yeah."

"And you didn't care what happened to me, how bad that made me look?"

Frank shrugged. "You tangled me in a lie," he said. "I cut myself free. If you didn't want to look bad, you shouldn't have tangled."

"It was a good lie," Rosy said.

"It was a good phone call," Frank said.

Rosy's mouth hardened. "Mum says you're to stay away or she'll involve the police."

Frank frowned, "She said that?"

"Yes. She said that."

"Oh, man." Frank leaned on the counter and sank his head in his hands.

The bell above the door dinged.

"GET OUT!" Frank bellowed.

Rosy turned in time to see a suited lady press her hand against her chest and stagger back out onto the street.

Rosy's mouth fell agape. "What are you playing at? Who was that?"

"No idea," he said. "She's not a regular."

"She never will be now, will she?"

"*Pfff*," he said and waved a hand.

Rosy pressed her hands on the counter. "Okay—"

"You said okay." Frank pointed at her.

"What I was going on to say, Frank, is I think I now have a good handle on the cafe, and how it's been working."

"Okay." Frank folded his arms. "If you can say okay, I can say okay."

"I've seen the good and the bad points—"

"Okay."

"Are you going to shut up for five minutes to hear me out?" Rosy said.

"Okay," he said. He ducked his head and held his hands up. "That one was an accident."

"Phyllis gave me a task." Rosy straightened her apron, dusted away crumbs. "My task is to turn this cafe around by the end of Summer. The key things we have to do are, number one: Renovate. Gut the place, get rid of all these hideous fixtures and fittings. If it's brown, it's out." She held up two fingers and touched the second. "Number two: Revitalise. We bring in an espresso machine—"

Frank blew a heavy raspberry.

"And we shift upmarket with a whole new range of breads and fillings, cakes, pastries and snacks." Rosy ignored Frank's raised hand. "And finally… Number three: Serve. We treat our customers as though they're VIPs. When they come in here, nothing is too much effort to please them. We do not shout at them. We do not point them at a seat and order them to sit down. We do not ask if that mess up there is all hair or does their brain have an upstairs."

"Can I speak now?" Frank said.

"Yes." Rosy nodded.

"Who put you in charge?"

Rosy folded her arms. "Phyllis."

"I think you'll find, Rosy, that my job title is manager. I'm in charge here."

"Tell you what, Frank," Rosy said, "shall we get Phyllis over?"

"Please do, baby," he said.

"Don't call me baby."

"You're my baby. I'm going to call you *baby*."

Rosy dialled Heidi, and once Phyllis was on, it was all Rosy could do to keep her voice level. "Phyllis, would you mind coming over to the cafe for a minute or two, please, to set Frank straight?"

Frank rolled his eyes. "You'll be the one she sets straight, baby."

Rosy's nostrils flared, ready for the fight. "Let's see." She crossed to the door and intercepted a couple of potential customers. "Really sorry. We have a staff awareness session for the next half hour or so." She turned the sign to *Closed* and waited.

———————

Rosy recognised Phyllis's petite frame and feminine walk as the woman crossed the road from the Shawford office.

"Now you're for it," Frank said.

The bell chimed. "Why does the sign say *Closed*?" Phyllis said.

Frank pointed at Rosy. "She did that."

"Something important has come up," Rosy said. "I wanted to discuss it with you."

"Go on." Phyllis folded her arms.

"I've just been explaining my ideas about the cafe to Frank," Rosy said.

"Oh, yes?" Phyllis said. "And when were you going to tell me about those ideas?"

Frank raised his eyebrows at Rosy.

"I'll tell you now, if you like."

"No," Phyllis said. "I'm busy now. I'd like a report I can read at my leisure. That's what I'd expect from a professional." Her eye bored into Rosy.

"A report?"

"You are a scientist, I believe, Miss Friendship? I'd like to see a little science brought to bear," Phyllis said. "A current model and a projection. A plan and some costs. Something measurable, not subjective."

Rosy felt her face and neck grow warm. "Of course."

"Anything else I can help with?" Phyllis set a hand to her hip.

Frank put his hand up. "Who's the manager, Phyllis?" he said.

"That would be you, Frank."

"And who's in charge of day-to-day running?" Frank said.

"Again, that would be you, Frank. Now, is there anything else? Frank? Rosy?"

Frank shrugged. "It's all really, really clear to me."

Rosy shook her head. Icy rage made breathing an effort. "Thank you for your time, Phyllis. You'll have my report first thing Monday morning."

"Good," Phyllis said. "Now, turn the sign to *Open*, please. We have a business to run."

# Chapter 16
# Collateral
## Boog

Boog dropped his ASDA carrier bags and lumbered over to the armchair where Crawford had propped up his *Chemistry* text book, now bound with a wraparound glossy picture of a grossly obese lady in her late forties, displaying a minge the size of an Arctic explorer's beard.

Crawford looked up from his laptop and laughed. "Thought I'd give you the chance to combine your two favourite pastimes," he said. "Pretending to study and jerking off."

Boog lifted the book, opened it at the inside cover and tried to pick off the picture. "You glued it on?" He waved the book in Crawford's smirking face, then threw it back into the armchair. "For fuck's sake, Crawford, grow up."

Boog steadied his breathing, gathered up his shopping, and carried it into the kitchen.

"Take a look at these pics," Crawford shouted. "Which one would be better as my desktop wallpaper?"

Crawford and his practical jokes. As if Boog didn't have enough to do. Now, he'd have to peel that obscenity off and find something else to glue over the top.

And of course he wouldn't be able to sell the book when he was done with it—which could be sooner than anticipated.

"C'mon, take a minute and tell me which picture," Crawford said, wandering into the kitchen.

"Piss off. I'm not interested in you or your porn."

Boog hauled open one of the cupboards above the sink. "Your Rice Krispies are on my shelf." He tried to stuff the box up onto Crawford's space but the pack was too tall, so he jammed its ass in horizontally.

"I think I'll use this one with Rosy in her bra," Crawford said.

Boog's chest filled with polar air. Despite himself, he stumbled around to look at the screen, a drum of Smash clutched against his heart.

The picture had been taken in the girls' flat: Jen in the foreground close-up, looking like she was applying make-up, and in the background stood Rosy, wearing a black underskirt and a black bra.

Boog's jaw lowered. "How did you…?"

"Interested now?" Crawford moved the cursor. Forward, rewind and play controls appeared.

A movie?

Crawford moved the mouse slowly back and forth over the play button, teasing, then he clicked.

"… nothing but roadworks," Jen said through tinny speakers. "How many times are they going to dig it up? Why don't they resurface the whole thing?"

"I know…" Rosy said, then said something indistinct, and put her arm into the sleeve of her blouse.

Jen sat upright and blocked Boog's view.

Ah, damn it. "When was that recorded?" Boog said. "How…?"

Crawford laughed. "Start of first semester. Spy cam pen, shoved into the spider plant on Jen's dressing table. That's where she sits to put her bra on. UV light, too, so it even works in the dark."

Boog set aside his morals to establish the most important facts. "Is there more of Rosy?"

Crawford looked at him, then said, "No, but there's more of Jen. A lot more. No girl-on-girl, sadly."

"Is the camera still in their flat?"

"What do you take me for?" Crawford said. "A perv? That was early days. I have full access to the real thing now, unlike certain fat bastards. Besides," he added, "the battery only lasts twelve hours."

Boog wanted to ask for the clip, but he could tell that's why Crawford had shown him it.

"What if somebody else picked those signals up?" Boog said.

"Nothing to pick up. It's all self-contained. Starts when it detects motion. Plant it one day, come back the next. Like a fishing creel. You never know what you're going to find in there."

"You're sick," Boog said, then realised he still hadn't put the tub of Smash away.

Crawford wrinkled up his nose, shook his head. "Not sick, just tech savvy. Everybody's doing it these days."

He closed his laptop. "Fifty quid, and that little movie could find itself onto a memory stick for your viewing pleasure."

There it was: the pitch. So fucking predictable.

Rosy in her bra. Boog shook his head. "I could just take a walk along the hall to Jen's and bust your ass."

Crawford laughed. "Now, that's the kind of thing I'd do, fat boy. But you…?"

Why was Boog even thinking about it? "No sale, sorry. Now, if you'll excuse me…"

"Okay." Crawford jammed the laptop under his arm, sauntered away, then stuck his head back around the door. "By the way, I lied. There is more of Rosy."

Boog froze.

"I started that clip near the end." Crawford nodded. "It's only fifteen seconds, but a lot can happen in fifteen seconds. A lot." He cupped imaginary breasts in front of him, then walked into the lounge.

How long to put a bra on? Less than fifteen seconds?

"I'll throw in the memory stick," Crawford shouted. "And a wad of tissues."

# Rosy

By the time Frank was locking up, Rosy's report was already clear in her mind. Anger with Phyllis had been replaced by embarrassment that the old woman had had to point out the obvious. The notes and tallies Rosy had been keeping, she could quickly turn into charts. For the projections, she could work out lost sales, including the impact of Frank's antisocial behaviour. Current model would be tricky, but she had an idea.

"Lamb chops tonight," Frank said, "with creamy potatoes, baby carrots and British asparagus. Apple and blackberry crumble for afters. With the homemade ice-cream you luh-luh-loved."

"No, thank you," Rosy said. "I have a report to write."

Frank shrugged. "Phyllis will always side with me," he said. "Get used to it."

"We'll see, Frank. We'll see."

Rosy straggled to the bus stop, her nose in her phone, aware that Frank kept looking over his shoulder at her. He disappeared into Shawford to deposit the cash. Rosy's bus came, but she stood back, let it pass. Frank emerged again, then headed uphill. Rosy waited until he'd slipped out of view between the buildings, counted to one hundred then doubled back and headed for the Shawford office.

An hour later, she had all the ammo she needed.

Smart girl, Heidi, and ever so keen for a change in the balance of power.

If Phyllis wanted a report, she'd have a report.

---

*Rosy collects her English essay, and wants to know why it's marked A-minus.*

*"English, Miss Friendship, is not science," says Mrs Broom. "At times I felt I was reading a report in* The Lancet.*"*

*"Isn't that good?" Rosy says.*

*"It was good, hence the A-minus, not a B-plus," Mrs Broom says.*

*Rosy shakes her head. "I don't understand."*

*"You were asked to write a piece discussing love, which you did, but only obliquely, via teenage pregnancy, rape and sexually transmitted diseases. Find yourself a boyfriend. Or girlfriend. A-minus."*

# Boog

Sitting in Pizza Hut, watching Crawford pick up his and Boog's side-salad bowl and hold them in place like breasts, Boog wondered why this always happened—why it was that, whenever Boog and Janek had agreed beforehand that they'd go out on their own for something to eat, Crawford always managed to guilt-trip them into inviting him along.

"When you and Rosy were making out," Crawford said, "did you take turns feeling each other's tits? Or did you stick with yours, because they were bigger?"

Boog stood up, "Think I'll skip the side-salad this time."

Crawford pushed the plate at Janek. "Looks like you're eating for two, Chubs. But then it always does."

Janek stroked his chin. "Were you a little caesarean crawfish, or did you slide straight out your mother's ass?"

Boog pushed through the door and into the toilets.

Sometimes he wished he hadn't talked himself and Janek into sharing with Crawford at all. But it had been the perfect way to get to know Rosy, smile at her in the morning, be there as she came and went.

Boog sat in the cubicle, unzipped, hauled out his semi-stiffie and flipped his phone to a picture of Rosy, holding a glass of red wine. With the right finger placement, he could hide that glass and imagine she was holding something else.

*I will not be carrying some worthless drop-out and making excuses for him.*

Making excuses for him… *being fat.* That's what Rosy meant. Making excuses to her stepdad.

No texts from her. No calls. Nothing. Nothing since Rosy's stepdad, that Findlay creep, had picked her up. And Findlay had acted like Boog was a pile of dog shit. Now, when Boog wasn't jerking off, or thinking about jerking off, he was thinking about Findlay Wormtongue, poisoning their relationship.

Boog and Rosy had been good up until Findlay showed up.

No, they'd been great. Rosy was so into Boog. He couldn't believe it, but it was true. He'd finally decoded his tattoo for her and she'd been so moved, she could hardly speak. Their whole relationship had been a miracle.

Boog had always been... well... hefty and girls weren't into hefty, and that meant Rosy wasn't just his one true love, she was his first real girlfriend. Which was like having a Lamborghini as his first car. Rosy certainly needed special handling and Boog would do whatever it took on that front. Whatever she wanted was absolutely fine.

But this... separation? Not seeing her? How could he study? And if he couldn't study, he'd flunk out, and lose her back to Ruben. Findlay approved of Ruben.

Maybe if Boog could just talk to Findlay, demonstrate his good character.

Boog studied himself. So now he had erectile dysfunction. He sighed, zipped and flushed.

He needed better jerk-off material.

Like spy cam footage of his own.

Boog washed his hands, careful not to look at himself in the mirror.

He could have coughed up the fifty quid Crawford wanted for that spy cam movie. Ultimately, it hadn't been Boog's morals that stopped him, but the thought of Crawford finding a way to turn it against him. Fifty quid for less than thirty seconds of bra —and possibly tit—to freeze-frame had seemed like a bargain. Fifty quid might buy a camera.

Boog dried his hands and hoped to God that was an air freshener up there, not a camera.

He knew where Rosy lived. And it wasn't like he was a pervert. He was her boyfriend, after all. He could fit a spy camera. Hide it, come back the next day. One little camera, like a NASA space probe on a mission for the good of mankind. Hypothetically.

Boog exited the gents and rejoined the table.

The pizzas were out in record time.

"Tuck in," Crawford said, "while it's hot."

Janek held up his hands in a go-easy gesture.

Boog inspected the pizza, lifted a wedge and bit.

The base was damp. And hot.

"Tabasco? You soaked my pizza in Tabasco?"

Crawford guffawed. "Bit of heat will help keep the weight down. Help you shrink down those titties."

---

Boog's beloved old Alfa GTV tipped and squeaked on its suspension as Janek squeezed into the passenger seat. They followed Crawford's low-slung silver Clio out of the Fountain Park car park.

"Sorry about the Tabasco pizza, dude," Janek said, and clamped himself in with the seatbelt. "He did that when I refilled my salad. What can I say? I have a crouton fixation."

Boog's tongue would survive. "Did you know that Crawford set up a spy cam in Jen's bedroom?"

Janek covered his face and shook his head. "Holy Jesus," he said, then sighed. "Don't know why I'm so surprised. It's a totally Crawfish move."

"Yeah. Totally Crawfish." Boog frowned.

He thought about the clump of hair he'd surreptitiously teased from Rosy's hairbrush and now kept in an envelope, along with a napkin he'd filched with her lip prints. Crawfish moves. And of course Boog had also downloaded the pictures from Rosy's phone. Was setting up a spy cam really any worse?

Crawford's Clio zoomed ahead through a late amber. Boog, like a good citizen, applied his brakes, heard a screech of tyres behind him then felt the shunt.

"I don't believe it," he said.

See what following the rules does?

---

*Boog leans over Rosy's shoulder as she updates Facebook with a picture of them both cuddling in the German Christmas Market. All Boog needs is the red suit and white beard.*

*"I look so fat."*

*"You look lovely," Rosy says.*

*Boog's eyes track to the other picture: Rosy with Ruben. Ruben has cheekbones. That photo of the pair of them could be an Abercrombie & Fitch advert.*

*"What do you see in me, Rosy?"*

*"Hmmm, nothing much." Rosy presses Boog's nose. "Just somebody I*

*can talk to, who's seen the same movies, read the same books, who buys me CDs I've never heard of and wind up loving, who doesn't talk about football, who sends me a message just when I'm thinking about him, who's kind and warm and cuddly." She shrugs. "Nothing much at all."*

*Boog looks at the picture of Ruben, the picture of Boog. They're not even the same species. What could Rosy possibly see in Boog?*

*On the physical front, things have stalled. He needs to give her more reasons to want him. He needs to dedicate himself to her, full-time.*

# Chapter 17
## Admiration
### (Monday, 6 June)
### Boog

This was the place then. A painted, pebbledash ex council house. Rosy's house. She grew up here. The most amazing girl in the world grew up right here.

Boog pulled up, parked, thankful his car was at least still drivable, then looked at the tan leather passenger seat with the chocolates and the single red rose. Was a rose too sentimental?

———————

*It's the last lecture before the break-up for Christmas and Boog has a gift for Rosy: a bracelet from Ortak. He's wrapped the box in silver paper and used a red rose instead of a gift tag. All during the lecture he's been waiting for an opportunity to slip the packet into her backpack but he's out of time, and when everybody is packing up he takes his chance. She grabs his wrist.*

*"Are you trying to touch my leg?" Rosy pulls his hand up and sees the gift. "Oh, Boog, that's beautiful. I'm sorry."*

*New to this girlfriend-boyfriend thing, Boog is confused about his status. He's put in the hours, but things haven't changed much. "Are we an item, Rosy? I mean, would you introduce me to people as your boyfriend?"*

*Rosy gazes at him, squeezes his arm. "Of course I would. Do you see anybody else? You're my cuddlemeister."*

*Boog lets out a breath he's been holding for three months. "Wish I could spend Christmas with you," he says.*

*"With my mum and Findlay? No you don't, believe me. Especially not Findlay."*

*"Why not Findlay?"*

*"He's the most boring man on the planet."*

*And all this time, Boog thought that was a title he himself held. Findlay must be a kindred spirit.*

# Findlay

Findlay was booing along with the Jeremy Kyle studio audience when the doorbell rang. Another fucking parcel for next door. He hit pause on parents against mixed-race marriages and stomped through.

"If this is for number twenty-eight——" Findlay said, then staggered back.

Jesus Christ, it was that fat boyfriend of Rosy's, crammed into a shirt and tie.

The kid smiled. "Hello, sir. Is it Findlay, or Mr Findlay?"

"Mr Dickson," Findlay said. "What do you want?"

"Sorry, Mr Dickson." The fat kid smiled again. "I'm Boog, Rosy's boyfriend. We met briefly. Could I come in, please? I'd like to talk to you about Rosy."

————————

Findlay brought through a tray with two coffees. He'd thought about bringing biscuits, then thought better of it. That greedy fucker would guzzle the lot.

"Sugar… er…? Forgot your name, sorry."

"Boog. No thanks," the kid said and slapped his belly, "Watching my weight."

Not closely enough by the sounds of that slap. "What's this about then… Boog?" Boog. What a stupid fucking name.

"Just a chat to introduce myself, and, oh——" The kid picked up the box of Thornton's Continental Findlay had been eyeing up. "I brought these…"

He handed the chocolates over, which Findlay was sure couldn't have been easy.

"Very nice of you."

"For Rosy," Boog said.

Findlay scowled.

The kid tousled his mop then leaned forward.

Great head of hair that, wasted on a fat kid. Findlay bet he had tits, that kid. Great big fucking hairy moobs.

"Thing is, when we met," Boog said, "I got the feeling you didn't like me much…"

"Oh dear," Findlay said, genuinely alarmed and quite taken aback. Was he so transparent?

"… and I was concerned that maybe you were just judging by appearances."

"Appearances?" Findlay said, carefully. "Appearances? How so?"

"Me being kinda… chubby, and all," Boog said.

"Chubby? Are you?" Findlay shook his head. "Not particularly. Can't say I'd really noticed."

"Well, that's really kind of you," the bloater said. "The thing is, I really love Rosy. Like, I mean, she's kinda my whole…"

Oh, Christ, the kid was gonna blubber. Ha-ha—blubber. Findlay had to hide the smirk at his own joke. One to write down, though.

The kid wiped his eyes and stared off into space, doing a weird jaw open kind of thing with his mouth that Findlay found himself copying.

"Sorry," the kid said, then sniffed and added, "We're having issues. And it's just that she's kinda, like, my whole… my whole world." The kid's voice broke and he took out a tissue to blow his nose.

God, this was embarrassing. Just embarrassing.

The kid took a minute and pulled himself together, thank fuck.

"Thing is, even if you don't approve of me—for whatever reason—I'd really appreciate it if you would let Rosy reach her own decision about me."

"Of course," Findlay said. "Of course. It's Rosy's life. I would never, never interfere in matters of the heart."

The kid smiled. "And I have to say, sir, I'm just full of admiration for you."

"You are?" Findlay frowned.

"Yes. Rosy is a testament to you and the fine job you did of raising her," the kid said. "She's not only beautiful outside, she'd beautiful inside. She's smart, and determined, and just a wonderful, wonderful person. And that's thanks to you."

"Thanks." Findlay sipped his coffee, feeling quite touched.

"It's not easy, raising another man's child."

"No, sir. Which makes your achievement all the more remarkable."

Findlay sat forward in his chair, and leaned in. "You have to do your best, knowing that you might not always be appreciated, but you're there. Supporting. Nurturing."

"I can see a lot of your character in Rosy," the kid said.

"You can?" Findlay said.

"Yes. You're very cerebral. Thoughtful." He shrugged. "I see that in her."

The fat kid had hit the nail on the head. Findlay studied his coffee mug. "I brought her up since she was a baby," he said. "Since eighteen months. Her biological father is rotten through and through. It's painful to think how she'd have turned out if I hadn't stepped in."

Boog nodded.

"And I did step in. Irene—Rosy's mother—was so unhappy, I couldn't bear it. I had my whole life ahead of me. I was only seventeen. I could have been anything. But I couldn't let Irene suffer." Findlay looked into Boog's earnest young eyes. "I stepped up to the plate. I set aside my ambitions. I became the husband Irene needed, the father Rosy needed."

"I never knew you did that. That's so brave."

Findlay shrugged. There was something about this boy he liked. He was deep. And wide, of course, but deep. "If there's one thing I've learned, son, it's self-sacrifice. That's what makes you happy: Making somebody else happy."

"That was my dad. Self-sacrifice," the kid said. "Nothing was ever too much."

"Was?"

"We lost him, couple years back," Boog said.

Probably a heart attack. Probably a fat bastard like his kid. "I'm deeply sorry to hear that."

"You were saying…? About self-sacrifice…?" Boog said. "I have to tell you—hope I don't embarrass you—if I had a pen and paper, I'd be taking notes. This is life. You don't get this stuff at university."

Findlay grinned and felt his back straighten, his chest widen. "Rosy's real dad threatened to come and snap my neck like a twig." Findlay nodded at the shocked look. "Oh, yes. His very words. I put my life on the line. I really did. Not for me. For Irene and for Rosy. For their safety."

Rosy didn't even know this next bit, but Findlay was in a mood to share.

"And I came this close to losing them both."

---

Findlay wasn't sure where the time went. The kid was a sponge and soon Findlay was teaching him about everything, from accordions and ventriloquism, to the secret of a good joke.

"Mr Dickson, sir," Boog said. "I'm still riveted, but those three coffees… Would I be able to use your bathroom?"

"'Course, son. Out into the hall, straight upstairs, the door facing you."

What a nice kid. What a genuinely decent, thoroughly nice kid.

Findlay listened to the stairs creak and groan, then the floorboards upstairs rock.

But what a fat bastard. Rosy needed a boyfriend with what's-his-name Renoir's body and that fat kid's brain. Mind you, that kid's brain would make Renoir fat in no time. Findlay had seen the movie. Kathleen Turner. *Romancing the Stone*. Or was it Meg Ryan?

Findlay picked up the coffee mugs, and took them into the kitchen.

That kid must have taken a wrong turn. Findlay could hear the floorboards shake overhead.

Still, a student at university would find the toilet himself. God, what if he needed a number two? Findlay would have to fumigate the house.

Those chocolates looked half-decent, though. A big box, too. If you wanted a decent box of chocolates, find a fat boyfriend.

And that was precisely the reason Rosy had to ditch Jumbo. Rosy would be like Kathleen Turner in no time.

The kid was coming downstairs again. Sounded like a wrecking ball.

"That's better," Boog said. "Where were we?"

Findlay frowned. "Actually, son, I have important matters I absolutely have to attend to." *The Jeremy Kyle Show*, for instance.

"Sure, Mr Dickson, no problem." The kid stuck his hand out.

Findlay shook it—even the kid's hand was fat—then showed him to the door.

"Mr Dickson? I can't tell you how much of a pleasure it was to get to know you, and to get the inside angle on Rosy. I hope you'll have a better view of me now."

Findlay nodded. He had a full view, all twenty-plus stone.

---

After waving back to the kid at the door, Findlay headed upstairs to empty his own aching bladder.

That's when something caught his eye through in Rosy's bedroom.

Something red. On the duvet.

A rose.

Sneaky bastard. The kid had gone into Rosy's room.

That rose would be going in the recycling. Well, what kind of a father would allow his daughter to have a romantic relationship with somebody like that?

# Boog

Boog's eyes returned from a fantasy universe where Rosy was eating a Thornton's Continental truffle, one of the buttons on her blouse undone, and refocused for a fraction of a second on his *Chemistry* textbook, before realising his phone was ringing.

But the caller wasn't Rosy, saying thank you for the chocolates and the rose.

"Ben?" Mum said. "If you have a pen, I'll give you the name of an authorised repairer for your Alfa."

Boog picked up his blank pad and pen, jotted down the address, then read it back.

"Thanks, Mum." He wandered into his bedroom and pushed the door closed. "Hope you're not mad."

"'Course I'm not, darling. Wasn't your fault, was it? Rearended. Nothing you could do about that."

There'd been no way to afford insurance, except on Mum's policy. New driver and all that.

"Once you have an estimate, Just let me know how much and I'll do a money transfer."

"Thanks."

"Not sure why you aren't coming home. Term is over, isn't it?"

Boog winced. "Me and Rosy are involved in some activities and things, Mum. You know. Obstacle courses, challenges. University stuff." Boog hoped that was only a white lie. "I'll spend some time at home back end of August. Honest."

After the re-sits.

"You be careful of those obstacle courses, Ben. Mind your back. Your dad hurt his back and he was never the same."

Mind his back. "Thanks Mum, I'll mind my back. Love you loads, miss you more… Bye."

Boog should go polish his car—

He clamped his hand over his face. Stupid.

Boog should study. Except he couldn't. He was too excited.

All he could think about now was how awesome he'd been on his visit with Findlay. Maybe one day they'd make a movie of that, the start of Boog's spy-diplomat career.

Rosy would text him at the very least. Then he could text her back.

Then he would study.

Once he'd had another wank in anticipation.

In fact, he'd have that other wank now.

# Chapter 18
## Balls
### Rosy

Rosy had posted her report through the Shawford office letterbox that morning. Heidi called her at just after 2 p.m. and arranged a taxi pickup from home at 7:30 p.m. for dinner at Balewood, Phyllis's estate.

But for the electric gates at the entrance and CCTV cameras along the driveway, the grounds of Balewood could be the woods around grandma's house in *Little Red Riding Hood*. The taxi drove past the big Georgian house, a stark, dark ghost of a building, and drew up outside a more modest structure in the same sandstone, perhaps originally a guesthouse.

Rosy regretted wearing only a T and jeans when Phyllis came to the door dressed like a duchess—ivory silk blouse, pearls and a Wedgwood blue skirt that matched her shoes. The woman did her best to smile past her landslip face.

"Thanks for coming," Phyllis said. "And thank you for a very comprehensive report, Rosy."

The girl followed Phyllis's clacking heels across a tiled lobby, and into a sitting room of golds and greens, filled with plants.

Rosy picked a low-backed Chesterfield chair, then regretted her choice when her jeans creaked against the leather. "I'm sorry you had to prompt me for the report."

Phyllis waved the apology away. "I won't beat about the bush, Rosy. I'm not prepared to invest in refurbishing the cafe."

Rosy opened her mouth then closed it again. "Well, that's disappointing. Not to worry. I still think we can significantly boost the profits by offering proper coffee and a more up-market food selection."

"Can we focus on the section of your report titled *Service*?" Phyllis said. "Treatment of customers. Seems to me, nothing else is worth doing unless we address that."

"I think service will improve as a side-effect of a more refined cafe experience."

"Let's park the fluffy words," Phyllis said. "You think fancy cakes can change Frank's personality?"

Rosy frowned. "I'm sorry, but changing Frank's personality wasn't in the job description, Mrs Long."

"I know, and I'm being a little unfair. But bawling at somebody to get out isn't the route to repeat custom."

"That wasn't in my report," Rosy said. "Have you bugged the cafe?"

"An excellent suggestion. But, no. That lady was an interview candidate for a personnel role in Shawford."

Rosy shook her head. Perfect. "Frank only did that because he was unhappy."

"Unhappy?" Phyllis said. "Rosy, how do you feel about Frank now?"

Rosy shrugged. "I'm very fond of him."

"Do you think you can cut his balls off?"

Rosy flinched, then was sure she'd misunderstood. "Bawls, as in shouts?"

"Balls as in nuts. Castrate him. Figuratively speaking." Phyllis leaned forward in her seat. "If I put you in charge, do you think you can keep him in his place, take over the cafe?"

"I thought I was in charge until you sided with him on Friday."

Phyllis dismissed that with a wave of her hand. "I needed to know what you had in mind."

Rosy bristled. "You haven't paid any attention to what I had in mind. You've ruled out renovating the place."

"I want to see if Frank can be renovated before I invest."

Rosy shook her head. "That's not how you sold me this job. You sold this as a business start-up consultant for a new cafe chain. What do I put on my CV now? Social worker? Behavioural therapist?" Rosy looked around the room at the art on the walls, the Persian rug, then thought about the quality of the fittings in the ladies' room at Shawford. "Before you knew

Frank had shouted at your interviewee, you said you wanted science and measurability. Well, me too. I want a target, and a budget."

Phyllis folded her hands. "What did you have in mind?"

"Did you read my report?"

"I don't want to spend thirty-thousand pounds on refurbishing the cafe, only to gut the place when you toddle back to university."

"Give me a budget of five thousand for the first month, and I'll recoup half that in increased profit," Rosy said. "Of course, we'd have to factor out Marek's wages, should he come back on board," she added. Fat chance.

"Monthly profit currently, according to your report, is nine hundred pounds," Phyllis said. "That's before we take your wages into account."

Rosy shrugged. "That's the business you've been running, Phyllis."

She fancied she saw a glimmer of amusement in Phyllis's eye.

"You can meet that target, can you? Because I'll hold you to it," Phyllis said.

"When I set a target, I don't miss."

"I'll have Heidi organise a credit card for you. Talk to her if you need to take cash. Now let's eat. We'll both need our strength for tomorrow."

# Findlay

Findlay sat in bed holding open an Ian Rankin he'd somehow missed, not reading it, but merely musing on the miracle of tits. Next door Irene brushed her teeth, probably not even thinking how lucky she was to have nice tits she could take out and hold, probably just thinking how she wanted a bigger house with an *en suite* bathroom.

That idea worried Findlay. The idea of mortgages worried Findlay. All it would take was Reward Biscuits to shut and then where would they be? Trying to live on the pocket money Frank paid Irene. Irene had nice tits. She should be happy with that.

When Irene came back, Findlay pulled the duvet aside for her.

Irene slid into bed, frowned at him, then leaned over and kissed him, long and slow, then smoothed his cheek with the back of her fingers.

Findlay blinked. "Bloody hell. You must have liked the Thornton's Continental."

"That's not because of the chocolates, Findlay. That's because I know why you bought them."

"You do?" Findlay wondered what anniversary he'd accidentally hit.

She nodded. "You're feeling what I'm feeling about Rosy."

Findlay stared at her. He fucking-well hoped not.

"She doesn't need us anymore. But I need you. And you have nothing to feel insecure about. All this business with Frank. You are a wonderful, wonderful person, and I love you."

Findlay put on a pained expression, then accepted a hug.

"Not sure if you noticed," Irene said, "but I'm economising so we're living on our own means." She combed the straggle of his hair with her fingers. "I'm saving Frank's maintenance money now, so if he stops paying, we know we can cope."

Findlay frowned. "Why would he stop?"

"Because, silly, Rosy's eighteen."

That didn't make sense. "But it's your money, Irene, not Rosy's."

Irene shook her head. "Doesn't matter. We're self-sufficient."

"'Course we are." And if Irene lost her job, she'd find another one. Findlay would stand by her.

"So, you don't need to buy me chocolates." Irene smoothed his cheek. "But I love that you did."

And to think Findlay had considered stashing those choccies and eating them by himself. He felt a stab of guilt about that. But he'd done the right thing.

"Shall we try for a baby?" Findlay said. It was their standard phrase. The only thing Findlay wanted less than an *en suite* was a baby. A low sperm count was no guarantee and he'd like to get the snip to be sure, but Irene might find out. He reckoned she must still hanker after a little Findlay, or Findlayette.

"Why not?" Irene said, then snuggled down and reached into Findlay's pyjama bottoms.

"I was wondering if maybe you could…?" Findlay said, "It's been so long since you… You know…? With your mouth…?"

"Oh," Irene said. "You want that?"

He nodded.

"Sure." She kissed him. "Why not? Anything you want. We'll try for a baby next time."

Findlay shimmied out of his pyjama bottoms and Irene's head slid beneath the covers. Then he played with her hair and pictured Rosy down there, with her miraculous tits.

"Uh, yes," he said. "Like that… That's amazing."

# Chapter 19
# New regime
## (Tuesday, 7 June)
### Rosy

When the Maclay's Bakery van arrived, Rosy told Frank she knew what to do, grabbed the empty tray and headed outside with it.

"Hello, doll," Jay said. "Daddy not worried about germs from the nasty Indian man today?"

Rosy cringed. "Sorry about that. Listen, do you do better rolls?"

Jay raised his hands. "What? Now you are insulting our products?"

"I mean, more variety. More up-market breads?"

"Certainly we do. Baguettes, ciabatta, focaccia, bagels, seeded rolls. We do all those stuffs for other cafes." He rummaged in his pocket and dug out a card. "Our website is on there. You can change your order online, or call Vince on that number."

"Fantastic. Thanks, Jay."

"My pleasure, doll," he said, then just stood there, smiling at her.

She waved the tray at him. "Our order?"

"Oh, yes."

They swapped trays, and Rosy ran back inside.

---

"What took you so long?" Frank said. "Wash your hands then do the tubs—"

Somebody had just knocked on the glass, and Rosy's stomach knotted when she saw Phyllis at the door.

Frank loped across the floor to let the little woman in.

"I won't hold you back," Phyllis said. "Just to let you know, Frank, that I'm putting Rosy in charge. From now on, whatever she tells you to do, you do it. Understood?"

Frank looked from Phyllis to Rosy then back. "But I'm the manager."

"You're on probation. For shouting at a customer." Phyllis pulled out a letter. "Here's your first written warning. You'll only receive one more written warning, and then you're out. Do you understand what I just said?"

Frank took the letter. "But, Phyllis—"

"One more written warning, Frank, and that's it. Third time, you're out the door, gone, no more cafe. Do you understand?"

Rosy squirmed and couldn't watch him.

"Yes," Frank said.

"Good." Phyllis clapped her hands. "Back to work."

The bell above the door dinged and Phyllis was gone.

Rosy couldn't meet Frank's gaze.

"I didn't tell her you shouted at that lady," she said.

He said nothing, just set his jaw.

"That lady was going for an interview at Shawford. She must have reported you."

"You're not in charge of me," Frank said. "I'm in charge. Phyllis can think what she likes, but this is my cafe, and I'm in charge. Now, wash your hands and do the tubs."

"Okay, I'll do that." Rosy wrung her hands. "But the tubs will have to go. And we'll need to talk about how we make the changes Phyllis expects."

"The tubs are staying. Everything is staying. We're not changing a single thing."

"Didn't you hear her, Frank?"

Frank shook his head. "No. I heard you. You went behind my back and put ideas into her head." He poked Rosy's arm where Findlay had bruised it.

"That's not what happened."

"When I dropped the cash off yesterday," Frank said, "Heidi told me you were having dinner with Phyllis."

She reached for his arm but he deflected her with raised hands.

"Germs," Frank said. He started to pop the lids off the tubs himself. "Now wash your dirty hands."

# Findlay

Findlay crossed out his two-dozenth stillborn gag, then set the notebook aside to grab a shower before Irene came home.

His thoughts filled with Rosy, first as he let the water play on him, then as he lifted the showerhead free and directed it upwards to play under his balls. Why, with all the geniuses in the world, had nobody invented a sucking-off machine? Sadly for his yearning dick, Findlay was an entertainer, not an inventor and, equally sadly, what he needed more than relentless lips around his shaft was a killer joke.

He held the showerhead level with his mouth like a microphone and reconstructed the joke he hadn't dared to write down. "My partner's husband hates me," he said into the water. "He doesn't mind if I bang his wife. But he hates sloppy seconds with his daughter."

How come it wasn't funny now? "Hates the sloppy seconds…?" He should have had the balls to write it down, but —let's face it—not a joke he could test on Irene.

"My partner's husband is so paranoid—" Findlay heard a door bang and Snuggy started to bark.

Irene? Back at this time?

Or Frank, here to kill him?

Findlay grabbed the towel, dried his front, then his head. Shampoo lather crackled in his ears. He told himself to take it easy, then stepped onto the tiles instead of the towel, slipped and had to grab the towel ring to save himself. The ring made a sick crunch like that time he'd chewed one of his own fillings. He gave a tug and the cheap piece of shit came away from the wall. He'd have to disguise the damage before Irene came home. Always assuming, he reminded himself, he wasn't already a corpse by then, with purple bruises around his neck the shape of Frank's fingers.

Did the stairs just creak?

Fuck.

Oh, Jesus, yes. He clutched his throat. Safest place to be, right now, the bathroom. The only room with a lock on the door.

———————

Findlay waited a good ten minutes, then counted to one hundred to calm down.

He opened the bathroom door, then—terrified by the prospect of crime scene cops mocking the size of his package— he retreated to pull his dirty Y-fronts back on.

Findlay edged down the stairs.

The bang had been the back door, he was certain. Snuggy had fallen silent and he pictured the dog pinned to the floor, a knife through his spine, a skewered sausage. But when Findlay, still only in his underpants, crept into the kitchen, the dog just tipped his head to one side and gave him a worried look.

He checked the back door. Closed but not locked. He smoked out there, so he wasn't exactly diligent about locking and unlocking.

The horrifying thought that a thief had come in and taken their TV made him dash for the lounge, but the TV was still there. And the hi-fi. Nothing personal missing, as far as he could tell.

But somebody had opened the back door and come up the stairs. Somebody had been in their home.

He wandered back upstairs for a final check of the bedrooms, then realised something that made him instantly horny.

Findlay was in Rosy's bedroom wearing only his underpants. He stood in front of her Cinderella dresser mirror and slid down his Y-fronts. His cock and balls were exposed in Rosy's bedroom, reflected where her face would be. And, look at that: had that box of tissues always been right there? Maybe, or maybe fate had placed them there.

He pulled out the top tissue and saw the print of her lips.

Destiny.

"Oh, Rosy," Findlay said, "of course you can kiss it."

# Rosy

All day, Frank wouldn't look at Rosy, wouldn't speak. Big baby.

After he turned the sign to *Closed* and locked the door, she took a great theatrical sigh. "Well, I'm glad we can forget about work for the day, Frank." She looped her arm around his. "What's for dinner?"

Frank unhitched his arm. "Go home, where you're wanted."

Rosy closed her eyes, then reminded herself who was in the wrong here. "Findlay will be very happy to see me."

And Findlay was. Very happy.

After dinner, Rosy visited Maclay's online portal and changed the bread order. See how Frank dealt with that.

Guerrilla action. Rosy would wage a campaign of renovation and Frank wouldn't stand a chance. She'd do it a little at a time and wear away his resistance. Rosy could hang in there to get what she wanted. She had skills in getting what she wanted.

---

*Rosy and Boog tour the German Christmas Market again and discover in the faux log cabins, amongst dodgy wood carvings and grotesque candles, a man with an alpine hat spit-roasting a boar, carving thick slices of pork for sandwiches, layering it onto crusty bread with dollops of apple sauce.*

*Boog salivates, then shakes his head. "I've put on too much weight. I'm being good."*

*"Go on," Rosy says. "It's Christmas Eve. We're on holiday. Be good after Christmas."*

*He thinks about it, then pats his stomach. "Better not. Better save myself for my mum's Christmas dinner tomorrow."*

*"Smells delicious. I could have one too," Rosy says, enjoying the hungry look on his face. "Go on. I'll buy. A delicious treat."*

*Boog smiles then rubs a hand across his mouth. "I'd still feel like a pig and I'll only hate myself. Better not. Come on."*

*"Everybody has to eat, Boog. You know you'd love to try that. Roast boar." Rosy sucks in through her bottom teeth.*

*"I'm getting too fat," Boog says.*

*"Not for me, Boog. You're lovely. I love you the way you are."*

*Boog blinks. "You mean that?"*

*"'Course I mean that. You're the cuddlemeister. You wouldn't be the cuddlemeister if you weren't cuddly."*

*Boog swallows. "We'll only get one and we'll share."*

*Rosy nods and buys one between them but she only has a couple of bites, because she knows he's enjoying it so much. When he's done, she kisses his open, greasy mouth, and rubs his belly. "Mmm," Rosy says. "That's hit the spot. I could eat you myself."*

Frank's anger had burned off by next day, and he was back to hugging Rosy. Yet as soon as she told him what to do, his thumbs went straight in his ears. Then when the Maclay's delivery arrived, Frank spotted the change and refused the order. He wouldn't let Jay climb back in his van until the man had gone through the other customer deliveries and picked out the requisite number of morning rolls to make up the old order.

"You can't do that every morning," Rosy said.

"I won't have to," Frank said. "The order is reverted. I'm now the sole approver."

Screw him. Guerilla action. And today, Rosy was going to fix the stupid trays. Just let Frank lift a finger to stop her and she'd scream bloody rape.

The dark wooden laminate food trays were all piled in a rack by the door. People would come in, walk right past the rack, then have to walk all the way back. Rosy began to ferry the pile, four at a time, over to a new place by the counter, half-expecting Frank to object or try to stop her. When he just stood there, doodling on an order pad, Rosy tried to get him to join in.

"Come on. You can be part of this, Frank. We'll both get credit from Phyllis."

"That's okay, baby," he said. "I'm looking forward to watching you shift the rack."

The rack was made of steel and, even without the trays, it was so heavy she thought it must be bolted down. Rosy managed to waddle the rack, one painful step at a time, into the centre of the floor, then her hands wouldn't grip anymore. She stood there, sweating, looking at Frank.

"Got yourself in a mess, now, haven't you, baby?" he said, and went straight back to his doodling.

Rosy marched past him, and retrieved a pair of rubber gloves from the sink. She pulled the gloves on over raw hands and gripped the metal, moved it one step closer.

"Good luck," Frank said.

The gloves gave Rosy the grip she needed to wrestle that stupid contraption the rest of the way until it was square with the counter. She filled it with the trays, and retired sweating, but satisfied, limbs turned to jelly.

"About that rack, Frank? Nothing to it. Thanks for all your help."

Frank nodded, "No problem," then walked around the counter, lifted the rack and the entire pile of trays, and carried it back to where it had been an hour before.

Rosy fought tears. "I'll tell Phyllis," she said.

"Tell her. I don't care. This is my cafe, not yours. Nothing changes, baby. Nothing changes."

------

*Rosy opens her Christmas gift from Boog. It's a silver bracelet from Ortak, with intertwining leaves and, as she turns it, she notices one of the leaves has a letter B then a heart then a letter R.*

*"Oh, Rosy, that's beautiful," Mum says. "Is that from Ruben?"*

*Rosy shakes her head, annoyed. "No, just a friend who has gone way over the top." She can't even make him take it back because he's had it engraved. Rosy gave Boog an Amazon gift certificate for fifteen quid.*

*She told him to be sensible. She told him, but he had to have it his way. Well, his loss.*

*And for some reason, Rosy can't quite bring herself to say that she's split with Ruben. There'd only be awkward questions. She's not hiding Boog. There's a picture of him, on Facebook. And of Ruben. It would be childish to remove Ruben. And her diplomacy avoids those questions.*

# Chapter 20
## Stasis
### (Tuesday, 14 June)
### Rosy

Inevitable that at some point somebody Rosy knew would come into the cafe, but she hadn't expected it would be "L'il Bunny" Patterson—Boog's nickname for his and Rosy's director of studies, on account of large teeth and a harelip. He had a lady friend in tow.

A week had gone since the nominal shift of power and it couldn't be clearer that Rosy had failed to cut off Frank's balls. Frank's balls hung unmolested, safe behind titanium armour. Rosy hadn't even managed a square-on kick.

She had annoyed him, though. Frank's sensitivity to change had become so acute, Rosy only had to be thinking of saying something and she'd feel him cool towards her. Open her mouth, and Frank's response was killer: instant withdrawal of affection. All her suggestions—internet access, proper coffee, different sandwich fillings, different teas—all of them had provoked Frank to move away from her, shrug off her arm, ignore her when she spoke, until she'd served her sentence in the doghouse.

"It's Ruby, isn't it. Ruby Friendship?" Dr Patterson said. "No luck finding a summer placement then, Ruby?"

"It's Rosy, Dr Patterson. I stopped looking. I'm working with my dad here."

"And a fine establishment it seems too." He looked around then frowned. "Well, just two small lattes, please." He rubbed his hands together as though they were cold.

"We don't do lattes here at the Tasty Bite, Dr Patterson," Rosy said. "We do filter coffee?"

"Ah. Okay. Two white filter coffees, then, please," he said, then frowned. "Why don't you do lattes?"

"Because, they stink," Frank said. "Now, sit down." He made shooing gestures with his hands. "Go."

Rosy closed her eyes. Frank's hand landed in the small of her back, and her frown relaxed.

"Take him his coffee, baby," Frank said.

"Okay, boss."

One week down, only three left to meet the target Rosy had so arrogantly committed to with Phyllis. Phyllis would be mightily disappointed. Ultimately, though, the cafe was only a summer job. Rosy's relationship with Frank had to survive a lifetime, hers or Frank's.

From the start, there could only be one winner: the only one prepared to play hardball with the relationship.

# Boog

Boog's *Chemistry* textbook might as well be a phone directory.

Weeks reading the same fucking shit and what had he taken in?

Fuck all.

Fuck all.

Fuck all.

"Gah." Boog covered his eyes.

"You okay, Boogie?" Janek said.

Boog nodded.

He felt Janek's hand rub his back.

"I can't do this," Boog said.

"Sure you can, Boogie. You're doin' great. You're doin' great."

"Whoa." Crawford stopped fast enough to slosh his tea on the carpet. "I'll take this back into the kitchen if there's gonna be a guy kiss."

"Scuttle back up your sewage pipe, Crawfish," Janek said.

"What's the matter with the fat boy?" Crawford said. "Pressure making him cry? Those re-sits are so close I can smell the fear. Half the time gone. Nothing learned. Tick-tock."

Janek rubbed Boog's back again. "Let's go for a walk, huh? Let's you and me go for fresh air."

Boog nodded, stood up, grabbed his jacket, and left the flat. He waited in the hall.

Rosy had sabotaged him. She'd brought him alongside then torpedoed him, holed him below the water line and Boog was sinking. He was sinking and there was nothing he could do to save himself. No time. No concentration. No breath.

He jammed his inhaler between his teeth, pressed and breathed.

Janek emerged, dressed in a T-shirt, jeans and a pair of sandals.

Boog managed three steps then the waterworks came on. "I

can't study, Janek. I can't stop thinking about Rosy. If I knew she wanted me—"

"'Course she wants you, Boogie. 'Course she does. You're a prize. You're a star prize."

They walked along the hallway.

Boog wiped his face, shook his head to be rid of the tears. "What's the secret, Janek? How did you breeze your exams without studying?"

"No secret. Maths is ingrained in me. I did all this stuff five years ago." He held the door open.

But Boog just stopped and gaped at his friend. "If you know all this, why not jump ahead?"

"I don't want to be a freak, Boogie," Janek said. "I want to meet a nice girl my own age."

They descended the stairs, two flights.

At the bottom, Boog shook his head. Janek didn't go near girls. "Why didn't you get out more during term?"

Janek shrugged. "Why didn't you study?"

Boog stopped.

"Fear," Janek said. "Fear of failure. 'Case you didn't notice, Boogieman, you're chubby and cute. I'm fat and ugly. Who's gonna want me? Who's gonna want fat and ugly?"

Janek held the door open and they exited the red brick building and headed toward Slateford Road.

"You're not ugly. Seriously dude. You'll find a girl," Boog said.

"You believe that, Boogie?" Janek said. "You really believe that?"

"Yeah, Janek. I really, really do."

"So if you believe in me, what's not to believe in yourself when you've come so far? What's that all about, Boogie? What's with not believing all of a sudden?"

Boog stared skyward. "What would you do if you were me?"

"I'd get me to the library," Janek said. "That's where I'd go. Every day. That Crawfish, he's sniping away at you, undermining your confidence. You don't need that. Nobody needs that. Nobody can handle that." He balled his fist. "It's his old man's flat and all, and I'm pretty laid back and all, but I've had just about enough of his ass."

Janek was the prize.

They crossed to the newsagent.

"What about Rosy?" Boog said.

"What do I know about girls, Boogieman?" Janek said. "But if girls are people like everybody else and I gotta assume they are, I think Rosy is fooling herself."

"Fooling herself?"

"She said she doesn't want to see you again. But her eyes didn't say that. Her eyes said a whole different thing. Her eyes said something maybe her head hasn't realised yet. She loves you, Boogie. She really loves you."

---

*It's the family's first attempt to celebrate Christmas since Boog's dad died. Mum hands him the carving knife and fork. "Ben," she says. "Will you do the honours?"*

*He starts to carve but hits something hard. His little sister Andrea laughs. Mum indicates with her hand to come over a bit. Boog starts to cut but the skin slides away. "You should do it, Mum."*

*"No. Keep at it, son. One day, you'll be a father, and you'll want to be able to carve."*

*Boog watches a tear fall on Andrea's plate, and onto the table cover beside her. But Boog will be the man of the family. He's not going to cry. Not this year.*

*And what does Boog have to be sad about this Christmas?*

*Rosy Friendship—the most beautiful girl he's ever seen, the girl all the other guys keep watching—loves him. She actually loves him.*

# Rosy

Near closing time, Heidi arrived and Rosy thought she'd have another battle on her hands over last-minute catering, but the woman ordered two pots of tea and sat at the bench in the window.

When Rosy delivered the teas, Heidi smiled and whispered to Rosy to sit.

"It's all right, honey. Sit down, please. Phyllis asked me to talk to you, to check everything is on track."

Rosy shrugged. "Yeah."

"Oh, that doesn't sound like a yes. Only, knowing Phyllis, it'd be better to say now if there's a problem," Heidi said.

"There isn't. Everything is on track. I'd better get back."

"Don't let him bully you," Heidi said, and made a tiny fist.

"How exactly do I do that, Heidi?"

When Rosy came back behind the counter, Frank was standing there with his arms folded.

"What was that all about?" he said.

"Phyllis sent Heidi over to check everything was okay."

"What did you tell her?" Frank said.

"I told her everything's on track."

Frank hugged her to him and Rosy rested her head on his chest, defeated.

"That's good, baby." Frank rubbed her arm. "Very good."

---

*Rosy is back from the Christmas break and has seen Boog's GTV in the car park. She calls his mobile from outside the flat door and he bursts out to meet her.*

*"Rosy." Boog throws his big soft arms around her. "Babe."*

*"Oh, I've missed the cuddlemeister," Rosy says.*

*His cheeks are pink, ripe with health.*

*She strokes his face. "You look amazing," she says, takes his hand and starts to lead him along the corridor.*

*"Amazingly fat, you mean?" he says. "I missed you so much, all I've*

*done is eat. Eat like a pig. My New Year's resolutions are to work harder and enrol in the gym."*

Rosy has breezed through her first semester exams to gain an exemption so will only have to sit one part of the second semester exams. Boog has scraped by and he'll need to sit both parts.

"Working a bit harder is a good idea," Rosy says. She heads downstairs, bound for the decking around the communal garden area so they can cuddle and catch-up. "Just don't go getting all skinny on me at the gym. Be who you are." She rubs his belly.

Boog pulls her hand away. "Don't do that. Not when I'm so fat. I'm one-and-a-half times who I am."

Rosy stops and folds her arms. "You won't want to go out to dinner with me, then," she says, her voice echoing in the stairwell, sounding angrier than she feels.

"Oh, I would, babe," he says, "But I'd rather stay in with you. We could study together."

Rosy rolls her eyes. *Study together? Yeah, that would be really productive having him asking questions all the time.* She picks up his hand. "Well, if I sent out for a Chinese, we could feed each other with chopsticks and we could snuggle. I could do with a cuddle."

Boog frowns. "Am I... sexy?" he says. "Or only cuddly? It's just that, if I'm sexy... I really missed you..."

Rosy drops his hand and folds her arms. "First day I'm back, Boog, a million things to catch up on, and that's all you're interested in?"

"Of course not. We'll do whatever it is you want to do, babe. You like tenpin bowling. We could go bowling and grab a healthy snack. Something light."

"Okay. Bowling then Chinese, Mr Sexy Belly," Rosy says, and kisses him, slipping her hand up his jumper to rub his stomach through his shirt. That clearly makes him feel happier about himself, because he holds her face and kisses back as if her mouth is his only supply of oxygen.

# Chapter 21
## Gorilla
### Findlay

The TV volume was down just so Findlay could hear Rosy come in. When the door banged, he ran into the hall, hands behind his back.

"Guess what I have?" he said.

"Another rash?" Rosy said.

He frowned and took the package out from behind his back. "This came for you. I think it's a book."

"Thank you, Dad." Rosy took the box from him but just put it down on the telephone table, then headed upstairs.

"Aren't you going to open it, Sweatpea?"

No answer.

Findlay heard her bedroom door close.

Frank-related injury, Findlay guessed, and although he wanted Rosy to see Frank-fucking-Friendship for what he was, Findlay was still Rosy's stepdad.

He followed her upstairs, knocked on her bedroom door and listened.

"What is it?" Rosy said.

He pressed his hands onto the door. "Would it help to talk?"

He waited.

"No."

He knocked again. "Can I come in?"

No answer.

"Rosy? Sweetpea? Can Dad come in?"

He didn't wait for an answer this time.

Findlay could tell right away she'd been crying, and that worried him. Rosy had never been a girl to cry, but recently…

He stood by the door, hands behind his back out of harm's way. "Tough day?"

Rosy nodded and Findlay's heart just about broke. He looked away, blinking, while she grabbed a tissue from the box.

"I made up a joke for my act today. Want to hear it?"

Rosy nodded and sniffed. "Sure."

"So a lady goes into the hardware store and takes a chipmunk out of her handbag."

Rosy smiled.

"The customer says, 'I'd like to return this.' So the assistant looks at her and looks at the chipmunk and looks back at the customer and says, 'But madam, it's a chipmunk' So the customer says, 'I *know* it's a chipmunk. But how am I supposed to plug it in?'"

Rosy's laughter carried Findlay with it.

"That's terrible," she said. "I don't even get it, so I don't even know why I'm laughing."

"But you're laughing. Mission accomplished."

He headed out of her room.

"Dad?" Rosy ran after him. "I've been meaning to say, there's a man I think could help you with your act."

Already, Findlay didn't like the sound of this.

Rosy held the tissue between her fingers, and dabbed her eyes. "You should meet him. He has a lot of experience with showbiz."

Findlay felt his chest constrict, but Rosy kept piling on the pressure.

"He has sell-out shows at the Edinburgh Fringe. His name is Marek. He's Polish, and," she laughed, "he's a naked magician."

Thank God, something tangible. "A naked magician?" Findlay looked up at her, shook his head. "That's a different kind of act, Sweetpea. There wouldn't be any point talking—"

She put her fingers to his lips. "You helped me. Let me help you."

Her fingers smelled of flowers. Findlay wanted so desperately to kiss those fingers but held back and when she took her hand away, he had to look down at his feet.

She picked up his chin with her hand.

For the briefest of moments, Findlay thought she would bend down, press her lips against his. And if she did that, then it would be okay. He'd know she wanted him.

"Please, Dad. Tell me you'll think about it."

She meant, meet the magician, that's what she meant. "I'll think about it, Sweetpea. I'll think about it."

Findlay pulled Rosy's bedroom door closed and looked at his shaking hands. Bricklayer's hands, not entertainer's hands. And in his underwear, his cock had gone rigid. Oh, God. How did he dig himself into such a deep and hopeless hole? And how the fuck would he climb out?

# Rosy

Rosy's phone vibrated with a message from Jen: *You up for the Opal Lounge Saturday? We could both go shopping for gorgeous outfits?*

Oh, yes. Rosy was up for that. She could try out Findlay's non-joke.

*It's a chipmunk. How am I supposed to plug it in?*

She felt so sorry for Findlay. He'd looked petrified at the prospect of meeting Marek for—

— some advice.

Nobody else had been able to handle Frank.

Until Marek.

---

Rosy was no psychologist, but she could guess what Marek's body was saying. He sat in the Widower's Fiddle with one hand along the back of the next chair, his legs wide and his other hand dangling at his crotch. Rosy's interpretation: Come sit beside me, young lady, and grab a firm hold of my wand.

Rosy had just told him about last week's tray rack incident and he had nodded. "Frank is a heavyweight and you are not," Marek said "Why go head-to-head with him? It's well known that when an opponent is bigger and stronger than you, you must use his strength against him."

"I'm not trying to knock him flat. I'm trying to make him cooperate."

Marek waved his hand. "Why oppose him, then? He is the silverback. Why go into his territory and piss all over his toys? He would have moved those trays if he'd wanted to. Make him want to."

"How?"

"Don't impose a solution when he doesn't even have a problem. Give him a problem."

Rosy frowned.

"If you give him a problem, you can give him your solution. But it must be his problem, not somebody else's."

She wasn't getting it. "How, Marek? How would you make him move the trays?"

"For the trays? Frank doesn't care about customers having to walk. That's their problem. What does Frank care about?"

"I have no idea."

Marek raised his palm from the chair back and gestured at his shoes. "Germs. So for the trays, I would say something like, 'Hey, Frank. If those trays were nearer, customers wouldn't keep trailing their dirty feet all over the floor.'"

Rosy fought to keep the smile from breaking out all over her face. "Simple as that?"

"Why not?" Marek said.

Rosy laughed, then stopped when she realised she'd made the biggest possible mistake with Frank. She'd used Phyllis to pull rank. Rosy hadn't just pissed on the silverback's toys. She'd tried to take his territory from him.

"Ah, and you are back to the same melancholy mood you arrived with," Marek said. "Are you having more problems with your boyfriend?"

"Boyfriend?" Rosy said, and felt her face go red. "Frank's not my boyfriend."

While the horror of her faux pas was still registering, Marek leaned forward and scanned her face, eyes darting like a machine recording the position and angle of every feature—click-click-click-done. His eyes locked back onto hers. His own smile didn't extend beyond his lips. "But of course he is not. Frank is your father," he said.

A sinkhole had opened in Rosy's gut. "Sorry, crossed wires," she said. "My boyfriend is great. We're great. He and I." Rosy stood up and almost fell back down again. "Oh, that beer was strong. Listen, I really appreciate your help, but I do have to go."

He took her hand. "My pleasure. I always have time for a damsel in distress."

---

*On Valentine's Day, after Jen has gone out with Crawford to leave Rosy on her own in the flat, Rosy answers a knock at the door to find Boog, barefoot, wearing only his pyjama shorts and T, holding something behind his back.*

*"Well, can I come in?" he says, and grins.*

*"I'm revising."*

*He raises his eyebrows.*

*Rosy relents then beckons him inside.*

*Boog tiptoes over the threshold.*

*"Seeing it's Valentine's Day," Boog says, "I thought I'd give you something extra special."*

*"You already gave me roses and a card."*

*"Well, I thought, what would be nicer than a cuddle on Valentine's day?"*

*Rosy smiles but before she can hug him he holds up his hand.*

*"I thought about that, and came up with an idea," he says. "Happy Valentine's Day, Rosy. Your extra special surprise is…" He produces an aerosol of Anchor squirty cream. "Me. With cream on."*

*Rosy glares at him, and folds her arms. "I beg your pardon?"*

*He smiles. "You can decorate me. With this." He waves the cream. "On my belly, if you like."*

*It's not his belly he wants her to decorate, though. What he really wants is what Ruben wanted and she's sickened. She walks past him and opens the door. "Congratulations. You're now as crass as Crawford."*

*His smile buckles. "Babe. It's Valentine's Day. It's a day to be crazy."*

*Rosy shakes her head. "Wrong, Boog. It's a day to be romantic, not a day to be a pervert. I'm going to forget this ever happened and I suggest you do too."*

*"Rosy? It's only a bit of fun. Please, say yes to a bit of fun."*

*Fun? What is wrong with him? "No," Rosy says. "Now go."*

*When he's gone, Rosy's thoughts wheel back to Ruben and she thinks she may throw up.*

# Chapter 22
## Pet
### (Wednesday, 15 June)
### Rosy

Rosy's bus arrived early and Frank didn't emerge to open the door when she rapped the glass. That's what made her walk around the side of the building toward the kitchen, where her feet came to a scraping halt.

Frank lurked by the dumpsters, his back to her, but not alone. Facing him, a wizened and grimy old man, a down-and-out in a raggedy coat of fur, fur that could only have come from skinned cats. As Rosy watched—

— the derelict parted his coat

— and appeared to be wearing nothing beneath.

Frank gazed down at the man's crotch. "Can I stroke it?" he said, then took a step closer, and reached his hand inside the coat.

A small gasp that must have been Rosy's made Frank turn around.

The old man, though bare-chested, wore baggy shorts. Frank's hand cradled a kitten. Inside the fur coat, a large pocket wriggled.

By the time Rosy recovered, the old man had already retrieved the kitten and was hurrying away.

"That's Catman," Frank said, and opened the back door for her. "He's usually gone before you arrive. He's kinda my pet. I feed him and when he has kittens I get to hold 'em."

Frank squirted soap on his hands.

Only Frank would keep a human as a pet. And wasn't that

what she'd become, too? A pet for Frank, grateful for his attention. Passivated. Claws clipped.

Why so content? Why, with so many unanswered questions, was she so unconcerned?

No fresh clues had crept out. No whisper to explain Alan McAdam's name in those clothes back at his flat, Ernesto and the jobs, or Frank's flat with nothing but a bed and a kitchen.

What did he do with himself?

And whatever it was, couldn't she be part of that life too? Couldn't he open up more to his own daughter? She wanted more of him.

Frank grabbed the towel and dried his hands.

Rosy shook herself. She'd spent too much time in Frank's company already, too much time thinking about him when she wasn't here. That's why she'd embarrassed herself with Marek yesterday. With Boog gone from the picture, Frank had become the only man in her life. *Frank's not my boyfriend.* How cringeworthy.

Roll on Saturday. Shopping and a night out. Time off the leash.

Rosy refocused and Frank inclined his head as though her brain broadcast on a channel and he could pick up her thoughts. He still stood by the sink and for a moment her heart clutched at the notion he would wash her hands with his, the way he had that first day, a reprise of that act of fatherly tenderness.

"C'mon, Rosy. Wash your hands." He walked away. "Germs."

---

When the cafe fell quiet, Rosy said with all the nonchalance she could fake, what Marek had said. "Hey, Frank. If those trays were closer, people wouldn't trail their dirty feet all over the floor."

Frank regarded her, then the trays, then settled his not quite straight gaze back on her. "The trays are okay there, baby. The regulars are used to the trays there."

At first, Rosy thought she'd failed, then she realised Frank hadn't pushed fat thumbs in his ears, hadn't sent her to the doghouse. He'd listened, and he'd come back with a reasoned rejection.

She settled for that for a while, then tried the same approach with another topic, her eyes downcast and away from the silverback, a submissive female. "If we had a wider variety of bread, we wouldn't lose customers to cafes serving badly drained tuna mush."

Frank frowned and that one bounced around in there a while before he spoke. "Customers come here because it's cheap," Frank said. "People around here don't have the money for fancy breads."

Rosy nodded. "Customers with the money will head into town, eat mushed up tuna, and we'll have to throw ours away."

Frank held her shoulders and his eyes captured hers. "Here's what I say, Rosy: Let them. People don't put enough value on loyalty. They only care about new customers, and they change things people liked. Things that didn't need to be changed."

"But Frank—"

He raised his hand, palm out, as though taking an oath in court. "The regulars keep this place open for business. The day a regular customer can't get his regular tuna roll, I've lost him. I'm here for my regulars. The Tasty Bite is my cafe. Nothing changes, baby."

---

In Rosy's absence, the package she'd left on the telephone table had climbed the stairs and thrown itself onto her bed, a sticky note affixed in her mum's handwriting: *Deal with this.*

*The Beancounter's Cafe Handbook: How to run a successful coffee shop.* She'd ordered the book the day Phyllis offered her the job. Only one hundred and twenty pages and as Rosy read, she recognised her every rejected suggestion, plus dozens more besides.

Vindication.

Except this was the wrong book. Rosy needed a book on how to coax a bone-headed silverback gorilla to stop pissing and start listening, before he lost his toys permanently.

They were on the same side, Rosy and Frank. She needed to hit him hard enough to make him see that.

---

*Ruben calls Rosy to apologise he won't be able to make their dinner date because he's been injured playing football and is in hospital.*

*As the conversation progresses, Rosy discovers that one of Ruben's perfect cheekbones has been fractured after the goalie in his own team punched him in the face. Rosy tells Ruben to take care and get well soon, but in reality, she'd like to buy the goalie a drink.*

Today turned out to be the hottest so far and customers who'd complained about the mediocre summer now had their wish: a day to really complain about. The sun, normally a lift to Rosy's mood, only beat her down, intensified her oppression. It baked her brain as they locked up.

"Read this, tonight, Frank." Rosy held out the *Beancounter's Cafe Handbook*. "It's small and it won't take long."

Frank looked at the cover, then pushed it back at her. "I'm busy."

He locked the door, and didn't hug her goodbye. No, of course not. He just walked away.

Frank-fucking-Friendship deserved everything he had coming. Everything. Rosy took a few steps in the opposite direction then turned and yelled loud enough for Phyllis to hear her over in the Shawford office. "She's going to shut the cafe down."

Frank's back stiffened and he stopped.

"Where will your regulars be then?" She closed the gap between them. "Where will you be then?"

Frank turned on her. "Shows what you know. Phyllis would never do that. Ask me how I know."

"How do you know, Frank?" Rosy said, stepped forward and pushed him in the chest, but didn't manage to budge him. "How do you know?"

"Because when nobody else would touch me," Frank said, growing bigger, wider, rising up over her, leaning in to seize every scrap of her personal space, "Phyllis gave me a job. When Findlay and Irene landed me in Young Offenders, Phyllis got me out, and guess what? I still had a job. Other, fancier places have come and gone. But, oh, look at that." He jabbed a finger at the shop. "My cafe is still there. I still have a job. Nobody can come between me and Phyllis. You want to know why?" he said. "Because Phyllis Long is my guardian angel." He glared down at her, then turned away.

"She's going to shut the place down. She told me. The day I first came to the cafe. You'll be moved out to work at her estate."

Frank turned and his face had gone white. "Her estate?"

"I'm trying to save your job, you stupid man," Rosy said, and strode off without a backward glance.

When Rosy's bus passed the cafe, Frank was standing in the same spot on the pavement, his holdall with the cash from the till down at his feet. Rosy faced forward and put all thought of Frank from her mind. Then his words came back to her.

Young Offenders.

Frank had been in prison?

---

Rosy came home to discover her mum and her stepdad had decided to humiliate themselves by sunbathing in the back garden. Mum's stretch-marked stomach blancmanged out between her two-piece Speedo bathing suit. Findlay looked like random bits of bleached driftwood the dog had dropped onto the sun lounger.

Mum peered at Rosy over her sunglasses. "Just grabbing ten minutes of this while it lasts. There's another lounger if you fancy joining us."

Findlay grinned at Rosy. "Definitely bikini weather. Lovely."

"I'll pass, thanks."

She backed up the steps, into the shadow of the house, but Mum called to her.

"You didn't accidentally take a pair of my panties, did you?"

Rosy laughed. "Those big white parachute things? Er… no."

Mum gripped the bridge of those giant sunglasses, squinted at her. "These were new from Marks and Spencer. Black silky bikini briefs with little lacy stars."

"Lacy stars?" Rosy pictured something Cher would wear. "I think I'd have noticed, Mum."

"Can't think where they'd be, then. They were hanging up on the pulley—"

Findlay's eyes couldn't bulge more if Cher had just waved at him with stars on her boobs and the panties around her ankles. "Oh my God, Irene. Oh my God. He's been in here."

"Pardon?"

"Frank. Frank was in the house. He took your panties. Last Tuesday… Was it Tuesday…? Anyway, I heard the door bang when I was in the shower. Snuggy was barking."

"What? Frank came all the way out here and nicked my underwear? Oh, please."

"I'm telling you. It's started. Time to call the cops," Findlay said.

"Was I at work when this happened?" Rosy said.

Findlay thought about that then said, "Yes…"

She shrugged. "So, how could it be Frank? And what do you mean, '*it's started*'? What's started?"

"Nothing's started," Mum said. "It couldn't be Frank."

"But—" Findlay said.

"Enough of your nonsense, Findlay." Mum stood up and threw her *Chat* magazine at him. "Enough."

---

Accordion music. Rosy listened at the door of the spare room for a break in the *Captain Pugwash* theme. She knew exactly where Findlay's fingers would falter. He'd rehearsed so long, he had the mistakes committed to muscle memory. She knocked and opened the door while the curse was still blue on his lips.

"Hey, Dad," Rosy said. "You were telling me about Frank a while back. I just realised I didn't ever hear you out."

Findlay gave her a long, wounded look, didn't say anything, then wheezed the bellows shut, turned his music back to the start, and began to play the sailor's hornpipe again.

"Dad…?"

"Busy," Findlay said, then *Captain Pugwash* hit a new rough patch and came to a stop in a discordant squall.

He pointed at her. "Are you starting to see now what you've stirred up?"

"No," Rosy said. "Because nobody will tell me anything."

Findlay impersonated a goldfish, mouth opening and closing. "I did tell you. Frank raped your mother because he couldn't bear to see Irene and me happy."

"Was Frank in a Young Offender Institution?"

Findlay bore his yellow teeth, goldfish to piranha. "No. Because Irene protected him, or by God, he would have been."

"Later, I mean. Did you and Mum go to the police? Was he

locked up?"

Findlay fidgeted with the tone switches of his accordion then nodded. "Yes."

"Why?"

"Because he wouldn't stay away, that's why."

"Is that when he threatened to kill you?" Rosy said.

Findlay nodded. "Yes. And that's why I don't want you anywhere near him. I'm scared if he knew what you mean to me..." He pinched the bridge of his nose. "He hates me and I'm afraid."

"And is that all?" Rosy said.

"What more do you want?" Findlay said. "A knife through my chest?"

"I don't think Frank would hurt me."

Findlay scrunched his eyes shut. "Oh, you don't? And you have some special ability to predict what a crazy man will do?" He opened his eyes again and the watery blue fear implored her. "Murder is in his genes. And someday, they'll find bodies. They'll find all the bodies of people Frank has been killing off and hiding away."

Was that for real, or was that just Findlay?

"Dad?" Rosy said. "Do you know somebody called Ernesto?"

His brow furrowed. "No. Should I? Sounds like somebody from a gangster movie."

Rosy nodded. "Doesn't he just?"

"Be careful, Rosy. Don't provoke him. I don't want one of the bodies they find to be mine."

# Findlay

Findlay rubbed his head, picked up his accordion, then set it back down. No matter how much he practised, he couldn't seem to ever get all the way through one tune. Captain-fucking-Pugwash.

Frank-fucking-Friendship well and truly back in their lives.

---

*Boxes crowd against the new sofa in their new lounge. Irene is upstairs, setting Rosy down in her cot in the nursery. Findlay has his feet up with a hot cup of tea when the telephone jangles him straight out of his chair.*

*He uses the cable to find where the phone is hiding. "Hello?"*

*"Peekaboo," Frank says. "Found you."*

# Chapter 23
# Beancounter
(Friday, 17 June)
## Rosy

When Phyllis had offered Rosy this job, she'd asked her to say nothing about the cafe closure. Rosy's fear now was that Frank might march into Shawford and confront the woman. But the moment Rosy's bus pulled in, he opened the cafe door. He'd been waiting for her.

"I can't work at Phyllis's estate, baby," he said. "She can't make me go there. She can't. What do we have to do to keep the cafe open?"

She stared at him, at dark rings beneath his eyes, at sweat droplets glistening on his lip, at his slumped shoulders.

Frank was scared. Scared he'd be sent to Phyllis's estate. Because his father, Gus, had worked there? Bad memories, perhaps?

Rosy fumbled out her *Beancounter's Cafe Handbook*. "Read that," she said, still studying him. "Then we'll work out a rescue plan."

Dare she even hope?

———

"This guy is a genius," Frank said, and waved the Beancounter's book.

"Helpful, isn't it?" Rosy said.

"Helpful?" Frank grinned. "Man, this changes everything. This is gonna be so easy."

Rosy gaped at him, Mr Intransigence. "Oh, you reckon?"

"Of course," Frank said. "I thought I'd have to be nice to everybody. I don't. If somebody's nasty, I just smile and recommend something expensive and fattening."

"Yeah," Rosy said, "you're picking up a slightly different message, aren't you?"

"No. It's all about making money, Rosy. That's Lesson One." He then reeled off something that sounded eerily like a word-for-word quote.

"Did you memorise that?" Rosy said.

"I read it," Frank said. "I told you before, I have a good memory."

She levered the book from his fingers, and flicked backward from his place. "What's Lesson… Three?"

"Lesson Three. Coffee is a Beancounter's Best Friend. The margin on coffee is so embarrassingly high, it's enough to make a beancounter blush—all the way to the cash register. Don't fret if you can't coax a customer to have lunch. Sell them that extra latte you both know they want, and you'll bankroll the same net profit. Ker-ching! Thank you, madam, and you have a nice day! Of course, great tasting coffee is the key to—"

"Stop," Rosy said. "Oh my God, Frank. You don't have a good memory, you have a photographic memory."

He shook his head. "I wish. I'll forget the words in a day or two. But the idea is in here now." He tapped his temple. "I'm never gonna forget an idea."

She handed the book back. "Keep reading."

Frank kept reading, even when he was serving customers.

"Can I recommend one of our home-baked scones with your pot of tea?" he said. He looked up and smiled.

That line produced a sale. Frank turned, winked and gave Rosy a thumbs up, and Rosy's toes curled. Once the customer had seated herself, Rosy elbowed him. "Those aren't home-baked."

"They're not?" he said. "Okay. Anyway, I'm just practising. We can buy in some home-baked, can't we?"

"Truthful descriptions only, please," Rosy said. "Say *delicious* or something."

Frank shrugged. "I could say *dry.*"

"This is why we need better quality products."

"Yeah, I'm totally with you," Frank said. "Let's dump this shit and bring in the expensive-looking stuff."

"It's not all about the money, Frank."

"Oh, but it is. Lesson One. Beancounters run the most successful cafes. Why? Because it's all about making money."

"You're dangerous." Rosy waved a finger at him.

He grabbed her hand, sandwiched it between his. "No-no-no, Rosy. Lesson Twenty-four," he quoted. "Body Language. How do you feel if somebody points at you? Exactly! There's never any need, so don't do it. Be aware of the subtle signals you're sending that send money walking straight out the door."

Rosy leaned in close and smacked his bottom, then pulled away, giddy and aghast at what she'd been about to do next. She'd been about to kiss his lips.

---

Frank had caught the Beancounter's religion and he was born again. After they'd locked up, he paced the floor. "You know how we could really screw money out of people? Homemade stuff. Real homemade. Made by me."

"I don't remember the phrase *screw money out of customers* in the handbook," Rosy said.

"He didn't say it, but he meant it," Frank said. "He says to create a house speciality. Get this." He moved his hand as though pointing out words on a sign: "*Frank's Special Coleslaw.* How much is a cabbage? And do you know how much coleslaw you get out of one cabbage? It's criminal."

What was criminal was Frank's smile. That's what sold the "homebaked" scone, not the description. Rosy couldn't help her own dopey grin. "I'm glad you're excited."

"Excited?" His big hands closed on her shoulders. "This is the best thing that ever happened at the Tasty Bite. The best thing ever. We can rip-off the entire world and they'll say *thank you.*"

"Hold that thought." She ducked free of his grip. "We'll pick up on Monday."

"Monday?" He shook his head. "We can't wait until Monday. We have too much to do. What are you doing tomorrow?"

Rosy raised her hands. "Oh, no. I'm not paid to work weekends, Frank. I promised a friend I'd go shopping with her."

"I could tag along," Frank said.

A crazy laugh escaped Rosy's throat. "No chance."

"But we have to fool people into paying more. We'll need something better than those cheap-looking tubs."

Oh my God. Was this the same person? "I'm busy tomorrow, Frank. If we had internet access in here, we could have shopped online together, right now."

"We could get a computer, right now." Frank ducked behind the counter, lifted the phone up and waved it at Rosy. "Call Shawford reception and ask for Darren in IT. C'mon."

"Hold your horses. I have to watch my budget."

"It'll be free, Rosy. We used to have one, but I kept breaking it."

"Clumsy."

"On purpose," he said, clearly put out. "The computer slowed me down. They brought in a new one six months ago for Marek. Titanium case, waterproof, rubber keys, but I cracked that as well."

"You cracked a titanium case?"

He wagged a finger. "No. That was their mistake, too. I didn't need to crack the case. I cracked Windows. That's an operating system," he added.

"It is? I did not know that," Rosy said, so that he would never ask her to do any troubleshooting.

"They wouldn't give me a password this time. But I did my research and I got a magazine with a cover CD. Have you heard of Linux? Just stick that in, boot it up, hello hard drive. Full access." Frank wiggled his eyebrows up and down. "Darren reinstalled Windows four times and still thinks it was a virus."

"Frank? Where did you learn about computers?"

He frowned like she'd just asked the most obvious question in the world. "In the magazine with the CD."

Findlay couldn't even start up the word processor, but Frank had bought one computer magazine and knew enough to sabotage an operating system?

Frank was still talking. "The point is, we can get Darren to set up a computer right now."

"It's Friday afternoon," Rosy said.

"So? It's a two-minute job. There's a box and a cable that connects to Shawford. The end got itself melted off on the panini grill, but Darren can fit a new one."

"You're a bit of a terrorist, Frank."

"I like to give Darren's face a good de-smug." He waved the phone receiver. "Call him. Tell him it's an emergency."

"Remind me again, who's the boss here?"

"You are," Frank said. "That's why you have to call him, baby boss."

She took the phone, and Frank hit zero. "Hi…" Rosy said. "Can you put me through to Darren from IT, please? Oh, he's gone for the weekend—?"

"Aww, the lazy shit." Frank covered his eyes.

"It's okay. I'll pick up with him on Monday." She put the phone down.

Frank folded his arms. "That's it. Now, I have to come shopping with you tomorrow."

———

*Rosy is in Princes Street Marks & Spencer, shopping with Boog for a fancy Easter egg for Boog's little sister, Andrea, when they bump into Ruben's sister.*

*The conversation is awkward but ends with a good suggestion to try Hotel Chocolat on Frederick Street for an extra thick egg.*

*"Everybody in that family looks like a model," Boog says, as they exit the Food Hall using the direct staircase to Princes Street.*

*"Do you fancy her?" Rosy says.*

*"'Course not. She must be mid-twenties. Anyway, you're the only girl for me."*

*"If you're tired of me, you should say," Rosy says.*

*Boog's eyes go wide. "Who said I was tired of you?"*

*"You never seem to be happy with what we have together," Rosy says. "You're always pushing the envelope."*

*Boog takes her hand. "I'm happy, Rosy. I'm so happy. I only want you to stay happy. That's all I want. I live to make you happy."*

*They emerge onto Princes Street and turn right.*

*Rosy swings his arm. "Good. Let's get you an extra thick egg, too."*

*Boog slows down. "The egg is for Andrea, babe. I don't want an egg."*

*"It'll keep your strength up for the exams," Rosy says.*

*He stops. "Extra thick chocolate? That's the last thing I need."*

*"You love chocolate. Ruben was pushy, Boog. Wilful and pushy. I don't want a repeat of the Ruben situation."*

Boog kisses her hand. "I'll never push you, Rosy, never. I'm so happy just as we are."

Rosy relaxes, and tugs him along. "Let's go get those eggs."

# Chapter 24
## The competition
### (Saturday, 18 June)
### Rosy

Rosy met Frank early on Saturday Morning at the St James Centre. She found him at a stall full of tat in the concourse, browsing furry hairbands with animal ears that maybe she'd have liked when she was eight.

"You were supposed to meet me at John Lewis," Rosy said.

Frank reluctantly hooked a fake fur hairband back on the rack. "I've been in. The clothes are for millionaires."

"Well, let's go look at their dishes first, and we'll have a baseline for comparison," Rosy said.

Frank ran in front of her and pointed back the way they'd come. "We should go somewhere else. Just in case."

"Just in case what?"

"Just in case I get blamed," he said. She frowned at him and he rolled his eyes. "I reversed a jacket that wasn't reversible. It kinda split open."

"Well, if it's not reversible, the lining was likely pleated. I doubt it actually split open," Rosy said.

"It made a ripping noise," Frank said, "and a bit fluttered out."

"Well, I really wouldn't worry. Sounds like it was badly made. Did you like the jacket?"

He shrugged. "I liked the lining."

"Tell you what," Rosy said. "Let's do our tour of cafes first, and come back to John Lewis later."

Frank nodded. "Yeah. Just in case." He took her arm, looked

back over his shoulder, then hurried her out.

---

Rosy and Frank concluded their reconnaissance of the— Frank's verdict—shit cafes on Princes Street and the less shit cafes on George Street in a few hours, then she managed to coax him back into John Lewis. Frank was a nervous shopper — would keep his hands in his pockets. "Just in case," he said. That made Rosy think of Franny, the bike thief. "I don't steal, I just destroy stuff," he explained, and for some reason, that set her mind easy.

She'd arranged to meet Jen for coffee at two, so if the gods had been smiling on them, she and Frank would have had lunch, then gone their separate ways, Frank bearing away the lovely little dishes, serving spoons and tongs they'd just bought for the deli. But the gods were in a mood for meddling, and when Frank and Rosy joined the up escalator from kitchenware in John Lewis, Rosy felt a tap on her shoulder and turned to see Jen.

"I came in a bit early," her friend said. "It's Crawford's birthday and I bought him a little iPod. It's just the one with the clip, but it's a really pretty colour and…"

Jen had stopped talking and was looking at Frank. Looking from Frank to Rosy. Then she covered her mouth.

"Is this…? Is this him?" Jen squealed and jumped up and down.

Frank looked off to one side as though checking Jen wasn't talking about somebody else.

The escalator levelled out and Jen stuck her hand at Frank, who shuffled the boxes and bags to shake it.

"I'm Jen. Rosy's flatmate from university," she said, then turned to Rosy, fanned her face with her hand, mouthed what could only be *phwoar* and grabbed Rosy's hand. "Have you two had lunch yet?"

---

They ate upstairs in an Italian cafe, nestled in the swanky wind tunnel precinct between Harvey Nicks and the rear entrance of the St James Centre. Frank gave a thumbs up when he saw the menu. "Criminals," he said.

Jen perched her chin on her hand. "Do you work out Frank?"

"Yeah," Frank said. "I jog, do some free weights. I used to do serious bodybuilding. I got really, really big…"

Jen nodded, eyes widening and roaming Frank's chest as he cupped it.

"But I was wolfing down two innocent chickens a day and clothes didn't want to fit me."

Jen sighed. "It became a problem."

"Yeah. I'm happier now," Frank said. "I kept a decent amount of mass."

"You look terrific, doesn't he, Rosy?"

"Yes, I'm still here." Rosy cast Jen a sour look. "We were going to do some clothes shopping, weren't we, Jen? For tonight?"

Jen sat up, picked up her Jimmy Choo looky-likey handbag. "Why doesn't Frank come out with us?"

Rosy's stomach lurched. "I don't think so, Jen."

"Why not? Are you busy tonight, Frank?"

Frank shrugged, looked left, then right. "Not really."

Jen patted his arm. "Ten-thirty. We're trying out the Opal Lounge. George Street."

"Okay," Frank said, then frowned. "Ten-thirty? That's kinda late."

"Yes, that is very late for him," Rosy said.

"But not too late," Frank said. He rubbed his chin. "What do I wear?"

"Whatever. We're not fancy, Frank," Jen said. "Wear a shirt and jeans. Wear whatever makes you feel good."

Frank's face grew thoughtful. "Whatever makes me feel good."

———

Rosy marched across Princes Street toward the entrance to Waverley Market. "I don't believe you, Jen. You were coming on to my dad."

"No I wasn't."

"You paid for his lunch," Rosy said.

"I wasn't coming onto him. He's thirty-odd," Jen said. "What age is he?"

"Thirty-four."

"Thirty-four. *Hmmm.*" Jen waved her hands. "Anyway, but

what's wrong with your mother? I mean, hello? Seriously? She dumps a hunk like him for Findlay? That's like you dumping Ruben for Boog. And, oh my God, Frank is so sweet."

"Just stay away from him, okay? He isn't even your type. Ruben was your type. Frank has a belly. You don't like bellies."

They grabbed an escalator down to the shops.

"But that's a sportsman's belly—a rugby player's belly—and he has the shoulders," Jen said. "I have no problems with a guy's belly if he has the shoulders to carry it. And the face. He's very like you." Jen fixed Rosy's hair. "That age difference is really not out of the question, you know."

"I don't believe I'm hearing this. You've got the hots for my dad?"

"Relax. I'm teasing. Admit it, though. If you met him and didn't know he was your dad, wouldn't you be all over him?" Jen laughed. "He has everything. Even a belly."

---

*Rosy watches Ruben move his pizza about, untasted. Their waitress has already asked if everything is okay, and Ruben said everything was fine.*

*Rosy finishes her spaghetti carbonara.*

*"If you weren't hungry," Rosy says, "you should have said."*

*Ruben looks at her. "There are lots of things I should have said, Rosy."*

*He hasn't even sipped his beer.*

*"I think this relationship has reached its natural end," Rosy says.*

*"You know what?" Ruben says, and looks up at her, "I think it has."*

*Rosy opens her purse and takes out a twenty. "I'll make my own way home."*

*Ruben crunches up the twenty and throws it into the pasta dish. "Haven't you emasculated me enough?"*

*Rosy leaves and is glad to be gone. Ruben is sex-crazed and unstable. Now, she can take things further with Boog, the boy she met at Freshers' Week. Boog is sensible and stable. He's a gentleman, and he's chubby. Rosy has always been embarrassed to admit she likes chubby guys. She can't explain why. Chubby guys are so cuddly, like Toff, her teddy bear with the pot belly.*

# Chapter 25
# Bust up
## Rosy

Rosy had planned to be at the Opal Lounge before Frank got there, but her bus was twenty minutes late, so by the time she arrived, the damage was already done. She could always claim Frank wasn't with her. She rubbed the centre of her forehead and laughed despite herself.

"Frank?" she shouted over the music. "Did you try something on and forget to take them off?"

He held his pint away, looked at his jeans, his lumberjack shirt, took an extra look at his shoes, then shrugged. "Nope."

"How about... on your head?" She pointed. "Like, for example... a pair of ears?"

"Oh, my wolf's ears," he yelled. "Cool, aren't they?"

She reached up to take them off but he pulled away. She put her hands on her hips. "You're wearing wolf's ears?"

"They make me feel good," Frank said. "Jen said wear what makes me feel good."

"You're the boss."

He stroked his chin. "I'd like a tail, too."

Jen came teetering in on five-inch heels. "Hello, hello—ha-ha, it's the wolfman," she hooted. "*Grrr.* Why do those ears look smoking hot? Am I crazy?"

"Yes," Rosy said, then her already dying smile slipped away, because she'd just seen who'd come in behind Crawford.

"Hey, Rosy," Boog said, and draped himself around her, kissed her cheek.

"Hey, fancy seeing you here." She glared at Jen, who just shrugged.

Boog pulled away, rubbed her cheek. "Missing you, babe."

Jen had just introduced Crawford to Frank. "Love the ears, dude," Crawford said.

"Thanks," Frank said, and nodded a smug told-you-so at Rosy.

———

Rosy, as usual, ended up with the kitty and ordered the first drinks for the group. She handed Frank another pint. "I thought you didn't drink beer, Frank."

"I don't," he said. "I'm already feeling funny."

"Maybe another one's not a good idea."

Frank grinned, drained a third of the glass and wiped his mouth. "Maybe," he said.

Jen set down her white wine and tried to pull Crawford up to dance, but he wouldn't budge, so she switched her attention to Frank. "Come on, Wolfman, give me a dance."

Frank tipped his head back, bellowed, "Howoooooo!" then almost knocked the bar stool over scrambling after her.

"How've you been, Rosy?" Boog said.

"I've been fine. Busy. With the cafe. Getting to know Frank. You know." She watched Frank wade through people. "How's the studying going?"

"That's kinda tough." He took a slug of his beer. "Finding it hard to concentrate." He looked at her with moist eyes. "Did your stepdad put you off me?"

Frank was a bad dancer. Rosy could see him nod his head, waiting for the chorus, then swing his arms to one side, then the other, trying to coordinate his feet before losing it again. He tipped his head back and laughed like he was having fun.

"I thought I explained myself, Boog?" Rosy said. "I think you lost the plot a bit, and I don't want that to be my fault."

"It's not your fault, babe. I just found something more important to me than university."

Rosy chopped the air. "No. It's not more important. You need to switch off your crotch, and switch on your brain."

"What about my heart, Rosy? Switch that off too? Because my brain can't work when my heart is breaking. And my heart is breaking because I've come so close, but you won't let me in."

Rosy took his hand and Boog gripped back, tight, pulled her

fingers to his cheek, then kissed her wrist.

Jen was shaking her ass and Frank watched, trying to copy her moves.

"Boog, please listen. Please," Rosy said. "You're a really attractive guy. I like you. I'm not ruling anything out. But right now, I don't feel the way you feel."

"You're dumping me," Boog said.

"Would you listen?" She smoothed his cheek. "I want somebody strong. I want somebody smart. I want somebody who can set his mind on a goal, and achieve it. You can be that man, if you'll only try."

"I think I've left it too late," Boog said. "There's too much to cram. I read stuff and don't remember a word, because all I can think about is, have I lost you?"

Jen had her arms around Frank's neck and Frank, still wearing those ridiculous ears, was bent over practically rubbing noses with her, shaking his big butt behind him. Married man, indeed.

Rosy raised her index finger. "I have enough to deal with without this." She smacked his hand away. "Congratulations, Boog. You weren't dumped, but you are now. I hope you're happy."

Crawford exploded into howls of laughter. "Fucking priceless. Too perfect. Oh, Bennie, Ben, Ben." He shoved his hands under Boog's arms and grabbed his chest, head back, laughing. "Just as well you have such big tits of your own to feel, you sad, sad bastard. You fucking sad sack of shit."

---

*Rosy sits at the edge of Boog's bed and watches the screen of his laptop as he shows each layer of his tattoo realigned. She feels sick. The layers of the tattoo form Rosy's name.*

*ROSY in hard black letters, obscene on his soft skin.*

*"Only you and I know that, Rosy," Boog says. "Not even the tattooist knows. It was my secret. Now it's our secret."*

*Rosy forces her mouth to smile. "Wow." She stares at the photo, horrified. He did that at the end of Freshers' Week. She remembers the bandage and feeling so angry he'd go get his skin messed up.*

*"I've never felt this sure about anybody, Rosy," Boog says. "I'm committed. I'm committed to you, babe."*

*"That's so... incredible," Rosy says.*

*Boog closes his eyes. "I love the kisses and cuddles. I love that. And I know how you feel about sex before marriage and stuff, and I respect that. I don't need that." Boog meets her eyes now, and there's a crazy edge in his voice. "I don't need to see anything. I would just like to touch you through your clothes. Like I let you touch my belly through mine. Please say yes. I'm committed, babe. Let me hold your breasts."*

*Rosy shakes her head. "I don't want to spoil this moment, Boog. It's so... moving. Do you understand?"*

*Boog clenches his hands then unclenches them and looks at her. "'Course I do, babe. You're right," he says. "A hug is enough."*

*Rosy hugs him and again she can feel him trying to press his hard dick against her body, like that's just an accident he can't help. She remembers Ruben, yelling at her: "Why must you keep denying me?"*

*Because she isn't ready. Isn't ready to bare herself. Isn't ready for sex. Because she doesn't feel it. Doesn't feel true love for Boog. And now she knows Boog is every bit as unstable as Ruben. And what happened with Ruben must never happen with Boog.*

*Rosy can't leave Boog's flat fast enough.*

---

The song was finishing and Rosy grabbed Frank. "Come here, you."

"Huh?" Frank said.

"What are you playing at?" Rosy waved a hand at Jen, the tramp. "She could be your daughter."

Frank pointed back to Jen. "I was only dancing."

Jen had a hold of Frank's other arm. "Rosy? What are you doing? Have you gone nuts?"

"Get your greedy paws off him," Rosy shouted, and smacked at Jen's hand. "He's married."

Jen let Frank go and Rosy made it back to Crawford, who was now throwing bits of a torn-up beermat at Boog.

"Wolfman," Crawford said and he and Frank high-fived.

Oh my God. Frank had just been trying to steal Crawford's girlfriend and Crawford was high-fiving him? Was he blind?

Frank lifted his pint and started to guzzle.

Rosy tried to pull the glass down. "Would you go easy, Frank?"

He drained half then came back for air. "Thirsty," he said,

downed the rest, then shuddered and belched. "I didn't know I could dance," he yelled over the music.

"Hate to break it to you, Wolfman," Crawford shouted back. "Your moves are even more shit than fat Ben's." Crawford grabbed Boog around the neck, pulled his head down and mussed his hair up.

"Fuck off. Fuck off and die," Boog said and tried to elbow Crawford in the gut, but Boog's skinny flatmate danced to his feet.

"Who wants another drink?" Crawford said.

Frank stuck his hand up.

Oh, no.

---

When Jen had exhausted her partners and came back looking for a dance with Frank again, she just missed Crawford being an ass and taunting Boog about getting himself dumped. Boog had actually started to sob.

Rosy stood but Frank waved her to sit down, and led Boog away, rubbing his back, those idiotic wolf's ears still on his head. Rosy couldn't sit still. She met Frank at the doors.

"Leave him," Frank said. "He needs space."

Frank led Rosy back, his hands on her waist. He smelled like a brewery. Rosy sat back down with Jen.

"Crawford says you broke up with Boog?" Jen said. "Good, and not before time."

Rosy nodded. "I know. But I feel like a heartless bitch now."

Jen raised her eyebrows and leaned back to study her. "Rosy, please. You fattened him up like a Christmas turkey."

"What?"

"He was scared to join the gym in case you left him. He's not your boyfriend, he's your prisoner. You led that boy on with promises you were never going to keep and tortured him for months. *That*," Jen said, "was heartless."

---

Embarrassingly, Boog didn't just do the logical thing and go home. He came back and took the table next to them, buying his own booze and getting progressively drunk, until he just sat there with his forehead pressed to the table.

"Smile, Bennie, it's not the end of the world," Crawford said.

"Oh, sorry, it is. You're fat, your true love dumped your disgusting ass, and you're about to flunk out. Did I mention how fat and stupid you are?" He prodded Boog's stomach. "Still, look on the bright side. Tattoo removal is getting cheaper."

Boog sat up. "What did you say?"

Rosy's mouth had gone dry.

Crawford laughed and made a sweep with his hand across his arm. "*Bzzzz*. Goodbye, Rosy. I bet when that laser starts to burn, you'll smell like pork crackling."

Boog was on his feet, coming at Crawford. Their table tipped over and Rosy made a grab for the glasses but was soaked in an instant. Boog hauled Crawford out by the arm and spun him around. Crawford tried to free himself, but somehow fell over Frank's feet. Boog threw himself onto Crawford and landed a meaty punch in his face that Rosy heard even over the music. Crawford lay pinned, choking. Boog, face twisted in rage, sat on him. Frank was the only one to move, half-lifting, half-helping Boog up, so Crawford could roll to the side, and push himself up on his hands, puking and gagging.

Somebody must have called security. A burly guy had Boog in a headlock, and another stood in front of Crawford.

"You broke my fucking bridge, you fat fuck," Crawford shouted, and curled his split lip back to expose a gap in his top teeth. "You stupid fat fucking flunk-out loser piece of shit." Blood spattered his shirt, ran from his lip.

Boog wasn't looking at Crawford. His eyes locked on Rosy and they burned with hatred. "My tattoo. That was our secret. And you told?"

The security guy and a colleague wrestled Boog away.

"Okay, folks," another bouncer with a coiled earpiece said. "Show's over."

"I don't feel so good, Rosy," Frank said.

"Me neither. Let's go."

---

Outside, Frank alarmed Rosy by sitting on the pavement.

"I'll get you a cab," Rosy said.

"I'm fine. Leave me. I'll walk," Frank said. "It's not far."

"Okay, well stand up."

He examined his feet. "Not yet," he said.

"Come on, Frank. Up you get." She looked around on the pavement. "Where are your ears?"

"Safe." He started to unbutton his shirt.

"That's fine. Keep them in there. Keep them in there, Frank." She buttoned his shirt back up, then smoothed his cheek with her hand. "Sorry. Sorry for bringing you here."

She called to arrange two taxis then changed her mind. "One taxi, two stops."

———

The taxi turned left at roadworks around the illuminated statue of King George IV onto Dundas Street and headed downhill towards Stockbridge.

Rosy studied Frank sitting there with his eyelids opening and closing slowly. How easy for him to find a new partner.

"Why don't you divorce Mum?" she said.

"Why should I divorce her?" Frank said, that little squint now more pronounced. "I'd be happy with Irene."

"But don't you get lonely?" Rosy said.

"'Course I get lonely," Frank said. "'Course I do. I need somebody to talk to. Everybody needs that."

"But Mum doesn't want you," Rosy said.

He sat back then leaned over. "Want to know a secret?"

Rosy nodded.

"She only says she doesn't want me." Frank wagged a finger. "But she does."

Rosy shifted across to face him. "No, Frank. She doesn't want you. Honestly. You need to let go."

He tapped his nose. "If she didn't want me," he said, "she'd have divorced me. She wants me. She loves me. Always and forever. Her words. She's testing me. I'm going to pass the test."

———

As they drove along St Bernard's Place, Rosy checked her purse. Ten quid and her ATM card was safe at home. The meter would likely end up at least four. Five or six quid wouldn't get her home. No chance.

"Do you have any notes, Frank?" she said.

He opened an eye and closed it again.

She slid her fingers into the pockets of his shirt.

"Tickles," he laughed, and grabbed her hand.

"Notes, Frank? Do you have any?"

She thought about reaching into his jeans pocket but couldn't. She checked the time. Two-thirty in the morning. Her clothes reeked of the spilled booze anyway. She should crash at Frank's.

———————

Rosy intended to sleep on the floor but Frank took away the choice by sitting down again. She gave him a pillow and the duvet, didn't want to go rummaging through his things for more bedding, so took his bathrobe from the bathroom and wrapped that around her, then fell asleep…

# Chapter 26
# It's serious
## (Sunday, 19 June)
## Rosy

… and woke instantly with sun shining in the window and Frank lying on the bed next to her, smoothing her hair with his fingers.

"You're prettier than Irene," Frank said.

Rosy jerked upright and pulled his bathrobe tight to her neck. "What are you doing?"

"Filling the bath," he said. "You want to go in first? I can squirt in Fairy Liquid for bubbles?"

He still wore his clothes from last night, thank God. So did she.

"I'll just call a taxi and stop by Jen's for a change of clothing."

Frank, as it turned out, had less spare change than she, but he knew the exact amount before he emptied out his pockets. That meant a taxi was out unless he nipped to the cash point. He offered to run her but he'd still be over the drink drive limit. The idea of climbing on a bus, reeking of booze didn't appeal.

"You can wear one of my T-shirts," Frank said. "Bath's ready. Go on. You need it more than me."

"Cheeky," she said. "You first. I'll boil the kettle. My tongue feels like a napkin." Her voice sounded hoarse and flat, though that might be temporary hearing loss. Jeez. How could Frank look so alive?

Frank fished out two T-shirts, threw one at Rosy, then headed into the bathroom. He closed the door but Rosy didn't hear the lock. She shook her head. Why would he lock the bathroom?

He was always here on his own.

She heard the thud of jeans thrown to the floor. Then an, "Ow, ow," and the trickle of water into the overflow, then skin juddering and sliding along the tub like whale song, then drips and splashes.

The door wasn't locked and Frank was lying there, naked.

Rosy shook herself. What was wrong with her? Was she still drunk? Jesus. Thinking such a thought. And last night when Frank had unbuttoned his shirt to show Rosy where he'd stashed his wolf's ears, she'd caught herself checking him out. She'd been too self-conscious to reach into his jeans pockets because she'd been worried about brushing Frank's package. Rosy would think nothing of reaching into Findlay's pockets if his hands were full.

She got out of bed and filled the kettle.

Jen was right. Rosy ought to have had sex with Boog. She hadn't just denied Boog, she'd denied herself. Always waiting for Mr Perfect and who turns out to be Mr Perfect?

God, Rosy's mother was out of her mind.

She'd found the tea-bags, but where was the coffee? She needed coffee, damn it.

Rosy tipped her head back and yelled, "Frank? Do you have coffee?"

A pause, then, "Just for cakes," he shouted back.

For cakes. There'd been a cupboard rammed with flour, sugar, paper cake bases. She found a Co-op coffee jar under small bottles of food colouring.

Frank's arms wrapped around her, then he pulled her aside. "I'll make it. You have your bath, stinky."

"I found the cof—" Rosy covered her mouth first, then her eyes, then peeked at him through her fingers. "Frank? You're not wearing underwear."

"So?" He tutted. "My T-shirt is covering my clobber."

Rosy shook her head. "Not from this angle. Not completely." She spread her finger and thumb apart. "This much," she squeaked.

He glared at her then banged the jar down. "Okay, if you can't just ignore it, I'll put my underwear on," he said, then muttered, "Everybody has a one-track mind. It's either tits, bums, fannies or willies." He snapped a pair of underpants up. "Happy?"

Rosy nodded and let her heart settle back down, but now the bulk of his legs distracted her. She stood by his side disgusted with herself.

She jabbed an arm at the cupboard. "You're into baking, then?"

"For the church. When they're having a jumble sale or a famine." He smiled. "Yes, you guessed it. I've already made stuff for the cafe. I made a rich man's walnut cake and a high-markup Victoria sponge yesterday. I was going to bake some premium brownies today. Wanna help?"

"I'd love to," Rosy said. "I've never baked a cake in my life."

"Go have your bath, then," Frank said. "The water's running for you. I'll make breakfast. Scrambled eggs okay?"

"I hate eggs," she said.

"Because," Frank said, "you've never had Frank's Special Scrambled Eggs."

"Special? What's special about them?"

He stepped behind her, put his hands around her waist and pressed his unshaven face against her cheek. "I make them. With love. For you."

She made it into the bathroom before she started to shake.

———————

Rosy couldn't relax in Frank's bathtub because she could only think of Frank's big body wedged in here.

The handle of the bathroom door rattled and she stood up, water streaming from her, and grabbed the towel off the rail.

"There's a T-shirt on the door handle for you, baby," Frank shouted.

When Rosy pulled the T in and looked inside the collar, there was that familiar nametag: *Alan McAdam*.

Now, she had a legitimate reason to ask. She just had to summon the courage.

———————

The brownies worked out great. Rosy watched Frank split one in half.

"Frank's Special Brownies," he said, and held a piece for her to bite.

"*Mmm.* That's a winner." The phrase made her think of Franny and her horses, then the biscuit tin. She shook the image away. "Next thing we need to work on is Frank's Special Sandwich Fillings."

"I'm on the case," he said. "How about... Frank's Special Cheese Orchardman's?"

"Orchardman's?"

"With homemade pear and apple chutney," Frank said.

"You make chutney too?"

"Nah," Frank said, "but I could." He lifted down a jar with a frilly label. "Ernesto's wife made this."

Rosy stretched out her fingers to grip the worktop for support before she asked. "Frank. I may regret this, but I have some questions I really need the answer to."

"Okay," Frank said.

"Who is Alan McAdam?"

Frank shrugged. "He's just a dead guy whose clothes fitted me."

Rosy closed her eyes. "Are you involved with the mob?"

Frank frowned. "I don't understand the question."

"The mob," Rosy said. "Organised crime. Are you a hit-man or something?"

Frank's frown turned into a scowl. "What kind of a question is that?"

"Doing jobs for Ernesto. Was Alan McAdam a job for Ernesto?"

"Pardon?" Frank said. "You think I... killed Alan McAdam? For Ernesto? Why? For his clothes?"

Rosy covered her face. "I don't know, do I? Why else would you be wearing a dead man's clothes?"

Frank pulled her hands away. "Alan McAdam was twenty-three," he said. "He scored a try in a rugby match and his heart stopped."

"His—? Oh, my God. Oh, no. That's so sad."

"Yeah," Frank said. "I never met him, but he must have been my clone. Everything fits, even his shoes. Alan's mum and dad gave all his clothes to British Heart Foundation, and I bought them all—everything—for five hundred quid. Most I ever spent but best things I ever bought."

Rosy shook her head. "Doesn't that make you feel creepy? Wearing a dead man's clothes. With his name still in them."

"You tell me. You're wearing them too." Frank pointed at the T draped over Rosy like a ghost.

"Thanks for that."

"But no, it doesn't make me feel creepy," Frank said. "Alan's mum wanted his story to be told. She sewed all those tags in so that people like me would ask. She wanted him to be remembered in more than flowers and stone. And I think of him every day. So it makes me feel good. I got nice clothes. The charity got money to help save the next guy. Win, win."

Rosy blinked down at the T.

"Ernesto," she said. "You always seem to be doing jobs for Ernesto. Why? Who is Ernesto?"

"Ernesto is the minister. He's the minister of St Monan's Parish Church. I do odd jobs up at the manse. DIY. Fixing fences. Painting. Laying slabs."

Rosy almost cried with relief. "Oh, thank God. I thought it was something illegal."

"It is," Frank said. "Cash-in-hand. No questions asked."

Mountains out of molehills. Findlay's doing, feeding her paranoia.

Rosy studied the brownies. Church baking. How come Frank had such a bad rap? Sure, he was rude, but for God's sake. She pushed the lid on the plastic tub.

"Customers will come in specially for those," Frank said.

Rosy nodded. "They will." She patted his arm, then met his eyes. "Sorry, there's one more thing, but if I don't ask, I'll only imagine the worst."

"Shoot," Frank said.

She picked up a crumb of brownie and nibbled it. "What were you in Young Offenders for?"

Frank shrugged and frowned. "Nothing much," he said. "Only abduction."

---

In the afternoon, Frank drove Rosy to Jen's, where she picked up some fresh jeans, undies and a T-shirt. Boog probably knew she was there but it didn't matter now.

"Justin's looking happy." Rosy pointed at the goldfish.

Bowl clean. And he had the plant, not the diver. Good. He'd never liked that diver.

"For the record," Jen said. "I wasn't coming onto Frank and he wasn't coming onto me. We were only having fun."

"It's okay, Jen. How's Crawford?"

"You mean apart from the fact he swallowed his bridge and his lip is three times the normal size?"

Rosy laughed.

"It's not funny, Rosy. That bridgework alone cost his dad fifteen hundred pounds. He's worried because the teeth on either side are loose now, maybe even cracked."

"Well, you shouldn't have told him about the tattoo, should you?"

Jen set her hands on her hips. "Excuse me, Rosy, but you told me about the tattoo."

"I also told you," Rosy said, "to keep it to yourself."

"And you think Boog wanted you to tell me?"

Rosy covered her face. "You're right. I'm sorry. I feel awful about Boog. How is he?"

Jen shrugged. "I have no idea. He didn't come back last night. Probably because he couldn't face Crawford."

God. What a mess.

"Rosy," Jen said and twisted her own fingers in her fist. "Crawford said Janek's pretty sure Boog bought a camera."

"A camera?"

Jen nodded and wrinkled her nose. "A spy camera. Crawford says to check your… your bathroom and stuff."

Rosy pressed her tongue against the roof of her mouth and stared up at the ceiling. "Unbelievable."

What kind of a person would do such a thing? They held a minute's silence for the death of trust.

Jen was first to speak. "You'll be happy to hear I decided eighteen is too young for a tattoo. Well, Frank decided me."

Thank you, Frank. "How did he manage that miracle?"

Jen wrinkled her nose. "I showed him the design. He asked me what it meant and I had to say, nothing. It meant nothing."

Like Boog's. A meaningless mess.

"There's another letter from N-BioCom for you."

Jen went through to the kitchen and came back with it. "It

was there when I got back from town yesterday."

She then handed Rosy another envelope, this one open. "That's their original rejection letter. Thought you might want that, too."

Rosy nodded. "Thanks, Jen."

"No worries," her friend said and smiled weakly. "Tell the wolfman, Jen said hi."

---

Rosy had her first well-lit, unobstructed view of Frank's flawless belly when he reached for a box of Kettle Chips in the cash-and-carry.

"We should get two boxes," she said.

He reached up again, revealing swirls and that light ridge of dark hair that sank into the deep well of his navel.

"Actually, no, sorry," Rosy said. "Let's see how we manage with one."

Frank stretched up to put the box back and Rosy looked away, ashamed of herself.

"These are expensive. That Beancounter's book better be right," Frank said, "or we'll be the ones getting screwed, not the customers."

"I can't wait for Monday, Frank."

"Me neither, baby."

Frank pushed the trolley along, and Rosy, walking along behind, fought to find a resting place for her eyes where they wouldn't swing back onto Frank's butt.

Oh, Jesus. When did this happen? And how was she going to make it unhappen?

---

Frank loaded the last of their purchases into the van and scootered the trolley into the trolley park, like a kid.

He jumped into the driving seat, flipped the glove compartment open and grabbed a deep yellow CAT baseball cap. After knocking it open with his fist, he jammed the cap on, curved the peak and smiled at her. "Keep the sun out."

The sun was in that smile and Rosy had begun to melt in its heat. "You should totally wear that to work. And a tight T. The women will hand their purses over."

"You need to get one too, for the men." He stopped, and

looked at her. "Can I say something that's been on my mind, Rosy?"

"Depends what the something is?" Rosy said, and held her breath.

Frank turned around to face her. "I'm really mad at you."

Rosy blinked. She twisted in the seat to face him. "Why's that?"

"You like that boy, Boog, don't you?" Frank said.

"It's complicated, Frank."

"It's not complicated. Either you like somebody or you don't."

Rosy shrugged. "I like him, yes."

Frank nodded. "Thought so. So why did you let that Crawford creep go on and on at him until he was crying? Why didn't you tell Crawford to shut the fuck up and leave him alone?"

"Why didn't you?" Rosy said.

"Because, Rosy, he needed to hear you say it. You. And you didn't. You let that nasty guy tell your boyfriend he was nothing but a fat, stupid loser."

She inspected her hands. "I wanted to say something."

Frank nodded. "Good. Well, next time, say it."

He took something out of his pocket and threw it into the tray beside the handbrake.

Rosy picked it up. The object was strangely organic, silver with struts and little loops and at the front...

She gaped at him. "That's Crawford's bridgework," Rosy said. "He thought he swallowed it. Why did you take that?"

"It looked expensive and difficult to replace," Frank said. "Give it to Boog. He won it, fair and square."

Then she remembered Crawford falling over Frank's feet. "You tripped Crawford up, didn't you?"

Frank shrugged. "Sometimes karma needs a little helping foot."

Rosy stared ahead at the road. Having horrible thoughts about Frank. Letting down her own boyfriend.

Without even trying, Rosy had become a despicable person.

# Chapter 27
# Truth
## Rosy

Rosy got home late Sunday afternoon with a neat cover story all worked out, but when Findlay asked where she'd been, the thought of another lie sickened her.

"Last night was a disaster: Too much booze, Jen's boyfriend earned himself a punch in the face, the whole works. I ended up crashing out at Frank's," Rosy said. "The good news is, I can eat scrambled egg if it's cooked right, and I can make brownies. I made them with Frank."

"Why would you crash out at Frank's?" Findlay said.

"Frank was with me."

Findlay slapped the table. "Suddenly it makes sense. Let me guess... Frank started the fight?"

"Wrong," Rosy said. "Frank split the fight up."

"Is Frank a bit of a cook now, then?" Mum said.

Findlay's hands shot up. "Whoa, stop. Rewind. Your daughter —your eighteen-year-old daughter—has been involved in a drunken brawl. And you, Irene, have moved on to cooking?"

"He's handy too, apparently," Rosy said. "He does DIY. Earns extra cash from that."

"That's two things you could easily do, Findlay," Mum said. "A little cooking, a few DIY jobs."

"Sure, why not?" Findlay said. "I could also be a psycho nut-job, too. Is that what you want?"

"A psycho nut-job?" Rosy said. "That's the term, is it, for a man who abducts his own wife and daughter because he isn't allowed to see his baby anymore?"

Findlay threw his hands out. "So he told you? Hallelujah.

It's out in the open."

"I grew up believing my own father didn't want me."

"Correct. He didn't want you," Findlay said. "That whole thing was a stunt. He only wanted your mother back. And he's pulling the same stunt again today, but you're too gullible to see it."

"That's not true," Rosy said. "You should have told me. You should have let him see me when I was growing up."

"Oh, that's right," Findlay said. "'Hey Rosy, sweetheart, here's the nice crazy man who raped your mum and kidnapped you both when you were eighteen months old. He says one day he'll come and break your stepdad's neck. Sweet dreams.' Would that have been better?"

Rosy's mum shook her head. "She's right, Findlay. In hindsight, we handled things badly. The important thing now is, everything has worked itself out, hasn't it?"

Rosy pressed her fingers to her temples. "No, Mum, it hasn't. You have no idea how much this has screwed me up."

---

Rosy checked the bathroom for the spy camera and found nothing. She shifted her search to her bedroom and spotted an unfamiliar object jammed in a desk tidy full of dried up marker pens and blunt pencils. The device was made to look like a pen, but was far too thick. The lens peeped from a hole above the clip. She pulled off the pen top and found two Panasonic AA batteries. Bastard.

Well, he'd have been disappointed—she changed underwear in the bathroom. Had done since she was little.

God damn him. It was all about tits for him, all about Rosy's body. That's all anybody was ever interested in. Except Frank. Cuddles were all Frank wanted. Cuddles from his daughter. And—like Boog—Rosy wanted more.

But Boog lusted after his girlfriend, not a parent.

Rosy sat on her stool with the Mr Men upholstery, beside her Cinderella dresser, hemmed in. A woman in a little girl's bedroom. No way back to innocent obsessions like Furbies and Bratz. No way to grow up with Frank as a dad like anybody else's, a sexless object, there for hugs and comfort like Toff, her teddy.

A sexless object, like Boog.

Rosy was as much to blame as Boog. More.

She rummaged her phone from her bag. Boog's number rang through to the answering service. "Hey," she said. "I was worried about you. I wanted to say sorry. For everything. Take care."

She used the spy cam pen itself to write a note:

*Boog*

*If you need this again, you've picked the wrong girlfriend again.*

*Present from Frank enclosed too.*

*Rosy x*

She found a Jiffy bag in her cupboard, tore off the label, wrote Boog's name and address on, then shoved the spy cam and Crawford's bridge inside and wound the package with Sellotape.

When Rosy dug in her bag for stamps, she found the new N-BioCom letter.

She held up the envelope to study the silky paper in the light, trailed her thumbnail across the ridges of the logo. Once upon a time, she'd have treated this with reverence, would have fetched the letter opener to keep the envelope neat. But the bastards had rejected her. She shoved her thumb in and burst it wide.

*Thank you for your patience. We have now completed our post-restructure review and are delighted to be able to offer you…*

Rosy sat up.

*… an undergraduate placement as Trainee Research Assistant within our Oslo facility.*

She looked at the dates. Starting 4th July, two weeks from tomorrow. She skipped to the bottom.

*N-BioCom is the world-leader in epigenetic analysis.… As yours was one of only four allocated places this year, competition was fierce, but you stood out in our process. Many congratulations. Please contact me, Arvid Madsen, at your earliest convenience to confirm your acceptance and to arrange travel and accommodation.*

Rosy grabbed the first letter, the letter Jen had read to her over the phone, fumbled it from its envelope.

*You recently applied for a post.… We are unable at this time to commit to our past levels of undergraduate places, but be assured… your application will be given full consideration for any suitable posts we identify in the coming weeks. We appreciate your continued interest in N-BioCom and have enclosed our information pack.*

The envelope was packed with brochures about Oslo and the labs.

Not a rejection, Jen—a holding letter.

Rosy breathed through her shaking hands.

Two weeks left with Frank.

# Boog

Boog woke to the sound of a girl asking, "Is that man an addict?"

"Are you okay?" the girl's mother, a woman in a navy Kangol top, asked as Boog oriented himself and worked out he'd spent the night in Princes Street Gardens, on the stone bench at the war memorial, site of his first real kiss.

The girl who'd asked about him looked just like Boog's little sister, Andrea.

"I was an addict," Boog said, his voice a croak. The stone had seeped into him, into his back, his muscles, his feet. "But not anymore."

He picked up his coat, and had no right to find his wallet and keys still in there, safe. Thank you, Edinburgh. Boog walked up the path and through a gate onto Princes Street.

Rosy had dumped him—hooray. At last, an end to the agony of not knowing.

And he'd hit Crawford—hooray. Not like the guy didn't have that coming.

Two cheers for Boog.

Time to put his life back into gear. His phone beeped and he read the message from Crawford:

*Hide all you want, you fat fuck. You are going to pay.*

---

Boog opened the door of the flat to find Janek fully clothed on the sofa, reading a battered Robin Hobb and Crawford sitting in Boog's study armchair, his face propped on his elbow.

"Fifteen hundred quid," Crawford said and displayed the gap in his teeth and swollen lip. "Minimum. And you, fat boy, are gonna pay."

"Crawfish," Janek said, and turned the next page in his novel, "you had a whole lot more than that coming, so suck it up like a good little crustacean, or this fatter boy will knock out the bottom ones."

"Oh, yeah?" Crawford said.

Janek got up tipped the armchair over onto its back with Crawford in it, and made a fist in his face. "Oh, fuck, yeah."

---

Boog shaved and showered and for once didn't beat off. Then he took out his *Chemistry* textbook, pad and pen and sat at the kitchen table. He made it all the way through Aldehydes and Ketones. One chapter. He measured the width of the chapter against the width of the book and panic grabbed at his heart.

"Lots to do?" Crawford said.

Boog jumped. "Yeah."

"I won't hold you back, but just so you know... After you smashed up my mouth, Rosy and me—we got to talking."

"Crawford, I'm through with Rosy. I'm through even thinking about her."

Crawford reached in his pocket. "Maybe that's just as well. Because after we got to talking..." Crawford pulled out his hand, and clenched it above the table. He held something black, balled in his fist.

"Girls are wired up different," Crawford said. "You'd think a guy with no front teeth would have zero chance. Like a fat guy. But I think Rosy felt sorry for me."

He opened his hand and spread out a pair of panties— skimpy, silky black panties. Lacy. Decorated with stars. Silvery stains threaded the material, the source of a smell Boog didn't want to smell.

"She was gagging for it. But she was only okay. Not as good as Jen," Crawford said. "Not as experienced. Wonder why?"

# Chapter 28
## Closer
### (Monday, 20 June)
### Rosy

Rosy tried a dozen different ways to phrase her rejection email to N-BioCom until she understood: her answer had to be yes. It had to be yes for her career. It had to be yes before her feelings for Frank made her do something insane. This was her escape route. Her ejector seat, and parachute. A rapid exit, an excuse that Frank and Phyllis would accept and understand.

But after she'd typed her acceptance email, she couldn't send it, couldn't press the eject button and land safely.

N-BioCom. N-BioCom was her dream job, her future. She couldn't say no. But she couldn't say yes. All she could do was procrastinate. Procrastination would allow her to see if Frank really had the heart to change.

---

Rosy decided she would say nothing to Frank, but his smile disappeared the moment she said good morning. He pulled out a chair for her and waited for her to explain.

And because Frank would smell a lie, she told him a different truth.

"I'm stressed out, Frank. I committed to a ridiculous target by the end of the month with Phyllis." Rosy rubbed her fingers, so as not to look at him. "Then I made it even worse because I told Heidi we were on track, remember? But we've lost two weeks. If we're going to hit the target… we have two weeks to show we can make a difference."

Two weeks until the start date at N-BioCom. If she decided to take it. Rosy could delay emailing them by a week, couldn't she?

Frank frowned. "I don't see why we only have two weeks, baby," he said. "But two weeks is forever. We can do it."

She shook her head. "There's so much we have to do."

"Like?" Frank said.

"Like, just look at this place."

Frank held up his hands. "You wanted to remodel. Let's remodel. We can do that in two weeks. I'm a fast worker."

"Remodelling is the next stage, silly," Rosy said. "We'd need a budget to bring people in for that"

Frank looked off to one side as though thinking that through. "To do what?"

Rosy pointed. "To get rid of that hideous bench, for a start. Or even that brown film on the windows."

"*Pfff.* Who needs people and a budget for that?" Frank said. "And the film's not brown. It's silver."

"Was silver, maybe," Rosy said. "It's brown now."

"How now, brown cow?"

Rosy looked at him.

He pushed the baseball cap back on his head. "Moo?"

She shook her head and laughed sadly. "I don't want to know what goes on in that brain of yours."

"Me neither," he said. "Have you tried picking it with your lady nails?"

"What, your brain?"

Frank pointed. "The film."

Rosy sighed. "I tried scraping it with a knife and it's baked on."

"Steam," Frank said, then his eyes went wide. "Ooh. Or fire." His fingers wiggled like dancing flames. "Burn it off."

She didn't even think he was kidding about the fire. "Steam would work. We could hire a steamer."

"Hire one?" Frank said. "Nah. Heidi will magic one up."

"Heidi, as in Phyllis's PA?"

"No, Heidi with the goat." He rolled his eyes.

"I mean, should you be asking Heidi to do things like that?" Rosy said. "She's not your PA."

Rosy watched him jab out a number faster than she thought the phone could work.

She shook her head. "Heidi won't be in the office yet."

"Hey," Frank said. "We need a steamer and two window scrapers for four o'clock." He hung up without waiting for an answer.

"What about 'please', and 'thank you very much, Heidi'?"

"She'll do it," Frank said.

"You're pretty nasty to her, Frank."

"I was nasty to her voicemail," he said. "Nasty or nice, you're still my baby, aren't you?"

"I'm still your baby." She put her hand on his cheek, then took it away and tucked it behind her back.

He resettled his CAT baseball cap on his broad head, and curled the already curving peak. Hair stuck out in a hundred directions, but Rosy couldn't imagine any image she'd rather capture on camera than Frank at that moment.

He grabbed a stool from the kitchen and set it down behind the counter. "You could sit on my knee for a minute, if you like," he said. He sat down and patted his thigh. "Nobody will see."

Rosy felt as though she'd sunk to her neck in ice water. Her breath left her and she knew her face must be burning red. "What?"

"You're my baby," Frank said. "It's allowed. You could sit on my knee and I could cuddle you."

"For what reason?"

"For the reason I'm your dad and you're my baby. For the reason I would like to cuddle you. For the reason you're still anxious, you need it and it would be lovely."

"There's no way I'm sitting on your knee, Frank."

"Come on. Make you feel better." Frank patted his leg. "You know you want to. And I want you to."

She knew she wanted to. "It's wrong."

"Wrong? *Pfff.*" Frank held his hands out. "What's wrong about it? Didn't Findlay ever cuddle you? Didn't your mum? Come on. Hop aboard. Before the bread van comes."

Rosy cast her gaze into the front of the cafe, licked her top lip, then walked towards him.

He spread his big hands, nodded. "That's my girl."

As Frank's arms closed on her, and Rosy let her weight rest on his legs, her mind refused to process this as reality. Then he cradled her. She let her ear press against his chest and she heard the slow thump of him. He rested his cheek on her head. And everything felt… right. She blinked away tears.

"That's my baby," Frank said, voice low so it rumbled through her. "That's my beaut'ful, beaut'ful baby."

---

Rosy expected Darren from IT to be a weedy geek, but he was way bigger than Boog, bigger than Janek, well beyond even Rosy's taste for chubbier guys.

"What the fuck has he done to my patch lead?" Darren said, twirling a black cable with brown welts down its length and an unrecognisable amber blob on the end. He held the lead up to Rosy's face. "Do you really need a PC?" he said, his breath rattling. "Because, Mr Friendship there is gonna just rape and pillage."

Darren was there for an hour and when he was done, Frank waved goodbye with the bread-knife. "Just gonna try it out wireless. Bye, Darren."

"Knife down," Rosy said. "Body language."

---

The first day of the Beancounter regime and even with the boring sandwich fillings, turnover was up by over a hundred quid on last Monday. Frank was keeping a running total in his head.

"Up by one hundred and-forty-one pounds and fifty-five pence so far," Frank said.

"How do you remember numbers?" Rosy said.

"Colour, mostly," Frank said. "And just the whole…" he moved his hands in the shape of a melon.

The bell dinged.

Colour? Rosy frowned. "Remind me to talk about that later."

---

Figures for one day were—statistically—completely meaningless, of course. Plus, they were only counting turnover, not profit, but in her gut Rosy knew this had a chance to work. And the proof had just walked through the door. A lady Rosy recognised from this morning.

"Any more brownies?" the woman said and made a grasping

gesture with both hands.

"I'm sorry," Frank said. "We're all brownied out." He shoved his baseball cap back. "But I can walnut-cake you? One tasty slice left."

Frank served the cake with a smile, and a fruit tea.

And that's when Marek walked in.

"Hello, my friend," Marek said. "I love your hat. Hello, Rosy." He peered in at the deli fillings. "Oh, doesn't this look nicer. I would like, let's see... I would like... to come back to work." He grinned, and folded his arms.

"Well, you can fuck right off," Frank said. "You've been replaced."

Marek raised his eyebrows, then gestured for Rosy to take the floor.

"I'm temporary, Frank, remember?" Rosy said. "And we're ramping up, aren't we? Phyllis was very happy with Marek's work..." Frank was staring at her and her throat had gone dry. "So I asked Marek if he'd consider re-joining us."

Frank jammed his hands behind his head and bent forward. "Oh, you went behind my back."

Customers were looking.

"No. Absolutely not. Phyllis wanted this," Rosy whispered. "And keep your voice down. Beancounters, remember?"

Frank made a grab for the laptop.

Rosy got there first. "No you don't." She clutched the computer under her arm and held Frank back with a hand on his chest. "Written warning, Frank, look at me. You're here to screw money out of customers, not to screw yourself out of a job. You worked with Marek before, you can do it again. With a Beancounter's hat on."

Marek leaned over the counter. "Hi." He waved. "I can start tomorrow."

Frank closed his eyes, then looked off to the side and just stood there, breathing heavily. Then he met Rosy's eyes. "Okay," he said.

"Is Beancounter's the new name of the cafe?" Marek said.

———————

Forty minutes after closing, forty minutes spent working away with the steamer on the window film, the sun cooking her, Rosy couldn't tell her own sweat from condensation. Water dripped off her nose. Her blouse clung to her stomach and across her chest. She angled the scraper in and once again managed to whack her elbow on the struts supporting the pine bar bench.

"Ow, ow, ow," Rosy said. "Stupid thing."

Rosy angled the scraper the other way, and skinned off a triangle of brown film about the length of her little finger.

"Argh, it's not budging. This crap is welded on." She turned the steamer off.

"You're doing it wrong," Frank said. "Wrong angle."

"Well, you could give me a demonstration instead of a critique, you know."

"I can't fit in teeny-tiny places." Frank drew a little box with his fingers. "I panic when I can't move my elbows."

"Steaming isn't working," Rosy said. "How do we get this mess off? And don't say burn it off," she added and Frank's mouth clamped shut. "There has to be an easier way."

"It needs muscle. If the bench wasn't there, I could do it in a minute."

"How about taking the bench down, then?"

Frank took off his baseball cap and resettled it. "Okay. Step aside, little lady."

Rosy pulled the steamer out of the way.

Without further warning, Frank landed a kick to the underside of the bench so hard Rosy's bones rattled. Another kick landed. She watched his chest and stomach bounce. Another. This time, wood splintered and the top lifted clear off its moorings. One more kick and the top slewed off and clattered onto the floor.

Frank moved in for the kill and Rosy backed away, watched him rip the carcass apart, her emotions a mix of awed delight and worry.

"Phew," he grinned at her, breathing hard, his belly peeking out beneath his T-shirt. "Just need a spanner and a screwdriver to take these off." He wiggled a broken strut that dangled forlornly from the supporting beam, and Rosy dragged her eyes away from those massive, squatting thighs.

Frank picked up the scraper, and swept it along the window. A two foot-long strip of film slewed off as effortlessly as a silk underskirt.

"Great," Rosy said. "There's only one problem now, Frank."

"And that is…?" he said.

"Where do people sit tomorrow?"

Frank studied the carnage. Rosy studied Frank, then forced her eyes away from the exposed strip of his stomach.

He tapped his watch. "B&Q will still be open."

---

They worked until after midnight, Rosy assembling stools while Frank scraped, measured, sawed and bolted himself into a saturated but happy heap on the floor. Frank's contribution was the more impressive, but the row of inviting stools made her smile too, and she could take credit for suggesting IKEA. The birch finish top and the glossy white and chrome seating had the clean, fresh look Rosy wanted. It may not last, but for now, it worked.

"You like it?" Frank said.

"I love it. You are so clever."

He wasn't at all worried about fitting the new lighting, either, nor about the new wiring they'd need for the light beneath the floating counter. All those jobs for Ernesto. Frank was amazing.

"I'm not clever, baby, but I do have a good memory." He looked at her expectantly, then said, "You wanted to talk about how I remember numbers?"

"I hadn't forgotten," Rosy lied. "If numbers have colours for you, I think you might have a condition known as synaesthesia." There'd been a documentary about it on TV. For some people, numbers had colours.

"Everything has colours for me, baby," Frank said, "and sounds and tastes and all the rest. My brain is damaged. It's all fucked up. It's like interference." He pointed at the bell above the door. "When that dings? Different shapes and colours for an innie or an outie. I can tell. I can be in the kitchen and I see if somebody came in—little orange sparkles, almond taste—or left—more yellow, flatter, no almonds." He stopped. "What?"

Rosy had remembered what Franny said about Frank. "You see things that aren't there."

*You taste of peaches.*

Tuna *sounds all wet.*

"That's how I remember numbers," Frank said. "That's how I remember everything. The whole…" He frowned and moved his hands slowly out and back in, tracing the shape of a melon in mid-air. "I remember that whole…" He made the shape again.

"Describe…" she made a melon shape, "for my name, for *Rosy*."

"Rosy is kinda lumpy like hard blue coal but a soapy tang."

"Synaesthesia," Rosy said. The people in the documentary had remarkable facility with numbers. "It's a gift, Frank. A wonderful gift." She laid her hand on his head and he looked up at her with those not-quite-straight eyes.

Rosy shook herself, folded her arms, then lifted an empty Kettle Chips pack, crunched it and checked the time on her phone. "I missed my last bus."

"Come on," Frank said, and heaved himself up. "I'll drive you home."

"Or…" She closed her eyes, steadied her voice. "I could crash at your place."

Frank shook his head. "Not tonight, baby," he said. "I'll drive you home. I need a long soak and a bed to lie on."

They could have found a way to share the bed.

Rosy didn't push it.

---

Frank was subdued all the way to Rosy's house. He parked on the street. The light was still on in her mum's and stepdad's bedroom window.

"That's their bedroom?" Frank said.

"Yeah," Rosy said.

"Just one bed?"

"Frank, don't."

Frank rubbed his chin. "No brownies ready for tomorrow."

"No, but it'll let us see if your DIY pulls more people in. That's more scientific. One variable at a time."

"I like having a scientist," Frank said.

N-BioCom would like to have her too. For real science. Epigenetics. Two weeks and she could be gone.

"I'd have liked to do that hill walk before it gets too busy," Rosy said.

Frank shrugged. "What's wrong with Saturday?"

"Okay," Rosy said. "It's a date."

She leaned over to peck him on the cheek but he held up his hand. "Germs."

She laughed. "Goodnight, Frank."

---

Rosy's mum was in the kitchen. The microwave spun with a jug of milk in there.

"Hey, thought you'd be in bed," Rosy said.

Mum drew her dressing gown up over her shoulders. "Findlay just hasn't been sleeping well. And he couldn't sleep with you not home. He worries about you on your own with Frank."

Rosy took a seat. "And you don't?"

Mum shook her head. "Should I worry?"

"Frank is… He's amazing, mum," Rosy said. "Yeah, he's not perfect, but…" She lowered her voice and looked behind her. "He loves DIY like you do. He cooks like you don't. He's so handsome like Findlay isn't. And he'd have you back in a heartbeat."

The microwave beeped.

"You will never have any idea how Frank made me feel," Mum said, "so you'll never understand why I'm so committed to Findlay."

"How could you not love Frank, Mum?"

"I'm glad you like him. I'm happy for him." Her mum stood, kissed Rosy's hair. "Goodnight, Rosy."

# Chapter 29
# Uh-oh
## (Tuesday, 21 June)
## Rosy

Rosy took an earlier bus to look at the cafe from the outside. They'd missed a couple of small strips of film, but the bench… Oh, the bench, the bench. She clapped her hands and danced around in a circle, then hoped nobody from Shawford had been watching. But it was awesome. Awesome.

Frank must have been out back feeding his pet human. He let Rosy in and she was still trying to pick the first of the residual strips of film off when Marek arrived.

"Ah, I cannot believe how wonderful a sight that is in the window," Marek said. "Frank, you have produced a beautiful work of art."

"Isn't it amazing," Rosy said.

"Oh," Marek said. "You mean the new seating? I was talking about your lovely self, Miss Friendship." He looked around, nodded. "But the seating is improved. Will it survive the customers? Let us see."

Did it matter, for a pilot in a cafe chain? Last night in IKEA, Rosy had seen just the perfect sofa. She could picture the place now. Lift the horrid vinyl flooring, sand the floorboards, neutral paint, a striking highlight wall with outrageous swirly wallpaper, that magenta sofa along the wall, an espresso machine taking pride of place on the counter.

Marek pointed. "There, and there also: you have more of the nasty brown stuff to scrape off."

"Thanks," Rosy said. "That's a great help."

"Speaking of nasty brown stuff," Marek said, "how are you, Frank? You have missed me, haven't you?"

Frank said nothing.

"And I," Marek said, "have missed our conversation."

Frank heaved a great sigh that could have been Rosy's.

"Wash your hands," Rosy told Marek. "Then there's a book you need to read."

————————

At busy times, Marek and Frank fell into a rhythm and Rosy, who couldn't keep up with Frank never mind both of them, drifted to till duty only. At quiet times, Marek scoffed at *The Beancounter's Cafe Handbook.* "Most of this is obvious. I have said you need to do this from the day I started. And the parts that are not obvious, are obviously wrong."

Frank looked put-out.

"We're not all psychology graduates, or marketing gurus," Rosy said, "and what you failed to do, Marek, with all your training, was inspire anybody."

"Yeah," Frank said, and pointed at Rosy. "Exactly."

"It does not take a genius to work out that selling Frank's homemade cakes is not a sustainable business model," Marek said.

"It doesn't need to be sustainable at this stage," Rosy said. "It's a pilot. If this cafe is successful, we'll roll it out."

"Who is we?" Marek said. "Aren't you only here for summer?"

"I mean, Phyllis will put money behind it and Frank will oversee the roll-out."

"Frank? Ha." Marek laughed. "Perhaps you mean Frank will oversee the buttering of rolls?"

Rage swelled in Rosy from nowhere. "Listen, to me, asshole. I will not have you come in here—"

"Quiet, Rosy," Frank said. "Marek's right. I'm happy to butter rolls. All I want is to keep the cafe open."

Rosy's eyes stung.

————————

Frank wanted to paint the ceiling and fit the new lighting before they did anything else, and when they locked the cafe up, and headed out to the van to collect equipment for this evening's activities, Rosy rounded on him.

"You wanted me to stand up for Boog, so, why wouldn't you let me stand up for you? I watched him bleed away all your positivity."

Frank shrugged. "Face it, baby. I could never run a business."

Rosy threw up her arms. "Why not? Have you any idea how awesome you are?"

"Could you just get in?" He tapped his watch.

Rosy climbed in and sat brooding. "Where are we going?"

"Up to the church hall for the work platform and my overalls."

Rosy touched his arm. "Do I get to meet Ernesto?"

"No," Frank said. "I have keys for every building."

---

But when Frank drove into the church hall car park, he pulled the handbrake on so hard, he rocked the van. "Fuck."

His outburst surprised Rosy. "What's wrong?"

"Look at all these cars. The hall's occupied."

"So?"

"So, I can't go clanking past them with a dirty big ladder."

"Well, let's forget the renovations for one day," she said. "We could bake some more brownies?"

"No." Frank chopped his hand down onto his thigh. "We only have two weeks. The ceiling needs three coats. That's six hours, minimum. The new lights, another hour, maybe two. That's a whole night's work. If I don't finish the ceiling tonight, there's no way I'll be done in time."

"In time for what?"

"Our big day," Frank said.

"Our big day? What do you have in mind?" She laughed. "A grand reopening?"

"No. Our big day, Rosy." He frowned at her. "Saturday? Don't you remember? You and me. Our hill walk. Off in the wilderness alone together."

Rosy swallowed. Alone together.

Frank gripped the steering wheel, rested his chin on top and stared out the window. "Everything has to be ready before Saturday." He sighed. "So, we'll just have to wait."

The two-week deadline was N-BioCom's, not Phyllis's, not

Frank's. But now, Rosy had managed to infect Frank with her own anxiety. "We shouldn't rush this, Frank. We have all next week too. And beyond."

He scowled, shook his head. "Not beyond, baby. Not if you're leaving."

Rosy felt dizziness surge and she gripped the seat. "Leaving? I didn't mention leaving."

He didn't look at her, just stared straight ahead through the windscreen. "I saw you put letters in your bag. A new letter," Frank said. "You told me all about that company, baby, the placement you wanted so bad." He shrugged. "Synaesthesia. I can see changes in people's voices. You got that letter, then got all anxious. And out of nowhere, we only had two weeks." He looked at her.

Jeez. What else could he see? "I have an offer. But I haven't said I'll take it."

"I have big plans for our last week." Frank said and smiled at her. "You and me, getting busy. And I don't mean baking brownies."

Rosy began to tremble. He knew what she wanted. He saw straight through her.

"You okay?" Frank said.

Rosy opened the van door and climbed out onto crunching gravel.

"Rosy?" Frank leaned over.

"No point in both of us waiting around," Rosy said, and forced her mouth into a smile. "I'll go try my hand at some baking."

"I'll run you home, baby."

"I'm good, Frank. I need the air." She swung the door shut, and *shuck-shucked* her way across the stones, back down to the road, rolling with the uneven surface to disguise her shaking legs. A slick warmth lubricated her thighs, and the cups of her bra felt hard as cardboard against her nipples.

Big plans for their last week. If Frank meant what she thought he meant, she couldn't let it happen. It was so wrong. Sick and wrong. She had to fight. But how, God help her? How?

---

Rosy hunkered down and peered through the oven door at the

tray of brownies. The mix looked too flat.

Movement in the reflections on the glass caught her eye—Findlay. Her stepdad dropped into a crouch behind her. Bony fingers massaged her shoulders. "Something smells good," Findlay said.

Rosy stood, shrugging free. "They're not for you. They're for the cafe."

"Why are you so obsessed with that cafe?" he said.

"It's a challenge, Dad. I love a challenge." She frowned and wondered if she'd missed an ingredient.

"I didn't say, but I'm so, so proud of you. I really am, Rosy…"

Maybe the temperature was too high. Frank's ancient old English Electric cooker measured in Fahrenheit not Celsius, so she'd adjusted. But this oven had a fan.

"Doing so well, getting into university from such a bad start," Findlay said. "University. Isn't that amazing? And you're not only beautiful inside, you're beautiful outside. You're determined and wonderful. You're very cerebral. If I had a notebook, I'd write down everything you say. It's like I'm in university."

"Huh? Sorry?" Frank's brownies had that crusty top, and chewy-soft middle. The worst would be if Rosy's were burned.

"Now you've grown up," Findlay said, "it's not easy for me to express myself—"

"Sorry, can I squeeze past?" Rosy pulled the oven glove on, and opened the door. Heat wafted into her face, made her gasp and turn her head away. She lifted the tray up and clattered it onto the hob. Too dark. She tutted, then pulled out one of the kitchen drawers and looked around for her mum's Betterware cake lift.

"Rosy?" Findlay waved his arms. "Please. I'm trying to say something important."

She took a breath. "Okay, sorry, Dad. Go for it. I'm listening."

Her stepdad looked at his hands. "I'm full of admiration. I hope I don't embarrass you. It's just that you're my whole world."

"Thanks Dad." Rosy shrugged.

Findlay reached out, squeezed her shoulder then drew his

hand back to make a thumbs-up sign. Then another thumbs-up with the other hand. He put his arms out, offering a hug.

She shook her head. "Cigarettes and baking? No." She smiled.

But the brownies would stink of cigarettes anyway. The whole house stank, even her room, even though he smoked outside. Findlay needed motivation to quit.

That's when Rosy remembered Marek.

"Listen, about that Polish guy I mentioned a while back? You know, the naked magician? He's started at the cafe now. I honestly think you two should talk."

She watched his barriers go up.

"I'd rather progress at my own pace, Rosy."

She folded her arms. "Do you even know how long you've been talking about this show of yours?"

He shook his head.

"Eight years. That's practically half my life."

"You know how to make a body feel old, don't you?" Findlay slumped down in a kitchen chair.

"Why not meet Marek? Where's the harm? Let me arrange it for you."

He scowled. "Let me think about it."

That annoyed her. "Frank just does stuff. He is a doing machine. You? You're always thinking about it. Well, tick-tock, Dad. Tick-tock."

He looked old and tired and tearful.

Where was that stupid cake lift?

Findlay's hand beat hers to the cutlery drawer. He studied his slippers. "I'll talk to your Polish pal."

Rosy nodded, satisfied. "Good." For once, she and Findlay had dialogued. "Help yourself to brownies. My treat."

He could eat what he wanted, eat the whole tray. She couldn't show those to Frank. They were only fit for the dustbin.

---

In Rosy's dream, Boog came into the cafe, but the cafe was somehow also Jen's flat. Boog kissed her then wanted her to step into the kitchen, and turn around so the camera could see. Then Boog lifted up her apron. No, not Boog. Frank. Rosy had nothing on under her apron. Frank was naked too. He kissed her—at last—pushed and ground into her, suckled her nipples and—

Rosy woke, heart hammering, breathless, the orgasm playing out in a throb of contractions and a slimy wetness soaking into her knickers.

No. No. No.

She closed her eyes and lay there in her shame, the smell of burnt brownies and cigarettes sickening her.

# Chapter 30
# Suspicions
## (Wednesday, 22 June)
## Rosy

Hard to credit the joy to be found in the simple act of flipping a light switch and having instant illumination. The light fittings looked modern and clean. The fluorescent tube from the deli was gone too and when Rosy flicked the switch—

The counter floated on light. That would look great in a before and after picture.

Frank did all this, and painted the ceiling, in one night. "Oh, you are so clever, Frank."

"Just paint and wires, baby." Frank yawned. "Nothing clever about that."

"The whole space has opened up," Marek said, when he arrived. "Sadly, we can now see how grubby the walls are. But a most excellent improvement. Well done, my friend, well done."

All morning, Frank kept yawning and rubbing his face. All he would say was the meeting in the church hall ran later than expected. When Rosy spotted Phyllis sashaying towards the cafe, she elbowed Frank, who groaned and levered himself out of his bleary-eyed slouch across the counter.

"Nice to see you back, Marek," Phyllis said.

"Thank you, Mrs Long. I am seeing leopard spots change before my eyes."

Phyllis nodded at the bench and the new seating, which Rosy took to be approval, though as usual the old woman's slewed face proved hard to read. Her attention appeared to be on the ceiling and new lighting.

"Super," Phyllis said. "You've changed the lights. Very professional job. Very nice. You are aware, I assume, that electrical work in a commercial building has to be done by a qualified electrician?"

Rosy covered her mouth.

"Not to worry," Phyllis said. "My people across the road can check it all. How long did everything take?"

He shrugged. "Seven hours, maybe?"

Phyllis whistled. "Seven hours." She put her hands on her hips. "Will Frank's seven hours of overtime be coming from your budget, Rosy?"

"It's not overtime," Frank said, cutting off Rosy's explanation. "I did if for free. For Rosy."

"And for the good of the business," Rosy said. "Because he really, really believes in re-energising the cafe and wants it to be a success. Isn't that right, Frank?"

He covered a yawn with his fist. "*Yuuuhhhp.*"

"Frank looks like he could do with some re-energising himself," Phyllis said. "I hope you're not too tired to help me solve a little mystery?"

"Mystery?" Frank said.

Phyllis looked up at the ceiling again. "Must have been hard to see what you were doing in the dark."

Good point. How had he managed to change light fittings at night?

Frank rubbed his eye.

Phyllis waved her hands. "But that's not the mystery. The mystery is, who used your alarm code at 1:38 this morning to enter the Shawford office, then again at 4:12 to re-arm the system? Any ideas?"

Frank nibbled his bottom lip.

"Oh," Phyllis said, "we do have some CCTV footage of a man—about your height and build, Frank—removing a desk lamp from the premises, then returning it at approximately 4:10."

Frank had taken off his baseball cap and was exploring the stitching with his fingers.

Phyllis kept going. "I say a man about your height and build because I can't believe that you, Frank, would wander about in the Shawford office—no matter how early—stripped to the waist."

Rosy closed her eyes.

"If that had been you, I'd have had to issue another written warning," Phyllis said. "Fortunately, I know you well enough not to ask."

Frank watched Phyllis, his baseball cap in a tight roll.

"Nice hat," Phyllis said. "That other character was wearing something much more unusual on his head." She tapped her wiry hair. "I'm only glad we don't have many customers out and about so early in the morning. It would have been very awkward to explain away a grown man, half naked, wearing clip-on animal ears."

Rosy stared at Frank. Why would he do something like that?

"Just so you know," Phyllis continued, "everybody's alarm code for the Shawford office has now been restricted to the hours that individual might reasonably need, which for you, Frank, is Monday to Friday, 07:30 to 18:30."

Phyllis rubbed her palms against one another. "Let's keep any future work to a sustainable pace, and make sure it's paid for. I don't want you killing yourself."

Now Rosy became the focus of Phyllis's attention. "How about you and I have a little chat now?" she gestured to a table, then hiked a thumb at Frank. "Sleeping Beauty. Go home. Marek and Rosy can cover for you today."

Frank objected.

"Go home, lie down and get some sleep," Phyllis said. "And no more nocturnal redecorating, please."

Rosy watched Frank wander out of the cafe, then wander back in holding his keys between finger and thumb. "Lock up, baby," he said. "I'll get the keys back later."

Phyllis pressed her hands onto the table and stared at Rosy. "May I see your project plan?"

---

Rosy floundered under Phyllis's glare, referring back to the summary steps in her report, and improvising a plan on the spot until the woman put her hand on Rosy's.

"That's enough, dear. I would prefer a straight, *'I'm sorry, Phyllis. I don't have a plan'.*"

"I'm sorry, Phyllis," Rosy said. "I don't have a plan."

Phyllis frowned. "After having to prompt you last time for a report, I had hoped you'd get the hang of this."

"I've been a bit distracted by Frank."

Phyllis tutted, and shook her head. "Would the university accept that excuse?" she said. "Another student distracted you from your work?"

Rosy thought about Boog and shook her head. "No."

"It's not acceptable at work, either, Rosy," Phyllis said. "You weren't hired to fill sandwiches and work the till. You're paid more than your father, and I expect you to earn it."

More than Frank? Rosy squirmed. She did so much less than Frank. Rosy had been taking a wage to watch Frank.

"I'm sorry, Phyllis. I haven't been applying myself. Frank was obstructive last week, so we've lost some time——"

"Oh?" Phyllis said, and the eyebrow above her missing eye rose then sank down, and Rosy was horrified to see the eyelid open a fraction. "You told Heidi you were on track."

Rosy scowled. She didn't need to take this. She had N-BioCom. Maybe. Wednesday already. Tick-tock.

"Frank and I had a small difference of opinion, but we're on track now because his position has flipped one-eighty degrees. He couldn't be more supportive."

"Of a plan that you've yet to set out," Phyllis said.

"Of the direction," Rosy said. "And we do have direction." She explained about *The Beancounter's Cafe Handbook*, but Phyllis's expression didn't waver. Rosy raised her hands to the ceiling and waved at the new seating. "Look at the changes already. He's moved mountains in only a few days."

"In other words," Phyllis said, "you've started an avalanche?"

"Phyllis, please. Don't judge. Give Frank a chance to show what he's capable of."

"I know what Frank is capable of," Phyllis said. "I don't need more evidence. I need to know he's under control, that he's behaving himself. Walking around shirtless, wearing animal ears? I'm not encouraged."

Rosy rubbed her face.

"Frank's judgement is poor," Phyllis said. "You need to compensate for that by applying yours. Keep him right, or who knows what would happen."

Rosy breathed out, nodded.

Phyllis stood. "I've taken enough of your time. Looks like Marek could use a hand. I'll expect a plan from you first thing Friday morning. Then we'll talk."

Rosy wiped her slick palms on her apron. Bollocking over. Time to get back to work. And to stop obsessing about Frank.

---

Phyllis was right again, damn her. With no Frank there to distract Rosy, even fifteen minutes at the computer was enough to spot a ton of gaps and to-dos. Rosy owed Frank a plan. A plan to follow so that if, on Friday, Rosy really did choose to go with N-BioCom, he'd stay safe.

Rather than proceed haphazard like one of Mum's projects, Frank could sketch the cafe interiors—an artist's impression—and Rosy could map out the paint colours. She'd always had an eye for that. Mum had hundreds of charts at home. Those sketches and colour maps would then be assets to reuse in other Tasty Bites.

Tasty Bites.

The cafe needed a new name:

*Phyllis's*

Yuck. Well, anyway, it needed a new name.

Rosy should use as much of the budget as she'd been given. She'd heard that somewhere before—best to use it, or you'd lose it. Items to include in her budget: The espresso machine. That big sofa. Tasty Bite baseball caps. And tight T-shirts.

How could she leave before the big sofa? And the tight T-shirts?

---

They worked well together, Marek smiling at Rosy and Rosy smiling back but as the hours dragged by, all she could think of was Frank. The cafe without Frank was like a movie theatre with no screen.

Marek expressed the same sentiment a different way. "I feel that work has strangely become pleasurable," he said. "I can move around with no fear of being squashed against the wall, or trampled into the floor." He picked up an order pad with one of Frank's sketches. "When a normal person draws a heart, it is a romantic heart. Frank draws a heart cut from a body."

Rosy scowled. "That's just Frank. There's nothing sinister behind it."

Marek laughed. "This is why psychology fascinates me. Humans pick up the most subtle of cues, yet are so willing to close their eyes completely."

"Have you ever seen Frank hurt anybody?" Rosy said, then added, "Physically?"

"Because violence is only violence if physical contact is made?" Marek said, then shrugged. "He once picked up a child by the hood of his coat and dropped him outside onto the pavement."

"Yes, Frank told me about that," Rosy said, annoyed. "But the kid had dog dirt on his feet."

"Nevertheless—" Marek cut himself off. "Forgive me. No, Rosy, I have never seen Frank physically hurt anybody. I myself have only ever been pushed around and verbally abused."

She swept her hands across her brow and back through her hair. "Why can't he just behave?"

"Because that's not who and what he is," Marek said. "The old lady has managed to cage a wild creature, but he is still wild. One day, I am sure, he will break free."

Rosy rubbed her temples.

"But enough about Frank. You asked some time back if I could help your stepfather, Findlay? With his act?"

She jolted, shocked she could have forgotten so completely about Findlay. "And, you know," she said, "I think I actually managed to convince him he needs help."

She gave the counter a quick wipe, then set the tea-towel down. Crumbs sure built up fast without Frank there.

"Dad—*Findlay* has this terrible comedy routine where the punchlines are accordion tunes. Which could be funny, except he keeps playing the whole tune—"

Marek held up his hands. "I am not a critic. The act is immaterial. I can only offer help on process."

"Of course," Rosy said.

"You have his phone number?" Marek asked.

She scrawled her home number on an order pad. Marek, to her surprise, began to dial.

"He will be out?" Marek asked.

"No, he'll probably be in but..."

He finished dialling, then handed her the receiver. "Introduce me."

"Ringing."

He stood with his fingers spread on the counter and she wondered whether he might be striking a pose for her—

"Hey, Dad. Listen, I have Marek here... Marek the magician. I'm going to put him on to talk to you about shows and stuff."

Marek nodded and took the phone. "Hello, Findlay," he said. "I am Marek Borkowski and I am so excited to talk to a fellow performer."

Rosy laughed and cringed.

"I would very much like to meet you to share with you my experiences, and help you to reach your audience..."

Rosy could hear her stepdad ramble on but when Marek rolled his eyes, she didn't like that, didn't like how fast he'd judged somebody he didn't even know.

"You could have a think about it, yes," Marek said, and shook his head like he was exasperated with Findlay already.

That, too, irked Rosy.

"Alternatively," Marek said, "we could meet at 6:45 tonight in Cafe Royal on West Register Street and I will buy you a beer.... Yes, 6:45 at the bar... So I'll see you tonight then...?" He replaced the receiver.

"Thanks," Rosy said. "He needs a little push."

"I help anybody," he said. "In this game, it's all about networking. Even if Findlay does not put on a show at the Festival Fringe, I have a feeling we will have some fruitful discussions, he and I."

Odd, that his *fruitful discussions* remark sounded so genuine. Was Marek thinking of some kind of a show tie-in? Wouldn't that be hilarious? Her stepdad playing accordion for the naked magician.

Marek was watching her. "Another reason to enjoy Frank's absence is, I can talk—*frankly*, as it were—to you."

"Please do. I'd like to know how you're finding things," she said.

"I'm finding things... perplexing." Marek said that with the tone of a doctor sharing news of an inoperable tumour. *It's not good, I'm afraid.*

Rosy swallowed. "Go on."

"I know you and Frank have only recently been reunited," he said, "and I know in such circumstances it is not uncommon to see this kind of behaviour, but to see it first hand…"

"Behaviour?" Rosy's? Frank's? "What kind of behav—?"

The bell dinged.

Marek held his hands up. "We must continue this conversation. Soon."

While Rosy served her customer, another came in and Marek handled him, but it felt to Rosy that in all that time, Marek held her in his blue gaze. Her hands had become slick and a knot formed in her innards, began to tighten with the certainty that Marek had peered inside her head.

What kind of behaviour?

Marek's customer took the table closest to the counter, within easy earshot. Rosy walked into the kitchen and waited.

Marek stepped onto the stone floor. "You love Frank, don't you?"

"Of course," she said. She couldn't look at the man. "He's my father. Why wouldn't I?"

"No, Rosy. That's not what I mean," he said. "I see the way you look at him. It is how Heidi looks at him." His diagnosis followed: "You are in love with Frank, aren't you?"

In the cafe, the bell dinged and the word escaped from Rosy's throat as a whimper. "No?"

Marek picked up her hand. "I find it moving and quite, quite beautiful."

The counter banged.

"Rosy?" said Frank.

# Chapter 31
## Diagnosis
### Rosy

Sleep had restored Frank but now that Marek had her figured out, Rosy found she could barely look at her father. And soon every time their eyes happened to meet, Frank seemed more and more confused.

By closing time, she was actively dodging him, and when she slipped past him again at the washing up, he spun her around, clamped his hands on her shoulders and pinned her against the sink. "What did I do?" he said, his eyes roaming her face.

"Nothing."

"I was hot, Rosy. I was hot and soaked in sweat. So I took my overalls and T-shirt off."

Frank was telling her about last night.

"I had to switch off the lighting at the mains," he said, "so I needed a light."

"It's okay, Frank."

"I like wearing the wolf's ears. It was late and… I like wearing them, okay? They make me feel good."

"Yes, Frank, it's okay," Rosy said. "Of course it's okay."

He pressed his hands together. "So what's wrong?"

"Nothing." Rosy crushed past him. "Really. Nothing's wrong."

———

Rosy had arranged to meet Marek in the Widower's Fiddle again, straight after work, but the bar hadn't opened yet. Marek pointed at a playground, deserted but for a mongrel dog, sniffing at the rusting roundabout. They took a swing each.

"The accepted term for your what you are feeling," Marek

said, "is Genetic Sexual Attraction or GSA. It is not a sexual deviation. It does not mean there is something wrong with you."

"Sorry to interrupt," Rosy said. "Did you cover this on a course at university?" she said. "Or did you dig it up on a website somewhere?"

"I still actively read about psychology, but—yes—I refreshed my memory with an internet search."

She kicked at the rubber matting beneath the swing. "On sick-in-the-head.com?"

"Don't worry, Rosy, it is a clinically recognised phenomenon, observed in as many as half of cases like yours." He then started to explain what he called the normal mechanisms of sexual attraction. "While it is true that we can be attracted to a genetic opposite—which helps increase diversity—it is more common to select a genetically similar partner. This helps strengthen desirable traits."

Rosy watched the mongrel approach a woman with a Labrador on a lead, then take a good old sniff. Attraction in action.

"Walk down any street and you'll see this." Marek continued. "Enormous men with tiny wives, or two tall people together, couples you might think brother and sister. Unchecked, this attraction to a clone would lead to a problem. Who is more genetically similar than a close family member—a brother or sister, a father or mother?" He raised his eyebrows. "If Mother Nature applied no controls, half the boys on the planet would turn into motherfuckers."

"Many do," Rosy said. She'd met her share.

"Indeed, but not literally," Marek said. "Growing up within a family stops us seeing those people as sexual partners. The very notion of sex with a sibling or parent or child turns our collective stomach."

"Yeah." Rosy was thinking about Findlay.

"But to you, Frank is a stranger," he said. "A handsome stranger. And there's a process you have no control over—the sexual attraction mechanism—that has worked flawlessly to select a match for you: Frank. Inside of you, Rosy, everything is yelling that this person is your ideal mate. Screaming at you to make him yours." He leaned back. "And that is Genetic Sexual Attraction."

"Thank you," Rosy said. "I really mean that. I thought I had to be the sickest pervert in the world." She looked up at the chains of her swing. "So now I know what it is, what do I do about it?"

Marek walked himself backward on the swing, lifted his legs to swing forward, then stepped off in a graceless rattle of chains. "You act on it."

---

Rosy left Marek and headed back to the cafe, then stopped.

Frank. Outside in the summer sun, up on a ladder, painting the shopfront.

She changed direction. Genetic Sexual Attraction. It made sense. Everything Marek told her made sense. Everything except... *act on it.*

When she'd pressed Marek, he'd explained. "You have been presented with an opportunity here, Rosy. Grab it. This is love, in its truest, deepest form. You know that. There will never be another love so true as the love you have for this man. And who else will Frank ever feel so deeply for? Who else can even approach him?"

"But it's illegal. It's immoral. It's wrong, Marek, it's so wrong."

He'd smiled sadly. "Then choke it off and never tell another soul. But whatever you do, whether you accept or reject him, you will be damaged. Do not think that by walking away, everything will be right. It will not be. It will never be."

"If I act..." she'd said. "If I act, it'll screw me forever."

Marek had nodded. "If you allow it to, yes. If you go in faint-hearted, the victim of the cruelty of fate, yes," he said. "But if you seize this as an opportunity, take responsibility for your own life, take the journey, no. No. You can do this and emerge a better, wiser person." Then he had shrugged. "I have told you what I would do if I could experience the drug of perfect love. I would take it. But I remove my clothes for strangers. This is your life."

Until Frank, love had been an intellectual abstraction. Rosy had wondered about Boog, if the feelings she'd had for him— truer than anything she'd ever felt for Ruben—might be love.

Until Frank.

Rosy's bus was coming. Another day gone, another day closer to the last with Frank, whether next week or at Summer's end.

Last days with Frank.

Rosy stopped.

What in the hell was she doing? It was just gone 4:50 p.m. Why go home to mope around the house when Frank was here?

Rosy stepped back from the kerb, waved the bus on, and ran back toward the cafe.

This wasn't her decision to make alone.

"Hey, Frank," she said.

Frank turned, smiled, unsure. "Hey, baby. I thought you'd gone home."

She wrinkled her nose. "Just coming to make sure you straighten up the T there." She pointed at the slanted letter. Bye-bye, Nasty Bite.

"Easy job," Frank said. "The screw's just rusted through. But I kinda like it hanging down."

Rosy frowned at him and laughed. Wasn't that just so Frank? "Well, is it okay if I watch?"

Frank pointed down by the paint cans, and grinned. "There's a half-inch brush for the details. We could do it together?"

Rosy nodded. "Yeah, Frank. Let's do it together. Let's get on and do it."

# Chapter 32
## Finding inspiration
### Boog

Boog recognised Rosy's writing on the Jiffy bag that was waiting for him when he got back to the flat, and he knew what would be inside: the Ortak bracelet. That pissed him off. Like he was so petty he wanted his gifts back. Like he could pawn it, or go give it to some other girl and be okay with her just wearing it.

Fuck the Jiffy bag. Let it wait until he'd had some food.

Janek was in the kitchen already. "Hey, Boogieman, you're looking real well. Real well."

Boog had taken Janek's advice and now he spent most of the day out at Heriot-Watt campus. Amazingly, it had worked.

Being in a study environment, being in a place with grass and trees, no prospect of bumping into Rosy, suddenly he could focus. The gym also helped. No longer fearful of Rosy's reaction, he'd joined the gym. His BMI was twenty-nine, one point below obese, so fuck you Crawford. He either had a ton of muscle, heavy bones or—most likely—they'd made a mistake, but for now, he was only too happy for the morale boost.

"Janek? I don't suppose you'd fancy starting at the gym?"

Janek looked down at his furry belly bulging out over his underpants. "You think I could shift any of that?"

"You could give it a go," Boog said. "Take the pain."

Janek nodded. "I could give it a go."

"And speaking of taking the pain…" Boog said.

The Jiffy bag. He might as well get it over with.

He began to bust the package open then had to get scissors for the shit-ton of tape Rosy had used.

He reached in, then pulled out…

"What the fuck is this?" Boog said. "An ugly-ass pen and…" He held up a knobbly silver plate.

"Crawfish's bridge?" Janek said.

Boog read the note, didn't understand.

Then he looked at the pen and he did. And for the first time in two days, he needed his inhaler.

He held the pen up, blinking away tears of anger. "What a cunt. What a complete cunt." He pulled the top off the pen, to reveal two AA batteries. "A spy cam. Crawford put a spy cam in Rosy's house. Is this why…?"

Janek just watched with his hand over his slack mouth.

But Boog knew why Rosy dumped him. She had said already. He hadn't made the grade, wasn't strong or smart or determined enough. Boog unscrewed the bottom of the spy cam and found a USB connector. "I'm gonna have to look at this now, aren't I?"

Janek frowned. "Are you, Boogie?" he said. "I wouldn't. I wouldn't look at that."

"What would you do, Janek?" Boog said.

"I'd give it straight to Jen." Janek said. "Straight to her, do not pass go. Crawfish stew, boiled alive in minutes."

Boog nodded. "What about the dental work?"

"I'd put that in the recycling," Janek said. "Or maybe in a little piece of dog shit then drop it in the toilet bowl. So he thinks it's an escape pod come back from the mother shit."

"And I thought you were such a nice guy, Janek"

Janek shook his head. "I have shortcomings."

# Findlay

Findlay must have been in the Cafe Royal before. He recognised the grand, old-fashioned bar and the tiled panels with scenes from great people's lives. Just the place for a pretentious Polish twat to arrange a meeting. Findlay scanned the bar for somebody weird looking. You could always tell a foreigner. He still wasn't sure why he'd agreed to come along anyway. At the time, it had felt easier to say yes than to argue.

No sign of the guy, and Findlay would be buggered before he'd buy his own drink. Marek was buying. No way the smarmy bastard would wriggle out of that.

"Findlay?"

He turned and a man about Rosy's height thrust a hand out. "Marek Borkowski." The shake was warm, two-handed. "Great to meet you. What will you have?"

---

Marek listened without interruption while Findlay told him what he wanted to achieve.

"I don't need to be on TV," Findlay said. "All I want is to have enough money coming in, so I can quit the day job."

"You have a day job?" Marek said.

"No," Findlay said. "Just a figure of speech. All I want, Marek, is an income."

He nodded. "You are not in this for a fast buck. Performing is in your blood, and pumps through your heart. Even if there were no money, you'd be in it for the love"

"Exactly," Findlay said. "My partner, she doesn't get that."

"Rosy's mother?"

"Yeah. Irene. She's always at me, you know, get a proper job. Yack-yack-yack. And it wears me down." Findlay couldn't remember the last time—or even the first time—Irene had said that, but she didn't need to say it. Findlay felt it.

"Psychologically, that's the worst thing she could do to a creative type, like yourself, Findlay," Marek said. "And that's what we need to work on together."

"Irene?"

"No," Marek laughed. "Silencing the critics so people can see how fucking awesome you are. Another beer?"

Findlay drained his glass. "Fuck, yes."

---

Two beers, that's all he'd had, so Findlay knew he wasn't drunk, but he felt high as Amy Winehouse's hairdo. This Marek guy really got him, really understood.

"It must be a bitter pill, Findlay, that Rosy dotes on Frank the way she does."

"What the fuck is she thinking? Frank-fucking-Friendship." Findlay's lip stiffened. "I cannot get through to that girl anymore."

"Rosy is a fine young lady. And she's that way because of her upbringing." Marek squeezed Findlay's arm. "Because of you and Irene and the wonderful job you've done. And it's in Rosy's nature to trust, to give people the benefit of the doubt. She cannot see Frank for what he is."

"A fucking psycho," Findlay said.

"Dangerous," Marek said. "And undeserving."

"Yeah," Findlay said. "Undeserving of Rosy, you mean?"

"Of everything. Yes, of Rosy. Of Phyllis Long's patronage."

"Yeah, he'd never get a job in the real world."

Marek laughed. "I don't just mean the job." The Pole leaned in close. "I am friends with Phyllis's PA. We have been very good friends in the past, if you know what I mean?"

"You fucked her?" Findlay said. "Oh, I envy you young bastards. You must be up to your neck in skirt with this naked magic act. It's genius."

"You are not wrong," Marek said. "But about Phyllis's PA…"

"Yeah," Findlay said. "How old is she? Is she a looker?"

"Heidi is twenty-seven. And, yes, she is very lovely. But that is not why I was telling you. Heidi sees everything that goes on. Have a guess who provides Frank a rent-free flat and pays his gas and electricity bills."

Findlay closed his eyes. "Phyllis Long?"

"Correct."

The jammy bastard.

"Also," Marek said, "Heidi was present when Phyllis drew up her will. Emails passed between Phyllis and the solicitor. Emails which Heidi saw."

Findlay rubbed his forehead. "Frank is in her will?"

"Yes, Findlay. Phyllis is not just leaving him the flat. She's leaving him... the building." Marek raised his eyebrows and nodded sadly. "A building worth—conservatively, on today's market—three hundred and fifty thousand pounds."

---

Findlay sat breathing into his hands while Marek bought him another pint. He wanted to vomit, wanted to cry. The man who'd deflowered Irene, whose daughter Findlay had been forced to look after, who had driven Findlay and Irene to the very brink, takes a job that could just as easily have been Findlay's and... wins the fucking lottery. Phyllis Long leaving Frank-fucking-Friendship an entire building? That didn't make sense.

"Cheers," Marek said.

"Cheers, mate," Findlay said.

"Where has your positivity gone, Findlay?"

Findlay was so upset he could barely speak. "He's destroyed my life, that man. And to think... to think..."

"What does it matter? Let Frank have what is coming to him, good or bad. I have my own prediction. My own prediction would be that Phyllis too will be made to see what kind of a man this is."

Findlay laughed without humour.

"Nevertheless, we must not measure our success by the success or failure of another," Marek said. "We must take responsibility. We must have many, many strings to our bow." He snapped his fingers, and Findlay looked up at him. The Pole's eyes sparkled. "I do not need to find a one million dollar idea. I am happy with a ten-thousand dollar idea. Because one hundred of them is all I need."

Findlay slumped back in his chair. "Even a one dollar idea is beyond me, mate."

"I do not believe this," Marek said. "I can see an inner strength shining from you."

Findlay's inner strength felt more like an inner tube.

A flat one, with a big hole.

"Let me give you an example," Marek said. "Think of a magic show. What is there for anybody to enjoy? We have all seen these tricks a thousand times. And there are a thousand magicians within a wave of my wand of here."

"I hate magic," Findlay said.

"Now, let us take the magic show idea and *combine* it with something else. How about… a strip show?"

"No offence," Findlay said, "you're a handsome young buck and all the rest, but I wouldn't pay to see your family jewels."

"Ah, but would you like to see my assistant's bouncing titties?" The Pole handed him a flier.

Findlay grabbed the paper, grinned then scowled and shook his head free of the titties. "But you're young. Ladies want to see you take your kit off. Nobody wants to look at a thirty-four-year-old's nut-sack."

"No, Findlay, you are missing the message," Marek said. "The message is not about nut-sacks. The message here is, do not do what everybody else is doing. Take two different ideas—entirely different ideas, and…" He brought his hands together in a ball. "Combine them. Do that often enough, and you will find gold." He sat back. "And that will be your homework. One-hundred combinations."

"My homework?" Findlay couldn't do homework. He'd rather take detention.

"I like you, Findlay," Marek said. "And I now understand why Frank is so antagonistic towards you. You possess every attribute he lacks. I think you have enormous potential and, if I look after you, one day you will look after me."

# Rosy

Rosy's mum poked a finger at Rosy's jeans. "Is that paint?"

"'Fraid so."

"Ruined."

The opposite. The paint splash made those jeans significant. Rosy would see that and remember the day she'd painted the cafe with Frank. Her Frank.

Mum offered macaroni-cheese from the fridge but Rosy had eaten at Frank's.

"You should go talk to Findlay," Mum said. "He met your Polish guy."

"And?" Rosy said.

Mum's eyebrows raised. "Go talk to him."

---

The astonishing thing about the lounge was that the TV was switched off.

Her stepdad sat with a spiral notebook and a pen.

He looked up and grinned. "Hello, Sweetpea. Can I just say, thank you?"

"For?" She looked at the pad but couldn't make out his scratchings. The smell of beer and cigarettes pickled him.

"For Marek," Findlay said. "Oh, Jesus, is he a breath of fresh air? That boy is a fuc— He's a genius."

Rosy nodded. "He's a switched on guy. Knows about all kinds of things."

"All of a sudden, I have a million ideas," Findlay said. "He's unblocked me."

"He studied psychology at University College London," Rosy said.

Findlay frowned. "Really? So maybe he manipulated my mind."

Rosy raised her eyebrows at him. "Psychologist, Dad, not telepath. If he gave you good advice, that's what matters."

"He gave me great advice." Findlay scrawled another note

that looked like *Drag V*-something. "I am smouldering hot." He stood and set down the pad. "Give your old stepdad a hug."

They hugged, but Findlay was all bones and ridges.

"*Mmm*," Findlay said. "What did you just do to me?"

"My phone vibrated, Dad," Rosy said. "And I think that's enough of a hug now."

Findlay nodded and pulled away, but his sweater stuck. He touched the sticky patch, "What's that—?" he said, then sniffed his fingers. "Oh, for fuck's sake. Paint? Is that paint? On my new fucking jumper?"

He stomped past Rosy. "Irene?"

Rosy pulled out her phone. The vibration had been a message from Boog. She knew from Jen that Boog was okay, but this was the first time he'd been in touch since the disaster at the Opal Lounge.

She opened the message:

*For what it's worth, the spy cam wasn't me. That's a totally Crawfish move.*

Crawford?

The dirty son-of-a-bitch. He'd sniffed about her during first semester, before he started dating Jen, and Rosy had rejected him flat out.

And she'd just worked out what Findlay had written on his pad:

*Drag Ventriloquist.*

Oh, please, God. No.

# Chapter 33
# Bad job
## (Thursday, 23 June)
### Rosy

Their exterior paintwork from yesterday looked good to Rosy but Frank assured her it would need a second coat, possibly even a third, so maybe there was still time to persuade him to straighten the T in the sign, at least until the cafe had a new name.

Today, Rosy had brought in some A3 paper and Frank, sitting at different tables while Marek and Rosy served the customers, drew various views of the cafe, first in pencil, then inked in.

"Now," Marek said, "tell me this is not a more productive use of your talents, my friend, than drawing oozing bodily organs."

Rosy simply shook her head and grinned at the perspective drawings—accurate and yet strangely comic-book. "Brilliant."

She squeezed Frank's shoulder, then met Marek's eye. He neither frowned nor smiled, merely nodded, impassive. Rosy's decision. And she'd made it.

"Now we have the new bench and seating at the front, we need to replace these other tables and chairs," Rosy said.

"Or," Frank said, and rubbed his hand on the pockmarked and scratched table top, "we could take them to a dip-and-strip, strip them back to the wood. Then I could bring the chairs and table bases up to an ultra-high gloss white, like the stools we bought. Sand down the table tops"—he swept his hand across the scored surface—"and varnish them." He shrugged. "Or lacquer them white. Or any other colour."

"Would you paint them with a brush?" Rosy said,

remembering the mess Mum had made with gloss paint on the kitchen door.

"Nope," Frank said. "With special paints and lacquers. We'd just need to hire a spray gun and compressor. Perfect finish. Faster too. I did a job like that for Ernesto."

Rosy smirked. "I think that might be acceptable, Frank."

"But that's not a job I can do by Friday." He slid his artist's impression back. "And no time to go get your sofa either, sorry, baby." He pointed at the sofa he'd drawn from the IKEA catalogue.

"We need to think up a new name for the cafe, so I can okay it with Phyllis," Rosy said.

"Nope," Frank said. "Cafe's got a name."

"A terrible one," Rosy said.

Frank stood up. "No, Rosy. I said no. I said no."

Customers were staring.

"Okay, keep your hair on," Rosy said, shushing him with her hands. "I'll use Tasty Bite then."

"For?"

"For baseball caps and T-shirts," Rosy said. "New uniforms."

"No," Frank said. "No Tasty Bite uniforms. No baseball caps. No T-shirts. No."

Hadn't he agreed to a tight T already? He was happy wearing a baseball cap.

He held his hand in front of her face. "No uniforms."

Rosy shook her head and sighed. "Okay, Frank. But you break my heart with all your stupid objections." Then she dropped her voice and said, "Between you and me, it's unattractive, childish, and probably why Mum left you."

She marched across to the counter and stared back at him. He'd tipped his head back and his arms hung down by his side.

Truth hurts.

———————

The job for the evening was to go buy filler, undercoat, paints, and patterned wallpaper, then come back and fill and undercoat all the walls.

Rosy found wallpaper with a bold swirl in B&Q, but Frank put her off by telling her wallpaper was like tattoos—seemed like a good idea at the time, then a pain to get rid of. Rosy picked a colour for the highlight wall instead.

"Are you sure, baby?" Frank said.

"Oh, yes," Rosy said. "Got to be bold," she said, then stepped behind Frank, wrapped her arms around his waist and rubbed his beautiful belly.

"Oh, Rosy, baby," Frank said when they were in the van. "You found my weakness." He wrinkled his nose up and patted her leg. "You've just gotta give me another belly rub."

Rosy smiled at him and almost cried. "I'd like nothing more, Frank," she said. "But not tonight. Tonight, I have to draw up a plan for Phyllis."

---

Rosy sat staring at a spreadsheet that contained nothing more than the items she could remember from yesterday's fifteen minute planning brainstorm.

Why couldn't she concentrate?

*Oh, Rosy, baby. You found my weakness.*

And Frank's weakness was Rosy's weakness too. Genetic. *The drug of perfect love*, Marek had said.

She replayed the memory of Frank at the cash-and-carry, reaching for the box of Kettle Chips. She remembered the phone conversation when Frank was in the bath, and he talked about washing his belly, saving the best bit to last.

Was that the best bit? She remembered him standing in his T, no underpants.

Rosy covered her eyes. Jeez. She was losing control.

And she had to finish this plan. Frank was utterly opposed to a uniform, but if she removed that line item, then there'd be even less to show Phyllis. How else could she pad this out? Maybe a graph of future target revenues? Maybe some of the sandwich fillings they expected to include?

In the spare bedroom, Findlay began to play *Captain Pugwash* on the accordion, and all Rosy could think of was Frank and his arms, legs, belly, and—

Snuggy. Rosy would walk Snuggy. Then she'd be able to concentrate.

---

Rosy sat at a bench outside, Snuggy at her feet, her eyes staring up at the collapsed remains of that kite in the tree, her mind on

Frank.

She realised now, she'd loved Frank the first moment she'd seen him. Love at first sight really was possible.

A jogger ran past, checking her pace on her watch, and Snuggy scrabbled to get up onto Rosy's lap.

Then Rosy felt a nip at her leg.

"Did you bite me—?"

Snuggy stared up at her, a fold of her jeans clenched in his mouth. Then, still making eye contact, he began to rub his crotch slowly up and down.

"*Ewww*, get off me, you dirty little mongrel," she said, and smacked his nose.

Eyes still on hers, teeth still locked in her jeans and now growling at her, the dog clung to her leg and pumped his little body.

Rosy stood and hauled on his lead and Snuggy snapped and barked at her, furious. Despite his size, she was trembling with fear.

Jeez. Raped by a sausage dog. "What's got into you? You dirty beast."

Dirty beast. Like Rosy, with lust on her mind.

*Act on it*, Marek had said.

She may not be able to help these crazy feelings for Frank, but she had to rise above sex.

First thing Friday morning, Rosy dropped off her three-page plan with Heidi, Frank's interior designs attached. Thank God for Frank's designs. With those to distract, it looked halfway decent.

Rosy's phone rang at 9 a.m. and her stomach shrank. She'd expected to see Phyllis's name, but the number was unrecognised. Even so, Rosy knew at once who was on the other end and what that call was about. The number began 47. An international call. From Norway. She silenced the ringer and let her answering service take a message.

An hour later, Rosy's phone rang again, again with the Norwegian number. She apologised to her customer, and when she had a free moment, she switched the phone to silent operation.

N-BioCom wanted an answer, but Rosy wasn't ready.

When, just before midday, the shop phone rang, Rosy thought for a moment that N-BioCom had managed to trace her to the cafe. This time the call was from Phyllis, and, boy, was she pissed.

———

Rosy clutched the phone to her ear, pressing hard so nobody else could hear, her sweaty hand sliding on the plastic.

"If I'm perfectly frank, Rosy, this looks like homework done at the school gate," Phyllis said. "Take away Frank's drawings and there is nothing of any substance here. Not a damn thing."

Even though Rosy knew the plan was lacking, Phyllis's words couldn't have hit harder if they'd been delivered with a slap. Rosy's heart thudded in her chest. "I'm sorry, Phyllis. You see, my stepdad was playing the accordion last night, and I already had a headache and couldn't concentrate—"

"You'll be blaming the dog next," Phyllis said.

Frank rubbed the small of Rosy's back and gave her a sympathetic smile.

Rosy bit her lip.

"This," Phyllis said, "is just nowhere near the standard of your first report. Nowhere near. And you know it. There's no point meeting to discuss this because there's nothing here. If you've lost your enthusiasm for the endeavour, tell me now, and we'll part company"

"I haven't lost my enthusiasm," Rosy said, desperate now to keep the cafe option open, in case... in case... "I couldn't be more enthusiastic. My mind has just been on the practical side. You'll see we've repainted the exterior—"

"I repeat," Phyllis said. "Your role, Rosy, is to stay in control. You are simply not in control unless you know what your plan is. And don't tell me you know what your plan is, because if you knew, you'd be able to write it down, and we would not be having this conversation."

Rosy stared up at the ceiling. The woman was right. She was right, damn it. "I understand."

"Good," Phyllis said. "If you can't do the job, you'll be passing the baton to Marek, and our relationship will revert back to chocolate Santas."

# Boog

Boog walked into his bedroom to find Crawford sitting with Boog's laptop open at a porn site. On screen, a flabby red-haired woman licked her lips, a baseball bat clamped between her pocked legs. Next to her, a form with payment details filled in. And on the computer desk lay Boog's open wallet.

"Thanks for that," Crawford said. "Your home address, all written out for me." He shook his head. "You know it's amazing the personal things you can find inside a guy's wallet." He shoved his fingers in and pulled out a flosser pick, then Boog's condom.

Boog grabbed his wallet and snatched back his debit card and the condom. "Crawford, if you've signed me up for anything…"

Crawford got up and shoved past him, pinched Boog's cheek. Boog knocked his hand away.

"Fifteen hundred quid buys one fuck of a lot of hardcore porn and toys," Crawford said. "But, no. I didn't use your name, *Ben*. Just your address and card details. The recipients are your mum and Andrea. Is that your little sister's name? Andrea?"

Boog closed his eyes. The transactions would clear. Mum had put money in his account for the car repairs.

"Now we're even, Boog. Or we will be, come delivery. Come delivery, arsehole."

———

Boog tried Jen's door a few times, but the girl wasn't there and when he went for a pee, his anger cooled as his bladder emptied. If Boog stooped to Crawford's level and handed over that spy cam—

A slap landed on the bathroom door. "Come on, Dumbo," Crawford said. "Stop stroking your bloated little trouser maggot. I'm bursting out here."

Why, exactly, was Boog holding back?

He flushed, washed his hands, and unlocked. "All yours, Crawford."

Crawford pushed into the bathroom, Boog stepped out, waited to hear the click of the lock, then ran to Crawford's bedroom, and for once, he had an even break.

---

Back in his own room, Boog finished a question from last year's Chemistry exam, then set his pad and paper aside, and picked up his laptop. The wording for the letter flowed like sewage from a treatment plant, and when he printed it and read it back, he smiled. He folded the letter into four, slid it into the Jiffy bag with the spy cam, sealed it, stuck on a new label, then nipped out and down the hallway to post the package through Jen's letterbox.

Now, all he had to do was wait for the nuclear blast that would turn Crawford into a shadow.

Janek, again, was Boog's benchmark. Boog had shortcomings too. Some people had no appreciation for nice guys.

# Rosy

4:45 p.m. Rosy had stopped looking at her phone so had no idea if N-BioCom had called again. She should be on the bus home by now to work on the plan for Phyllis, but knew she wouldn't be able to concentrate. She was too hyped about tomorrow's hill walk, their first real father-daughter adventure. Frank, also, was raring to go.

And Rosy wanted to be in the cafe this evening to paint the walls. Frank had already made a start, doing the cutting-in with a two-inch paintbrush on one wall in the neutral shade, while Rosy used his power drill to mix the paint for the highlight wall.

Rosy, painting. Her mum would be dumbstruck.

"Wow," Frank said, when she rolled her first test stripe. "That's just… wow."

"Wow," Rosy agreed, and her earlier certainty wobbled. Teal. An iridescent finish. Brazen and brash. "Is it too… wow?"

"No," Frank said. He came over to double-check her painting platform was secure, then patted her leg. "Do the cutting in around the edges first, baby, like I showed you." He blinked. "Wow."

She mussed his hair, then clambered down to get a two-inch brush for herself.

Now, Rosy smelled of Frank, too. The moth-eaten Fred Perry T-shirt she wore for painting was an old one of Frank's, and not part of Alan McAdam's donated wardrobe. A little girl, drowning in her dad's shirt. She smiled.

She climbed back onto the paint platform and began to do the cutting in.

"You could make a design for the wall, Frank," she said.

"*Pfff.* My diary is already booked out solid, baby, and so is yours," Frank said. "Oh, and you need to make sure Irene knows you'll be staying with me next week."

Rosy's brushing stalled. "Oh, yeah?"

"Yeah," he laughed. "Oh, yeah. I'll be needing your full

attention, all night, every night."

Rosy swallowed. "Why's that, Frank?" Her voice had no volume. Was he hoping to give her his full attention? She remembered him standing calmly in his T with no underwear. That'd be a lot of attention. Her hand began to shake at the thought of them alone in that tiny flat. She pulled back from the line.

"I think the T gave the game away, didn't it?" Frank said.

Rosy's breath had halted.

"Couldn't be more obvious, right?" He laughed. "Doesn't take a scientist to work out what I was up to. After I just left it dangling down like that. But I knew you wanted a sign, baby, soon as I saw how you were looking at me. We're on the same wavelength."

Genetic Sexual Attraction was a two-way street. She'd read all about it on the internet and was an expert now. There'd been bad stories, regretful people. She'd ignored those. Ignored the advice to resist, swept up in Marek's enthusiasm: *Who else will Frank ever feel so deeply for?* Who else would Rosy ever feel so deeply for?

She clutched the neck of his old Fred Perry to calm down.

"Look at you, all worried." Frank laughed. "Whatever picture you have in your mind, forget that picture. Because I promise you, it'll be better. It's not gonna be cheap and tacky. It's gonna be classy and beaut'ful. But we have to keep it a total secret."

"As secrets go, it's a biggie," she said.

"It's a biggie, all right. You don't know the half of it." Frank laughed at his own innuendo. "I'm going to surprise you in a really good way. You might even cry when you see this beauty go up." He tugged at the crotch of his overalls.

Rosy steadied herself against the wall and for a moment, she thought she would topple from the platform. Frank didn't notice. He was busy painting, totally relaxed, lacking the judgement to know any better.

"Nobody can know what we're up to. We'll sneak off to my flat," Frank said, "and we'll let people think we're just having dinner, building jigsaws. You mustn't breathe a word about what we're really doing." He shook his head. "*Pfff.* If Phyllis found out, she'd string me up by the balls—" He ducked his head. "Oops, language. Sorry."

"I think we can talk frankly as adults now, don't you?" Rosy said.

He fell silent for a while then said, "Could I wear my wolf's ears? Not now. I mean when it's just the two of us?"

Rosy wanted to say, *I can't go through with it.* But when her lips moved, she said, "Yes," then nodded, not sure if he was watching her. "'Course you can. Like Jen said, you look... hot in your wolf's ears."

Rosy climbed down off the platform. "Well, I'm happy with the paint colours," she said. "Just going to use the ladies."

She slipped into the toilet, bolted the door and stared at herself in the mirror. Oh, Jesus. This was going to happen. It was going to happen despite Rosy. Because Frank wanted it and Frank got what he wanted.

But didn't that make everything easy again?

*Take responsibility for your own life,* Marek had said.

She wouldn't. She'd let Frank take responsibility. Let him be a dirty beast, an animal.

If they took precautions, nobody else needed to know.

------

Back home, after dinner at Frank's, Rosy retired to her bedroom and took out her phone. Four missed calls from the Norwegian number. She dialled the answering service. One new message:

"Urgent message for Ms Rosy Friendship. Rosy? Arvid Madsen from N-BioCom here. We sent you already a letter and multiple emails to advise you have an undergraduate placement. We need confirmation today, please, if you wish to accept your placement, otherwise we must release it sadly to another applicant. Please call back as soon as you get this."

He gave the number twice then added, "Even if your wish is to decline, your call would be appreciated. Thank you."

9:42 p.m. Too late.

Multiple emails. The email address she'd given them had been lost when Mum had changed internet service providers.

But N-BioCom wasn't important. Rosy had found something that mattered far more:

Love.

Whatever happened between them wasn't Rosy's fault. Not Frank's either.

*It is not a sexual deviation. It does not mean there is something wrong with you.*

*If I could experience the drug of perfect love... I would take it.*

She opened the Lloyds Pharmacy bag and, fingers trembling, took out the box of Durex Elite. On the bus, she'd already opened the cellophane. The condoms came in strips of two. Might not need these until Monday, but just in case... She slipped a strip into her smaller backpack for tomorrow's hill walk, then added a change of knickers, and the pack of Simple cleansing wipes from her toilet bag.

Toff, her teddy bear, was staring at her, eyes wide, horrified. She turned him to face the wall.

Frank Friendship couldn't be denied. Rosy's very existence proved that.

# Chapter 34
## Ascent
### (Saturday, 25 June)
### Rosy

Saturday. The day of their hill walk. Rosy slipped out of the house at 7:00 a.m. Frank was waiting for her in a smaller Shawford van.

She didn't lean over to kiss him as she had kissed Ruben on that earlier trip, just squeezed his knee.

"Do we have any music?" Rosy said, and reached for the radio.

Frank put his hand on hers. "Leave that off, baby," he said. "It makes things dance in the road."

She guffawed. "Dancing deer? Dancing rabbits?"

Frank laughed too. "I meant synaesthesia, not a badger, breakdancing over the roof."

But for some reason, the image of a badger spinning across the top of the car had set Rosy off. The laughter clamped her chest, stopped her from breathing properly, so funny and so sore her eyes had started to stream. Then, just when she thought she might be able to bring herself back under control, Frank gave her a sour look that set her laughing again.

"Man," Frank said. "I hope I don't say anything that's actually funny, or I'll have to shampoo your seat."

———————

The roads along Loch Lomond wound this way and that. She remembered from Ruben's drive, but Ruben couldn't bear to be behind anything and kept overtaking on blind bends. Frank made rapid progress, and at times went too fast also, throwing the van into wooded bends that made Rosy hang on. But Frank waited for sensible places to zip past caravans and tractors. The loch stretched out to their right and then speckles of rain turned into a deluge the wipers couldn't keep up with.

"Nice day for it," Frank shouted over the drumming on the roof.

Let it rain. Rosy had the sun right next to her.

# Findlay

Findlay lifted the phone ready to tell whoever it was that Irene wasn't at home.

"Hello, my friend."

"Marek?" Findlay grinned. "You are a fucking genius. You want to see the ideas I'm coming up with. It's unbelievable."

"I'm delighted to hear that," Marek said. "Maybe it's time for another tip, to boost you higher still?"

"Are you kidding? I'll be in orbit."

Marek tutted. "We cannot have that. Orbit is round and round. You must break free of orbit to reach the stars. I think you do need another tip."

"Same place, same time next week?"

"There is something else I need to speak to you about," Marek said. "Can you be at Cafe Royal for opening time today? 11 a.m. And of course, I will be buying the beers."

# Rosy

They hit slow-moving traffic and arrived at just after 9:30 a.m. Rosy remembered this car park, and her relief on coming back to the car last time.

Beinn Narnain was the first and last Munro she and Ruben had climbed together. Ruben had already bagged it months previously and no doubt that had contributed to his mood the whole day, because it "didn't count". Rosy hadn't been as fit then and had straggled, holding him back. No bra and a new T-shirt had been a major mistake. By the time she and Ruben had got back to the car, her nipples were so tender, she felt every movement of her arms.

Today, in her sports bra, Rosy was prepared. "This is it," she said.

"Do we park here then?" Frank said, then rubbed her arm. "You okay?"

Rosy nodded. "We park here then cross the road to the path. And, yes, I'm okay. I'm great, Frank."

---

As before with Ruben, the hill walkers they'd seen in the car park and at the base of the hills headed off in a different direction. Rosy remembered the name of the lower peak Ruben had mocked: the Cobbler.

Frank pointed at the people heading the other way. "Cobblers," he said.

That made Rosy laugh again, and Frank looked bemused. "You've got the giggles today."

"Nervous laughter," Rosy said.

The downpour by this time had eased back to no more than a delicate swirling drizzle.

Frank picked up Rosy's hand. "You don't ever need to be nervous about me, baby," he said.

She had to look away. The Ruben who'd descended this hill was a lesser human being than the Ruben she'd set out with.

But Ruben was a boyfriend, nothing more. Frank was irreplaceable. If she let him—

"Say something, Rosy. When you don't speak, it's not as easy to work out what you're thinking."

She pointed up the hill.

———

Trouble began about an hour into their walk. Rosy, fitter now than on that climb with Ruben, enjoyed staying ahead of Frank. She'd stopped to look back, then spotted him coming towards her, waterproof trousers and coat gone, now wearing a T-shirt, and a pair of red shorts way too tight. Way too tight.

"What's up, Frank?" Rosy said, her gaze firmly on his face, not down below.

"I'm not sure these fit me anymore." He pointed at his shorts. "They're kinda tight around here." He rubbed a hand around his crotch and thighs.

Oh, Jesus. Frank's bulge was massive.

"I heard a noise. Can you check my shorts haven't split up the back?"

Rosy covered her mouth. "Can't you tell yourself?"

"Not easily," he said, and turned his butt to her. "Can you check?"

The shorts were intact but his buttocks were so clear, the red might have been sprayed on.

"Perfect," she managed, then set off.

# Findlay

Marek set Findlay's beer down. "I believe your homework has been effective? Has the exercise sparked any ideas for your show?"

"Has it ever," Findlay said. "I put my skills together, combined them, like you said."

He turned the pad around and watched Marek intently.

The man smiled, and Findlay laughed. "Well?"

"These are fascinating. *Ventriloquist Accordionist.*"

"That'd be hilarious," Findlay said. "It's the kind of thing that'll make people say, '*What the fuck?*'."

"Yes," Marek said. "It had that effect on me."

"And then you've won their hearts, haven't you?" Findlay said. "They have to find out more."

"Indeed," Marek said, and returned Findlay's pad. "These are ideas to bank, and decide later if we follow them through. Your new assignment is to take something mundane and reverse the normal expectations. For example, dog trainer. What if the dog stood there, waving its paws and a man with a collar on his neck jumped through hoops?"

Findlay gaped as half-a-dozen new ideas parachuted down from the brain he thought had crash landed. "*Aw*, man. You are the business. High five."

Marek high-fived him.

"Do you have a mobile phone, Findlay?"

Findlay shook his head. "I know this is gonna sound bad, but I don't really have any friends."

Marek pointed at his own chest. "What about me?" he said. "I feel hurt."

"Present company excepted."

"You should have a mobile phone so we could share inspiration when it strikes." He smiled. "I have an old handset. I shall bring it for you next time."

What a guy.

Findlay watched Marek sip his Guinness. He exuded charisma. How old was he? Mid-twenties? Ten years younger than Findlay, maybe? And such a wise head on his shoulders. Findlay would buy the next round. It was past his turn.

"I'm afraid there is a less pleasant topic we must discuss now, Findlay," Marek said, his eyes worried.

Findlay felt his smile slip. "Oh, yes?"

"It concerns the nature of the relationship that has developed between Rosy and Frank."

# Rosy

Sweat ran down Rosy's back. From a wet start, the day had become baking hot, the only relief came from the occasional eddies of wind around the hill. She didn't want to stop here, not here where she and Ruben had sat that day. But she'd lost Frank.

Rosy took in Loch Long far below, then unshouldered her backpack and sat. Her watch told her they'd been ascending for two hours.

Where was Frank?

She gave him a few minutes more then walked back down a ways, but when she saw him, she saw he'd taken off his T-shirt, and the wave of desire that ran through her sickened her.

"*Pfff,*" Frank said. "I'm not as fit as I thought. Need to do more aerobic again." He had those stupid wolf's ears in his hand and he clipped them on.

"Still some way to go," she said, eyes on the fake wolf fur.

"Hot," Frank said.

"Well, don't get sunburned."

She rummaged in her pack again and handed him out the sunscreen. She didn't allow her gaze to drop from his face. "Rub some on your neck and shoulders."

He read the instructions, sniffed at the bottle, "Coconut. Tasty," hauled off his backpack, handed the bottle to Rosy, and turned his back. Feet planted, he stuck his arms out by his sides. "Squirt me."

Ruben's back had been muscular—glamour photography muscular, male model muscular. After their Prague holiday, when Rosy flipped through their photos with Jen and they reached the sequence of Ruben at the hotel pool, Jen took control of the laptop, and at each picture sighed, "*Mother-of-God.*" And when Rosy dumped Ruben for Boog, Jen had clamped her hands over her mouth and staggered wide-eyed around their lounge, moaning as though Rosy had shot her in the face. Ruben, perfect as a sculpture, left Rosy cold. Boog's hefty frame stirred Rosy's emotions. But Frank, muscular yet soft, bulkier by far than Boog, yet solid… Mother-of-God.

Rosy pumped the spray until first a creamy white spittle, then a mist of the liquid dampened the smooth foothills of his shoulders.

"Cold," he said.

Rosy's breath stalled when her palm touched Frank's burning skin, and she bit her lip at the easing rush in the crotch of her shorts.

"Oh, yes," Frank said. "Lovely."

No, no, no. This was her dad. Her dad, God damn it. And spraying him with sunscreen should be about as sexual as Turtlewaxing the Fiesta.

"I like sunscreen. I like sunscreen a lot." He turned to face her. "Squirt me again." He grinned, and pointed at his belly. "You know what I like. Squirt lots and lots."

"Squirt yourself." Rosy pushed the spray at him. "I'll do my arms when you're finished."

He scrambled after her. "I'll do your arms, Rosy. Then I'll lie down and you can do my front."

Rosy turned on him, her breath short, face aflame. "I'm not doing your front, Frank. Got it?"

"Okay." He backed away. "Crabby. *'I'm not doing your front.'*" He mimicked, mumbled something about no point having a daughter, then cut himself off. "Look at all that yummy grass down there to munch on and see how bare this path is? But look." He pointed, shook his head. "Sheep poop. Glad I'm not the dumbest one up here."

A sudden fury descended on her. "Stop bringing yourself down, Frank. Stop it. You're not dumb. You're wonderful, and beautiful, and I can't bear to hear you criticise yourself," Rosy looked down at him and, down, down at the grass below, and the words lost their grip. "Oh, Frank. I love you so much, it hurts."

# Findlay

Findlay wasn't sure whether his head or his stomach would be the first to give out.

"And this GAS," Findlay said. "You're sure she has it?"

"GSA. Genetic Sexual Attraction," Marek said.

Sexual attraction to Frank. Findlay pressed his fingers against his eyelids. He felt he was about to lose his pint.

"It's not a disease, my friend," Marek said. "It is more pernicious and you do not need to catch it. In up to fifty-percent of such reunions, it is a sad but inevitable hazard. I didn't want to say anything until I was sure. I am sure now. She is in its clutches."

It was just so wrong. So sick. "What do we do?" Findlay said. "What do I do?"

"For now, be vigilant," Marek said. "For obvious reasons, you do not want to share that you got this information from me. Any criminal case will be stronger if you can say you had your own suspicions, and I can corroborate independently. I will be a silent observer, your informant, an agent in the enemy camp, with your family's best interests in my heart."

Findlay felt his eyes sting with gratitude.

Marek swilled the dregs of his Guinness around in the glass. "Frank is still married to Irene, isn't he?"

Wasn't Findlay low enough already? "I gave up talking to her about it. Why, what are you thinking?"

The Pole took a minute then said. "Idle thoughts, nothing more at this point. But it puts the criminal seal firmly on any relationship Frank might have with Rosy. He is her father. He is married to her mother."

"Oh, he's a criminal, all right. He'll end his days in jail for something, I promise you."

"I believe you, Findlay. You are a man of action. A man who keeps his promises."

# Rosy

*Rosy sighs with relief when she sees Ruben has waited for her. She takes a seat beside him and looks down at the grass and the loch below.*

*Ruben starts to kiss her.*

*"Not here," she says.*

*"What's wrong with you, Rosy? What's wrong with me?"*

*She kisses him to shut him up. He kisses back, ravenous, and Rosy's the meal. He pinches her nipple through her chafing T.*

*"No, Ruben, stop it."*

*But he's unzipped his trousers.*

*Rosy is horrified when he pulls out his dick.*

*"Suck me off," Ruben says. "I need this, Rosy. Just this. I need something or I'm going to fucking explode."*

*She stands up but he grabs her arm, then he pulls her head down to his crotch and his dick is against her lips.*

*"Do it, Rosy. Do it, or I promise I'll find somewhere else to shove it."*

*Rosy opens her mouth and in, in he goes until she chokes.*

*"Ah, at last. Ah, yes. Yes. Yes. Take it."*

*He shoves her face back and forth, back and forth until she doesn't know if she's gagging more on him or on her own saliva. All she can hear is the bilge squirting and slopping and the pressure drumming in her ears. It lasts two, maybe three minutes. He ejaculates on her face and into her eyes and in her hair. Wipes himself on her chin.*

*"Oh, fuuuhhhck, Rosy."*

*Then he kisses her and she tastes him. The girl Ruben says he loves. He's just used her like she's a hooker.*

---

Frank met Rosy's eyes, then he studied the sunscreen bottle, small in his hands. "Wow," he said. "Oh, wow."

"Wow? Is that all you can say?"

"Well, one minute you're crabby and won't squirt my front, next minute you love me so much, it hurts. I'm confused," he said. "But it's great. Wow."

"Great? How is this great, Frank? It's terrible. And what do I tell my mum?"

"The truth." He beckoned and before she could stop him, he hugged her, pressed her face against the soft down of his chest, laid his cheek on the crown of her head.

The truth? Rosy needed Frank to be her father. She didn't want this. She didn't. And she couldn't do it. "You love me too, don't you?" she whispered.

"I already told you I love you, didn't I?" Frank rumbled.

Pain. In her chest. And, just like love, she'd always assumed she'd never experience a broken heart. She'd found her father —the best thing in her life. Now, she had no choice but to walk away and try to forget him.

Frank was still talking, as though this weren't the parting of the ways, the end of everything for them.

"I love you, Rosy. I loved you from the first moment I saw you. You were so, so beaut'ful. Irene's gonna have to listen. You love me, not Findlay, 'cos you're still my beaut'ful baby, not Findlay's. Irene will have to take me back now." He gazed into her eyes. "We're gonna make her."

"Oh, Dad," Rosy sobbed—so grateful to be so confused— and held him as hard as he held her.

---

*When Rosy and Ruben descend and walk, still wordless, under pylons and past the substation, back toward their car, he breaks the silence. "And that's what happens if you tease a guy for long enough. A guy needs an outlet. Not hugs and kisses."*

*Rosy says nothing.*

*"Admit it. That was sexy."*

*Rosy ignores him.*

*"God damn you, Rosy. You're a fucking robot."*

# Chapter 35
## Pinnacle
### Frank

Frank looked out over the mountain. The wind raised spectral wisps that fizzed in his eyes. The band of his wolf's ears gripped his head like a hand, like his dad's hand when he was little, comforted him. Rosy, his precious Rosy, his newfound direction sat watching him, smiling at him, kinda happy, kinda sad too, stirring up his own emotions and making colours and shapes and noises not quite visible, not quite audible, yet there, eddy around him.

Today had been good, might have been perfect if only Rosy had rubbed that sun cream into his front.

"You okay?" he said.

"I'm fine, Frank. I'm better than fine. I'm always better than fine when I'm with you."

He was relieved her voice had gone back to almost the normal colours and lines. He picked up her hand and held it in his cumbersome fingers. Still perfect, like when she was a baby.

"I'm not sure why I need to stay at your flat next week," Rosy said.

"Told you already. We'll have to pull all-nighters. You'll understand when you see the size of the job."

"A job for the cafe?"

"'Course for the cafe." Man, he couldn't make sense of Rosy's behaviour today. They'd talked about this last night. The reason he'd left the T in the Tasty Bite sign dangling down.

"Tell me how Mum can bear to live without you?" Rosy said. "Tell me why she's with Findlay?"

Frank opened his daypack and reached into the bottom for

the plastic box with the sandwiches he'd made. "Cheese, tomato, lettuce and orchard pickle," he said. "Or... ham, cheese, tomato, lettuce and orchard pickle?"

Rosy laughed. "So they're both the same, except one has ham too?"

Frank loved the sensations when Rosy laughed. He mostly knew her sense of humour now.

He looked at her. She wasn't a child. Still, he could spare her the details. "Irene wanted me to do things I just didn't like to do. In the bedroom."

Rosy was giving him one of those mystified stares. *Aw*, fuck it.

"She wanted me to kiss her mouth. She wanted me to—" He didn't need to tell her everything. "She wanted me to have sex. And I didn't want to."

"Frank?" Rosy said. "Are you gay?"

That made him mad. "I do have a willy of my own, Rosy. It's right down here. I could show you the bits you haven't already seen." He poked it but the extra pressure on those too-tight shorts hurt his balls and made him angrier.

She was still staring at him.

"I don't want to look at women's fannies. I don't want to look at other men's willies," Frank said. "They're unhygienic." And ugly. So, so ugly. What was wrong with people? Once they'd seen genitals, why did they want to keep looking at them when faces were so much nicer? His eyes roamed the hills. "Everybody has a one track mind. Tits, fannies, bums and willies. Me? I'd be happier if more people discovered jigsaws."

Rosy pressed her fingertips to her temples and her mouth hung open.

"Can we just change the subject?" Frank said.

"Frank?" Rosy said. "Are you telling me you're asexual?"

He gazed into the sky, exasperated. "I'm not any kind of sexual, okay? The whole sex thing goes way over my head. It's supposed to be adult but everybody behaves like kids. And I just don't get it."

"Asexual means, you don't feel sexually attracted to men or women."

His gaze snapped back to his daughter. "That's a real category?"

She nodded.

"Okay…" he said. "In that case, I'm asexual." He grinned at his scientist. "I thought I just had another thing fucked up in my head. But now I'm asexual. And I have synaesthesia. And it's all thanks to you."

"And now, I'm really confused," Rosy said. "If you're asexual, why would you"—her voice lowered—"rape my mum?"

"Eat your sandwich first," Frank said and hoped that by the time she'd finished she'd have forgotten. Frank loved his daughter dearly, but like practically everybody else, her memory was utter shit.

# Chapter 36
## Descent
### Rosy

Rosy watched Frank's big legs thump their way down in front of her. She felt as though somebody had zapped her brain, because everything—everything—had shaken loose.

Their conversation last night had been about a job, somehow, although Rosy couldn't work out what that had to do with Frank leaving his penis dangling below his T. The mystery could wait until Monday.

She smiled watching him, those beefy thighs, the great supple bulge of his butt, the pack so small on his back. Frank was asexual. He was her father. She could admire her father. She could still love him. She could still hug him, guilt-free, like a big teddy bear. Like a big, beautiful teddy bear.

Rosy's smile shifted to a frown. What would drive an asexual man—a fourteen-year-old asexual boy at the time—to rape her mum? She'd tried to ask again but he'd pointed at a bird and told her to keep quiet or she'd scare it.

"Frank?" She ran up to him. "Franny has something in a biscuit tin."

He stumbled and almost fell over, then pushed his thumbs into his ears. "Don't say it. Please, don't ask me about that."

"I have to know, Frank." She pulled at his hand. "I have to know who it is."

Frank put his hands up as if she'd pulled a revolver on him. "It wasn't anybody, okay?" He bawled at her. "Because she never got born. She never got the chance to get born. Now, just stop asking me questions you won't like the answers to."

The baby was malformed. Oh, please, don't let that foetus be

Frank's baby.

Not Frank's baby by Franny.

---

Twisty roads, even surrounded by beautiful scenery, could grow tiresome and Rosy felt her stress levels drop once they were back on a major road. This was a time she was glad she couldn't yet drive.

Hey. Maybe Frank would take her for lessons.

She wasn't sure if Frank was still mad at her.

"I had a lovely day, Frank," Rosy said.

He thought about that for a while, then smiled. "Me too."

"Looks like you have some sunburn on your chest and belly."

He sighed. "Because somebody wouldn't do my front."

"I'll rub some aftersun in when we get back home," Rosy said.

He gave her a monster smile. "Okay. I'll remind you about that."

"I didn't mean to upset you… about Franny," she said.

His knuckles went white on the steering wheel. "Leave it."

They drove on in silence for a while, then Frank said, "You didn't say you'd help me get Irene back."

Rosy puffed her breath out through puckered lips. This again. "Mum isn't going to have you back, Frank."

"Why not?" He punched the side of the van. "I knew Findlay when we were at school. He had a teeny tiny little willy. He can't be giving her anything she'll miss."

Rosy gritted her teeth and tried not to imagine Findlay's teeny tiny little willy. No good. "I don't think this is just about willies."

"Well, what's it about then?"

"You know Heidi really likes you," Rosy said.

"I know Heidi has a one-track mind. If she was really interested in me, she wouldn't always be shoving her tits up and fluffing her hair. Heidi is after something else. I know it. I don't know what, but I know she is."

"Paranoia," Rosy said.

"Synaesthesia."

"Pardon?"

"That's how I know Heidi's no good. That's how I know Marek's no good. That's how I know Findlay's no good.

Synaesthesia."

Rosy sat forward. "You see colours and stuff? Is it when they talk?"

"It's not colours. It's sick. And it's not like it's all the time. But sometimes when they say stuff, normal stuff like 'Hello', or 'Have a nice weekend', or 'Stay the fuck away from us, you psycho'. I get this horrible fish taste and a feeling like I'm gonna be sick."

Rosy stared forward at the road. Was this all true?

Frank rummaged behind the seat, pulled out his wolf's ears, and clipped them on.

"Your boyfriend, Boog?" Frank said. "I think he's a good person."

And yet all Boog wanted was to feel her tits.

And all Rosy had wanted to do was tear Frank's clothes off.

Rosy hadn't been fair to Boog. She simply hadn't.

---

Frank refilled the van with petrol and parked in a hatched area marked private, not far from the Shawford office.

"You mean you're going to make me walk to your flat?" Rosy said.

"I could give you a piggyback."

"Or we could park in the street at your place?"

He looked at her as though she'd suggested taking a hovercraft. "It has to be here or somebody would know we took it."

Rosy gaped at him. "You didn't ask? You took a van and didn't ask?"

"Of course I didn't ask," Frank said. "They don't even like me driving the big van. I'm only supposed to use that for the cash and carry." He frowned. "It's gonna be tricky to sneak the keys back in, now my alarm code is limited."

"Frank," Rosy sighed. "Let's do everything by the book from now on, okay?"

"Might as well cancel next week, then," Frank said. "That's not by the book at all."

Next week. Rosy cringed at the memory of just this morning, when she'd thought she and Frank might be having all-night sex. How crazy was that anyway? Had she been doped? Or only duped? By Marek. "What's this secret job?"

"You've forgotten? Already?"

She shrugged. "No, it's not that. I thought I'd guessed what it was, but something you said made me realise I didn't. So what is it?"

"It's a surprise," Frank said. "Two surprises. Two big surprises."

# Findlay

Findlay undid his shirt button, rolled his sleeve up and bent his arm, fist balled to swell his bicep. He'd let himself go, but at thirty-four, he could bring it back. A naked accordionist had novelty value, and he could certainly play up the danger aspect based on what might get trapped in the bellows.

Knuckles wrapped on the bathroom door and made him jump.

"That's your Polish pal on for a chat. Handset's by the door."

Pal. Findlay had a pal. Fancy that?

"Hey, mate. How are you?" Findlay said, buttoning his cuff.

"Findlay, my great friend. This may be nothing but…"

"Go on, mate," Findlay said.

"I saw Rosy with Frank. They went hill walking alone today, and after an exhausting day, I would have expected Rosy to go straight home to recover."

"Go on," Findlay said.

"They just arrived back. I saw them park the van. They left holding hands. Frank was wearing shorts and his shirt was off. They were headed in the direction of Frank's flat."

*Aw*, fuck. "Are they in there now?"

"I do not have cameras inside Frank's flat, unfortunately," Marek said.

Findlay should call the police. He should do it right now, before they consummated this revolting relationship. But did he have the balls?

# Rosy

If Rosy had been asked what might happen today, she might have guessed that it would end up like this—with Frank stripped to his underpants. But she wouldn't have guessed how she'd be feeling about the whole experience: Not exactly like waxing the Fiesta but she felt safe and free of guilt, almost.

Frank stood with his arms stretched out and when Rosy squirted the first of the aftersun and smoothed it across his chest and down onto his belly, he wiped a tear from his eye.

Rosy looked at him. "Is it sore?"

"Nope," he said. "If Irene would come back, this is what I want."

"You could pay for a massage. Plenty of masseurs do home visits."

He looked down at her. "You have to help me get rid of Findlay."

"What do you mean 'get rid of'?"

"I don't mean kill him or anything. I just said I'd kill him so it'd always prey on his mind."

"Well, that's a pretty mean-spirited thing to do, don't you think?" She smacked his chest. "As well as stupid."

Frank laughed. "I told him I'd be watching him. I did at first. I told him I'd be waiting in the shadows for him and, one day, I'd step out and I'd snap his neck like a rotten branch. But I won't."

"Pleased to hear it."

"If it was back in the days before laws and stuff," Frank said, "then, I would have killed him."

Rosy winced. "You really hate him, don't you?"

"Yeah. But he hated me first."

Rosy squirted more aftersun and smoothed it on his perfect belly. "I think, Frank, you would easily find a nice lady prepared to give up sex just to have you around. You're beautiful." So beautiful.

"I just need Irene back."

"You really love Mum, don't you?"

He shook his head. "No," he said. "I never loved her. But she's mine."

---

Rosy pointed with a fork. "This is a tasty curry. Make it a bit hotter and it'd be perfect."

They sat at Frank's tiny table. Frank had his wolf's ears on. "Hotter." He scowled. "Everybody wants food to hurt. Why is that?"

Rosy shrugged. "Dunno." She looked at him. "Why can't you meet up with Findlay and Irene? Offer to take them out for a meal somewhere and just explain to them how you feel. Get all this stuff aired." She shrugged. "It seems to me you'd understand each other better."

"What's to understand?" Frank said. "She's my wife."

Rosy let the handle of her fork drop. "But you don't love her. You told me that. Findlay does love her. What's this about? Is it about hurting Findlay?"

"It's about right and wrong, Rosy," Frank shouted. He stabbed a fat finger at his table. "It's about truth and lies. It's about promises. Irene made a promise before God. She promised she would forsake all others. That means, she's mine. Mine, get it?"

"She broke her promise. She's not prepared to be that person for you," Rosy said. "This is like the cafe all over again. You wouldn't change. You dug your heels in and then—hooray— you saw sense. You relented, and it's better. Why can't you forget Mum?"

He pushed his plate away and gazed up at the ceiling. "I want Irene to come back because I didn't do anything wrong, and I want her to admit that."

Nothing wrong, except raping Mum in the first place.

"I want Irene back and I want you back," Frank said.

Rosy held her eyes on him. "I'm back, Frank."

"I want you back as a baby," he said. "I want you back to watch you grow up. I want you back to go to school and go on holidays and bury me on the beach. I want to buy you ice-cream and birthday presents and read you stories."

"I want that too but I don't have a time-machine," Rosy said. "And neither does Mum."

"That's what Findlay took away," Frank said. "That's what he stole."

"Findlay thinks you took Mum away from him in the first place—"

"No."

"That you were his friend and you only took Mum because Findlay loved her. You took her away to hurt him."

"That's not what happened. Irene wanted me. She did. She loved me. Me. Not Findlay Dickson."

"But she doesn't love you now," Rosy said.

He folded his arms. "Are you sure about that, Rosy? Did you ask her that direct question?"

# Findlay

A cushion smacked Findlay in the face.

"Don't bite your nails," Irene said.

He looked at her then saw Rosy in her face and had to look away.

"What's wrong, Findlay?"

He shook his head. "Where do you think your daughter is?"

Irene shrugged. "I don't know. But she's eighteen. Whatever it is, I'm sure it's perfectly legal."

If Rosy was with Frank, Findlay wouldn't just call the police. He would kill her. But before that, he'd fuck her himself.

---

*Findlay arrives home from a wet day on the building site to an empty house. No places have been set for dinner. Perhaps Irene is out walking Rosy.*

*That'll be it. Out for a walk with the little one.*

*He waits.*

*The hours pass and a voice in Findlay's head starts to whisper. Irene still loves Frank. She already admitted that. And the voice tells Findlay that Irene has shaken off her daze and realised Findlay is worthless, realised he only wants her, not her baby, realised she belongs with her husband, Frank —with tall, handsome, exciting Frank, the man she loves, not with short, ugly, boring Findlay. Findlay, the marriage-wrecker.*

*Findlay has been resisting checking whether the suitcase has gone, but he knows what he'll find when he opens the wardrobe doors.*

*Yes, it's gone.*

*And not dwelling on why, Findlay goes into his work tools and takes out his four-pound club hammer.*

*As Findlay drives and the wiper blades struggle, hatred and anger rise. Not just for Frank, but for Irene. And Findlay knows why he picked up that hammer. Because Findlay is going to bash in their heads.*

*He drives to Frank's flat and Frank buzzes him in. He just buzzes Findlay in, dripping water like blood, hammer and all.*

*The door at the top of the stairs is open and all the way up, Findlay's arm gauges the weight of the hammer.*

*He's really going to kill them. He knows he can. He knows he will. He'll bring that hammer down in Irene's face first so Frank has nothing.* Bam. *Then the baby.* Bam. *He'll leave the best to last.*

*But when he steps through the door, hammer raised, Irene is standing there in her coat, Rosy asleep in the push-chair.*

*"Goodbye, Frank," Irene says, then to Findlay, "Can you manage the suitcase, darling?"*

*Findlay waves the hammer at Frank, almost cries when he says, "Stay the fuck away from us, you psycho."*

*Frank's mouth turns down as though he might throw up. "I'll come for you and when I find you, I'll snap your neck like a rotten branch."*

---

*Down in the car, Findlay shakes too much to drive, horrified at what he almost did, at what Frank almost turned him into. "He kidnapped you. We have to call the police," he says.*

*"Forget it, Findlay. He didn't hurt anybody. Let's just go home."*

*"He's dangerous, Irene. He's dangerous and we have to put him away behind bars."*

# Chapter 37
# Virgin sacrifice
## Rosy

Rosy walked down to the bus stop by herself because Frank had "stuff to do". Not a job for Ernesto, but he wouldn't say what. Still holding out on her, damn it. After all today's revelations, he was still this tight little box she couldn't prise the lid off.

But Rosy had opened a box in her own head, and once it opened, there was nothing inside. Even the box itself had gone. The virginity box.

Sex before had seemed so complicated, so scary. She'd held Ruben at bay, because he'd always scared her, even before the assault. After what Ruben did to her, she'd given Boog no leeway. But there'd been another reason to hold Ruben in check. She'd only dated him because everybody else said how dishy he was. She'd dated Boog because...

Because he was just lovely. Sure he was overweight. Rosy liked chubby. She liked how he looked. He looked...

He looked sexy.

Sexy, God damn it. Boog wasn't a freaking teddy bear, he was a big handsome sexy man-beast. He turned her on, pushed her buttons.

More important, she liked him. He'd just had the misfortune to come along after Ruben, and to like her an awful lot, way too early.

Now, after what she'd gone through with Frank, sex wasn't complicated at all. And Boog wasn't scary.

And, God, Rosy was so, so horny.

---

Boog didn't answer until the sixth ring. Getting sloppy.

"Hey," Rosy said. "How's it going? I was thinking about coming over."

"Yeah," Boog said, "well, I'm studying."

"I was thinking we could… get together tonight?"

"I told you, Rosy, I'm studying."

"Are you still angry with me?" she wheedled.

"Is this a joke? You dumped me, remember? You dumped me."

Rosy started to talk but he'd hung up.

She redialled. "Can we have sex, Boog? Please. Now."

---

By force of habit, Rosy almost pressed Jen's number on the door entry system.

"Is that Janek?" Rosy said. "It's—"

The remote lock made a grinding buzz and she pushed the door open with a *snick* then headed upstairs.

Boog opened the flat door.

Janek leaned on the back of the couch with a piece of bread in his hand. The bread drooped beneath the weight of peanut butter. He grinned. "Hey, Rosy."

"Hey," Rosy said.

Crawford, too, was watching from the kitchen door, his arms folded.

"Hey, Crawford. Did you get your bridge fixed?"

He bared his top teeth. The gap was still there. "Don't worry," he said. "My revenge will come soon enough."

"Revenge? Do everybody a favour and grow the fuck up," Rosy said, "And for information, I dress in the bathroom, next time you want to plant a camera."

"The camera is your fat boyfriend's," he said.

Rosy put her hands on her hips. "I don't have a fat boyfriend. I have a beautiful boyfriend."

Boog took Rosy's hand and pulled her to his room.

"Did you tell Crawford and Janek that we'd be… doing it?" Rosy said.

He shrugged. "I think maybe they guessed."

The bed was strewn with papers and two textbooks lay open. One she recognised as *Chemistry* by Blackman, the other she wasn't sure of. Boog lifted stuff and deposited it on top of clothes lying around the bed. It didn't smell too fresh, but she guessed by the time they'd finished, it wouldn't matter.

Boog held up his hands. "To be clear, you still want to have sex?"

Rosy nodded.

"And you said *boyfriend*. Am I still dumped?" he said, but before she could answer he held his hand over her mouth. "Doesn't matter. Where do you want me?"

Rosy rolled her eyes. "Should we try the bed?"

---

If Frank's body was a polished marble statue, Boog's was the sculptor's rough first pass, but when he dragged his shirt up to expose his furry belly, Rosy's eyes moistened. She helped him pull the shirt over his head, then locked her mouth over his and groaned. She pulled away. "Toothpaste," she said.

"Curry?" Boog said. "I prefer yours."

Rosy still wore her T-shirt and sports bra from today's climb. Skank. She pulled off the T.

"Love this," Boog said, and pointed at the bra. "Super-sexy. How do I get it off?"

"I'll deal with that," Rosy said.

Boog's mouth found hers again, kissed her. "You were right," he said.

"What about?"

"I wasn't applying myself." He kissed her neck and shivers cascaded down her collarbone. "I've been in a daze." He kissed her ear and she gasped. "All I could think of was you," he whispered.

Rosy swirled her hands through the fluffy soft hair of his belly. "Your tattoo kinda scared me off. I panicked," she said. Her hands had found his belt buckle and she unlooped the leather flap, pulled it and failed to free it.

"I'll do that," Boog said. "I've been letting myself go. I've started at the gym. It's helping…"—a kiss on the back of her neck beneath her hairline—"my concentration."

Rosy looped her fingers around the back of his jeans and pulled them. He levered himself up off the bed and she hauled the jeans, together with his underpants, over his butt. "Muscles are good. Muscles are great. Just don't go getting all skinny like

Ruben on me." Her hand found his lolling dick. "Oh. Well, that's not so skinny, is it?"

"No," he squeaked.

She shed the bra.

Boog gave a little whimper—"Oh, my God"—kissed her throat then laid a path of stepping-stone kisses down her neck, across the top of one breast then around it. He kissed underneath her nipple. "I'm finding out I knew more about the course than I gave myself credit for." He suckled her nipple, gave it a tiny bite then a kiss. "There's still a shit-load of work," he kissed between her breasts then moved over to the other side, and while Rosy's fingers gathered around his dick, he repeated the pattern. "But I can do it. It's achievable. Oh, I love your breasts. I love all of you but I love your breasts most."

"I love your belly. But this is nice too." She wasn't sure what in the hell she was doing, but what came to mind was a porno she and Jen had gaped at. She tugged him up then licked her thumb and slid it into the warm pocket between his foreskin and the head of his dick.

Boog gasped. "Ooh, that's nice. That's so nice."

At the door, Rosy heard shuffling and muffled laughter. At this stage, they could be filming with Crawford's spy cam and she wouldn't care, just as long as they stayed out.

Boog kissed down her stomach then her panties. He pulled her panties down.

"Oh, that's so, so pretty," he said.

He kissed between her legs and started a rush of pleasure there.

Boog kissed his way back up then grew serious. "There's no going back, Rosy, for either of us. If you tell me you don't want this, I'm gonna cry, but I have to ask. Do you still want to?"

She kissed his minty mouth again. "I've never wanted it more than now, and you're the one I want to do it."

Boog lumbered off the bed, his erection leading the way. She watched him open his wallet, take out a blue shiny square, tear open the packet and roll the condom on. The bed sagged when he climbed back on.

"Can I be on top?" Rosy said. "I just think it'd be easier."

For a girl who still had a hymen, Rosy had examined it more

often than was respectable. It didn't look like much at all, just a sort of an inner ring, no more than a membrane. It had been so important to keep that for her one-day prince. And here he was.

She'd thought it would hurt like hell but in the end it felt a little like the jab of a stitch when running. Boog was in her and she gripped him through her discomfort, enjoying grinding down onto him. She lifted her butt up and down—slowly, for her own sake, but Boog stopped her with an urgent gasp and a grab at her arm. She watched him tip his head back and grit his teeth then scrub his chin with his hand before looking back at her. "I don't think I'll be able to hold it in." He covered his face. "I gave up… you know… because I was doing it too often. I haven't spanked one off since… you dumped me."

Rosy smiled. "It doesn't matter, Boog."

"I want this to be amazing, Rosy. For you."

She held her hand over his lips. "It already is."

She rode up and down him slowly, pushing him deep. He lasted another minute of that. Then he cried out, his whole body shook, his chest and his belly shivered—

And Rosy felt something she absolutely should not feel.

She felt him spray inside her.

"Boog?" Rosy said, "How old was that condom?"

"What? Why?" His face had turned to ash. "A year. The date was good."

Rosy pulled off him and translucent milky liquid oozed from the nipple of the condom, and dripped off into her blood.

Boog covered his face. "*Ugh.* The son-of-a—" he said. "Crawford was in my wallet." His voice had become a whine. "He even said it: We'll be even, come delivery. Come delivery. He sabotaged my fucking condom."

Rosy heard a crazy, howling, hooting laugh at the door.

Boog's face had contorted in fury but she clambered over him, pulled the clammy condom free of him, pushed him back onto the bed.

"Rosy?" Boog said. "I'm sorry."

"He wanted to spoil this for you, Boog." She kissed him. "Well, we are not going to give that asshole the pleasure." She gripped his dick with her hand then guided him in.

"Rosy?" Boog said, "What if you get pregnant—?"

She had those condoms in her daypack, but it made no difference now. "I'll get a morning-after pill," she said.

Boog closed his eyes.

"Come on, baby," Rosy said and rubbed his fuzzy chest. "Forget Crawford. This is for us."

———

Rosy lay in Boog's arms. He looked so serene, so beautiful, she could lie there forever. But she had a confession.

She cringed. "I didn't ever tell you the summer placement with N-BioCom would have been based in Oslo."

He sighed. "I already knew, babe. Jen told me."

Jen and her big mouth again. Thank God.

"Well, I actually managed to get a placement," she said. "They wanted me to start there in a week's time."

He kissed her nose. "You've got to do it, babe. Just like I need to pass my re-sits. And get myself in shape." He shrugged. "It's our future."

She nestled against him. "I'm too late. I had to accept by Friday, and I missed the deadline."

Boog picked up her hand in his, and kissed it. "There's still time. There's always still time."

She blinked at tears. "I kinda need to get away," she said. "I know it's horribly selfish but I really do. Meeting Frank, it's messed with my head." She mastered herself. "I worry about leaving him, though. About what would happen to the cafe. He doesn't need me now. He just needed a catalyst." She laughed. "Frank is awesome. Except the cafe owner doesn't see that. Nobody seems to see that."

"It's a summer job so you'd have to finish some time," Boog said. "Why not talk to N-BioCom and say you'll start a couple of weeks later?"

Rosy kissed him. "Oh, I do love my cuddlemeister."

He studied her face. "Would you stay with me tonight, Rosy?"

"You mean you thought you were kicking me out? Boog, how could you?"

She closed her eyes and wondered what was going on in her belly right now. Had a baby Boog just popped into being?

# Chapter 38
## After
### (Sunday, 26 June)
### Rosy

In the morning, Rosy nipped out to knock on Jen's door, in urgent need of a change of clothes. Bad enough she'd have to visit a pharmacy for a morning-after pill without looking like the night before. She knocked again.

"She's at her mum's," Crawford said. He wore only Y-fronts. He clutched his package. "See anything you like down there?" he said.

"Crawford?" Rosy said. "You are just so much smaller than Boog." She flicked his crotch. "In, oh, so many ways."

"Least I don't have a sexually transmitted disease," he said. "Better get tested, that's all I'm saying."

---

Rosy had turned down Boog's insistent offers to drive her to the pharmacy. "I'll manage by myself," she'd said. "I'm not with-child. You need to focus on your work."

She made it through the door of the pharmacy only after an effort and when she was next in the queue at the counter, a hand to hold would have been welcome. "I was looking for," she lowered her voice, "a morning-after pill."

The assistant raised his eyebrows and gave a small, disappointed sigh. "There are a few questions I need to ask first, I'm afraid." He laid his fingers onto the counter and the gesture reminded Rosy of the church minister. "Is it less than seventy-two hours since you had unprotected sex?"

Unprotected sex. Crawford had tried to spook her about

diseases. "It's ten hours," Rosy said. She looked behind her. Nobody. But still. "Could we maybe go over there?" She pointed toward the dispensing area.

He shrugged, then gestured. "Sure. After you, Miss."

Rosy answered the questions in a daze. When it was done, he put a box and a leaflet in a dispensing bag and handed it to her. Rosy was walking away before she realised she hadn't paid.

He held up his hands, like the minister again. "In Scotland, it's free."

"Thanks again," she said.

"Good luck. Take it as soon as possible. And see your GP."

---

Rosy spotted her stepdad at the window and held tight to the daypack with her hill walking gear, the pharmacy bag stowed safely in a side pocket. She let herself in.

Findlay slid into the hall, white-faced and white-knuckled.

"Hey, Dad."

"Don't *hey-Dad* me. Look at the state of you."

"You look nice too. Where's Mum?"

He stopped her from going upstairs. "Never mind Mum. Where have you been all night? With Frank?"

Rosy shook her head. "No. Now if you'll excuse me? I'd like to have a shower and get changed."

---

Rosy sat on her bed, drying her hair with a towel, and staring at the orange foil package, at the single tablet in the centre. One poison pill for Boog's baby. Possible baby.

Ninety-five percent effective up to one day later. Eighty-five percent effective up to two days later. Fifty-eight percent effective on day three.

She'd searched on the internet and confirmed what she well knew. The most fertile days were midway through the menstrual cycle. Perfect timing. She touched her belly and imagined the egg splitting.

Her phone began to ring: Frank.

"Hey," she said. She shifted the daypack down from her Mr Men stool onto the floor, those condoms still in a pouch.

"What're you doing?" Frank said.

"Nothing much," Rosy said and managed to smile. "You?"

"Nothing much."

They both fell silent.

"Why are you phoning me, Frank?"

"Just to talk," he said.

"You're not saying a lot," Rosy said.

"Just to listen."

She rubbed her brow through her damp hair. "I don't feel much like saying anything."

"Okay," Frank said. "I have cakes. You could come have a cake. You could come have a cake and just say, '*Mmm.*'"

She closed her eyes and a tear escaped. She blinked it away. "Sold. See you in a bit," she said, and hung up.

Rosy smoothed her belly, looked at the packet again. How could an aspiring geneticist be sentimental about disposing of a few cells?

Ninety-five percent effective.

Against Boog's baby. Her baby. Frank's and Mum's grandson.

Possibly.

She left the tablet inside its protective foil, put the foil back in the box, the box in the pharmacy bag and the pharmacy bag in her underwear drawer.

# Findlay

Findlay blocked Rosy at the bottom of the stairs.

She'd put on perfume. He could smell it. "Where are you going now?" he said.

"Frank's made cakes," she said. "When Mum gets back, tell her not to worry about dinner for me. See ya." She barged past his arm.

"Rosy—?"

The door banged.

Findlay wondered if an ulcer were chewing a hole in his gut, if ulcers chewed holes. That's what it felt like: munch, munch, munch. The idea of Frank's dirty big mouth closing on Rosy's — Ugh. It made him want to throw up. Sex with her biological father? Ugh. He shuddered.

If Rosy was prepared to do it with Frank and had even been prepared to do it with that fat fuck of a boyfriend, then why not Findlay? Why not, eh?

Findlay put his fingers in his mouth and bit down, then tramped upstairs.

Why was he beating himself up about these urges? He was only human. And he was only Rosy's stepdad after all. No relation to her. Not even married to her mother.

Findlay walked into his bedroom and snatched up the picture of him and Irene.

Irene. He still loved her, but Rosy was so much... fresher.

He clattered the picture down.

There'd have to be something wrong with him if he didn't have these thoughts. She'd changed so much from when she was a girl. That bony, gaunt girl had filled out so magnificently —lips, tits, hips.

And now he'd gone and given himself a hard-on and wouldn't be able to service it without wondering if Frank was—

If Frank and Rosy were—

Fucking Frank-fucking-Friendship.

Findlay slipped into Rosy's room, and slid her underwear drawer open. He picked out a delicate little pink pair this time, the type of material—if he were very, very lucky—that hair might get trapped in. He sniffed them. Flowers, again. Might as well take a bra too. He pulled the drawer a little further and saw a paper bag.

A bag from the pharmacy.

Was Rosy on medication? On the pill?

# Rosy

Rosy finished her cake and wondered just how fat her mum would have been if she'd stayed with Frank. Rosy too, for that matter.

Frank patted his own belly. "There's a good boy," he said.

She smiled, pushed her plate away and sighed. "When you found out Mum was pregnant, what did you think?" Rosy said.

Frank frowned. "I thought, *uh-oh, I made a baby.* Then I started to think up names, but Irene had picked one already: Ross or Rosy."

"Didn't you think about an abortion?"

Frank shook his head. "I didn't. The subject didn't come up, so I guess Irene didn't either."

"But you were fifteen. Fifteen, Frank. There must have been a huge amount of pressure."

"Yeah." He nodded. "But mostly, I stayed back so she wouldn't kiss me and stuff."

Rosy squeezed his arm. "What would your life have been like if I hadn't come along?"

"I don't like to think about that," Frank said.

She watched him pick up the empty plates and cups. Grandpa's genes would be in her baby. Those big arms, the hefty wrists.

She followed him to the sink. "What are the two big surprises for next week?"

"You'll have to wait," Frank said.

"At least tell me one of the surprises."

"Nope," Frank said.

"You're pretty good at keeping secrets, Frank." She thought about Jen and her blabber mouth. And her own blabber mouth. Poor Boog.

Frank nodded. "I'm really good at secrets."

She leaned against the worktop. "When you're not working at the cafe and doing jobs for Ernesto, what do you get up to?"

"Secret stuff." He tapped the side of his nose.

Rosy sighed. "I have a surprise on the way too on Monday. I hope you won't be mad. It's something we need."

"An espresso machine?" Frank said.

She smacked him. "You ruined it."

"No, you ruined it, Rosy," he said. "And, no, I'm not mad. I hate the stink of coffee, but it's a beancounter's best friend. I already have one stinky friend."

"I hope that's Catman and not me," she said.

"You stank at the end of the hill walk," Frank said. "I didn't say because I thought I might not get a belly rub."

"Thanks." She must have stunk at Boog's. And she'd tasted of curry. How embarrassing. What a complete skank.

She studied him, still wondering what he did with himself all the time. Yes, Frank was very good at secrets.

"How would you cope if I quit the cafe and went to Norway," she said.

Frank shrugged. "I'd miss you, but I'd cope. Long as you kept in touch."

She nodded. "Oh, I'd keep in touch, don't you worry."

Frank patted her hand. "Keeping any other secrets, baby?"

"From you, Frank? Never."

Rosy smoothed her stomach.

Still ninety-five-percent effective, the pill.

# Findlay

Irene was back home, preoccupied with a self-assembly shelf unit when Findlay finally saw his slut of a stepdaughter come through the gate. He intercepted her at the front door, and walked her back down the path, so Irene didn't hear.

"You're hurting my arm," Rosy said. "What's this about?"

Findlay pulled himself to his full height. "You know incest is illegal, don't you."

"Why?" Rosy said. "Are you thinking about committing it?"

"We're not related. But you and Frank…" He glared up at her. "Why do you need a morning-after pill?"

Her slutty mouth gaped. "How do you know about that?"

Findlay had anticipated that one. "The nice pharmacist phoned to check you'd taken it."

She closed her eyes. "The nice pharmacist didn't even take down my name, *Dad*."

Not one Findlay had anticipated. He fell back to his original story. "I was suspicious. I searched your room."

She met his eyes, then looked away just before he chickened out.

"I'm eighteen," she said.

Findlay felt sick. "Just take the fucking pill, for God's sake," he said. "We don't want another one of Frank's monsters to take care of."

# Rosy

Rosy held Toff her fat teddy bear.

*We don't want another one of Frank's monsters to take care of.*

What did that mean? Rosy herself? Or the foetus in Franny's biscuit tin?

Rosy checked that the morning-after pill was still there.

Still ninety-five percent effective.

But only just.

———————

Able to think, at last, Rosy worked until 2:00 a.m., taking points from the Beancounter's book and transforming the list into a plan she hoped would be good enough to salvage her reputation with Phyllis. She also updated her original report, showing the before and after pictures she'd taken along the way.

One piece of Beancounter's advice was to run small ads in local papers and highlight an employee or a product, a differentiating factor. Rosy produced a profile for Frank, turning his bad people skills into a quirky asset, then read it back and had to scrap it because the only question it would leave in anybody's mind was, why wouldn't you sack somebody like that?

Frank's future was in his own hands. As was Rosy's. As was Boog's. All you could do was love people.

Rosy knew what was right for her own future. But she'd sleep on it.

# Chapter 39
# Found out
## (Monday, 27 June)
## Rosy

Rosy—never a light sleeper—had set two alarms, just in case, but the act of setting them seemed to set an internal alarm, and she woke at 5:55 a.m., five minutes before the first was due to go off.

Norway was only one hour ahead, but she called at 6:00 a.m. and was relieved to get the answering service; apologising to a machine, and asking a machine for a delayed start-date was so much easier than speaking to a real person who could ask awkward questions.

But her relief was brief and Rosy was on the bus when—too soon—the Norwegian number called again.

"I'm sorry," Arvid Madsen said, "but we cannot accommodate even a single day's delay. This running after people consumes far too much of my resources. I will need a yes now, or the place is gone."

Rosy bit her knuckle. "Are you sure there's no way to delay? Could you speak to Dr Stein?"

"Dr Stein? Our CEO?" the man said, and laughed.

"Dr Stein interviewed me himself," Rosy said.

"I cannot talk to our CEO about an undergraduate summer placement," Madsen said. "The notion is ridiculous."

And just as Rosy was about to throw a tantrum, she thought about silverback gorillas.

"I completely understand," she said. "I'd love to have started, and I'm only sorry I can't save you having to go around that tedious loop again. Oh, but maybe I can…" She paused as though the idea were only just occurring. "You know, I've actually been working on an entrepreneurial project here. Very much in line with the N-BioCom ethos."

"A project?" Madsen said. "A genetics project?"

"No, but with your permission, I could send an email to you and Dr Stein within the hour. It would explain why I'm duty-bound to complete this project before I start at N-BioCom. Just an idea… Might help all concerned…"

"You may send your email, Miss Friendship, but I'm not optimistic," Madsen said. "Not optimistic at all."

Rosy was optimistic. As long as Dr Stein got to the before and after pictures in her report.

## Findlay

Once Rosy had disappeared off to work, Findlay marched into her bedroom, drew open her underwear drawer and found the pharmacy bag. Still where it had been. He popped open the end and—

   — the fucking tablet was still in the fucking foil.

Findlay moaned and held his fists to his face. First Irene, now Findlay's Rosy. His sweet, sweet, beautiful Rosy.

Time to deal with this.

Past time.

# Rosy

The espresso machine arrived before the doors opened. It cost over two-and-a-half grand, half Rosy's entire budget from Phyllis, but when Rosy tore back the protective cardboard sheath, she beamed.

"It is exactly the colour of the highlight wall," Marek said. "You have a good eye."

"It's shiny, like a car," Frank said. "I like it. I like it a lot. Let's get it set up. Where's the coffee?"

"It will, of course, need to be plumbed in," Marek said.

Rosy and Frank said, "Will it?" at the same time.

Marek nodded. "I know a Polish plumber. And, no, I'm not kidding."

"Can he come in tonight?" Rosy said.

"As a favour for a fellow countryman, I am sure."

Rosy laughed and gave him the thumbs up, but when she smiled at Frank she saw he'd gone pale.

"Are you okay, Frank?"

"They'll have to run pipes?" Frank said. "Pipes up through the floor?"

"Certainly. They will have to lift up much of the floor," Marek said.

"Frank?" Rosy laughed. "What's the problem? You haven't been stashing bodies down there, have you?"

Frank just closed his eyes.

# Boog

Boog passed a maintenance man who was replacing a carpet tile in the library, and the man gave him a monster smile, and Boog smiled back. Everybody was smiling at him today— everybody—and Boog was smiling right back, walking with a bounce, and a confident bob of his head. Boog felt good. He felt better than good.

Having sex with Rosy, that had been a risk. That could have destroyed him, destroyed his concentration. But, no, he'd had his most productive morning so far. Keep this up and, come August, he might even be ready for the exam.

When he'd been taking off his clothes, he realised he'd had a fear. A fear that if Rosy were to actually see that belly she was so fond of, minus the shirts and pullovers, if she were to see those stretch-marks his mum had given him cream for, those marks like fingernail scratches, Rosy would be as disgusted as Boog himself. But Rosy's face had said it all. She really did think he was lovely.

That thunderhead over Boog for so long had broken and the sun was lighting every step.

And Jen had come back last night. At this moment, she could be taking a little look at Crawford's spy cam. That spy cam was just like any other memory stick. Files could be copied on as well as off. And that's what Boog had done. He'd left the recordings from Rosy's house on there, but he'd also copied back all the spy cam movies Crawford had made previously. All those movies of Jen.

The moral of the tale: If you're gonna be a bastard, always lock your laptop, even when you're just off for a pee.

Boog took his seat.

He'd found a nice image to cover the porno picture Crawford had glued to his *Chemistry* textbook—something that would always remind him of Crawford. Rows and rows of perfect, white, shiny teeth.

Even Boog's textbook was smiling. He cracked the book open at his page, and got back to work.

# Rosy

Rosy watched Frank pace back and forth. He asked her where the espresso machine would go, exactly. Wanted to know exactly. Couldn't the espresso machine go in the kitchen? He asked her that so plaintively, she began to talk through with him where it might go.

"In the kitchen?" Marek said. "Are you crazy? This must go on show. It must. It is magnificent. You are worried about a few pipes?" He pointed at the counter. "Here is where all eyes will be. Pipes through the floor will never be seen."

Rosy did like the way the counter floated, but all eyes really would be on the espresso machine.

"He's right, Frank," Rosy said. "That machine is for show, not for locking away in a back room. Beancounter's Handbook. A killer feature."

"Killer feature," Frank repeated and went back to pacing the floor.

---

Just before closing time, a stocky young dude in overalls came in. He and Marek exchanged a few words in Polish and they bumped fists.

Rosy winced at her own poor planning. "Marek? Would you mind supervising the cafe while the plumber works?" she said. "I'll pay overtime. It's just that Frank and I have long-standing plans for this evening—and every evening for the rest of the week."

"I do not want overtime. It will be my pleasure to supervise, if it will take Frank's mind off the floor." He smiled. "Besides, I want to be here the moment the first real coffee is brewed."

They deposited the day's takings at Shawford, then headed uphill, bound for Frank's flat. Frank kept looking backward toward the cafe.

---

Rosy finished her helping of rhubarb crumble, watching Frank.

"Delicious. I'm looking forward to this week. And I'm looking forward to the surprises."

His gaze flicked over her, distracted.

Was something bad hidden beneath the floor? She held her breath, then asked him. "What's the problem with the floor, Frank?"

He rubbed his face and she thought he might cry. "You need to see the surprises now." He lifted the dishes and deposited them in the washing-up bowl.

"Not going to wash those up first?" she asked.

"Nah. Let them sit," he said. "There'll be knives and things to wash later."

Knives and things. He meant knives and forks, cups and plates. Of course he did. Not bloodied knives. Rosy was freaking herself out. She needed to lighten the mood. "Haven't you forgotten something?" she said, and made the shape of ears.

He smiled, thank God, clipped them on and patted his head. "Good boy."

She rolled her eyes. "So, where do you want me to sit. On the bed?"

"The surprises aren't here, Rosy. The surprises are in my secret dungeon."

"Your... secret dungeon?" Rosy said.

He nodded. "Everybody thinks I spend my time in the flat." He shook his head. "I told you I'm good at keeping secrets."

Foo Fighters thrashed from Rosy's phone, and she practically fell over, didn't even register the caller. "Hello?"

"Rosy," Jen said. "This is about Findlay. It's not good."

"Jen, this is a really, really bad time."

"Just listen, babes, please... Crawford's spy cam in your bedroom. Well, it didn't just record you." Jen hesitated. "Findlay came into your room and—" She stopped "Babes, Findlay took a tissue with a lipstick print on it. Then he masturbated into it."

Rosy closed her eyes.

"It gets worse..." Jen said.

Worse? How could it get worse?

Rosy listened to what her friend had to say, then just said,

"Thanks, Jen."

One dad down… Rosy turned to Frank, struggling not to cry.

"What's up, baby?"

She shook her head. "A secret dungeon, Frank? If this is bad…"

He opened his front door and beckoned Rosy. "You first. Downstairs and stop at the bottom."

---

Rosy's shoes echoed in the stairwell. Her hand slid along the steel banister, and made a ringing noise. He'd switched on the landing light and it cast the shadow of a beast. Massive and with great animal ears. Horns, she thought. They're like horns. Frank's breathing echoed too.

And at the bottom of the stair, right there by the entrance, she realised, there was a door that looked as innocuous as a broom cupboard. Frank leaned against her as he unlocked the mortice. He clicked a switch beside the door but no light she could see had come on. "Okay, baby. You can go in."

Rosy stepped into a high-ceilinged space the same size as Frank's entire flat. This was, in effect, the ground floor of the flat. Once a stable, a stall still occupied one corner. A rectangle of sunlight cut through: the lockup garage door. In front, racks of weights and a weight bench inside a cage made of builder's scaffold. A mirror leaned against the wall, giant, with an old-fashioned frame. And shelves. Shelves against the three remaining walls, stacked with boxes, everything sealed or covered over so she had no idea what might be in there.

But her eye went to a box in the middle of the floor, and flat sheets of something, covered over in newspaper.

"What's under the newspaper, Frank?" Her voice was a whisper.

"That's the big surprise," Frank said. "See for yourself."

Rosy stepped into the dungeon.

"This was meant as a tribute to my dad," Frank said. "And when Beancounter's said about a killer feature, something just connected in my head."

Rosy lifted the newspaper and saw a curve of crimson and knew at once why Frank was so worried about those pipes.

A buzzer sounded somewhere.

"I'll see who's at the door," Frank hissed. "Don't make a sound."

A tribute to a child killer. She pulled the newspaper back and covered her mouth.

The dungeon door swung open and Rosy turned to see Frank, his face rendered skeletal by the light. "Baby? It's the police."

# Boog

Boog answered the door.

"Hello, Boog," Jen said, and smiled at him like a schoolgirl. "Is Crawford there, please?"

"Sure," Boog said. He called into the kitchen. "Crawford, Jen's here."

Crawford emerged, chewing. "Hey, Jen."

Boog retreated a step or two.

"Crawford?" Jen said, and took one hand from behind her back. "Do you recognise this at all?"

Crawford's mouth fell open. "No way. Is that Boog's spy cam?" He picked it up, then shook his head at Boog. "So Janek was right. You really did buy one, Boog?" He tutted. "Oh, you sad, sad bastard."

"I have something here for you too, Crawford," Jen said, and took her other hand from behind her back, her smile gone. "Have some pepper spray, you shitbag."

Crawford's mouth dropped open as a translucent fizzing liquid flowed over his eyebrows and nose and dripped down onto his mouth.

He blinked once, twice then screamed, squeezed his already red eyes shut and brought his hands up to protect himself, but Jen shoved the spray between his raised hands and emptied that sucker.

Boog could feel his own eyes and nostrils prickle and backed away from the stinging mist.

"Ssshhhhhhitbag!" Jen yelled, then threw the spray after Crawford's blinded, stumbling, retreating ass.

The girl breathed out, dusted her hands, then smiled. "Thank you very much, Boog. Oh, and can you tell him from me, please, he's dumped?"

# Chapter 40
# Confrontations
## (Tuesday, 28 June)
## Rosy

The police car dropped Rosy off at her house. She'd never felt so abused, so violated.

She slammed the front door, walked into the lounge, past Findlay and pulled the plug out of the TV.

Findlay sat with a mug of coffee in one hand, the remote in the other. She took them out of his hands, and slammed the mug down, spilling it over the TV guides, leaned into his face.

"Incest?" she said.

Findlay shrank into his chair. "I had to do something."

Rosy shoved his chest. "I have had to be swabbed by a doctor to check that I hadn't just been having sex with my biological father."

Findlay looked away, but Rosy turned his face back to hers.

"My boyfriend has had to come down to the police station with his two flatmates to swear that, yes, on Saturday night, I did have sex with my him, and, yes, the condom did leak."

"Your boyfriend? The big fat kid. Oh, thank God."

"Thank God?" Rosy was so furious her voice shook as though her throat was about to detach from her chest. "No. What you should be thanking God for, Findlay, is that I didn't tell them to come check out my stepdad. My stepdad who goes through my knicker drawer. My stepdad who whacks off at my dresser mirror." She shoved him again. "My stepdad who comes into my bedroom at night, sits on my Mr Men stool and masturbates right next to me when I'm asleep." She shook her head.

"Where the fuck is the man who brought me up? Where is he? The man who used to take me to school? Or were you sniffing my knickers back then too?"

"No," Findlay said. He had started to cry, but she was too angry to stop.

"In all your endless hours of reality show drivel, Findlay, have you ever heard the word *asexual*?"

He blinked, then blinked again.

"Do you know what that word means?"

"No," he said. "Somebody who's into himself?"

"It means, having no sexual desire. None. And what I found out is that Frank, my mother's alleged rapist, is asexual. Now do you see why that doesn't make much sense to me? Somebody with no sexual desire rapes my mother?"

"No sexual desire?" Findlay said. "Did he tell you that? If he did, he's a liar and you're a fool."

"Where's Mum?"

"I don't know," he said. "She went to B&Q, I think." He rubbed his head and his hand shook. "No, I remember. She came back. She's just out walking Snuggy."

---

Mum had let Snuggy off the lead—not something Rosy ever did—and was sitting on a bench.

"You're here," Rosy said.

Her mum sat up, hand to her breast. "Rosy? Has something happened to Findlay?"

"What?" Rosy said. "No. He's… No."

"Oh, thank God." Mum closed her eyes then opened them and frowned. "So… what are you doing out here?"

"We need to talk," Rosy said, and sat beside her mum.

---

"Remember a long time ago," Rosy said, "might have been five years, there was a documentary on TV about asexual people."

Her mum frowned. "No. I could barely remember a documentary from five days ago."

"But you know about asexual people, don't you? People who experience no feelings of sexual attraction?"

"I do actually remember that documentary now," Mum said. "The girl who's boyfriend wasn't allowed to—" She touched her mouth. "Oh, Rosy. Are you asexual?"

Rosy held up her hands. "Oh, my God, no. Not me." She picked up her mum's hand, and her mum stared at her. "Hasn't the penny dropped yet? It's Frank. Frank is asexual."

Mum stood up, pulled away. "Snuggy," she shouted. "Snuggy."

Rosy took her mum's arm, turned her. "Was it really rape, Mum?"

"Yes." Mum started to march across to the dog, and Rosy followed her.

"Snuggy," Mum said. "Come when I tell you to come, you little shit."

"I don't believe you. I don't."

Her mum turned on her. "It was rape. It was non-consensual sex." Her mother's eyes filled with tears and her hands clutched at her breast. "But—God forgive me—Frank was the victim."

---

Rosy walked back to the bench with her mum. They sat there, Snuggy warm against Rosy's shaded legs, but facing safely away, dirty little sausage.

"Frank was one of Findlay's friends." Mum dashed her eyes. "I loved Frank from the moment I saw him. He would never really talk to me. But Findlay and me, well, we connected. And I should have known back then, it wasn't about looks. But Frank… he was… beautiful."

Rosy nodded. "I understand."

"It happened at a Halloween party." Mum said. "I invited Findlay in the hope that he'd invite Frank. And I couldn't believe it when he showed up. It was fancy dress and Frank had this stupid—"

"Pair of ears?"

"Ears?" Her mum frowned. "No. No. He was dressed as an oil sheik. No, Saddam Hussein. He had this towel around his head, and a dressing gown cord, and a moustache he'd made out of wool that wouldn't stay on. He had a faint little moustache of his own. It was the finest, softest, most beautiful…" She looked down at Snuggy. "Anyway, Frank was drinking beer. Lots of people were. But not me. I'd been keeping my eye on Frank and then I looked and he wasn't there.

I found him in the room with all the coats. Lying fast asleep." Mum closed her eyes. "And I bent down and I kissed him."

Rosy bit her lip.

"Except I didn't stop at a kiss." Mum took a shaking breath. "I will never understand what made me do it, but I undid his trousers, and he was... up." Her mum rolled her eyes. "I can't believe I'm telling you all this."

"It's okay, Mum," Rosy said.

"Well, that was it really. He woke up but he just lay there. Perfectly still. Perfectly... terrified." Mum swallowed. "I don't even know how I got pregnant. He didn't... you know. Nothing. But there must have been enough... just there."

Rosy nodded. Sat for a while. Watched the kids play, no idea what was ahead of them.

"Why did you say he raped you?" Rosy said.

"I didn't say that. Not at first. Not until we visited Frank's mum. Franny. My parents were there and Franny put her arm around me and asked me to whisper *yes* in her ear if Frank had done something to me without my permission." Mum straightened. "I made a terrible mistake. But I set it right."

"What do you mean, you set it right?" Rosy said.

"I stuck by Findlay," Mum said. "The one who really loved me from the start."

Rosy gawped. "What about Frank?" She lowered her voice. "He got the blame for you... doing that."

"Frank's mother hated him already, Rosy. I didn't make things any worse."

"Frank is still waiting for you, Mum. He wants you back."

"Frank didn't treat me like his wife. I loved him, but to him, I was some disgusting, germ-ridden thing he couldn't even bear to kiss."

"He's asexual. Everybody is a disgusting, germ-ridden thing he can't bear to kiss."

"Well, that's different then, isn't it?" She stared Rosy straight in the eyes, then hauled Snuggy's lead. "Come on."

"You have to let Frank off the hook, Mum. You have to divorce him."

Her mum stopped. Poor Snuggy had no idea what was going on. "Frank is a dangerous man, Rosy. A point you fail to grasp."

"Dangerous, says the wonderful Findlay," Rosy said. "Did Frank ever actually hit you? Did he hit Findlay?"

"No," Mum said. "It's not just Findlay. He did something unspeakable to Franny. Why do you think Franny hates him?"

Rosy balled her hand into a fist and cupped it. "Oh, I know why," Rosy said. "I'm going to have a little chat with Franny."

---

*At the police station, when Rosy and Frank are waiting for a car to take them home, all Rosy can think about is whether the foetus in the biscuit tin is Frank's little monster. Frank seems to have zoned out, but then, without Rosy even prompting, he starts to speak.*

*"You asked about the baby in the biscuit tin," he says.*

*Hairs at the back of Rosy's neck bristle and she can't breathe.*

*"She's my sister," Frank says. "My sister Jessica. That's why my mum hates me. I killed Jessica before she was even born."*

*Rosy's breath exits in a gasp. "No." She rubs his back. "No, you didn't. The baby was deformed. If she'd been born, she'd have died."*

*"I deformed her," Frank says.*

*It's so awful but so funny, Rosy laughs.*

*"I did," Frank says. "It's true. That's why my mum drowned Frankie."*

*Rosy clamps her hands over her mouth and her eyes scan his face as he speaks.*

*"She held him under the water. I couldn't breathe. I mean Frankie couldn't. And he wanted her to let him up. But she held me down. She held me in the water until I had to breathe it."*

*Rosy stays perfectly still.*

*"I have some of Frankie's memories," Frank says. "Before memories. I have Frankie's memory of being drowned. Know what he was worried about?"*

*Rosy shakes her head.*

*"He didn't want the taste of soapy water in his mouth. And the funniest thing was, it didn't have any taste. It just came right in his nose."*

---

Rosy waited for Franny to open the door.

"Come in my darling. Are you here with more biscuits?"

Rosy followed the woman's retreating back into the kitchen. "No, Franny, I'm not, but that's not what you keep in your biscuit tin, is it?"

Franny folded her arms. "You looked, didn't you? You looked

at my angel. My Jessica."

"Frank told me what you did to him," Rosy said.

"He made that up," Franny said.

"Made what up?"

Franny waved her hand. "Whatever he told you. He sees things that aren't there."

Rosy shook her head. "He's like an elephant, remember? And he remembers what you did. You drowned him."

Franny waved her arms. "Lies. Frankie fell in the bath. He must have been climbing up to get the shampoo. He fell and hit his head. I was busy with dinner."

"The bathroom is next door and you didn't hear him?" Rosy said. "I can tell if somebody has enough bran in their diet, and you didn't hear a four-year-old fall into the bath and hit his head?"

"I didn't hear him fall."

"Because he didn't fall," Rosy said. "You blamed him for your miscarriage, and you drowned him."

"No, you have it all wrong," Franny said. "That's just not what happened."

"And then, to shut him up, you showed him that corpse in the biscuit tin and told him it was his fault."

Franny nodded. "Oh, he killed his sister, all right. He drove Gus away from me."

"What about that growth on Jessica's back?" Rosy said. "She would have died anyway."

"He did that to her, Rosy. Frank did that. Frank made her—" She swiped at her eyes. "Frankie stressed me out. If he hadn't stressed me out, my Gus and my Jessica would be here."

"You killed him, Franny," Rosy said. "You killed Frankie. But thank God he fought his way back."

"Frankie never came back," Franny yelled. "My Frankie never came back. A hateful, unloving monster came back. That *thing* came back. That zombie. That creature came back. Ask your mother why she left him."

"I already did," Rosy said. "She left Frank because he didn't want sex. He'd rather do a jigsaw. Frank didn't rape my mum. But you knew that, didn't you? By then, you hated him. You hated everything about him. You'd side with anybody but him to reassure yourself how bad he was. And you were happy to tell my mum's parents the pregnancy was all Frank's fault. Happy to tell me he was a rapist. You blackened his name." She shook her head. "And my mum—my mum—to her shame, went along with it."

Franny waved a hand. "He's poisoned you with his lies, like he poisoned Gus."

"The poison is in you, Franny," Rosy said. "In you and Gus. Not Frank. Not my father. You're the monster, Franny. You."

---

Rosy banged Franny's front door so hard the porch light rattled.

The neighbour's door opened, almost immediately, and the old man who'd protected Rosy from his wife's attack with the hoe stepped out.

"I heard," he said. "The walls are paper thin."

"Poor wee Frankie," Rosy said. "Go. Run. Don't come back. Don't come back." She shook her head. "You both knew what she did to him. You and Isabelle knew, but you said nothing. Why?"

The neighbour looked like he wasn't going to respond, then he started to talk. "I was at work. Gus was fixing his car. Isabelle heard Jean shouting at Frankie, then heard Frankie…" He looked away, mastered himself, then looked back. "She heard Frankie calling for help. Help, Daddy, help. By the time Gus got the door open…" He shrugged. "Gus got him breathing again, called the ambulance but asked us not to involve the police. Jean was pregnant, couldn't sleep. She couldn't cope with Frankie. She wasn't thinking straight. We all thought Frankie was okay."

"Stop," Rosy said. "She was still pregnant? She was pregnant when she drowned Frankie?"

"Yes."

"You're sure? She hadn't miscarried?"

"She was pregnant. I'm sure. She miscarried a few weeks later."

Franny drowned Frank, then miscarried. There was no motivation, just a bad mother who got angry with her son. Rosy had to get out of here, or she'd break the door down and smash Franny's head in.

"After Gus was gone, Jean lost all control. It broke Isabelle's heart to hear the shouting. Terrible, terrible woman. We would have reported her, but we were scared we'd make things worse. The boy had nowhere else to go. Then you were born. Jean couldn't be nicer with your mum around. Then your mum and Frankie got married and moved out."

Rosy calmed herself. "Thank you for telling me."

He sighed. "When he was little, he was an amazing kid. Brilliant mind. An artist too. He could have been something special."

Rosy nodded. "He is something special."

# Chapter 41
# Dungeon of the beast
## Rosy

Rosy buzzed Frank's intercom and he came straight to the door. The police had clearly given him his wolf's ears back. "We've lost a whole day now," he said.

But Rosy had gained a two-week delay in her start at N-BioCom. What Arvid Madsen hadn't known was that Dr Stein, the N-BioCom CEO, wasn't just impressed by Rosy's grades, and her research into and enthusiasm for N-BioCom. His eyes had widened when she'd walked in for her interview. Smitten. What was she going to do? Apologise to a geneticist for having great genes?

Rosy followed Frank through to the dungeon. His art studio.

Frank held out two sheets of paper. "This was the original design of the big surprise."

"I think we can stop calling it a surprise now, Frank."

She looked at a scale drawing of a circular mosaic, three metres or almost ten feet in diameter. Two outer concentric circles formed a ring about thirty centimetres or twelve inches wide. In that ring, amid leaves and flowers and forest creatures, nestled "A Friendship" in the upper half and "1956 – 1983" in the lower half.

"The A is for...?"

"Angus," Frank said. "Gus."

The centre circle—about a metre or three feet in diameter—depicted an adult hand, palm upward, holding a child's hand.

Rosy compared the first drawing with the second.

In the second design, the letter A had gone and the dates had been replaced with "Cafe," so the outer ring now read

"Friendship Cafe." The smaller hand in the centre had gone and in its place were coffee beans.

"Those are the changes we have to make," Frank said.

"You haven't changed the hands yet, have you?"

"No. That's gonna be a real slog. It'll take ages to redo an area that big."

Rosy frowned. "Is that your dad's hand holding yours?"

Frank said, "Yes," then choked up with tears and just nodded.

"We should keep the hands as they are, okay? They're beautiful. The whole mosaic is stunning," Rosy said. "Forget the coffee beans."

He nodded. "Okay. I like that better."

"Where will the pipe have to come through?" she said.

"Well, that's the great thing. The plumber couldn't be bothered lifting the floor," Frank said. "Man, he was a real cowboy. He brought the pipes up at the door then ran them along the underside of the counter." Frank grinned. "We just need to lay it down. No holes. No pipes to box in. The counter still needs to float over the top edge, but people coming in will see the whole thing, right from the door."

"The second surprise," Rosy said, "is the name of the cafe, then? Friendship Cafe. I'm not sure how Phyllis will like that." The name *Friendship* must stir up all kinds of emotions for the woman.

"It's Friendship, not Friendship's. What's not to like?" Frank said. "And now you can order the baseball caps and T-shirts." He poked her. "See? I had a reason to say no."

"I'm glad you did say no, Frank," Rosy said.

So glad.

Frank scratched under his wolf's ears. "Did Irene say no? To coming back."

Rosy nodded and sighed. "She did. I'm sorry. Like I told you, she felt unwanted. And she's devoted to Findlay, now. But the main thing is, everybody knows you didn't do anything wrong."

"Not everybody. All everybody knows is, Irene left me."

"The people who matter know," Rosy said.

"*Pfff*," Frank said. "Well, at least I have my baby back."

"Yup. You're stuck with me."

Frank smiled. "There's another surprise that shouldn't be a

surprise." He pulled out another drawing. "More mosaic, sorry."

This one was a long rectangle that simply said "Friendship," which was acquiring two decorative swirls like rising steam on coffee.

"A shop sign," Rosy said, and beamed.

"Of course, a shop sign," Frank said. "Man, Rosy, your memory is crap. I told you that. I said, I knew you wanted a sign. I could tell by your face after I left the T in the old one dangling down."

"Ah." Now everything made sense. "I remember now. I just had something else on my mind."

He rolled his eyes.

She looked at the sign. "The swirls are beautiful, but do we need them?"

"We're not cowboys," Frank said. "The sign has to be long enough, and deep enough to cover the panel, so we're also adding a border."

Rosy smiled through clenched teeth. "Hate to tell you this, Frank. I can draw a bit, but I can't match a standard like this." She waved at the mosaic.

He nodded. "That's why all you'll be doing is breaking up coloured tiles into squares."

She rubbed her face. "Great."

"Better get cracking then," Frank said and laughed at her.

"Now that's as bad as one of Findlay's jokes." Rosy tweaked his wolf's ear. "First, if you'll excuse me for one minute, I have to use the ladies'."

---

Rosy sat on the toilet and reached into her pocket to remove the morning-after pill. Not the morning-after now. She popped it from the packet, then dropped it into the toilet. If she was having a baby, she'd be having a baby. Stretch-marks, and everything else that came with it.

And if Rosy did have Boog's baby—if—then she'd have Boog's name tattooed discretely. Under her arm, maybe. Or on the sole of her foot.

Well, she hated the freaking things.

# Chapter 42
# Flight
## (Saturday, 16 July – eighteen days later)
## Rosy

Rosy shoved her purple Karrimor in the back of the Fiesta, using her left hand out of habit, even though the blisters from cracking mosaic tiles had all but gone. She'd break a million more tiles to see the end result—a cafe that shone as bright as the devilment in Frank's eyes. And the emotion in Phyllis's steely little eye. The woman faked disapproval, but there was no doubt the artistry of those mosaics had moved her.

On the spur, Rosy had told Phyllis she'd be happy to stay on all summer at Friendship Cafe, half-hoping the woman would insist she do just that.

"No point hanging around after the mountain has been moved, dear, is there?" Phyllis had said. Then she'd taken off a bracelet and given it to Rosy as a "heart-felt thank you", the bracelet Rosy wore now, on the same wrist as Boog's.

Rosy fastened her seat belt and gave Mum and Snuggy a wave, then found her hand had settled on her belly. Again. She lifted her arm away, shook her head. A home pregnancy test had shown no baby from their misadventure and Rosy couldn't have cried more if she'd lost it. Funny that.

"Thought you'd ask Frank to drive you," her stepdad said.

Rosy had come within an inch of telling Mum about Findlay. But as her molten rage cooled to mere anger, she'd thought back to her own urges—the overpowering, animal desire she'd felt for Frank—and how close she'd come to acting on them, the way her mum had all those years ago. Yes, Findlay had behaved shamefully. But so had Mum and so had Rosy.

She studied the pain in the lines of her stepdad's forehead.

A wise man once said, "Let he who is without sin cast the first stone." Rosy wasn't the religious type but some messages had a power all of their own.

"I'm not shutting you out," she said. "But if you ever cross the line with me again, Findlay, you're toast. Do we understand each other?"

He dashed a glance at her, then nodded fast. "Like I said, I don't know what came over me. Irene's all I want. I swear nothing like that will ever happen again. I swear on my life."

Rosy nodded. "Good. In that case, you can be one of my dads again. Just so you know, I haven't forgotten the man who brought me up. I still love that man."

Findlay looked straight ahead, blinking, and Rosy gave him a moment.

They were exiting Northfield Terrace before he spoke again.

"I haven't worked hard enough, Rosy. That's going to change. Marek has shown me how much effort needs to go into instant success, and I'll do it."

Rosy smiled. "Nice to have you back, Dad."

# Findlay

Findlay dropped Rosy off in the Edinburgh Airport car park, hugged her and wished her good luck, then patted his pockets for his cigarettes before he found the Nicorette gum and remembered he was giving up.

He burst out a square and began to chew.

Marek, that magical Polish genius had told him, "Every failure prepares us for greater success." Then he'd told Findlay about a plan already underway and for the first time Findlay could see how his own greatest failure could become his greatest success. It was so perfect, and so easy, Findlay had cried.

"Animals, you see," Marek had said, "often turn on those who seek to help them. Look at Gus Friendship. Wouldn't it be tragic yet unsurprising if Frank were to follow in his father's footsteps? Who would ask questions if Frank were to murder Phyllis?"

Rosy would be inconsolable, but Findlay—as always, when Frank let her down—would be there for her.

Hope you enjoyed book one in the Frank Friendship series.

Who did Gus Friendship murder and why? What's Marek's plan? Will Findlay get what's coming? And why is there a severed hand in Frank's freezer?

Find out in Pursue Friendship.

———————

Thank you for making one of my books one of yours.

For giveaways and to hear about new books, why not subscribe to my newsletter (visit rgmanse.com)?

Planning to review Screw Friendship? Thank you. Send me a link to your review—good or bad—and I'll send you an ebook advance reading copy of the next book (rg@rgmanse.com).

———————

Follow the story through the other books in the series. Here's the current line-up:

Screw Friendship

Pursue Friendship

Deny Friendship

Books four and five are in plan. Be first to hear about the next book via my newsletter (visit rgmanse.com).

## ABOUT RG MANSE

RG Manse's school teacher told the ten-year-old RG, "You think you're God Almighty," and, "You're a right little Adolf Hitler." Thus encouraged, it was inevitable that the young RG would be torn between writing and IT.

"Not sure what became of that teacher," RG says, "But don't listen to her—I certainly didn't."

You can (and should) email rg@rgmanse.com or you can keep up with all things RG Manse at the website, rgmanse.com.

Printed in Great Britain
by Amazon.co.uk, Ltd.,
Marston Gate.